NIGHT VOICE

By the Author

Stick McLaughlin: The Prohibition Years

Exchange

Night Voice

NIGHT VOICE

To Patrice & Wendy — Thank you for your support! Have "fun in P-town"! — CF Frizzell Pride '17

by

CF Frizzell

2017

NIGHT VOICE
© 2017 By CF Frizzell. All Rights Reserved.

ISBN 13: 978-1-62639-813-9

This Trade Paperback Original Is Published By
Bold Strokes Books, Inc.
P.O. Box 249
Valley Falls, NY 12185

First Edition: January 2017

Credits
Editor: Cindy Cresap
Production Design: Stacia Seaman
Cover Concept and Composition by Deb B.
Cover Design by Sheri (graphicartist2020@hotmail.com)

Acknowledgments

Sometimes a story writes itself, and *Night Voice* pretty much took its own course. That's not to say there weren't long moments (days?) spent searching for the best route to happily-ever-after, but, overall, this story felt as alluring as any visit to Provincetown. However, as every author knows, a story rarely gets a chance if its cover fails, and goes nowhere at all if it's not worthy of a reader's investment.

Graphic artist Deb B. didn't just understand my cover concept, she "got it." Her amazing talent shows in this intimate, sultry cover, and I'm immeasurably grateful.

And credit for the tale itself goes as much to my wife, Kathy, as to the words that spilled out of my head. Her feedback and insight lent direction and helped round out this story from the very beginning. Far more than a sounding board, she's become a part of my creative process I can't live without. She's proof that "happily-ever-afters" happen in real life, too.

To Kathy, whose voice I will always need to hear,
day or night.

CHAPTER ONE

Good evening on this, yet another snowy Friday night. This is Sable turning on *Nightlight* for all you hardy women of Cape Cod. Let's hunker down and keep each other company with some good music and intimate conversation." She tipped the extended microphone more directly to her lips. "So. What's on your mind tonight? Winter's not a month old and you're sick of the snow already? Ready for something... *hotter*, perhaps? Have a dedication you'd like to make? As always, we'd love to hear from you, right here at 555-201-1112 at WCCD's Provincetown studio. Or, if you'd rather just listen, send a little good karma to those in need. We can never get too much of that, right? So while you fluff those pillows in your comfy chair and settle in with your special someone, your dog, or your favorite beverage, we'll let Cris Williamson's "Woman" lead us into *Nightlight*."

Taking her cue from her engineer, Razor, disc jockey Murphy Callahan removed her headphones and rolled away to reach the coffee she'd absently set on the studio's rear table. She took a quick sip before kicking off her UGGs and fumbling beneath her counter for the fuzzy Elmo slippers. She couldn't care less that, at forty years old, she cherished them as much as her L.L. Bean floppy-eared hat. Comfort was everything, especially when working the ten-to-two time slot in the dead of winter on a New England seacoast.

"How bad were the roads?" Razor asked, her voice that of some omniscient deity emerging from the ceiling speaker.

"Horrible." Murphy poked her keyboard several times to cue up two commercials as Williamson's song wound to a close. "I was all over the place. I left a half hour early and I *still* just made it in time."

"I noticed. Supposedly, there'll be five inches out there by the time we're off."

"Swell. I'm buying a team of huskies tomorrow."

"Better than the Chihuahuas who pull you around now."

"Hey. Don't make fun of my Beetle."

"Right. Ten seconds."

Murphy ran both hands through her disheveled hair and reset her headphones with a glance at her call monitor. A single light blinked. She had hoped to ease into this shift, catch her breath through a couple of tunes before things picked up. *Maybe this will just be a song dedication.*

Razor feigned shooting her with her fingers and the studio fell silent. Murphy raised her mouth to the mike that scissored toward her from the opposite edge of the counter.

"Cris Williamson. Timeless, always beautiful. And speaking of time, we have our first caller of the evening standing by, so let's not waste any of it." She clicked the call button. "Hi. This is Sable and you're on *Nightlight.*"

"Hi, Sable. Love your show. We look forward to it every night."

An early-twenties local. After two years on the job, Murphy could usually "see" her callers quite well. To pass the time, Razor kept a completely haphazard tally and currently had Murphy at approximately eighty percent accuracy.

"That's so nice to hear. Thank you."

"Friday nights, especially. The four of us hang at my place and tune you in. This is the first time we've called, though. We need another opinion on a…a situation."

"We love first time callers. Hope you'll become a regular with us. Give us a name, if you want."

"Okay, um…I'm…I'm Bangles."

"Nice to meet you, Bangles. Now, what's your situation?"

"Well, see, my girlfriend finally got her dream job in town, but… her new boss is coming on to her already."

"How so?"

"Well, first there were the 'looks,' y'know? The extra long ones that say 'Can you guess what I'm thinking?' And then she started with the touchy-feely stuff, the hand on the back, the shoulder bump. But today she actually took her by the hand—until my girl pulled away. I want to scratch the bitch's eyes out."

Murphy grinned at the mike. "Your girlfriend must want this job very badly."

"You know how hard it is to get winter work around here."

"You realize you're probably talking about sexual harassment. There are laws—"

"Yeah, right, and that'll kill the job."

"Your girlfriend has made things clear to her boss?"

"Yeah, Sable, but this woman thinks it's all a joke."

"Is it feasible for the two of you to speak with her, as a couple?" Two lines came to life on her monitor. "Say, at the end of her workday?"

Bangles hesitated, apparently considering the idea.

"Well...um...I suppose, but...See, I...I tend to get..."

"Excited?"

"Yeah. Excited."

"Our listeners might offer some ideas, but I suggest you rein in that excitement—for your girlfriend's sake—and give talking to the boss a serious try."

"Hm. I guess. Yeah, okay."

"Good. You can do it. And let us know how things turn out?"

"Sure. Thanks, Sable."

"Good luck. And thanks for the call."

Murphy clicked on the next button.

"Hi. This is Sable. Welcome to *Nightlight*."

"Hi. I say the girlfriend better start job hunting. Sounds like trouble."

"Let's hope not. Is this Digger?"

"That's me. Hi, Sable. You know I can't go a night without calling."

"You've worked in the area a long time, Digger. You can't blame Bangles and her girlfriend for trying to avoid a job hunt." She grinned at Razor and shook her head. Digger and her sandpaper voice could always be counted on to pop into conversations, when she wasn't starting debates of her own. In her late thirties, Digger worked for the Provincetown Highway Department year-round, one of the fortunate few to land such secure work, and as such, had appointed herself *Nightlight*'s expert on local employment.

"Times are tough, I know, even when it's not January," Digger went on, "but bosses like that one are trouble. I mean, it almost figures, y'know? Woman in charge, has a hot one on her payroll, a newbie practically eating out of her hand. She's bound to be tempted eventually."

"Come on, Digger. That's over the top."

"Call 'em as I see 'em, that's all."

"First of all, your 'woman in charge' premise—"

"Hey, I'm old-school and I *do* think women give in to temptation easier. They're softer. Of course, that's also a wonderful thing."

"Okay, so we have one vote for changing jobs. So noted." She refused to be baited into inviting another of Digger's chauvinistic diatribes. "Let's see what other listeners think. Thanks for the call, Dig." Murphy disconnected the call and clicked the next button.

"Hi. This is Sable. You're on *Nightlight*."

"Ah...hello," a breathless female began. "Look, I just think Bangles's girlfriend should tell the boss to cut the crap."

Murphy looked up and found Razor shaking her head. "I see. And risk losing her job?"

"I'd tell her I would spread her name all over town. It'd be a stalemate."

"Sounds like you've figured this all out."

"Pretty simple. That's all I got. Thanks."

Murphy connected the other waiting call.

"Hello. This is Sable. Welcome to *Nightlight*."

"Hello." The easy alto caught her ear. She stopped scrolling through song titles on her monitor and stared at the lone light, waiting. "Yeah...hi. If I were in that girlfriend's shoes, I'd ask the boss out."

"Would you? As in call the boss's bluff?"

"As in, be waiting with my girlfriend when the boss arrives."

"Intriguing idea." She drew her mike closer. "Any chance you're speaking from experience?"

She enjoyed this woman's relaxed delivery, the richness of her voice, and wanted to hear more. The pause lengthened, though, and she checked to see if their line was still open, the light still lit.

"A chance? Oh yeah."

Murphy picked up on a brief muffled laugh. "Care to enlighten *Nightlight* listeners with your story?" She pressed her right earpiece to her head tighter, but heard only silence. "No pressure here. You don't—"

"Let's just say I learned my lesson. The police chief made it pretty clear I'd missed his wife's signals."

"Whoa." She straightened in her seat, inadvertently rolling slightly away from the mike. She gripped the edge of the counter and pulled herself back into position. "Police chief?"

"Smart, I know."

"You missed or ignored the hints?"

The answering snicker was unmistakable. "Ignored, I suppose."

"So…the police chief, the tactic worked on you."

"It did."

"What lesson did you learn?"

"To be a very good listener."

Smart woman. "We treasure good listeners. And we love it when they call in."

"It's a first for me. I guess…I wanted to get that off my chest."

"Sounds like it's bothered you for quite a while. How long ago did this happen?"

"Many years ago. I was young and foolish and ruined a very good relationship of my own."

"Oh. You were with someone at the time you…Young and foolish, I'd have to agree. And since then? Those days are behind you now, correct?"

"They are. Gone but not forgotten, if you catch my drift."

"I think I do." Murphy imagined this woman alone in her living room, dwelling on the past. "However, we move on." She tried not to hear herself. "Have you?"

"I try. It made me a much different person, someone who values depth in a relationship more than I ever did. That can be hard to find today."

"That's true, but commendable. It takes strength and it sounds like you have more than you give yourself credit for. Patience and self-respect go a long way and they will for you, I'm sure."

"Thanks, Sable. Thank *you* for listening."

Murphy could listen to this woman all night. Sometimes weeks went by without a caller who actually *learned* a life lesson, who spoke well and knew her mind, who made the fine hairs on the back of Murphy's neck stand at attention. This one did. "Well, I hope it won't be your last call. We're always here to listen. I'm glad you called."

"Me, too. Have yourself a good night."

Chapter Two

I figured that's what you did. Jesus, RB. You parked that damn Jeep halfway up the snowbank last week, too, and brought the cops in here." Didi's meaty arm jiggled as she shook her finger. "You know what I think of that."

"No place else to park, Didi." Riley Burke stroked the back of Didi's hand, overtly teasing. "I wasn't about to let that keep us apart."

Didi yanked her hand away. "You and your bedroom eyes just keep on dreamin'. You won't be smirking when the cops shut down this hideout, now, will ya?"

"Relax." Riley pulled on her black knit cap and slapped a twenty-dollar bill onto the bar. "They only came looking for me because my back bumper blocked the street. I didn't block it tonight. Besides, it's only been an hour."

Riley stood and zipped her thick, hooded jacket. "Nobody will give you trouble and you know it." Didi shook her head, reaching for Riley's empty shot glass, and Riley rapped the chubby hand with her gloves. "Hey, Deidre's Den is the hideout all of us late-nighters can't live without."

"Right. And don't you forget it." Hands on her broad hips, Didi narrowed her eyes. "Hear that?" She tossed a thumb up toward the portable radio next to the Glenlivet on the top shelf. "Damn snow's not going to break till lunch time tomorrow. Wish Sable had more juicy drama tonight instead of depressing weather updates."

"It's only midnight. She's got another two hours to get you all hot 'n bothered."

Didi's belly laugh rolled through the tiny basement bar. "Never would've pegged you for a follower of the show, RB."

Riley shrugged. "The show keeps me company whenever I fall into one of these late-night jobs."

"Uh-huh. Wouldn't have anything to do with Sable's pillow talk voice, I'm sure."

"Sexy and sophisticated. I'll give you that."

"Oh, Jesus, yes."

"And I like recognizing the places, a caller now and then."

Didi checked to see if the other two patrons in the room could overhear and leaned toward her from behind the bar. "My money says it was Digger who plowed through the door at Nina-and-Pinto's Café. Wonder if she'll admit it on the air."

"We'll have to stay tuned to find out."

"She hasn't been on yet tonight that I've heard."

"So she's probably still out plowing and might not have time to call in. The plows will be out all night with this storm."

"Nah. Digger's a regular *Nightlighter*. She'll call from the damn truck."

"Good point. She's on a lot. Sable's very patient."

"With everyone, actually." Didi buffed her reflection in the six-foot oak bar top. "So, you headed home now or off to another job?"

"Home," Riley said and drew her hood up over her hat. "Hopefully, nobody else will call with a crisis. Sealing up the café in the blowing snow was enough for now."

"Until the next plow jumps a curb."

"Shit, at this hour, Didi? Don't even think that." She headed for the door. "I've got a hot shower and a comfy bed waiting."

"Bed already warmed up?"

"No." Riley sighed and knew Didi would never pass up the opportunity for a smartass quip.

"Still? Bad time for a dry spell. Valentine's Day's just a week away."

Riley gripped the doorknob, focused on returning to the third snowstorm in two weeks. No way would she engage Didi on the subject of her non-existent love life. "You just watch it getting home."

"You're the one who's slipping, RB."

"Yeah, yeah. See ya, Didi." Ducking her head, she leaned out into the sideways snowfall and shut the door quickly. Snow had filled her inbound footprints, and she grabbed the mangled aluminum shovel by the door and did a rush job on the steps.

Deirdre's Den operated a few hours beyond its license for the handful of the town's true nightshift workers and, just like them, Riley treasured the little place. But she never shared too much of herself. Some things Didi didn't need to know. The fact that Riley still occasionally reeled from a year-old break-up was one of them, and even though her pride was a bit dented these days, her self-respect remained intact. The dream of saving to buy their own home had shattered when her partner declared that "another woman" promised more than Riley's obsession with work. Riley emerged from that nightmare, shaken and wary, but all the more determined to build her own home, to fill each day with work, if necessary, and create her own happiness.

She tested the snowbank's density with an adamant boot stomp and climbed up and over to her driver's door. *Damn snow. With six new inches on top, this old stuff underneath probably won't melt till June.* She found the snow brush behind her seat and, hunched over and head bowed, slipping, squinting, and sinking in the snow, she rounded the vehicle and cleared all the windows. Finished, she swiped the snow buildup off her arms, shoulders, and hood, slashed at her jeans with the brush, and dove into the Jeep.

Her cheeks burned and her nose dribbled. "Jesus. Summer, where are you?" She took a moment to let the adrenaline subside, then pushed off her hood and dug in her jacket pocket for her keys.

Radio conversation about the storm filled the confined space, picked up where she'd left it in the bar, and she drew a moment of comfort from the talk and the minimal illumination of the gauges. *Pretty much the same as home.* She clicked on the heater and defroster, and her heavy sigh formed a stream of frosty air onto the dashboard.

She guided the Jeep down off the banking and onto the snow-packed alley—an official street in this compact town, one not yet plowed. Too many snowy nights, she mused, too much time to think about her too-empty loft apartment.

Riley's rebellious streak reared its head, something she hadn't permitted in ages. She shifted out of four-wheel drive, tapped the accelerator, and slid the Jeep around the corner onto Commercial Street.

She loved the look of Provincetown's main street at any time of year, but this scene was always particularly striking. Riley stopped the Jeep. This was a living postcard, the heart and soul of a little village cherished by so many, now deserted and under siege by Mother Nature and the Atlantic Ocean. Half caked in white, streetlamps mustered only an eerie, filtered light that took strength from the snow's reflective power but cast no shadow. And like silent and brave survivors of summer, storefronts stood shoulder-to-shoulder against the battering and soldiered on through the windswept snow.

She never tired of looking, of appreciating, of feeling that she was a tiny part of it all. Capturing one of these rare solitary moments, as only she bore witness between swipes of her windshield wipers, she felt singly entrusted with the heart of this fragile, isolated world. The respect she held for it humbled her, and instead of submitting to its pervasive helplessness on this night, she realized that she, like this dogged little street, didn't battle these elements alone. *They* battled the elements here tonight. *Maybe that's why it always feels so personal, so intimate.*

Wishing she had the skills of an artist, Riley simply shook her head at the dusty white scene before her and imprinted it to memory one more time. A friend would razz her for waxing romantic, she thought with an inward laugh. A lover would relate.

A calm, reassuring voice spoke from very close range. *"You know I'm only a phone call, a keystroke away.* Nightlight *shines on, regardless of the weather."*

Riley stared at her radio as if she could see the woman behind the words.

CHAPTER THREE

"Mm-mm. Well, I'd say *Nightlight* is really beaming now, wouldn't you? That reading raised the temp in here by twenty degrees." Murphy grinned at the two women sharing a microphone opposite her. Although rare, having guests in the studio was a nice change, even if they had to sign a confidentiality agreement regarding Sable's identity. "What a great selection to read on this Valentine's Day evening, terrific dialogue in a *very* romantic scene. Thank you to local author Rose Keegan and her wife Nancy Rich. Reading from *Banking on Love* like a script was a delicious tease." She gestured to the blinking lights on her monitor. "Looks like listeners can't resist."

Tightness in Murphy's chest subsided just a bit once she connected a caller to her guests. Their conversation allowed time for memories roused by the reading to withdraw, back into storage where she kept them. The steamy scene paralleled a happier time for her, distant some three years now, but nonetheless vivid in its passion and longing. Rose assured the caller that the novel, like her first, had a happy ending, and Murphy wished her own love story had featured less tragedy.

"That's what we search for in romance, isn't it?" she said, endorsing Rose's statement. "A happily-ever-after ending means so much."

"The buildup is the tough part," Rose added. "Coming up with just the right scene, setting the mood with just the right amount of romance, can be harder than you'd imagine."

"Now that's worth exploring," Murphy said. "How about that, *Nightlighters*? Give us a call at 555-201-1112 or drop a note. Have you set a scene similar to that in *Banking on Love*? What kind of scene would you or have you set for a romantic moment?"

"Rose almost used one of our moments in the book," Nancy said.

"Many years ago, I think we'd only been dating a couple of months, we thought we'd scalp some tickets for a concert near the beach." She eyed Rose as she spoke into the mike. "Well, we didn't have any luck, so Rose set up a picnic, blanket and wine, the whole shebang, right outside the venue in the sand." She squeezed Rose's arm. "It was a *very* romantic evening."

Murphy's thoughts strayed. She had enjoyed many such evenings at Herring Cove and other beaches along the Cape, nights that featured sunsets and moonrises, and kisses broken by whispers of future plans. But after just nine years, illness swept Bryce and those dreams from her life, and Murphy hadn't spent an evening on any beach in the three years since Bryce's passing.

Two more lights sparked to life and seized her attention. Grateful, she clicked on one.

"Welcome to *Nightlight*. This is Sable and you're on with Rose Keegan, author of *Banking on Love*, and her wife Nancy."

"Hi, Sable, and hi to your guests. I bought your first book and I'm buying this one as soon as it comes out. My wife set me up in a way similar to your story, but that's not why I'm going to buy it, though." The caller laughed. "My wife's nodding at me right now. She told me she once wrestled with just the right thing to do...you know, to...make the moment perfect."

Rose chuckled. "It can be just as difficult to create on the screen as it is in real life."

"It is!"

Murphy leaned into her mike. "So...tell us? What did she do?"

"Oh, Sable! She wanted to propose on the deck of this fabulous beach house, so she finagled a way to get hired as the house sitter. She dealt with the homeowner's Realtor and everything, just to have the perfect spot."

"I like the way your wife thinks." Rose chuckled. "My protagonist *bought* her lover the house."

They all laughed and Murphy connected the next caller.

"Hi. This is Sable and you're on *Nightlight* with local author Rose Keegan and her wife Nancy Rich."

"Hi, ladies. This is Belle, Sable. It's been a while."

"Good to hear from you, Belle. To our guests and *Nightlighters*, Belle may be familiar to many of you as one of the outstanding summertime DJs at the Boatslip. You've got a romantic setup to share, Belle?"

"Well, maybe not the most romantic, but it certainly was great. Terri was deejaying at the Labor Day tea dance and the place was packed, bouncing off the walls. Well, right in the middle of a song, she stopped the music dead—and proposed over the PA system."

"Wow!" Rose exclaimed.

"Yeah, a big wow!" Belle said. "And God, the whole dance scene turned into this wild engagement party!"

"Well, *Banking on Love* doesn't have a huge party scene like that," Rose said, "but it does have some special moments on the dance floor."

"I've read my advance copy," Murphy offered, "and I can attest to those scenes. Both sweet and hot."

"Excellent," Belle said. "I'm sold. Good luck with the book. And good talking to you, Sable."

"Same here, Belle. Thanks for the call." Murphy clicked the next blinking light. "Good evening and welcome to *Nightlight*. This is Sable and you're on with author Rose Keegan and her wife Nancy Rich. Do you have a setup for us tonight?"

"How about outside in a light snow, like the one falling now. Alone beneath the streetlamp at town hall, say…the wee hours of the morning?"

Murphy stared at the illuminated button, taken by the same easy, relaxed alto that had struck her several weeks ago. She glanced up to find Rose gesturing toward Murphy's microphone, urging her to respond.

"Sounds like an intimate rendezvous."

"Could be the end of an evening…or…"

With an amused look at Rose and Nancy, Murphy added, "Or the beginning?"

"Or the beginning, yes."

"I see. Not many options at that hour, are there? Do you envision anything in particular?"

A gentle sigh came through the line. Murphy was sure this was the intriguing caller who had encountered a police chief's wife, and she was delighted to have her on the phone again.

Rose leaned away from her mike and whispered, "Keep her going."

"In your scene, is this the couple's first meeting or…a makeup meeting? Maybe a final meeting?"

"Hm…A first meeting."

"Accidental?"

"Sure."

"And what's accomplished in this intimate first meeting?"

"A date for a second."

"Oh, I like it," Nancy said, and elbowed Rose.

"I do, too," Rose said. "I'd run with that for sure. The concept is exciting."

"Are you a writer?" Murphy asked into the mike.

"God, no. But I do work with my hands."

All three in the studio chuckled.

"Have you ever encountered someone in such a setting?"

"No, Sable. Have you?"

Murphy sat back in thought, touched by the unexpected personal question. Despite Rose and Nancy egging her on, she chose to avoid it. "So you think this would be romantic, as opposed to…opportunistic?"

She heard the familiar muffled chuckle. "Definitely."

"Well, it's certainly a unique addition to our list of ideas tonight. Do you have a romantic setting of your own to share?"

The caller paused. "A chance meeting at Race Point. It was a long time ago, but I do remember the full moon."

"Oh," Rose said with a dreamy sigh. "Now, that's almost too perfect."

"I suppose it was," the caller said, her voice dipping. "The ex of my ex. Just one night of mindlessness and we went our separate ways."

The lowered tenor of her voice piqued Murphy's interest further. "Have you met since?"

"No. She went back to my ex, and last I knew, they were living in Chicago. Like I said, it was a long time ago."

Nancy sighed at Rose. "Where would we be without the drama of our exes?"

"Some scenarios we can do without," Rose told her.

Murphy leaned closer to the mike. "Sounds like you feel it was… it was an opportunity lost."

"No regrets, Sable. I think it was just one of those moments in life that you have to pass through to get where you're going."

"Well said. I like your attitude."

"And I like yours. You make *Nightlight* a good friend to us all. Thanks for doing what you do and doing it so well."

"Well, I…I'm moved by that. Thank you very much," Murphy said, about to stumble. "You've called *Nightlight* before, haven't you?"

"Yes."

"I thought so. Don't be a stranger. Please call again."

"Thanks. You have yourself a good night."

"And you do the same." Murphy disconnected the call and, with the signal that they were off the air, Murphy set a string of commercials to play.

"Three minutes," Razor said.

"Well." Murphy dropped her headphones onto the counter and ruffled a hand through her hair.

Rose and Nancy clapped, relaxing in their seats.

"*That* was interesting," Rose said. "You get many calls like that at this hour?"

Murphy took a long drink from her bottle of water. "Lord, no. Once in a while after midnight but not in the ten-to-eleven hour."

"Great voice," Nancy said.

"Plays with the imagination, doesn't it?" Rose asked.

Murphy nodded, still taken by the caller, still hearing that voice in her ear. "It certainly does."

❖

Swirling wind off the ocean had built a two-foot drift of snow on her doorstep by the time Murphy saw her driveway at three o'clock. The usual fifteen-minute trip had taken an hour on the slippery roads, and she had precious little energy left after such a long, rather emotional night. But adrenaline, necessity, and the prospect of bed pushed her onward. Gunning her engine and summoning courage, she rocketed up and just barely over the barricade created by an earlier pass of a plow, and managed to deposit her Beetle in her driveway with an exhausted, relieved sigh. Next challenge, she thought grimly, shoveling out the damn front door.

Twenty minutes later, she exited the hottest shower she could stand and took a cup of tea to bed. "Enough with the snow, already," she grumbled to the empty house, and settled in, listening to the storm rattle her windows.

Light from the nightstand lamp flickered, and she groaned at the likelihood of losing power. The most serious storm in memory here, several years prior, had dropped the seaside neighborhood into darkness for a week, and she just as easily remembered snuggling up to Bryce in front of their roaring fireplace. They weathered all kinds of storms back

___

then, all kinds, except for the one that mattered most, Bryce's recovery that never came. And times like this tested her resolve.

Recalling those happier, carefree days, she met Bryce's excited eyes in the framed picture of them on her bureau. "I'm getting all weepy again, aren't I?" She wiped her misty vision with a tissue. "Sorry. Don't give me that 'I told you so' look. I've been doing better and I know you're proud of me. I'll always be proud of you, too." She sipped her tea and tried to set those special recollections aside as she usually did, and look ahead, giving thanks for what used to be and for the opportunity to carry on.

Unbidden, the smooth alto of that caller replayed in her head. The pensive, maybe winsome air about her threatened to tap memories and tug them back out of hiding. Murphy sipped her tea again and realized she'd welcomed the replay. She shook her head at herself, lying there, musing about the caller, her physique, her past... Abruptly, she tossed aside the bed covers and went for the novel in her briefcase.

"Like you should get swept away by a caller's voice," she mumbled, studying the book's cover as she slid back into bed. It had been too long since she'd let herself escape into fictional romance, but tonight she sensed that another Rose Keegan novel would fit the bill perfectly.

And it did. When blinding sun greeted her at ten thirty the next morning, she wondered where she'd ridden with the tall, dark-eyed Texan in the smoky duster, why her body yearned, and how she ended up with spilled tea on her expensive comforter.

CHAPTER FOUR

Riley unplugged the extension cord from the portable power pack behind her driver's seat, coiled it up as fast as she could, and tossed it into the back of the Jeep with her tools. Snow had fallen steadily as she boarded up the broken window for the night, and now she left an impression almost four inches deep as she climbed the steps to the beachfront rental. She left the keys to the unit on the little table just inside and shut the door, testing the knob to make sure it was secure.

She brushed her vehicle windows and herself free of snow and drove out onto Commercial to head home. It was twenty minutes to four, and she knew Didi had closed the Den more than an hour ago, so there was no sense drooling over a fiery shot of schnapps to warm her bones.

Here she was again, she thought, moved by the isolation on Commercial in yet another blustery storm. *A week into March. The winter that has no end.* Her windshield wipers built long, thin snow barriers at the apex of their reach, narrowing her field of vision. To concentrate, she turned off the 1930s radio drama airing on WCCD. *I know you're done, Sable, but at this hour, I could use more of you, not that.*

She crossed to Bradford Street and headed east, trying to remember if she had any of her landlord's beef stew left over. The Angel's Landing repair call had been her third since six thirty, and her stomach had been complaining since four that afternoon. Just get to bed, she told herself, and worry about eating on a normal schedule tomorrow.

She slowed cautiously as she reached the top of one of Bradford's many hills and the tiny lane to her loft, but before she began the turn, her headlights reflected off a taillight halfway down the slope. The vehicle sat tilted severely over the snowbank, completely covered in new snow. "How long have you been there? Little shit car out in this... What'd you expect?"

Riley motored down slowly, careful not to slide past, and stopped alongside. The Volkswagen was dark and Riley grabbed her flashlight off the floor and shone it into the driver's side window. Empty. She checked the road ahead as far as the blowing snow would allow and saw no movement, no house lights where a neighbor might have been awakened to help. And she'd seen no one walking as she'd driven along Bradford this far.

She shifted into four-wheel low and climbed the snowbank in front of the Beetle, well off the road, and snapped on her flashers.

"Nothing like asking for trouble." She drew her wet hood over her cap, zipped up her jacket, and pulled on her gloves. "One more for the road. Hope you're watching, Santa." She trudged up the hill and onto the banking to the car.

The window was down an inch and she pressed her flashlight to the opening. A red gloved hand slapped onto the glass, and Riley leaped back so fast, she lost her footing and fell onto the street.

"What the fuck!" She snatched up the flashlight and shone it at the car. "Hey, you in there!"

"I'm so sorry!" A woman's ruddy face enclosed by a furry hat and earflaps appeared in her light. The spoken words fogged the glass and blurred Riley's view of the woman's features. "I can't open the doors," the woman said. "I...I sank."

Riley shined her light along the side of the car and found it had indeed sunk into the snowbank. The driver's side sat sealed from the bottom up by nearly a foot of snow. She knew the other side was a lost cause, angled downward into deeper snow.

"Are you okay? I mean, are you hurt or anything?"

The face moved sideways in Riley's light. "Just humiliated. And cold."

"Okay. Hang on. I've got a shovel."

Riley hurried to the Jeep, her head down against the biting snow. "What are people doing out in this shit?" She pulled out a shovel and headed back. "God knows what. Same as you, stupid."

The woman spoke from the window opening. "Thank you so much! I can't believe this. And I'm so sorry I startled you."

Riley didn't bother looking up. She started shoveling with abandon.

"Really, I'm sorry," the woman tried again, her voice raised against the wind. "I come this way in all kinds of weather and I've never had trouble."

"Bad storm," Riley said, breathing hard now. "Can you open the window?"

"My battery is dead. No."

"You have a phone? Did you call for help?" Riley's words came out sporadically as she tossed one load of snow after another over the car's hood.

"I forgot it."

"Big surprise," Riley grumbled, heaving another shovelful.

By the time she'd cleared the length of the vehicle, Riley felt like a pack-a-day smoker who'd gained thirty pounds. Snow had accumulated on her head, shoulders, and arms, and she imagined she looked like a yeti tromping around in the Great White North.

She returned to the driver's door and the woman's face reappeared at the window.

"Gotta free the front end next, before I can try pulling you out. Meanwhile, you should come sit in the Jeep and get warm. Leave the car in neutral." She opened the door, and the woman shifted the car out of park before accepting Riley's hand.

"Jesus. I can't believe this happened. You're my savior. Thank you so, so much."

"Look, I can't help but ask. What the hell were you doing out in this mess at this hour?" Riley stomped a path into the banking to reach her own passenger door. The woman followed dutifully, arms wrapped around herself. The hem of her quilted parka dragged through the snow.

"I work late. I knew it was bad and I thought I was prepared, dressed for it and all, but…I…just slid."

Riley helped her up into the seat, shut the door, and climbed around to get in and start the engine. The woman held her palms to the heat vents.

In the dim light of the dashboard, her profile was all Riley could see of her face. That funky skull cap and earflaps, gray-ish imitation rabbit fur, she guessed, hid most of the woman's features, save for an aristocratic nose and slight chin. Long, graceful eyelashes tipped with drops of melted snow fluttered as she sighed.

"How long have you been stuck here?"

"About an hour or so. I thought I'd see a police cruiser or a plow, but no one's come by." She turned abruptly, biting her lower lip. "I can't begin to thank you." She extended a handshake. "I'm Murphy Callahan. What's your name, please?"

Riley shook her hand, her own thick leather-covered fingers enclosing the smaller knitted glove. "Riley Burke. You sit a while. I'll be back." A humble smile grew across Murphy's lips, and some of the anxiety appeared to ease from her features.

Riley spun out of the Jeep, back into the gale, and spent another fifteen minutes shoveling out the front end of the Volkswagen and a sizeable portion of the snowbank.

"No phone," she mumbled as she returned to her Jeep. "Jesus Christ. When it goes bad, it really goes bad." She opened the tailgate and pulled a thick coil of rope out into the snow, aware that Murphy watched from the front seat. "I'm going to drag the car to the edge of the banking, close enough to the street so I can push it free. I don't want to try towing you downhill and have you slide down into my rear end."

Murphy nodded and Riley almost grinned at her own words. She shut the tailgate and connected one end of the rope to her Jeep with an industrial-strength steel hook, then took the other end to the Beetle, dropped onto her back, and attached a similar hook to its frame. She returned to the Jeep, shook off most of the snow on her body, and jumped in.

The heat was oppressive and she broke out in a sweat. She pushed her hood off and fought back a shiver.

"Please buckle up, just to be safe." She eased the Jeep forward and crept off the banking until the rope drew taut. "This is where we pray for a little traction," she said. Murphy just nodded, her hands folded in her lap.

The Jeep's rear axle sank several inches as her tires dug in, and Riley released a heavy sigh of relief when both vehicles moved forward. Inching steadily onto the street, she looked back to see the Volkswagen roll through the snow and level off. She stopped gently, turned her wheels into the banking, and set the brake.

"Stay here."

She hustled out and unhooked the rope, then opened the Beetle's door. Snow blew into the car and swirled around her face. She fumbled to find the ignition, but managed to turn it on and angle the steering wheel slightly toward the street. With a hand on the wheel and one braced on the open doorframe, she set her boots firmly and pushed. The car resisted, and Riley eased up, then pushed again, and then repeated the actions until the rocking motion set the car free.

Riley jumped behind the wheel as the Volkswagen began to move. She turned the key, but nothing happened. Silently, the car picked up speed, rolled past her Jeep. Riley turned the key again. On the third try, the engine kicked in, and she revved it up as she coasted to a stop at the bottom of the hill. She held the accelerator down slightly, keeping the motor active, its alternator supplying power to the dead battery.

Murphy and her furry hat appeared at the window and Riley jumped.

"Oh my God. You're a magician!"

"You're supposed to stay in the Jeep!"

"But the car's good to go now, right? It's run—"

"I doubt this will last if I take my foot off the gas. How far away do you live?"

"Wellfleet. Just twenty…Well, tonight, probably a lot more."

"No kidding. Your battery needs a jump." As if proving her point, the car died when she stepped out. "Come on. We'll bring the Jeep down and get you hooked up."

Within ten minutes, Riley had her vehicle positioned nose-to-nose with Murphy's, both hoods raised slightly, and jumper cables transfusing life into the dead battery. To pass the time, they relaxed in the Jeep's dashboard light, while the snow whirled outside and the silence inside lengthened. Riley removed her gloves and tried to ignore the irony of the moment, two women connected by an electric lifeline.

"Water?" She produced a bottle from a cooler behind Murphy's seat.

"Thanks. Again." Murphy tugged off her furry hat and then her gloves and stuffed them into it. She ran long, manicured fingertips through her hair and shook her head. "I'm surprised you don't have an espresso machine in here. You've got everything else."

Riley wiped condensation off the windshield with a paper towel. "The thermos of coffee I started out with was gone by five. Sorry." Tempted to get a good long look at her now, Riley fussed with the heater instead. She shut off the fan, figuring it wiser to stick to business than to get distracted by tousled dark waves. Besides, the temperature in the Jeep was unsettling. Sweat trickled down the back of her neck.

Murphy sipped her water. "So, you've had a very long night. Do you make a living rescuing people?"

"Property maintenance," she answered, settling back and opening her own bottle. She gestured to the window. "Winter's never been this bad. We'll probably set a record for snow." She rubbed another paper towel across the back of her neck. What she wouldn't give for a shower right about now, she mused, and almost chuckled out loud at her present situation. *Not long ago, I'd have taken you home. It's less than a half-mile away. And encouraged you to stay. Don't look now, Didi, but maybe I am slipping.*

"Well," Murphy set her hand on Riley's arm, "tonight you're my knight in shining armor, Riley. No doubt about it."

"Glad I could help. But...you've got to be more careful." She met Murphy's eyes evenly then, and swallowed hard when they took hold in the poor light. They were deep and soft, and narrowed when those glamorous cheekbones rose. Riley forced herself to make a point. "Forgetting your phone was a big mistake."

"Tell me about it." Murphy brought her water bottle to her lips, and Riley watched her drink, noted the smooth glide of her cheek, the sway of her throat as she swallowed. The temptation to touch suddenly rose from nowhere, and Riley hurried to think of something to say.

"Were you sleeping when I pulled up?"

Murphy shrugged. "It seemed harmless. I mean, someone was *bound* to come along."

"Are you always so...brave?"

"Brave?" Murphy laughed, a bright, spirited sound rather out of place, considering, but Riley liked it nonetheless.

"Well, I wanted to say reckless. Are you?"

"God, no. I'm not reckless. It was just a crazy evening and I guess I wasn't thinking."

"You could've been hurt out here, you know."

"I know. You're right. And I'm thankful."

"What if you'd rolled over? Did you notice how close you came?"

"Oh, trust me. I noticed."

"If you hadn't sunk in the snow, you would've gone right over, and there's a hell of a drop on the other side. Out here in this...this mess, you could've ended up unconscious for who knows how long. It's after four in the God damn morning, for Christ's sake."

"Hey, whoa." Murphy held up a palm. "Hold your horses, there, Rough Rider. Sounds like a lot of 'would haves' and 'could haves' in there. I was lucky, I know, and luckier still that you arrived."

"I take it there's no one waiting for you? Who'd come looking?"

Murphy arched an eyebrow, her look challenging and rather irritated. "As a matter of fact, no."

"I bet you don't even have an emergency blanket in your car."

Murphy turned in her seat and squared off with her. The dim light allowed only the side of her face to show, but Riley could tell from the keen look in one eye that she'd probably overstepped.

"As a matter of fact, I *do* have a blanket in the car. In the spare compartment beneath the carpet in back. Which, as you well know, I could not get to."

"Through the backseat," Riley countered. "You could have. More than an hour in a blizzard dropped the temperature in there so low—"

"I'm well aware of how cold it was, thank you. I'm not an idiot."

"I didn't call you an idiot."

"Just because I don't know how to turn a car inside out, doesn't make me a fool."

"I didn't say that it did."

"Well, you certainly implied as much."

"Okay, look. I'm sorry. I'm not in the mood to argue."

"Neither am I." She tightened the cap on her bottle. "How much longer will this take?" She jutted her chin toward her car.

Riley adjusted her hat and pulled up her hood. This conversation was over. "Should be enough." She got out and shut the door. "Better be," she mumbled into the wind.

She thanked God when the Volkswagen purred. Fifties music blared from the CD player. *Cool, she likes the old stuff.* She shut off the music and dashed back outside and unhooked the cables. She jumped back in, switched off the heater fan, and disconnected the useless cell phone charger from its port. Around her, an empty coffee cup and wrappers from two breakfast bars littered the passenger floor. A bulging laptop case sat on the seat, and she wondered how much comfort it provided as a pillow.

Could have had a few sweet moments getting to know a very alluring lady. But no. Now, she's pissed off. Nice work, knight in shining armor. Rough rider. She grinned at the term.

The driver's door opened abruptly and wind and snow barged in. Murphy bent down, earflaps on that funky hat loose and swinging at her cheeks.

"What's the verdict?"

Riley nodded as she unfolded herself from the small car. Murphy backed up to let her out and they stood toe-to-toe, squinting at each other, shoulders hunched.

"You're good to go, but take it slow and steady." Riley stepped aside and unconsciously guided Murphy by the arm into the driver's seat. She leaned into the opened doorway, blocking the storm. "Don't use any accessories. Just the defroster on low, if you have to."

Murphy nodded at the gauges, then reached for her laptop case.

"I want to pay you for all you've done."

"No."

"Yes." She put a checkbook and pen on the dash and pulled off her gloves. "Don't argue."

Riley reached in, grabbed the checkbook, and tossed it onto the passenger seat. "No. Now, do you have enough gas to get home?"

Murphy glared up at her. "Jesus, Mom. Are you always this stubborn?"

"Yes." Riley bent closer to check the gas gauge herself, and her cheek brushed the top of Murphy's furry hat. The faint scent of sweet spring rain reached her, a perfume seductive and welcoming, and she withdrew immediately. *What did the fuel gauge read?*

"Listen, Riley." Murphy touched her arm again and the sensation struck her as tangibly as if her arm was bare. She suddenly wished she wasn't wearing three layers of clothing beneath her thick jacket. "I *do* thank you. Maybe we'll see each other around town—under different circumstances?"

Hungry, wet, exhausted, and even a bit irritated, Riley heard sincerity in Murphy's words and thought of how wrong it was that no one was out there losing her mind, worrying, waiting for Murphy Callahan to come home.

"You're welcome. Maybe we will. Take care now."

She shut the door and backed away, back to her Jeep, where she stood in the snowy wind and stared after the disappearing taillights.

CHAPTER FIVE

Murphy opened her front door. Razor looked her up and down, and the piercings above her right eye glittered in the porch light.

"Sweats. Nice outfit. Surprised there isn't a line of butches sniffing around your door."

"God, you're gross. Get in here. You're scaring the neighbors."

"You don't have any." Tall and ridiculously thin in baggy jeans and olive fatigue jacket, Razor and her deadpanned humor were as striking as the gold and red stripes in her spiked hair. She headed for the kitchen, raising and lowering a large Spiritus pizza box as proof she could open and close the straight edge razor tattooed down her left arm.

"Figured you'd be staying in tonight."

"I've been working here all day and I'm beat." Murphy leaned over the box and inhaled. "And I'm starving."

"Tell me you have beer."

"Help yourself and grab my wine." She put plates and napkins on the table. "Want to go over that Easter theme show for next week while we eat? Or wait?"

"Wait." Heineken in hand, Razor retrieved a wine glass for Murphy and sat. "It's Saturday night, for God's sake. Besides, mixing religion with pepperoni makes me vomit."

"Good point." Razor could always be counted on to make them— like everything else she did—graphically. Murphy opened the box and laid a broad slice on each plate.

Being a transplanted New Yorker, Razor folded the crust in half and aimed the point of her slice at her mouth. "Are you really going to be able to unload all that crap you have out there?" She tipped her head toward the cluttered living room as she bit off the first couple of inches.

"It's not crap, and yes, I will. Shoes and handbags are big sellers. Sorry the room's such a mess. I was taking inventory." She pointed at her as she raised her own slice. "How many times have I told you that you, too, could make money by running an eBay store?"

Razor spoke around a mouthful of food. "You spend your free time collecting other people's junk and cleaning it—hoping it'll sell. Now *that's* appealing. Fumigate your dinky little car lately?"

"Stop picking on me. It's not junk and it's not disgusting work. Bryce and I had a ball getting it off the ground and it's paid off." She filled her glass and took a sip. "And you love this place, my little piece of heaven on the water. It's not just *Nightlight* paying the bills."

"Speaking of *Nightlight*...Have you checked your email today?" Murphy shook her head and took another bite. "Well, go fire up the laptop. Management dropped an email bomb this morning."

Murphy stopped chewing. WCCD management never interfered with what the DJs put on the air. In fact, when she and Razor proposed *Nightlight* and landed contracts two years ago, they hadn't dreamed of winning such creative freedom. Management had only required anonymity for the Sable character, and all parties had readily agreed. An "email bomb," as Razor put it, really piqued her curiosity.

Murphy wiped her mouth and hands and hurried into the little room off the kitchen for her laptop. "What's going on?" She returned just as fast, pushed the pizza box aside to make room, and opened her mail.

"I'll let you see for yourself."

Murphy snorted after just a couple seconds. "They want us to participate in Carnival Week?" She took another bite and pointed her pizza slice at the screen. "Looks like every business in town is listed here, doing something. What are we...?" She sat back. "A live broadcast? How's that supposed to work if we're—"

"Read the whole thing."

After a few more seconds, Murphy looked up again. "God. A masquerade party."

"Yup."

"Oh, I don't know about this, Razor. How will Sable still be the aloof, secret friend to listeners if they can get up-close and personal, even in costume?"

"Doesn't look like we've been given a choice." Razor reached for more pizza. "Actually, I think it could be pretty fun."

"Well, it's for a good cause. I'm all for raising money for HOW, but I'm not thrilled about the whole damn town knowing who I am." She closed the laptop with finality. "I like our privacy just the way it is."

"We have till August to come up with costumes, Murph."

"Costumes. It's going to take suits of armor to keep us anonymous. *Nightlight* is a smash for a reason." Murphy drank half her wine at once. "I don't like messing with a good thing."

"You don't like going out any more, period. And you know it. A hot, single woman dropping out of circulation," Razor posted air quotes with two greasy fingertips, "is never a *good thing.*"

Murphy went to the counter. "Don't start." She refilled her glass, scowling. "I've recovered well since Bryce died, thank you very much. That has nothing to do with exposing Sable to the world."

"Listen a sec." Razor leaned back. "Jesus. I hate it when you make me think like an adult." She waited for Murphy to take a mouthful of wine before continuing. "You work around here all day and play Sable at night. You don't date. You don't even go out with Tina and me unless it's some special occasion. Want to show me your little black book?"

"You're pushing, Razor."

"I'm your best friend. I'm entitled." She saluted Murphy with her beer bottle. "What if, just to get out of the damn house, mind you, you picked up a little part-time job?"

"Seriously?" Murphy set her glass down hard. "Maybe I can flip burgers at McDonald's for the social stimulation." She folded her arms across her chest.

"We don't have a McDonald's around here. Eat your pizza. Just give the idea a little thought, that's all." Razor put on the oblivious, cavalier act, which irritated Murphy even more. "For instance: You like animals, and I doubt the CASA shelter would turn away a volunteer. Oh," she raised her slice triumphantly, "the senior center—"

"Stop it. Next you'll have me in training as a home health aide."

"Hey, you have the heart for that, Murph. Remember, the organization that came here all the time for Bryce *was* looking for help."

"I don't believe you!" Murphy threw up her hands. "Am I a recluse now? Jesus, Razor."

"Calm down. You're not Miss Social Butterfly, either."

"Too damn bad. I'm not interested in hooking up, which is what you're not very subtly aiming at."

Razor concentrated on her pizza, repositioning slices of pepperoni to make sure she got at least one with each bite. Murphy watched the meticulous process until she couldn't stand it any longer.

"So, are you finished harassing me?" On the verge of her next bite, Razor obviously wasn't going to respond verbally. "Don't eat that. Speak."

"Okay. I'm you're bestie, remember, so here's the deal." She put the slice down. "I know you've made progress, Murph, and I'm proud of you for it, but, seriously, your head and heart are still in Bryce's world here." She swung her arm around at the room. "I worry because the rare times you venture out, you go somewhere anonymous and safe."

"You think I'm hiding? Is that it?"

"Are you? That caller with the creamy voice, you're very comfortable with her. And she's *anonymous and safe*."

"Oh, please, do not go there."

"You do get a little—"

"I get a little what?"

"Well...I don't know, soft." Razor took a quick swig of beer. "I have to watch your levels when you chat with her. You...you soften up."

Murphy rolled her eyes. *I don't believe this.* "Not true."

"It is, and I think you relax because she's—"

"Yeah, yeah. 'Anonymous and safe.' Couldn't be because she's got the most seductive alto in freaking America."

"You do realize she calls at least once a week now. She likes you, too. A lot...and I think it's pretty obvious."

"Razor Delaney. You put something in that Heineken? We have a lot of regular callers. There's nothing different about—"

"Oh yes, there is and you know it."

❖

"Patent leather shoes. With straps that cut into the tops of your ankles." The woman's craggily voice belied her amusement. "I mean, torture on Easter? Was that supposed to be appropriate or something?"

Murphy laughed as she nodded toward her mike. "Another line just lit up, Grunt. You've touched a nerve. I remember them well, too. God forbid our mothers ever realized that patent leather reflected up."

Grunt chortled. "You got that right, Sable. Thanks for letting me chip in."

Murphy reached for the next call but heard Razor cut in.

"After church, I wore high-tops with my dress all day."

Still laughing when she hit the blinking button, Murphy fumbled over the air. "H-hi. Hello. This is *Nightlight*. Welcome."

"Hello, Sable."

Murphy's head swiveled to the monitor. That easy alto was back. Mentally, she scurried to compose an image, as always, whenever that voice tripped her senses.

"Well, hello. Glad you could join us tonight." Distantly, she wondered if her voice "softened," as Razor claimed.

"Same here. I just couldn't resist this topic. I want to contribute a Swiss dot dress that scratched and itched. Along with those damn patent leather shoes that hurt. White ones."

"Oh, my."

"And the broad hat with little flowers in the band."

Murphy had yet to formulate a clear picture of this woman but somehow knew the Easter outfit didn't suit her. She chuckled. "Wide satin ribbon flowing from the hat?"

"You got it. Really, really awful."

"And what's more evil than Swiss dot?"

"Exactly." The smooth voice broke into a muffled laugh. "Nothing is."

"And the stiff, ruffled slip underneath."

"Aw, hell, yes. Like a bristle brush."

"I bet you begged to get out of it."

"I had to suffer through Easter dinner in it. That'll ruin a kid's appetite in a big way."

"And after dinner, you were in play clothes, outside getting dirty."

"Baseball in the neighbor's backyard. Happiest memories of Easter. Do they still make Swiss dot?"

"They do. And little girls are still subjected to it."

"Hopefully, fewer than years ago. Moms are more tuned in these days."

"A well-deserved shout-out to smart moms everywhere. I was forced into the navy blue dress with the white trim, patent leathers, the hat, the tiny white purse—for a whole day. We were up and out from eight till dark visiting relatives. No time for this girl to go out and play."

"And now you're this bewitching woman, crooning to an adoring audience that takes you in every night. All sight unseen."

Murphy just looked at the mike, lost for words. She glanced at Razor and received a sideways, cautionary look back.

"Well, ah, thank you, but, more accurately, it's the ex-folk/rock DJ who counts her blessings that she has such thoughtful, generous listeners." She blew out a breath toward her lap, relieved she'd overcome her fluster and produced some worthy response without accruing too much dead air.

"Thanks for taking my call, Sable. You have a good night."

Murphy disconnected the call with a touch of reluctance.

"Time for *Nightlight* to pay some bills, everyone. We'll be back for more Easter delights after this break, so stay close."

"Four minutes." Razor's voice settled her nerves.

"I need coffee."

"I just made a fresh pot," Razor said, "and a kick of sambuca should bring you back to earth, *crooner*."

"Who *is* that woman?" She still sat in her chair, staring at the monitor. "And…yes, she knocks me off my stride."

Razor chortled over the speaker. "She wishes you a good night with each call."

"She does, doesn't she?"

"Very sleepy voice," Razor said, coming in with coffee. "She needs a name."

"She doesn't."

"We'll call her Sleepy, then."

"No, you won't. I doubt she's one of Snow White's—"

"Then you give her one."

"Will you stop? If she wants to be known by something, she'll tell us. Besides, I'd feel funny asking."

"Since when?"

"Since her mother put her in Swiss dot. Damn, that's awful."

Razor laughed as she returned to her booth, but Murphy knew she'd admitted to feeling differently about this caller.

CHAPTER SIX

R azor lifted her foot off the gas as they edged through the foot traffic on Commercial Street and then braked so slowly she made the wheels grind. Murphy shook her head.

"Why are we stopping?"

"We're just being courteous." She grinned impishly and nodded toward a woman about to walk across their path. "She's worth slowing for, don't you think?"

Murphy checked her watch impatiently before following Razor's line of sight. "This luncheon you're dragging me to begins in five min—oh."

"Yeah, oh."

Razor brought her old Subaru to a complete stop, and they watched the woman in cargo shorts and T-shirt, her concentration on the Portuguese sweet roll in her hand. After a nonchalant wave of appreciation, she hefted a worn, dirty tool belt farther up onto her shoulder and her tanned, well-defined biceps flexed in the midday sun.

"Mm-mmm." Razor shook her head. "If I wasn't attached…"

"You'd jump out and end up getting arrested."

Razor sighed. "Yeah, probably." She drove on. "Can't fool me, Murphy Callahan. You'd like a feel of those muscles. You see her thighs? Those calves? Jesus. I bet she's got abs you could bounce a dime—"

"Will you concentrate on the road? There are people walking here."

"Admit it." Razor crawled around a bicycle. "She was hot. Work boots, ball cap, Oakleys. You wanted her, didn't you?"

"You are awful," Murphy said with a laugh.

"And I'm right. She got your hot spot a-tingling, didn't she?"

Murphy howled. "Jesus, shut up."

"Hey, Tina wants to know when we'll get an answer, by the way." She sped up a bit as they reached the West End. "She's taking nothing less than 'yes.'"

Murphy looked out the window, dreading this discussion. She didn't want to be a third wheel on a night out with Razor and Tina, and she *definitely* didn't want to be set up with a date.

"I'm still thinking about it."

"Well, Memorial Day weekend is coming up fast. Think harder."

"I just don't know, Raz."

"Come on. Remember, we've been over this issue. How many times?" *Plenty. No way I could forget.* "The Larsons had their barn all done over and it's spectacular. It'll be sweet. We'll dance and drink and laugh all night."

"A country night, Razor? You know that's not my thing."

"Oh, like country is *my* thing? They're calling it a 'hoedown' for a reason," Razor said, that wicked grin back on her face. "We'll have fun. We can be as outrageous as we want."

"Now *that's* appealing."

"Quit being a fart. Say yes."

Murphy exhaled hard. Razor could be relentless.

"Okay, yes."

Razor shouted, "Yee-ha!" out the window as they parked at the Provincetown Inn.

❖

Riley pulled a Coors Light from the six-pack in her tiny refrigerator and flopped onto the futon in the corner. The long day had her aching in spots that the shower hadn't helped, and she vowed never to work in the sun for nine hours again, not when she had night commitments, too. The new deck she finished for an East End rental took far longer than estimated, especially when the tide came in. She hadn't even had a chance to grab supper when Pawz called with a crisis about a collapsed rack of shelves that she *had* to fix immediately. In all, it made for a fourteen-hour day on nothing but a sweet roll.

Too tired to eat, she clicked on the television and zoned out. Two hours later, she awoke to the *Tonight Show*'s opening monologue and laughed until her hunger returned. She canvassed the fridge to no avail—beer, ketchup, pickles, and something in an old Chinese takeout box she didn't feel courageous enough to open.

She returned to the futon with the jar of sour pickle wedges, shut off the television, and opened her laptop. She brought up WCCD Radio's page and sat back as a rickety voice came from the tiny speaker.

"I don't go for those sexy clothes, showing everything the Lord gave ya. Takes all the mystery away, not to mention what it says about the woman."

"You think it's demeaning, then, showing a lot of skin?"

Sable's voice crackled out of the laptop, and Riley frowned at it. Note for tomorrow, she told herself: buy Bluetooth speaker.

"I do. Take that...that Mariah Carey. Now, I know I'm way past over the hill and too old-fashioned, but she practically pops right out of those dresses. How does she sing so good without flopping out everywhere?"

Riley laughed right along with Sable.

"Very carefully, I'd imagine, and with the help of some strategically positioned tape. She's a beautiful woman, caller. Sorry, but I can't share your position on that one."

Riley muttered, "Atta girl, Sable."

"Y'don't think it makes her look...y'know, cheap?"

"Personally, no."

The elderly voice sighed. *"Guess I gotta get with the times, then, huh?"*

"Everyone's entitled to her opinion. There's nothing wrong with that at all."

"Okay, I suppose. Well, thanks for listening to this old crone rant, Sable."

"Correction: You're not an 'old crone.' You're a wise, experienced woman."

"And you're a sweetie. Love ya."

Riley bit into another pickle and stuffed a second pillow under her head. Too comfortable now to get up and turn on her old stereo, she underscored her mental note about the Bluetooth. Damn, if she wasn't hooked on this woman. Try otherwise as she might, most nights ended this way, alone with a voice. She sighed, reminding herself that her punishing workload ultimately would brighten her life. She set the pickle jar on her stomach and assessed its contents.

"Well," Sable said, sounding a bit winded. *"It's been a very busy*

night. Who would've thought our topic would be so hot going into our third hour. In case you've just joined us, tonight we're hip-deep in women's attire, the what, how, and whys of it—on others as well as ourselves. Don't be afraid to chime in. Our direct line is 555-201-1112 or drop a note to nightlight-dot-com. We'll be right back after this little break. Stay close."

Riley watched the color needle on the screen bounce with the station's signal strength. She hardly ever resisted the temptation to call anymore, but did limit herself to once a week. She figured she'd be perceived as a stalker if she called more frequently. But tonight, the thought of sending a note struck her, and she sat up and started typing madly. Halfway through, she stopped and reread what she'd rattled off, then added more.

Riley grinned at her composition, arrowed over to the "Send" button, and stopped herself short. Her name. It would show up on the email. Provincetown was a very small town, and she wasn't sure she wanted it to attach her name to such personal thoughts.

She picked up the phone and dialed instead. *Screw the stalker thing.*

"WCCD Radio," the always-official voice answered.

"Hi. I'm calling for *Nightlight*?"

"Great. Do you wish to give your name?"

Riley wondered if this woman who always screened the calls recognized her by now.

"Ah, no, I…"

"Can be any name you choose."

"I know, but…Well…" Without thinking, she blurted, "RB." *Why in the name of God did I do that?*

"Arby. Got it. Sable will be on with you in a few."

And she was on hold, listening to the commercial currently running over the air.

RB. Real smooth move, dude. Didi will bust a gut laughing. I'll never hear the end of this.

"Good evening. This is Sable and you're live on *Nightlight*."

As usual, Riley's throat tightened. She hurried down a sip of Coors and took a breath.

"Hi."

"Hi there. This is…Arby?"

"Eh, yes," she managed, still regretting giving her name. "Hi, Sable."

"First time calling?"

"First? No, no. We've spoken quite a few times before." Riley thought she'd been disconnected. Sable had gone silent. "Hello?"

"Well. Hi, Arby. Sorry, I didn't recognize the voice at first. I'm happy you called. It's great to hear from you again. Are you going to add to our hot discussion tonight, I hope?"

"Just my humble opinions."

"You know I'm always eager to hear your opinions. Fire away."

Riley took another sip of beer and read aloud what she'd typed.

"I'm old-fashioned, too, and love the classy lady look. A dress and heels, subtle makeup, it's a turn-on."

"I see. You're...you're not alone in your opinion, that's for sure."

"And too much skin? Is there such a thing?" She smiled when she heard Sable laugh. "No, seriously, the mystery is a big part of it. Just what the lady shows and how she shows it, tell me a lot, but also say a lot about her. And one on one? I enjoy the discovery, and I appreciate the lady who enjoys granting it."

Sable missed a beat and Riley caught it. The idea of really reaching *this* woman made her day. *Another note to self: meet this woman some day.*

"Arby, I can't say I've heard it said any better."

"Like I said, just my opinion. How about you? Sorry if you've been over this already tonight. I just tuned in, but I'm sure your listeners would love to know where you stand."

"Just tuned in, you say?" The playfulness in Sable's seductive voice was, in itself, a turn-on. "Does that mean *Nightlight* is your last resort this evening? I'm deeply crushed."

"Oh no, really. I...I worked late and just crashed." Riley mentally shook her head, rushing to reassure this stranger on the phone. She relaxed back onto the futon, admittedly comfortable with Sable. This game they played more often lately grew easier with each call. "So how about it, Sable? Where do you stand on the issue?"

"Well, we did touch on it earlier, but I'm a dress-up kind of girl—but only on special occasions. Jeans and T-shirts are my first choices."

"And on other women?"

Sable chuckled. "I appreciate the Mariah Careys of the world, too, believe me, as well as the tailored suit and the jeans-and-shirt look on a woman. And...I confess to drooling over hard-working butches in shorts and tanks, too. I'm as taken by toned muscles and broad shoulders, the hard abs as much as any woman. I'm only human, after all, and…well, as you put it so succinctly, is there really such a thing as too much skin?"

Riley was smiling so hard her face hurt. She ran a palm over it briskly. *I should get off the damn phone. This woman could make me come in my shorts.*

"Arby? Are you still with us?"

Riley upended her Coors for a severe blast. *She's loving every minute of this. Just as much as I am.*

"Oh, I'm right here. Thank you for being so honest."

"Goes both ways, my friend."

CHAPTER SEVEN

Murphy kicked off her shoes, left her clothes in a heap on the rug, and fell into bed. More exhausted mentally than physically, she lay staring at the ceiling for the next hour, listening to one low, buttery soft voice in her head.

The alto lingered over her memory of Bryce's voice, and with a twinge of guilt, Murphy acknowledged that it was louder. Uplifting and welcome. She pulled a pillow over her face, then tossed it away and stared at Bryce's picture across the room.

"Am I losing it? You're the one, you know. Always will be."

Without a second thought, she went to her closet and revealed Bryce's favorite suit, the black one she'd wear to court whenever a case required she impress a judge. Murphy hurried back to bed, thankful she'd made the right decision when parting with Bryce's clothes and kept that suit. She could see it from the bed now, while snug under the covers with memories of long loving arms around her.

The phone rang and she hesitated to answer. At this hour, it could only be one person. The only one she dared open her mouth to at this moment.

"Yes, Razor, I'm still awake."

"So, I repeat: What's an Arby?"

Murphy sighed heavily as the present swirled over the past in her mind. "We did this in the parking lot an hour ago."

"Seriously, though. What kind of a name is Arby?"

"Go to sleep. Tina will boot you onto the couch."

"I mean…What? Does she make roast beef sandwiches?"

Murphy had to laugh. "You're an idiot."

"I can't believe we *finally* get a name after all these weeks and it's friggin' *Arby*."

"So…" Murphy tried, shaking her head, "so what?"

"Couldn't be something sexy, like…Alex or Reese or…or Shane. No, it's *Arby the Sandwich Dyke*."

"I'm hanging up now."

"No way you'll be able to keep a straight face when she calls again. I promise you."

"Not if you keep this up."

"Murph, listen."

Murphy yawned. She didn't need to listen to *any* voice, not for at least the next eight hours.

"What?"

"It really is time to start thinking about what's going on."

Murphy sat up. "What are you talking about?"

"You know what I'm talking about. Don't lose sight of the big picture."

"Cripes. Go to bed."

"You two were on the phone for ten minutes straight tonight. Calls sat in queue, waiting. I know you saw them."

"Oh, we just got carried away. It was fun."

"Uh-huh. You're lying there now, I just know, thinking of how much *fun* it was listening to her voice."

"Actually, right now I'm lying here thinking I'm losing my mind. So I'm going to hang up."

"Don't get so close, Murph. It's not real."

"Razor. Cool your jets and get some sleep."

Razor hesitated on the line and Murphy hoped she'd come to her senses. *It's just flirting and there's no harm in that. It's all part of* Nightlight*'s schtick…right?*

❖

Murphy set the Aussie-style hat on her head just so and rolled her eyes in the ladies' room mirror. Razor will love this, she thought, and she'll stop nagging about the damn hoedown.

"So come out of there and show me!" Razor yelled as she entered her booth.

Murphy posed in the doorway, a sideways stance complete with suggestive, over-the-shoulder look.

Razor's eyebrow piercings danced in the studio lights. "Oh yeah!" She hurried closer. "It's great, Murph. I love it. Do you?"

"Well, yeah. I guess I do." She took off the hat and went to her position at the microphone. "It *is* cute, isn't it?"

"Sexy is what it is." Excited, Razor followed closely. "Now, what've you got for an outfit?"

"An outfit? Like what? Farmer overalls or something? Because, if you think—"

"Hell, no. Just some tight jeans, a western shirt. How about a midriff—"

"No. Next, you'll have me in Daisy Dukes. It's just a get-together, right? This hoedown?"

Razor nodded. "And you want to put on a good show." Murphy sent her an icy look. "You *do*, because the place will be crawling with eligible women."

Murphy rolled up to her counter and adjusted her mike. "I'm beginning to think a blind date would be better—and I hate them."

"But—"

"But nothing, Raz. I'm not 'on the make.' I'm just hoping you'll quit bugging me."

"Murph." Razor rested a hip on the counter and Murphy cringed at the pregnant pause. *Here we go again.* "Do you even remember your last date? Wasn't it, well, last summer, when you went out with that cop?"

"Toni, yes. And we went out a few times, *if you recall*. She just lived her job twenty-four seven…and wooing me at the gun range didn't work. Sorry. She carried a gun everywhere and made me a nervous wreck."

"My *point* was, that was all you did. You haven't seen any—"

"I did so. I dated Naomi, remember."

"Naomi was a flake."

"True."

Razor hugged her where she sat. Murphy hated being reminded that her solitary life needed fixing and Razor's persistence was getting old. But this tender side of Razor never failed to move her deeply.

Razor pressed her cheek to Murphy's ear.

"It took two years before you went out again, Murphy, and there've only been a couple dates in total. I want you to find somebody because you deserve it. I just want you to be happy."

Murphy gripped the arms around her. "You're such a mush. Where would I be without you?"

"Probably not stuck at a mike talking to voices in the night." Razor stood and tapped her watch. "You still going with the 'April Flowers' topic tonight?"

Relieved Razor dropped the subject, she straightened the little framed picture of Bryce next to the call board. She should have known those other women wouldn't meet her expectations; she'd set the bar pretty high. Without question, no other woman ever would. *In a lifetime, there's always that special someone.* Granted, Razor's rationale made sense; there really was nothing wrong with a little fun, but there was no way she'd drag herself through such drama again.

"Yeah, so, I thought we'd start with flowers, then broaden things to gifts, tokens in general."

Back behind the glass now, Razor nodded. "I remember the time my brother gave his girlfriend a snake in a shoebox."

"No way?"

"Yeah. She ran screaming from the kitchen, fell down the back steps, and split her lip open on the cement." Razor looked up from her work and grinned. "They were seven."

Murphy laughed at Razor's demented amusement. "My best gift ever was Bryce's diamond."

The absence of the commitment band still made her heart catch, always reminded her that, while diamonds lasted forever, people didn't. Memories of them did, however, and she knew theirs were worth preserving. *How dishonorable to let them fade.* Some days the urge to put the ring back on was hard to resist. She couldn't imagine anything ever taking its place.

"No slipping into a funk, there, Sable. Four minutes."

CHAPTER EIGHT

Murphy jumped across a puddle and hurried through the rain toward the entry of Shepley's home design center. *Why does the weather have to suck when you have time off from work?*

A shopper about to leave held the door open and Murphy scurried inside. Deep in thought about ideas for the addition to her house, Murphy hardly noticed the woman, except to see she dabbed at her face with a tissue.

"Thanks," Murphy said. "Too bad we're not ducks." She removed her windbreaker and shook off the rain. She glanced up and the woman's vivid blue eyes stopped her in mid-motion. Shaggy blond hair fell over the woman's forehead and was immediately stroked back by her broad hand.

"Well, I'll be." The woman's raspy voice spoke of laryngitis. She offered a handshake and flashed a brilliant smile that danced right down Murphy's spine. "It's…Murphy, isn't it? Murphy…Callahan, right?"

The woman was ruggedly attractive, relaxed, and obviously toned in a snug white long-sleeved T-shirt beneath a black vest.

"Um…Hello. Yes," Murphy stuttered, obligingly shaking the wide, calloused hand. "We've met, haven't we?"

The blonde dipped her head rather shyly. "Looks like I have to work on my first impression." The words came out in an agonizing croak.

"Forgive me, but your name escapes me. I'm sorry."

The curious expression felt comfortable, somehow, just like the familiarity of the woman's thin lips and rocky jawline. Murphy mentally cursed her inability to recall more details of their meeting.

The blonde's tanned, captivating face softened as tiny laugh lines formed at the corners of her eyes and mouth. "You don't remember, do you?' she asked, a teasing lilt evident in her gravelly sound. "I'm Riley. Have you sunk into any snowbanks lately?"

Stunned, Murphy took a sideways step and knew she looked shocked. She could feel the gap between her lips. *Shut your mouth, fool.*

"Jesus! Riley! H-how are you? It's great to see you." She pressed a hand to her forehead. "I can't believe I didn't recognize you. I'm so embarrassed."

Riley rocked back on her heels as she laughed. "Don't be embarrassed. It's been, what? Two months or so? Besides, you don't look the same either, not without the earflaps."

"Oh, dear God. I love that stupid hat." Their hour-long winter adventure came to mind in perfect detail. For some reason, it felt like so much more. And she sensed there was so much more still to share than what they'd exchanged that night along the road. "It really is great to see you again."

A crew of carpenters exited the store laughing and walked through their conversation.

"I feel the same way," Riley answered around the men. She pointed at her throat. "Sorry about this. Woke up with it. A total pain in the butt."

"Tea with honey," Murphy suggested, surprised that she cared.

She watched as Riley deliberately inspected her, a look that tingled through her sweater, blouse, and bra, and over her hips and down her thighs until her toes twitched. *That was bold. Flattering, but bold.*

"I had no idea I had a supermodel in my Jeep that night."

Murphy smirked. "Oh, that's rich, coming from someone who sounds like an obscene caller. Tell me how you've been."

"Good. Busy. I'm glad the winter's over. That storm after Saint Patrick's Day was the worst." They dodged a couple with two children in tow and Murphy debated suggesting someplace less distracting for this reunion, but Riley talked over them. "It had me out for three hours around nine and then, after I was all dried off and warmed up in bed, I had to go out at four."

"Any damsels in distress?"

"No, but I thought of you."

"Is that right?" Murphy was touched by the sentiment.

"Well, my power pack ran out of juice for my saw—" Two workmen eyed them for standing in the doorway. One bumped Riley on his way by. "Excuse you," she snapped. "Anyway, I was stuck in the Jeep for an hour while it charged."

"How flattering to know a problem brought me to mind."

Riley laughed. Murphy enjoyed the look of it on her, was sorely tempted to return the full-body inspection. She considered teasing further, but a busy store's entryway was hardly conducive to hanging on an attractive woman's every word. The distractions irritated her.

"I had the radio on, that talk show, *Nightlight*," Riley said. "Do you ever listen to it?"

"Yes, I do." Murphy bit her lip.

"Women were complaining about having another storm, and the host, Sable, she had a tale very similar to ours."

Murphy felt her nerves ignite. She remembered that show. She remembered mentioning how she'd been stranded unprepared in a snow bank, remembered being careful to avoid specifics that could jeopardize her identity and ruin the show's premise, its mystique. She also remembered second-guessing herself for even bringing up the topic on the radio in the first place. *Serves you right.*

But Riley didn't wait for Murphy to respond.

"Damn, that Sable melts me with that voice. A puppy at her feet. It's pathetic." She uttered a painfully gruff chuckle. "She could recite the phone book and women would swoon, I swear. Anyway, it made her story very personal. Made me think of you."

"Riley the Rough Rider, the knight in shining armor, has a soft side." As soon as the words were out, Murphy wondered what Riley would think of her.

"Listen, ah," and Riley shuffled nervously, "it's been great bumping into you. I'm glad. I mean…finally, our paths have crossed again."

Murphy found herself pleased by it, too, and she didn't want them to part, definitely not so soon. But now that nagging deception poked her in the back, the role she was obligated to maintain. *It would be nice to level with her, if I could. Wonder what she'd say if she knew. Hell, I'd embarrass us both.*

"This has been a fun surprise," and she extended her hand. "I'm sure we'll continue to cross paths around town."

"Sorry to have kept you, Murphy. I hope I'll see you again soon. Have a good weekend."

"Thanks, Riley. Same to you." She entered the store and forced herself not to look back.

❖

"I stay away from the dunes on Memorial Day weekend, Sable. Let the tourists enjoy them. I head to the beach if the weather's decent."

"The forecast is promising, Digger."

"Yeah, I'm excited. We're planning on spending each day, all day, the old-fashioned way, y'know? Blanket, coolers, portable radio, slathering on the suntan lotion."

"No partying for you, Dig?"

"Nah. Getting too old for that stuff." She laughed gruffly. "Lose precious hours in recovery."

"Unfortunately, I know what you mean. I prefer a laid-back, relaxing time myself."

"Uh-huh. I figured you were the quiet type. Have a great weekend."

"You, too, Dig, and thanks for the call." Murphy clicked open the next line. "Welcome to *Nightlight*. This is Sable and you're on the air."

"Tea dance, Sable!" The young female voice bounced into Murphy's ear. "It's the only place to be."

"That you, Belle?"

"Sure is. Friends are having a party Saturday night, but as of Sunday afternoon, it's time to go out and dance. Why don't we ever see you there? You know it's the best party in town."

"Sable needs to maintain her mystique. Once upon a time, you couldn't tear me off the dance floor, but a few years have passed since then, and it's quiet time I cherish now."

"Bummer. Well, if you ever do come, make sure you look me up. I'll be in the DJ booth most likely."

"I'll certainly do that."

Murphy let a Melissa Etheridge song loose and went to make coffee at Razor's desk.

"Do I sound staid and stodgy, not wanting a wild weekend?"

"Hell no. Well, stodgy, maybe."

"Thanks a lot."

"A tea dance sounds like a good idea, don't you think?" Razor grumbled when Murphy just returned to her seat and raised her lips to the mike.

"Looks like Melissa will be back at the Melody Tent in Hyannis again this year. Did everyone see the events calendar? Let's hope we have a great summer. We've certainly earned it, after the never-ending winter we had, don't you think? So, I'm still eager to hear your plans. Are you looking forward to tourist season on the Cape?" She dragged the cursor on her monitor to the "Play" button, where a song by Mary

Chapin Carpenter waited. "I'm staying close to home this summer. I know I'm fortunate to live here, but I confess to having a love-hate thing about tourists. No question it would be hell for us without them and the more, the merrier, and all that, but I'm also grateful for the restaurants, entertainers, businesses, and property owners who cater to them. Let's remember to support our locals. We're all in this together."

She tapped the button and sent music out over the airwaves.

Privately, Razor's voice crackled into her headset. "You'd be a shoo-in for mayor."

"Just what I need." Being one of P-town's most popular personalities had its perks, even if shrouded by the mystery of night radio, she mused. That anonymity was an integral part of life now, a part she'd learned to play—and depend on. *Since losing Bryce.*

"Next call, Murph. It's her."

She cleared her throat and refocused.

"Good evening and welcome to *Nightlight*. This is Sable."

"Good evening to you, too. Thanks for taking my call."

Murphy bit her lip at the familiar voice. *Razor thinks you have such influence, such power over me.*

"My pleasure. What's on your mind tonight? This is Arby, am I right?"

"As always. I just thought I'd chime in about the holiday weekend."

"Let me guess. A barbecue bash on the deck with a cooler of liquid refreshment."

"No," the laugh came with a subtle, private feel, "but not bad."

"Sailing?"

"Also, not bad."

"Hm. You're stumping me, Arby. Okay, how about a gallery tour all over town?"

"Sorry, but that's not me."

Murphy chuckled. "All right. I give. Tell us what *is* you."

"If I could, I'd take a bike ride somewhere and camp."

"Ah. So, you're the outdoorsy type? A cyclist?"

"Motorcycle."

"I see." And she wished she actually could. "But…it sounds as though you can't do this."

"No bike."

Murphy laughed. "Definite problem."

"But if I had one, I would."

"With a girlfriend who shares your enthusiasm?"

"Don't have one of them, either, but…I don't mind going solo."

"I don't believe that. You're so soft-spoken, my guess is you're tenderhearted and considerate. Girlfriends like that are in high demand."

"Oh, I look a lot, but I'm done being burned. I learned those lessons and focus on my future now. It would take a special woman to get me to commit again."

Murphy relaxed in her chair and drew the mike closer. "What's a special woman?" She couldn't resist asking. She couldn't deny being curious about whether she fit the bill.

"Eh…Well, she's smart and self-aware, considerate, funny… She'd have to put up with the kid in me, I suppose. Someone who's learned from her own lessons and isn't afraid of being herself, who she's become."

"A woman who wears her heart on her sleeve?"

"Not necessarily on her sleeve, but not buried so deeply it can't be found."

"Ah. Well said, as usual."

"What's Sable's definition of a special woman? Does she have one?"

Oh, she certainly does. Murphy shifted in her seat and sipped her coffee. She could feel Razor watching, knew Razor expected to hear a description of Bryce. But Bryce wasn't alone in her head, not with Arby's dusky voice in her ear.

"Sable lives a private life, Arby, but she values honesty and humility…a sense of humor and has a strong romantic bent."

"So Sable's also a softie, at heart."

"I think she'd admit to that. Sometimes to a fault."

"Oh, no. There's nothing wrong with that. There's no fault in a glass of wine at sunset, a hushed, intimate conversation with a special lady, maybe tucked into a cushy chair together, stealing kisses." Arby paused and Murphy took a breath. *Who are you?* "So, no, there's nothing wrong with being a softie at all."

"Well, I think there's a softie in a woman who'd ride her motorcycle off to some campsite by herself. How does that jive, Arby? I think you're holding out on us."

A hearty laugh came across the line, and a rush of satisfaction made Murphy grin at the mike.

"Yeah, well…There's an intimacy in going solo, too. Alone under the stars or taking that deep breath of morning air…Lends you strength. It'll fill you up and settle your mind."

Murphy closed her eyes as the truth of the statement hit home. The voice carried her back to breathtaking sunrises on the dunes with Bryce and then without her, tender moments that would never recur, romantic memories Arby accessed too easily. Too publicly. She sat up straighter.

"You're secret's out, Arby. The woman with the bedroom voice is a member of the softie club. We're wise to you now."

"I guess you are." Arby chuckled, and Murphy was touched by the shyness she detected.

"Thanks for sharing that. I think we needed a serious dash of the romantic tonight, considering everyone's out to celebrate the holiday weekend in big ways."

"Ah, well, not me. Work puts crazy limits on my time, but your show always…*You* always get me thinking, and I like spending time talking with a friend, especially a woman who puts her arm around you with her voice."

Murphy's mouthful of coffee stayed right where it was. Her throat jammed so quickly she couldn't swallow, or, obviously respond. *And how long has it been since I felt an arm around me?*

"Hello? Sable?"

She forced down the coffee, wishing it would flush out her traitorous mind.

"Right here. *Nightlight* appreciates devoted fans like you very much, and we're happy to be your entertainment of choice this weekend."

"I'm glad you're here, too. Thanks for listening. Hope you have a relaxing weekend."

"Thanks, Arby. Same to you, of course." She watched the line go dark. "Don't go anywhere now. We're taking a short break but will be back with some sweet Brandi Carlisle and plenty more of *Nightlight*. Stay close."

She removed her headset and gulped down the rest of her coffee as Razor arrived at her chair.

"What?"

"'Stealing kisses'? I thought you two were gonna start making out over the air."

Murphy frowned and busied herself making insignificant notes on her clipboard. "You're losing it, Razor. That conversation was perfectly fine. Stop reading into—"

"*That* conversation was just shy of sweet nothings in your ear. Maybe you don't hear yourself."

Murphy looked up. "I certainly do. Do you think I've drifted off somewhere?"

"I'm not positive where you're going, but I can guess. You need a dose of reality, not that." She jutted a thumb toward the mike. "Don't you see?"

"God, you're *so* overreacting. Calm the hell down."

Razor shoved her arms into a folded position across her chest. She pivoted and stalked toward the door, then returned. "Would Bryce want you getting all gooey over the air with some Romeo?"

Murphy was on her feet immediately.

"Do *not* bring Bryce into this. I've done nothing that Bryce would've disliked—*if* she was here to speak for herself. Which she isn't. And never will be." She blinked away tears.

Razor sighed toward her running shoes. "Okay, yeah. That was— I'm sorry for that."

"I like talking to that woman and I'll continue to do so."

Razor set her palms on Murphy's shoulders. "Just…please give some thought as to why, Murph." She kissed her forehead and walked out.

CHAPTER NINE

O h, good heavens! Murphy! It's been how many years? How've you been?"

The exclamation cut through the strains of Martina McBride's peppy "Independence Day," and stopped Murphy in mid-sip of her beer. A redhead emerged from the crowd, flipped her ponytail over her shoulder, and pecked Murphy's cheek. Names flew through Murphy's head and not one stuck.

"I think too many," she said, desperately hoping a recollection would arrive. *Jesus, is my mind so jumbled lately I can't remember a damn thing?* "I'm so sorry, and it kills me to admit it, but—"

"Oh, silly. We're not *that* far gone yet, are we? It's Nan. Nan Coggins, from the sandlot days, remember?" She feigned a batting position at home plate, hands clasping an imaginary bat too high over her right shoulder.

"Oh, God, Nan!" Murphy hugged her quickly. "Has it been eight years since that crazy summer?"

Nan pulled her aside.

"Eight that have been just fine to you! Not a touch of gray and you're just as svelte as ever." She patted her own rounded hips. "I'm still the steamroller in search of steam." Their laughter faded when Nan touched her arm. "I'm so sorry about Bryce, honey. She was such a doll."

"Thank you. Sometimes three years feels like yesterday, but I've come around, I think."

"Good for you. We have to bounce back, you know." She looked quickly at the string of women laughing and struggling with the quickstep. "So did you come to this hoedown on someone's arm tonight? Is there a special woman?"

Oddly unsettled, Murphy heard "special woman" in Arby's voice. "I'm here with friends, the kind who don't take no for an answer."

Nan chuckled. "Oh believe me, I hear you. After Gretchen and I split up that summer?"

"I remember. That was bad."

"Damn softball drama. Anyway, I had friends on my case, too. Shut them up by making a really squeaky third wheel out of myself. They left me to my own devices soon enough, but you *do* have to get out and about eventually."

"I know." *Is that why I'm here?* She stifled a frustrated sigh.

"Well, I'm glad you came. This country stuff is kinda fun after all, don't you think?" She leaned closer confidentially. "Plenty of prospects here tonight, so we have to keep our eyes open." She poked Murphy's arm. "Time to mingle. Got to get my money's worth out of this new pearl-button shirt."

"It's a dandy," Murphy said, grinning.

"Darn tootin', it is. Catch you later."

Murphy watched her cross to the opposite side of the crowded barn and wondered where the years had gone. In a previous life, she and Bryce brought their own crowds to such get-togethers and danced till they could barely crawl into bed—and then made love till dawn. Age limitations aside, she knew too well that those days were behind her now. She tamped those thoughts back down into hiding.

Wearing a plaid shirt and skintight jeans that told everyone she weighed less than a corn stalk, Razor slipped her arm beneath Murphy's.

"Let's go, gal pal." She drew her onto the dance floor.

"I don't know these country dances, Razor!"

"I just learned so I'll teach you."

"God help me."

Side-by-side, they fumbled over their feet and struggled to keep up with Kelly Clarkson's latest hit, and laughed too much to really hear any instruction Razor managed to offer. They finally fell into sync as the song ended.

Murphy joined the rest of the dance crowd in taking a collective breath. "Just when I was getting the hang of it." She found her beer on a nearby table and finished it.

"Next dance we'll do as a group," Tina said, appearing out of nowhere and tugging Razor close by her belt. "I'm liking this leather. Very handy."

Razor kissed the tip of Tina's nose and beamed at Murphy. "Lady can't keep her hands off me."

Tina elbowed Razor. "Wouldn't surprise me if one Murphy Callahan's got dance partners all lined up." Murphy laughed. "I mean it. Very sweet look, Ms. Callahan, the *country girl* red gingham, slick jeans, and where'd you get those sparkly boots? Damn, they're fine."

Murphy looked down at her brown wingtip boots, inlaid with contrasting cowhide and accented with rhinestones. "A friend at Spiritus loaned them to me. If we weren't an exact size match, I never would have risked wearing them tonight."

Razor snorted. "You'd be home soaking your feet already and it's only ten o'clock."

Tina eyed Murphy's hat hungrily. "Well, I wish *I* had gone with a sassy hat like yours. This leather on my head is too damn hot."

Murphy loved Tina's blunt honesty. Her bubbling personality never ceased to lift Murphy's spirits. *Razor, you're one lucky nut.* Suddenly, Tina dipped her head and stepped closer.

"Warning: Christine Ross headed your way at two o'clock. Quick—let's dance!"

"We need drinks, though, don't we?" Missing Tina's signal, Murphy caught on too late.

"Well, if it isn't Murphy Callahan."

Murphy turned to P-town's most successful developer and had her empty beer bottle removed from her hand.

"Allow me."

"Chris. It's nice to see you."

"Nice to be seen, Murphy." Chris never missed a thing, and the sharp cut of her silver hair enhanced the keen look of her long, angular face. Decked out in red shirt and black jeans, Christine Ross stood tall, confident, and close. She sent a glance to Razor and Tina. "I'm stealing her, ladies."

Murphy tossed them a hopeless look as she was guided toward the bar.

"Another Sam Adams?" Chris asked. "Or a zinfandel? Martini?"

"Sam Adams would be fine. Thank you."

Chris spoke to the bartender, and Murphy simply observed, admittedly taken by Chris's assertive bearing—and the attention. Chris shared Bryce's height and sophisticated good looks, as well as the years of education, accreditations, and successes that legitimized her self-assured air, but that's where their similarities ended. Murphy was just one of many who knew why Chris's relationships notoriously fell apart like badly funded charities.

"I hope I haven't ticked off your date," Chris said, handing her the bottle.

Murphy let the backdoor inquiry slide. "How've you been? What's new with you these days?"

"Ah, let's see..." She leaned back, a hand in her back pocket, and scanned the barn's upper reaches. "Closed on the old Genoa motel parcel last week. Twenty units by next summer, I hope."

"Wow, that's a major victory, isn't it? That family has held the land for generations."

Chris nodded vigorously and her face brightened. "These old-timers...It's hard for them to look forward, never mind let go. And we all know the area needs more units on the water. Property like this is a gold mine. It took eight months, but they finally came around."

Murphy raised her bottle in salute, while hearing radio callers in her head bemoan the continued development of precious oceanfront. And it saddened her whenever a long-time owner surrendered to financial demands. Obviously, Chris Ross wasn't as empathetic.

A small roar came from the little raised stage in the corner, and the gaggle of women surrounding the DJ hurried onto the dance floor. More women joined them, and the catcalls and laughter intensified. The DJ upped her microphone volume to be heard.

"If I hear 'Boot Scootin' Boogie,'" Chris said, raising her voice, "I'll scream."

Murphy laughed. She didn't particularly want to hear the song either, but the prospect of a frazzled Chris Ross carried a rather naughty appeal.

At the intro to the Dixie Chicks's "Let 'er Rip," the bouncing throng whooped and began clapping and stomping along to the beat. Chris placed a palm on Murphy's back and guided her toward the barn's rear doors, which were open to the field and night sky.

"Can't hear yourself think when there are *five* lesbians in one place, let alone a hundred."

Again, Murphy laughed lightly, politely. She appreciated the respite, but her guard rose with every one of Chris's personal touches. *I could* so *do without the contact.* Murphy walked only out to the broad doors, not wanting to convey an interest in intimacy, and sipped her drink as she searched for a topic of conversation. But, never at a loss for words, Chris beat her to it.

"Didn't I hear, quite some time ago, that you were working from home now? An Internet company?"

"I am. And loving every minute of it." She cocked her head when a familiar voice piqued her interest. The noise in the barn camouflaged it, however, and thwarted her professionally hewn listening skills. *I know that laugh.*

"Well, that's courageous. Correct me if I'm wrong, but the last time we met, you were running the entertainment for us, my commitment ceremony…eh, my first, that is." Murphy nodded, only partial thought recalling that huge paycheck. "And now you've started your own company? In what field?"

Murphy supplied the usual answers but only half-heard Chris's responses, and cared even less. Most of her attention zeroed in on the snippets of conversation at the refreshment table, just inside the barn. That hearty, sexy laugh struck her again, but disappeared too soon into the maelstrom of voices. Razor's familiar sound also carried to her for a moment, and vanished just as quickly.

"I'm impressed, you know," Chris was saying from within an arm's length. *When did that happen?* "I know you enjoy the luxury of the work-at-home world, but would you ever consider developing a side business for a client?"

Being drawn from her audible surveillance—the most captivating part of her evening—seriously irked her, but she gave herself a mental slap.

"I've never given it a thought, because what I'm into suits me so well. At least right now, it does."

"Right now, exactly, but what about down the road?" Chris leaned on an arm against the barn door and effectively boxed Murphy in place on three sides. "What you've done sounds perfect for someone looking to expand her business, as I am."

Close to losing her avenue of retreat, Murphy quickly weighed her options. She doubted that an advance by Chris would send her screaming into the woods; kissing her probably would be…okay…and lack of interest would take it from there. Of course, she could return to the chaos of one hundred drunk, stomping lesbians…

There's that laugh again. I know I've heard—

Something akin to electricity sizzled down Murphy's spine, and she froze with the realization. *It's you.* Without thinking, she looked back at the crowd in the barn, as if she could literally see the voice, match it to a face.

Chris turned her chin back with a fingertip. The touch instantly derailed Murphy's delinquent train of thought.

"Chris."

"There's no reason we couldn't talk about it, is there?"

An unexpected memory of Bryce, approaching her that first time at a New York party, gallant and polite, flashed through Murphy's mind. It illuminated her current situation so brightly, she almost cringed. "Seriously, I have a lot on my plate right now, but I'm really happy with the way things are."

Arby. Who are you?

Chris curled a wave of Murphy's hair behind her ear. "Would you consider dinner some night?" Her voice dropped to a whisper. "We're not kids, Murphy. A few drinks and some serious talk. Maybe some *not* so serious talk. No harm, no foul."

Arby. No harm, no foul. I know...and shouldn't know. Let it go.

A loud stutter-step at the doorway broke them apart, Chris backing away and Murphy exhaling subtly with relief, and they looked on as a woman wearing a black cowboy hat stumbled out of the barn. She muttered slurred words to someone she'd left behind.

"Dyke drama," Chris grumbled. "Lesbians and too much booze set us back decades. That one's old enough to know better, too."

"Too much alcohol affects everyone," Murphy said, still following the woman's progress toward the shadows. Defined muscles and a broad back filled out the yellow Henley she wore quite well, in Murphy's opinion. Her bearing grew steadier with each cautious stride. A jolt of awareness straightened Murphy where she stood. *Riley. Our paths cross again.*

Murphy sighed, disappointed to see her in such a state, and returned to searching the crowd for that voice. Arby's voice. *Why am I doing this?*

"So, what do you say, Murphy?" Chris persisted. "Can I give you a call sometime? Maybe we can get together? Talk business, at least?"

Her search abandoned, Murphy faced Chris and tried to ignore the surprising wave of defeat, of resignation that threatened to overwhelm her.

"Maybe lunch sometime, Chris." It was the best she could do.

CHAPTER TEN

Riley tossed back the rest of her Scotch and groaned. Didi snickered and Riley tried to wave her off.

"Go…count your millions or something. I'm recovering here."

Didi poured her another. "Hair of the dog, they claim," she said, "but in your case, looks like it would take a friggin' wooly mammoth."

"Hey, I tried working it off today, but it didn't help." She straightened on her stool and stretched her back.

"What? You think God was going to heal you just 'cause you spent Memorial Day Sunday working?" She made a disgusted noise.

"Sixteen by sixty-five feet. *Feet.* You have no idea what it's like to lay that many pavers. And then, tonight, the Sachez Grill dragged me out of bed for a broken freezer door."

"Don't be bitching to me, RB the Wonder Woman. You could hire help, but noooooo. *Somebody* wants all that cash." Didi sank back on her hip. "If it's body building you're after, don't bother. Just like the bankroll, you've already got what it takes. You need a woman, a babe to keep you in check."

Riley sent her an evil look. "No. That's not what it's about, Di. Not anymore." She knocked on the bar three times. "A year or so from now, I'll be out of that damn loft and in my own home, with a little luck." She winced into her drink when her back muscles spasmed.

Didi bent down so far they were eye to eye. "Why don't you call up your girlfriend Sable and ask her out? Settle down with that voice from the goddesses. Best of both worlds: cool your workaholic jets while the sex keeps your body in shape."

Riley straightened again and groaned louder. "Jesus Christ. Pick on a girl when she's down, why don't you."

"Pick on you, my ass. She's got a thing for you, RB." Didi laughed as she poured a draft for another customer and was still laughing when she returned. "Whenever I heard your name on the radio I almost peed my pants."

"Yeah, well, I was dog-tired and got a little nervous. The initials just came out."

Didi leaned on both elbows and lowered her voice.

"Couple guys in here Friday night? They got a real charge out of you two. They said you're the town's newest drama."

"That's bullshit."

"No bullshit. They said the regulars at the A House started a pool, betting on when you two will hook up."

"Well, that's just stupid. Jesus, it's not like we're having phone sex on the damn radio, Didi. We just enjoy talking."

"Uh-huh."

"I *do* wish I knew what she looked like, though."

"Well..."

Riley looked up over her glass. "Well what?"

"Well, go get her."

"Oh, sure. That's keeping my priorities straight, isn't it? No, I'm staying on track. I told you that." She ran a hand through her hair and returned to slumping over her drink. "God *damn*, my head hurts more than the rest of me."

"Gee, must be those 'priorities' acting up. What the hell were you thinking, drinking into oblivion at that thing, anyway?"

Riley shook her head. "Obviously, I wasn't thinking a whole lot. I don't even know why I went."

"Well, when George Larson shows off, he does it in a big way, and he'd bragged about your work in that barn for weeks. I can understand that. But, cripes, RB. What happened?"

"Aw, probably no food in my system and two hours' sleep." She scrubbed at her face. "George brought out some wicked stuff for just us. Some home brew bathtub shit that blew the top off my head. It was good, but, God. It turned into Napalm or something when it hit the four beers in my stomach."

Didi gushed appreciatively. "You dummy. Hope you learned your lesson."

"Too old to miss that message, Di. I can't remember the last time I slept in the Jeep all night."

"And then went to work. You're crazy, you know that?"

"Yeah, probably."

"I think you were less crazy when you were a regular dating machine. Maybe you ought to revive some of the old RB. Your little radio love affair ain't going anywhere, you know."

"Love affair." She snorted. "Please." She pulled money from her wallet and stood up gingerly. "I'm going home to soak these old bones."

She purposely drove home in silence. Hearing Sable's voice would just reinforce Didi's assertion, and it was loud enough in her head already. *Girlfriend. As if.*

❖

Murphy typed "The Wow Factor" notes into the system, then pulled the old-fashioned logbook off the shelf and scribbled in the night's show info. The duplication bugged her, but there was something nostalgic about the antiquated process that she enjoyed. Plus, Razor insisted they maintain thorough records, and Murphy preferred a happy Razor to a cranky one. Like tonight. Razor still wasn't overly thrilled with the topic. Murphy slid the book back onto the shelf and lined up several songs appropriate for that special occasion that carried the convincing touch, what she amusedly termed, the "Wow Factor."

"It's going to get hotter than that," Razor mumbled when Murphy ended a call and went to commercial. "We need to weave this off in a different direction before we get into trouble."

"July Fourth isn't that far off, Razor, and summer's in full swing. A hot date is a great topic. You worry too much for the both of us."

"There are three calls already waiting, and Digger's one of them. You should strap on a chastity belt."

"Sex has never been taboo on *Nightlight*. And won't be."

"Damn straight. And I haven't had to cut anyone off since that nutcase back in April, but I'm not going to hesitate."

"I know. I know. Please try not to worry."

"Uh-huh. Three, two, one…"

"Welcome back. We're sharing some of our finest memories and taking notes tonight, and if the lights on my board are any indication, you're eager to tell all." She clicked open the first line. "Good evening. This is Sable, and thank you for joining *Nightlight*."

"Ah, yeah. Hi. My story is…Well, it was a date my brother set up, right after I came out to him."

"A good date or bad?"

"Pretty good, actually. He made sure his teammate's sister and I showed up at the same game and…I mean, I hit the jackpot. She was way prettier than I expected, and we clicked, y'know? We did a lot of beers and…" she took a breath, "we ended up in the dugout once the park emptied. I think my new silk blouse was my wow factor, because she really liked it, then she wasted no time taking it off me."

"I see. So was this the start of a good thing?"

"It was a *great* start. A great middle and a great finish. *Four times* that night. I never knew I—"

"Ohhhh-kay."

"Oh. Um…well, yeah. *Four!* She even broke the zipper diving into my jeans."

"Okay, caller. I think we get the picture. So did this encounter lead to a relationship?"

"Sure did. A whole summer. Well, actually, it lasted for our brothers' baseball season." Now, the caller laughed heartily. "Then I guess we struck out."

"Who knew the impact of buying a new blouse, huh? Thanks for sharing." She disconnected the call and heard Razor purposefully clear her throat. She clicked open the next line.

"Welcome to *Nightlight*. This is Sable. Have a 'wow factor' to share? A special song request?"

"Wow factor, Sable."

"Hi, Digger. I knew we could count on you. What do you have?"

"A fifty-seven Chevy Belair. Two-door, turquoise and cream, and enough shiny chrome for a dressing room of showgirls."

"Oooo. A classic car definitely gets a 'wow.'"

"And got more girls than I could handle, although I made a noble effort—many times, if I do say."

"I have no doubt." She relaxed into her chair, anticipating another wild tale from the gravelly voice.

"We did it on the hood, in the front seat, the backseat, and even in the trunk."

"Now that's exhausting just to think about."

"Once, a friend and I took our girls out in it and it was so roomy, we each had plenty of privacy and we got down to business simultaneously. The fifty-seven was a-rocking that night."

"Do you still have it, Dig? Not that I think you'd *need* it today, of course."

"I sold it back in nineteen ninety-eight. Was a sad day, lemme tell you. I couldn't afford to keep replacing parts. My gal and I gave it a proper send-off, though."

Murphy laughed. "I can only imagine."

"Rolled it into the backyard, set her iPad on the dash, and brought up *Texas Chainsaw Massacre*. We had microwave popcorn and three bottles of Strawberry Hill and screwed till the sun came up."

"Well! I…I suppose that was…fitting."

"Something you'd tell your grandkids about, don't you think?" Digger laughed. "All right, maybe not. I just wanted to give a salute to the ol' fifty-seven. Thanks, Sable."

"Consider it done. They don't make 'em like they used to, that's for sure. Thanks, Dig." She clicked the blinking light on her monitor. "Good evening and welcome to *Nightlight*. That's a tough act to follow, I know."

"Digger's hard to top," the easy alto said, "but I bet she'd admit she likes it."

Murphy nearly giggled at that but was too focused on the voice. *What have you been up to lately, Arby? I heard you at that hoedown.*

"You might be right," she said. "It's good to hear from you, Arby. It's been a while. Can I play a certain song tonight? Or do you have a 'wow factor' to share?"

"Well, my 'wow factor' isn't a first date story or even *mine*. It was my girlfriend's, and she set a new standard for me. We were just college freshmen, and I stopped playing the field pretty quickly."

Murphy's continued inability to form a mental picture of this woman frustrated her to no end, but she was sure a sensitive, young Arby and her enthralling voice had no problem dating in college.

"She had that special something, I take it."

"Oh yeah. Well, we'd gone out before, typical fun stuff, a concert, a sorority party. But for the third date, we planned dinner, dancing—we had great fake IDs in those days—and then spending the night in her dorm, because her roommates were away."

"Getting serious."

The wistful accent in Arby's sigh had Murphy eager for more.

"She answered her door that night, the most beautiful woman I'd ever seen. Gorgeous red dress to her knees, high heels, earrings and necklace that just sparkled in the overhead light. And she took my breath away." Murphy grinned as she doodled on her clipboard. She'd floored Bryce that way more than once. "And I thought, 'God, she's done this for me. *For me.'* And every thought of other women vanished. I wanted to move heaven and earth for her, be everything she dreamed of."

Murphy reached for her coffee, her tether to reality. She glanced at Razor, and the pierced eyebrow rose. It didn't matter what Razor thought of Arby's touching story. At that moment, Murphy didn't care that Razor knew Arby's words had stroked an aching nerve. *Yes, the special ones still exist.*

She heard the smile in Arby's voice when she added, "I was shaking when I took her hand."

"*She* was your 'wow factor.'"

"What she did said everything about her."

"It changed your approach to the rest of your night together, I bet." Murphy's curiosity brought an instant message from Razor onto her monitor.

Drink more coffee.

"It changed everything. It changed me. I was on my best behavior." Arby laughed softly. "The 'perfect gentleman,' if you will. I was determined to give her my best, and I'd never wanted to make an effort like that before. And when we arrived back at her dorm, I even offered to leave."

"My guess is she insisted you stay." Murphy simply wanted it to be so.

"She did. And she turned her roommate's little CD player on low and we slow-danced in her room for...Well, not for long, but we did."

"I gather you didn't leave that night."

"Would you?"

"Hm. Highly doubtful."

"Something about dancing in the dark, isn't there?"

"Honestly? Only one other situation comes to mind that's more intimate."

Arby paused for so long, Murphy quickly checked to see if their connection was still lit, but then the soothing voice returned, deeper than ever.

"*Nightlight* is a dance in the dark."

Murphy put down her coffee.

"Thank you, Arby. That's sweet of you to say."

"You feel it too. You're too intelligent a woman not to."

"Well..." Dancing with Arby created a dangerously distracting fantasy. "I like to think listeners and callers feel comfortable here."

"Comfortable is a pair of old shoes, Sable. *Nightlight* is far beyond that. It's anonymous, and you make it intimate."

"Callers like you make my job easy, Arby."

"It *is* dancing in the dark, you know…Close, soft words in your ear, personal thoughts being shared effortlessly, like taking those little shuffling moves that are safe, with no worries about stepping on your partner's feet. Intimate."

Jesus, this is being intimate with you. And, it's so easy.

"I confess that I like the 'dancing in the dark' corollary. What's not to love about this job?" She had to turn away to clear her tightening throat. "Boy, a while back when I called you a softie, I was spot-on."

Safe. Intimacy with no commitment. That's what I take from this gig, admit it. Who am I fooling? Not Razor and certainly not this woman. Not even myself.

Arby added, "Well, Sable's warm and welcoming, thoughtful, smart, and open-minded, fun. I look forward to dancing in the dark with her. I guess…that song Suede sings fits, because I like to lead when I dance—and Sable likes it."

Murphy grinned. "I look forward to our dances, too, Arby. You're considerate and insightful, and, as I've said before, tenderhearted." *Arousing, disarming…* "And yes, I rather enjoy following your lead."

Another instant message appeared on Murphy's screen.

End the love fest.

She ignored the directive, actually resented Razor's "cutting in" on them.

Arby paused again. "I'm humbled by every dance you accept."

"Every one is a delight, I assure you."

"Dancing is such an unsung pleasure. Not the bouncing and thrusting stuff, the hold-her-in-your-arms stuff, when you're moving as one and the fit is perfect, when the feel of her body against yours is all there is."

Jesus, make this tough, why don't you.

"An unsung pleasure, how true."

"*Nightlight* is the ultimate dance partner. I can't say I know how others see it, but it's clear to me. *You* are that perfect fit."

"I…ah…" Murphy purposely avoided looking toward the booth. "I guess, maybe…sometimes, there's just a special touch to the spoken word, Arby."

"Your touch—" Arby stopped. Murphy could hear her own

breathing in her headset and inched away from the mike. "Sable, your touch is compelling and sure. It lingers."

And I've fallen to sleep at night with yours in my head...on my skin...

"*Nightlight*'s all about memorable dances, isn't it?" she offered, urgently dodging the physical allure. "Sharing old ones, new ones. I'm happy to play a part in that."

"Well, you own the dance floor, graciously, and make it so easy to be swept away."

"Sometimes we yearn to be swept away."

"And sometimes a dance just ends too soon."

"I feel the same way," Murphy said, as losing Bryce rushed to mind. She squeezed her eyes shut. "The good ones are never long enough."

"The music hasn't even stopped and you can't wait for the next one."

"It can't come soon enough." *Did I admit that out loud?*

"That's when you take a big-girl breath and tell her how much you enjoyed the honor, politely say thank you." Riley's sigh was barely audible. "It's been a pleasure, Sable. Thank you for this dance."

"You're quite welcome, Arby. And thank you for making my night."

Chapter Eleven

The next morning, Murphy hit the supermarket right away, hoping not to hear Razor's inevitable phone call. She also hit Riley in the ass with her fully laden shopping cart.

"Oh, Jesus!"

Riley stumbled forward, regained control of a bottle of orange juice, and turned to face her assailant.

"Riley! Hi—or, sorry's more like it. I was looking the wrong way."

Murphy eagerly recalled their reunion at Shepley's, gladly put it ahead of the glimpse she'd taken of the drunken Riley leaving the hoedown.

"Y'know, Callahan," Riley began with a fake growl, a hand on her hip, "even though you're sexy as hell in those cutoffs, you're still a menace behind the wheel."

Murphy felt the heat rise in her cheeks but didn't care. Flirting face-to-face with *this* woman somehow settled her mind, restored her faith in her sanity. It muted the bewitching loop of Arby's seduction that played endlessly in her head, kept her awake at night, and refused to stop. *This is much healthier.*

"Now, listen, you," she countered. "If that tight little ass of yours hadn't been sticking out into the aisle, I wouldn't have hit it." The words flew out of her mouth and she felt a full blush take hold. Riley grinned, and Murphy practically swooned. *Damn, if this woman isn't flaming hot.* "So…So you're showing your domestic side today?"

Riley glanced back at her groceries. "Eh, a few things. My fridge is lonely."

"Mine, too, especially when my best friend plants herself in my kitchen for the day. And I'm sure she's already waiting in my driveway."

Riley's posture shifted from attentive to anxious. "Oh, well…

Hey..." She set a hand on Murphy's cart. "Would you like to meet for a drink some time? I mean, it beats passing like ships in the night." Her cool and casual sound had Murphy ready to accept anything.

And the impassioned blue of her eyes commanded all Murphy's concentration at that moment, the flecks of amber shimmered in an ocean that mesmerized her. Steady and now hopeful, that gaze from beneath sunny, rowdy hair gripped Murphy so completely, her talent for words abandoned her. *A summer dream.* Murphy's mind flooded with wild scenarios, and, surprisingly, none of them included declining and walking away.

"Well, I...That would be nice."

"You in town Friday?" Riley's voice became a mumble as she checked her cell phone, apparently for her schedule. "Mid-afternoon okay?"

"It is, yes."

Riley held up the phone. "I'll be between jobs by two. Is the Pig okay?"

"The Pig at two. Sounds good."

"Great." She slid the phone into a thigh pocket of her work pants. "Looking forward to it."

"Me, too. I'll see you there."

"Just make sure the menace parks downtown and walks up. It'll be safer for everyone." She grabbed her cart and escaped around the corner.

"Hey!" Murphy yelled after her.

"See you Friday!"

The teasing put a smile on Murphy's face she hadn't felt in too long. *Riley* put it there, she mused, and, man, if it didn't feel good.

She paid for her groceries and loaded the Beetle. *What's not to smile about?* Riley's quick and economical speech and polite, considerate manner underscored what Murphy saw as a very appealing sense of humor, and she figured time spent with her promised to be refreshing, and a good excuse to get out. Razor would be proud of her. Of course, that Riley was indecently delicious to look at was a bonus. For the first time in ages, Murphy allowed her thoughts to wander as she drove home. *Hard to imagine complete surrender, beneath that body...Whoa.*

She blew out a calming breath and turned down her street, trying to picture the Riley who had rescued her that snowy night. It was difficult, as only a hooded ball cap and shadowy face came to mind. When they had been face-to-face, they'd squinted and dodged gusts of biting snow, and in the Jeep, the dashboard lights hadn't helped much.

The healthy, though often distracted, look she got of Riley at Shepley's lost a bit of its shine in her memory when the image at the hoedown surfaced. She wondered if Riley was a serious drinker, how often she let herself go that badly, but she decided to let their upcoming afternoon at the Squealing Pig answer those questions.

Getting to know a new friend is nerve-wracking, no matter how old you are. There's so much ground to cover, so much to discover...

And as she pulled into her driveway behind Razor in her Subaru, Murphy remembered how that reunion at Shepley's had ended. *Sable is just someone on the radio. That's where I have to keep her.*

Murphy tried tuning Razor out the minute the tirade started. She loaded bundles into Razor's arms, grabbed the rest herself, and slammed the hood with her elbow.

"Can't you wait till we're in the house?" Balancing things on her hip, she managed to unlock and open the door.

Razor trailed after her. "We're putting this away and you are sitting down and hearing me out for five straight minutes. Do you understand?"

Murphy pulled chilled items from the bundles and pushed them toward Razor. "Fridge." She filled the cabinets with the rest of the groceries. "We had this discussion last night before leaving. You already made your point, Razor. On numerous occasions, in fact."

"I still can't believe you let that call go that far," Razor said into the fridge. "Do you hear what it says about you, your emotional state?" She straightened and shut the door. "You've always been sharp as a tack on the air. Tuned in to every voice, every nuance and innuendo."

Murphy placed bottles of water for them on the counter and sat on a stool, feeling a bit like a child told to sit in the corner.

Razor cracked the seal on the bottle cap and sat heavily.

"If I didn't know better, I'd think you'd fallen for that voice." Murphy lifted her head to speak but Razor threw up a hand. "What am I supposed to think? What are the listeners supposed to think?" She made kissing sounds, then exhaled a poor imitation of Sable's seductive croon. "'Every dance is a delight, Arby.'"

Murphy smothered a chuckle. "Do I sound like an asthmatic witch?"

Razor took a long drink. "Jesus, Murph."

"It was just all innocent chatter."

"The hell it was. 'Thanks for making my night'? *Your* night? What happened to 'our' night, as in that little thing called our friggin' radio show?"

"Okay, I slipped up there. I'm sorry that came out so personally."

"Murphy, that whole thing was personal. 'Your touch is compelling and sure. It lingers. You're a perfect fit.' Holy crap. You think that's not personal?"

Murphy reached for a paper towel to wipe the water rings off the counter. "Yeah, it was, wasn't it?" *There's no getting around it.*

"Murph. It's like you've let her cast some spell over you."

"I guess I've grown to...to like it." She spoke so softly, Razor leaned forward. "I know that's pretty stupid of me, immature, but..." She met Razor's discerning look with one that felt almost desperate, and realized she was hoping Razor would see a need for compassion. "I'm sorry I let you down, Raz." She toyed with the water bottle. "I let us down."

Razor set their bottles aside and took Murphy's hands over the counter.

"Okay, so, maybe I'm overreacting some. But what I'm seeing and hearing here makes me want to protect you. We're sisters in our own way, Murph, and you're the finest woman I know, next to Tina, that is. You're kind and giving, a true romantic at heart, and...I know there's a hole in your life. It makes a woman vulnerable, no matter how strong she thinks she's become. A part of her yearns more each day. It's only natural. I get it."

"Razor, stop, please." *Do I need to hear this? Can I?*

"More than anything, I want you to have what Tina and I have, and I know you will again. No one will ever take Bryce's place in your heart, sweetie, but a real someone's out there who will claim a different piece of it. I just care that you give it to the right someone for the right reasons."

Murphy lifted their joined hands and kissed the back of Razor's.

"Y'know, for someone with striped hair and metal stuck in her head, you're a pretty perceptive girl." Razor beamed. "Now I know why I've kept you around all these years."

Razor brought their water bottles back. She tapped on her temple. "Not all just good looks, you know."

Murphy smiled. She loved this woman. Their wild days of rock 'n' roll might be relegated to some dusty, reckless era, but the soul of the woman who became a stalwart friend so long ago hadn't gone anywhere.

"When it happens, it happens, and I'm good with that, but I'm... I'm picky, okay? It has to be right, Raz." She turned her bottle with her fingertips. "I *do* wonder if I'll be able to get past Bryce's memory when that time comes...if I'll be able to let go."

"You have to, Murph. And you will. It sucks, it hurts like hell, but you'll come out okay on the other side."

"So I've heard and seen." She nodded. A tired but true fact of life, one that always involved others, not her. Until now. "Do you think I'm really just fitting Arby into a fantasy?" She searched Razor's face. "Maybe I am."

"Look, she's romantic. She hits all your buttons. She even strokes your poor, neglected little hot spot with that voice, for God's sake. And she's *safe*. No strings required. You have the best of both worlds, in a way: Arby, the romantic fantasy, and Bryce, the active memory. But a *real* someone is who you need, Murphy, eyes you can find answers in, hands to hold, lips that'll deliver you." She stood up. "We're going girlfriend hunting."

Murphy sighed. "Jesus, here we go again."

"See? That's the wrong attitude. I'm going to get you out of this... this funk bef—"

"Okay, hang on there, Woman on a Mission." Murphy raised her hand. "Listen." She took a breath. "I have a date." Razor's jaw dropped. "I do. Well, sort of. Friday."

Razor sat back down. "Who is she? When did this happen and why didn't you tell me?"

"Will you give me a second?" Murphy wasn't sure meeting Riley for a drink at the Pig constituted a real date, but it was the closest thing to one she'd agreed to in ages—and it would ease Razor's distressed, ever-devoted mind. *And it will be fun because Riley is fun.* Razor sat with her lips obediently pressed together, as they were prone to do when she was ready to burst. "You've seen her around town, Raz—"

"Do I know her?"

"No, I doubt it. Remember that business luncheon at the P-town Inn?"

"Back in May?"

"Yes. We—"

"Was she there? Were we introduced?" She seized the edge of the counter with both hands. "Oh, God, Murphy. Not Meredith Bronsworth from the West End Club. It's not her, is it? She's a sleeze. Cute, but she's had every—"

"Will you shut up?" Razor slammed her mouth closed. Murphy shook her head. "Now, don't speak and let me finish." Razor nodded eagerly. "You stopped the car on Commercial that day and let her cross in front of us. A tradeswoman. She had a tool belt—"

"No, shit! That hot butch?" Razor almost fell off the stool.

Murphy pointed at her. "*Quiet!*" She sat back and tried to collect herself. The "hot butch" image messed with her thought process. "Yes. Turns out we met last winter. And we've bumped into each other since then. Quite literally, actually. Anyway, we ran into each other again, just this morning, shopping, and she asked if I'd like to meet her for a drink Friday. I said yes." Razor was red-faced with restraint. "Okay, you can speak now."

Razor flew around to her side of the counter as if launched. She took Murphy's face in both hands and kissed her quickly on the lips. "Hot damn!"

Murphy laughed. "Go sit down. It's just a drink at the Pig. Apparently, she has a break in her workday. It's not some secluded rendezvous or anything, just a drink."

"Who is she? And tell me again how you know her. You didn't recognize her that day in May."

"Her name is Riley. I think her last name is Turk or Clerk... something like that. Damn, I can't remember. But prior to May, the last time I saw her was in a snowstorm in February, and she looked a *whole* lot different crossing the street in May."

Razor snorted. "I bet! She was the one with the shorts, that great body, wasn't she?" Murphy nodded and knew her face was coloring. Razor's smile twisted knowingly. "Oh, Ms. Callahan. You might just be in for a real awakening, girlfriend."

CHAPTER TWELVE

By lunchtime Friday, Riley had trimmed nearly all the gangly branches in a cute little yard near the Pilgrim Monument when disaster struck. She'd just started on the last meaty limb when the leather strap that held her to the tree some fifteen feet off the ground slipped several inches. Her gaff's spikes in the trunk gave way and she dropped.

Luckily, landing on her back only knocked out her breath, but the chainsaw that followed chewed her shin to the bone.

Just as her consciousness faded to black, her lungs refilled, and she fought back a howl of pain. Up on her elbows, she fought the scorching and throbbing of her shin. She scanned her extremities through fuzzy vision and gratefully found them in working order, but the sight of blood pumping from the ragged six-inch trough on her left leg curdled her stomach. She fumbled for the phone in her pants and cursed the safety belt, the gaffs, the tree, the saw, her stupidity, and her pricy accident insurance policy. She hated to call for an ambulance, but couldn't drive in this condition. Depressing the clutch in the Jeep's standard transmission would make one hell of a bloody mess. Not to mention the pain.

"Good heavens, Riley!" The property owner shuffled as quickly as her little legs could travel to where Riley lay and bent down to catch her breath. At eighty-two and recently widowed, white-haired Mary Bridget O'Hara was far smaller than her name and too feisty for her feeble condition. She also was Riley's favorite customer, and upsetting her just added to Riley's misery.

"I'm sorry, Mrs. O."

"Oh, my dear girl. What are you apologizing for? Look at you!"

She adjusted her spectacles and examined the gory wound without hesitation. The woman's spunk was inspiring.

"I'm so sorry to put you through this," Riley said through clenched teeth. "Makes me so mad."

"You hush. I'm getting a towel to wrap around this ugliness." She straightened with effort. "And I'll bring my car around, so don't you move." She marched off.

Riley dragged her butt across the grass to where her saw lay sputtering. *Thank God the damn chain wasn't spinning when it hit me.* She switched the motor off and flopped back onto the ground, not too happy about the fog in her head. "Really, I can call someone for a ride!"

"Nonsense!" Mary yelled without looking back. "I don't keep that Ford as a lawn ornament, y'know!"

Within minutes and with the help of her late husband's cane, Mary had Riley sprawled across the backseat and was motoring with purpose toward the clinic.

"Now when we get there, I'm going to get comfy and read while I wait, so you're not to be worrying."

"You don't have to wait, Mrs. O. You have bridge club today. The ladies will be worried to death when you don't show."

"Phooey. They'll be glad to have someone else win for a change. I'm staying."

She parked the Taurus with extreme care. Hot knives dug into Riley's shin as she slid off the seat, and she bit her lip to silence her whimpering, determined to get out before Mary could overexert herself helping.

"I'm wise to you, Riley Burke." She put a slim but firm arm around Riley's waist. "You're not stopping me from doing this right. You can bet your ugly boots, you're not."

An aide met them at the door and hurriedly produced a wheelchair. Riley figured he probably could have seen her bloody lower leg and saturated sock and darkly stained work boot from a mile away.

"Please head home, Mrs. O. I don't know how long this is going to take and you've already done so much." She lifted her T-shirt, bent forward, and wiped sweat from her face. Someone handed her a clipboard and a pen.

Mary settled into a waiting room chair and retrieved a novel from her large purse. "You fill out that paper and behave yourself." She looked up at the aide. "Please take her away and fix that mess now."

Riley was down the hall, into an exam room, and being seen by a rather attractive nurse before she knew what was happening. She blinked back tears several times and spoke only when she was sure she wouldn't gasp as a physician's assistant numbed, cleaned, and then stitched her wound. She tried to focus on the nurse nearby, thought she filled out her uniform extremely well, but something about the waves of brown hair that gathered on her shoulders reminded Riley of a certain beautiful lady she was supposed to meet—very soon.

She checked her watch.

"Going somewhere?" the PA asked and completed the closure. He wrote on her clipboard and handed her a prescription for Percocet. She wasn't sure he expected an answer.

"I am. Two o'clock downtown."

"Don't think so."

"Why not?" As if she hadn't been ticked off enough.

He issued the okay for the nurse to begin wrapping Riley's leg, then turned and flashed his penlight into her eyes.

"You're going home to rest. Two days." He put the light away. "Keep the leg up at least until this time tomorrow, but no activity for two days."

"I have to work. I've got clients expecting jobs to be done."

"And when your brain rattles so bad you pass out, what'll get done then? Maybe you fall off a ladder, or drill a hole through your hand, or worse, drive into somebody." He nodded at her stare. "Right. Home. No activity. Become a slug for two days. Take the Percs for the leg, and that should be a plus if any headaches come around. Any dizziness, nausea after today, you come back. Understand?"

She sulked as she limped back down the corridor but brightened for Mary's sake in the waiting room.

"All set."

"My. That hardly took no time at all."

Riley grinned at the remnants of Mary's Irish brogue. "Nothing to it."

"And what instructions did you get?"

"Just some rest," Riley lied.

"Looks like a prescription in your hand."

"Yes," the nurse injected, "and should be filled promptly, plus two days of rest, no activity. Elevate that till tomorrow afternoon."

Great. Thanks a lot.

Mary put her book away and jingled her car keys. "Nuh-uh." She eyed Riley sideways then pointed at herself. "You're a sly one, you are. Don't think you're pullin' one over on Mary O'Hara. Now here's the cane. Let's go."

Back in the car, in the front seat this time, Riley pleaded her case. "Just drop me off. I'm sure she'll give me a ride later."

"The doctor didn't prescribe courting a lady in a beer hall."

"I'll introduce you to her when she brings me back for the Jeep."

"As much as I'd enjoy meeting a lady friend of yours, no."

"I've got to drive the Jeep anyway."

"I'll flatten those tires."

"Come on, Mrs. O. It's already ten past two."

Mary lifted her chin and drove toward the pharmacy, undaunted.

Riley dropped her head back onto the headrest and sighed. *If it weren't for bad luck...*

Mary finally pulled into the pharmacy and ordered Riley to "sit and don't move" while she went in for Riley's medicine.

With no recourse, Riley pulled out her phone and called the Squealing Pig.

❖

Murphy removed the clip at the nape of her neck, fussed with her hair, and re-clipped it. She dabbed away a tiny smudge of mascara, slid her sunglasses back on her head, and left the ladies' room. Her table by the window, which opened onto Commercial Street, now sported her second glass of iced tea, but no Riley. The absence worried her. She didn't want to think she'd been stood up.

She checked the clock above the bar as she returned to her table. Twenty minutes.

"A Murphy Callahan here?"

Startled, she turned and acknowledged the bartender, who stood near the back room. He waved the handset at her.

"Thank you." She skirted the tables in the center of the room to take the phone promptly. "Hello?"

"Murphy? It's Riley."

"Riley?" She blocked her other ear to hear over the noise from the bar and the kitchen nearby.

"I'm sorry, Murphy. I've had a little job accident and left you stranded."

"Riley, can you speak up please? Did you say an accident?"

"Yeah, I'm sorry to leave you waiting, but I'm restricted by the doctor. Could we reschedule?"

"Restricted by a doctor? What happened?"

"Hurt my leg, but I'm only out of commission for a day or so. Would you mind if we did this another time? I'm sorry, really. I've been looking forward to this since the supermarket."

Murphy grinned despite her disappointment.

"Of course I don't mind. I was looking forward to it, too. Are you going to be okay?"

"Yeah, but I have to lay low. Can we reschedule?"

Murphy hoped Riley wouldn't suggest an evening during the week. With Sable's identity practically a national secret, weeknights were not very feasible. Weekends, however, were her own. "Yes, certainly, Riley. Would...would you be up for something this weekend?"

"This weekend? Like tomorrow night?"

Riley's eagerness was flattering. "If you're up for it."

"Yeah. I'm sure I'll be on my feet by then."

"Well...let's...Why don't you come by the house?" she heard herself say. "It'd be easier on you. I'm in Wellfleet on Duck Harbor Road. Just look for my Beetle."

"Okay. Music to my ears. I'm sorry about today. If I hadn't been so stupid, this wouldn't have happened."

Murphy leaned against the wall, happy just to know they hooked up at all, even if it seemed as if she lived on the phone. "Save that 'stupid' business for tomorrow night. Rest up and I'll see you then, all right? Around seven? That will give you more time, and I'll throw together a light supper. Nothing fancy, mind you."

"Wow, sure. What kind of wine do you drink? Or...do you drink wine? Beverage of choice?"

"Riley, no. You don't have to stop and do that." She warmed at Riley's effort to please.

"Uh-uh. The lady's beverage of choice, please?"

"If you *insist*, then a red, please."

"Got it. Thank you, Murphy. This is awfully nice of you." Riley's voice dropped and she sounded both humbled and embarrassed. Murphy was touched.

"Don't worry about this today. Honestly, it's all right."

"Yeah." Riley chuckled quietly and Murphy listened harder. "Thanks for taking my call."

"Thanks for calling. See you."

The closing lines echoing in Murphy's head stalled her brain, and she was slow to put back the handset. She heard only those lines all the way back to her table and for the next half hour. She didn't give the prospect of Riley in her home a second thought. She watched but didn't see all the auto and foot traffic pass by. There was only the echo of those lines, as clear as if written on paper. Familiar lines, there was no doubt, but there was more…

She left plenty of money to cover her drinks and time occupying the table, and made it to her car in a haze. Her mind still wasn't her own when she sank into her couch and flipped open her laptop. *Nightlight*'s Facebook page appeared, and she noted all the comments, the "likes," but had no reaction to any of them.

She sat back and closed her eyes. That gently muted chuckle… *"Thanks for taking my call."* If it had been recorded, she'd play it back till she was certain, one way or the other. And she wasn't certain which way was best.

"It can*not* be," she said. "You are losing your mind. Seriously."

She decided that Razor's campaign about Murphy's attachment to Arby and her reclusive lifestyle had to be driving her, affecting her more than she realized. Some identity transference *had* to be in play here because she was just too close to associating a fantasy voice with an acquaintance she knew. *It's just too farfetched to be true. All this talk about being the lost and lonely woman in need, creating a fantasy love to fill the void…I'm dumping all that on poor Riley. Razor would agree.*

She snickered at herself as she poured a glass of wine and went to sit on the deck.

"I can't even remember your last name," she said and laughed lightly toward the beach. "You're clever, charming, and, cripes, the handsomest devil I've come across—maybe ever—and that's saying a lot, especially coming from me. You deserve better than a woman who has a few loose screws."

She sipped her wine and another thought made her laugh again.

"Do you believe this, Bryce? I don't want to go certifiable and make a fool of myself here. It would cheapen everything we had, everything we were together." She swirled the burgundy liquid almost to the rim of the goblet. "But she is something else, and I do like her. There's this *thing*, a jittery *thing* between us I can't explain. Probably because we sort of know each other but really don't. It's sweet, that's all."

She scanned the pale blue summer sky and sipped again.

"Get a grip, girl. Are you even *considering* something more than friendship here? Since when is there room for that?" She stared out at the water. *Since life changed three years ago.* She didn't want to consider the possibility of pain at the end of a road. Losing Bryce had supplied enough pain for a lifetime, and she had no desire for more.

She drank the rest of her wine straight down and stood, satisfied that she'd given herself a good talking to and steadied the dizzying turmoil in her brain. *A long hot shower should snap me up to par.* Friday night was *Nightlight*'s most popular night, and she couldn't tackle it if her head was bouncing between fantasy and reality.

Chapter Thirteen

"I was forced out of a great apartment in New York many years ago," Murphy said into the microphone. "My building was sold and they instituted a no pets policy. It broke my heart to leave, but would have killed me to give up my dog."

"I gave up my cocker spaniel, Sable, and swore I'd never do it again."

"As a writer posted on *Nightlight*'s Facebook page an hour ago, it's like surrendering a child."

"Exactly," the caller said and sniffed into the phone. "My parents couldn't take Sophie, and I had nobody else, so she had to go up for adoption."

"Consider carefully, that's the only advice I can give."

"I know. Thanks, Sable."

"On the flip side, and we can use some flip side right about now, let me share part of a note *Nightlight* received from an Orleans woman. Her four-year-old Sheltie helped *get* her owner a home. At the time, she was a New Jersey college senior, and dogs weren't allowed in the dorms, but she'd smuggled hers in for a weekend."

Murphy paused as she scrolled down the screen. "Just bringing up the best part. Okay, check this out: 'When the alarm went off, she started running from room to room, all ten of them, until everyone opened their doors and got out. She barked constantly and led the last girl through the smoke and down the stairs to the door. Our dorm burned to the ground, but then that girl's dad found out my Chippie saved his daughter—saved everybody—and he paid to build a brand-new one. And when I graduated six months later, he bought me my own condo in Boston.'"

Murphy drank her coffee. "Talk about rescue dogs. Well. While we all try to find a dad to buy us a special place, let's wax nostalgic with some of the bravest, finest music in our history. Turning things over to Ferron, Jane Oliver, and Meg Christian, now, so stay close. *Nightlight* will be back in a bit."

She set her headphones on the counter and strolled into Razor's booth.

"What are you grinning about?"

"You and your supper date tomorrow night."

"It's really not a big deal, Razor. I just thought it would be nice, especially considering she's injured. I'm sure she's beside herself about that, knowing how hard she works. Why are you still grinning?"

"You don't know squat about how hard she works, and you're all gooey over making her feel good. I love it."

"I do *so* know. She's no slacker."

"She's earned that body, huh?"

"Yes," Murphy stated. "I'm sure she has. The old-fashioned way."

"Well, I'm happy she called instead of hanging you out to dry at the Pig, and I'm thrilled that you took this step. Asking her over to the house is big, Murph, and I'm proud of you."

"Thank you." She really didn't see having a friend over to be the big deal Razor saw. She and Bryce had done it dozens of times over the years. She had done it a few times herself, although couldn't remember the last time. She wasn't anti-social, for God's sake. "Now, no more teasing."

"No promises."

"Brat." She slapped Razor's rear with a clipboard.

"Calls are a little on the slow side tonight. I thought we'd be inundated with animal lovers."

"The night is young. Who knows where we'll end up after midnight."

She waited anxiously for Arby to call. She wanted to hear that voice tonight, as soon as possible after hearing Riley's. She knew it really was wildly preposterous to think they were one and the same, but she couldn't get the suggestion to go silent.

"You look perplexed." Razor drank the last of her Red Bull and clanged the can into the recycling bin across the room. "Two points. What's bugging you?"

"Nothing. Just wondering what topic we'll end on tonight. I've got two more emails on this for the next hour, and a cute Facebook comment about summer theme parties. I think we should've gone with the theme parties."

"But we like animals."

"Yes, we do, hon." Murphy patted Razor's shoulder. "That's why we're doing it. But I don't know if it'll keep flying past midnight, and I don't want to waste a great topic like theme parties on the last two hours of a Friday night."

"Hm. Good point. We should have a fill-in topic in case. You're right."

"Such as…?"

"Sex."

"Anything else?"

"Makeup sex."

Murphy looked up from writing on her clipboard. "What else?"

"First time sex."

"What else?"

"Getting caught sex."

"Razor. How about kissing?"

"Too Valentine's Day."

"How about shifting to stupid pet tricks?"

"Or just stupid pets. I had a roommate whose hamster ate his own poop."

"Eww!" She whacked her with the clipboard this time.

"Well, he did!" Razor put on her headset. "Thirty seconds."

Murphy sighed heavily and returned to her chair. "Stupid pets and tricks. Should get us through." She settled the headphones onto her head and drew the mike close. "Since when is a Friday night this tough?" *Tougher still because Arby will never call about stupid pets or pet tricks.*

With thirty minutes left to their night, and both Murphy and Razor coming off a welcomed, hysterically funny call, another light blinked to life on Murphy's monitor. Razor spoke privately into her ear, over the commercial that was ending.

"Not sure about this one. Froggy and maybe buzzed, but promised a good bird story."

"Last one of the night, then. We can stretch a while and I've got plenty of tunes queued."

"Good. You're back in three, two, one…"

"Welcome back. Have we recovered from our dialing dog story? Let it be a lesson to us all: keep the cell phones out of the dog's reach and you keep the 911 responses where they should be." She slid the cursor over to the blinking call button on her screen. "Let's try another, shall we? This caller has been waiting patiently." She clicked open the line. "Hello. Thank you for holding. This is Sable and you're on *Nightlight*."

"I've been listening all night 'n haven't heard a parakeet story yet."

Murphy studied the mike. The deep, lazy delivery piqued her curiosity.

"Not yet, you're right, caller. What's your story?"

"Well, see, dogs 'n cats weren't allowed in our first apartment so we had a parakeet. Quite a social guy, always had things to say, songs to sing. Never shut up, 'specially when friends came over. Till we came home from work one day 'n found he'd mowed down my baby pot plants."

"Oh, God, no. Did he get high?"

"Hell, yeah. Act'lly, worse, I think. Brain damaged. He...he thought he was a hawk." Murphy laughed outright. "So, y'know... y'know we had those...little mirrored perches on three sides of his cage. He'd sit on one 'n get all pissed off at the other birds he saw—his reflections, y'know? Jesus, he thought a crowd had moved in on him, dumbass bird." Murphy laughed at the tale, but noted the caller's voice had faded, and Murphy wondered if the woman had paused to take another drink. "Yeah, he'd squawk 'n flap 'n bounce around, totally bull...eh...real furious. Eventually, he got so mad, he wrecked 'em all, grabbed the plastic frames in his beak and slammed 'em around till they broke. Had the cage swingin' like...like a pend'lum. Tore his place apart."

Murphy heard the caller laughing along with her. "That's wild. Poor little guy." She glanced at Razor and found her smiling broadly, shaking her head.

"Was never the same. Y'reached in to fill his dishes 'n he'd attack you, draw blood, even. He'd flip open the damn cage himself 'n dive-bomb us at the kitchen table."

"Remind me never to grow pot in my house."

The subtle laugh struck a familiar chord.

"You, Sable? Naw, doubt you ever would."

Murphy focused hard on the voice. "In my house? Seriously, never."

"Mmm. Nope. Not real bright, 'specially if you got pets or kids around. Uh-uh."

"Especially."

"From then on, that damn bird was always escaping into the apartment. He'd land on ashtrays and peck at butts, loved to chirp along to 'Stairway to Heaven.' Chris'mastime, we'd find'm sitting in the tree like a decoration. I fig'red he thought he was outside in the woods."

Murphy couldn't help but laugh, and the caller did the same. *There it is. That laugh.* She peeked at Razor, but there was no recognition on her amused face. *I'm pressing. Imagining it. Can't even be sure it's you, Arby, let alone compare your voice to someone else's. You're a bit loose tonight, aren't you?* She felt an urgent need to confirm the identification, at least.

"How did he react to music after that, caller? Did he still sing? Did he dive-bomb you if you danced in the apartment?"

"Nope. Didn't sing much anymore. An' there wasn't much dancin' 'cause he'd land on my shoulder 'n I's always afraid he'd attack one of us or...or bite my ear."

"Well, that was a bummer, I bet, killing the dancing." She was pushing and she knew it.

"A wicked bummer. Love dancin'. I know you do, too, Sable."

"Have to say I do."

The instant message she knew would come popped up on her monitor.

WTF ?????????

Razor was catching on.

"So, Sable, um...you...D'you dance often?"

"Not as often as I'd like, no. Do you?"

"Nope. Same here." The muted chuckle again floated across the line. "An' won't for a while now, I s'pose..." *Why not? No perfect setting? You're going through a breakup, aren't you?* "But...whenever the feelin' strikes, y'know?"

"I do. No parties or bars necessary."

"Don't even need music playin'."

"Sometimes, the music in your head is all you need."

Razor's instant message appeared—in capital letters this time.

YOU STARTED THIS!!!

"As usual, y'nailed it, Sable. When it's right, y'don't even need a melody, just words."

"Killer parakeet or no."

The answering laugh had Murphy grinning.

"Damn bird couldn't spoil this dance."

"No way. It's been fun, Arby."

"With you, it's always fun. Have a good night—'n thanks for dancin'."

"You're welcome. Good night."

Razor sat with her headset in her lap and her head back when Murphy stepped into her booth. It appeared she was ready to spend the night.

"She was drunk as a skunk," Razor grunted.

"Cute, though, and coherent and entertaining."

"Just when I thought you'd come to your senses, you bring up the damn dancing."

"I had to know, Razor."

"Oh, *well*," Razor flailed grandly from her prone position, "by all means, slow dance on center stage for everyone. Don't let some safe reality cool your libido."

"Now, you're definitely overreacting. It's late and we're both tired." She stepped up to Razor's board and shut everything off. She unwrapped the headset from round Razor's neck and hung it over her mike. "Come on. Let's get out of here."

Razor grumbled as she got to her feet and gathered her things. "I guess it wasn't so bad."

Murphy elbowed her as they stepped out into the parking lot. "It wasn't bad, and when you run it through your head tomorrow, you'll feel better about it. You're just upset you didn't recognize her."

"I did almost turn her away, because I heard the slurring right off."

"It turned out fine." Murphy rose on her toes and pecked her cheek. "Go to bed. I'll talk to you in the morning."

Razor stopped and looked back from her car door. "The dinner date! Yeah, that's right. I'll be over."

"I don't need help getting ready, Razor. I'm a big girl."

"You're a rookie. I'll see you later on." She slid behind the wheel and shut the door.

Murphy sighed. *I know you mean well, but, Razor, you're probably the last thing I need to think about tomorrow.* She drove home, lost in a myriad of thoughts.

The evening hadn't been a dud after all. Arby had been fun and restrained. She's someone to look forward to when the sessions in the dark of night tend to drag, she thought. Maybe the credit for the night's success, for keeping their repartee on the proper level went to Arby's buzz. She'd never called in such a condition before, and deep down, Murphy actually hoped she wouldn't again.

Arby at less than her quick-witted articulate best left Murphy feeling a bit diminished, cheated out of their usually honest, challenging conversation. She always felt a person shortchanged herself as well as others when inebriation dimmed the shine of her personality. And then Murphy's busy memory presented Riley stumbling out of the hoedown and into the dark. *Two different people, I'm sure, but the same applies to you.*

CHAPTER FOURTEEN

Hey, the name just hit me! I know her. She does the upkeep on my grandfather's place in the West End. *She's* the one who saved your ass that night?" Razor finished arranging cheese and fruit on the platter and put everything in the refrigerator. "Her last name's Burke, isn't it? She works all over town and everyone knows her. You *do* realize that, right?"

Murphy emerged from the bathroom in a terry robe, talking into the towel she was using to dry her hair.

"How much beer do I have? Should I have a lot or just some? Did you drink it all?"

"I beg your sweet, frazzled pardon. I did not." Razor reopened the refrigerator. "You've got a six-pack of Heinies and a six of your lemonade."

"It's not lemonade. It's Blue Moon."

"Whatever." Razor shut the door and leaned against it with her arms crossed, grinning as Murphy zipped around the kitchen. "Do you even know if she drinks beer?"

"Well, I know she drinks." Murphy ripped the towel off her head. "I have wine, don't I?"

"Jesus Christ." Razor checked an upper cabinet. "Yes. Two pinot grigios and a cabernet, plus the two noirs in the rack—the rack right there on the counter in front of you."

"God, and I said she could bring some." She stopped and addressed the refrigerator. "Steak tips are marinating. I'll throw the salad together once I'm dressed. The fruit—" She turned to Razor. "Did you cut some—"

"Yes. Chill. Throw the tips on the grill while you guys hang out, and the salad will be perfect. Stop worrying."

"What time is it? I have to get dressed."

"It's six thirty-five. Five minutes later than the last time you asked."

Murphy gathered WCCD paperwork off the counter, spun to Razor, and dumped it in her hands. "Please put all this somewhere out of sight. And take the CCD magnets off the fridge."

"Quit freaking out."

"Please."

Razor sighed. "You don't have to take these down." She peeled off the magnets. "So, you're not going to tell her, right?"

"Right. Well, I just don't think I should. I-I still can't decide."

"Decide what, for crissakes?" Razor stuffed the paperwork and magnets into Murphy's desk draw in her office. "What's to decide?" she yelled into the bedroom.

"If it's wise, still keeping Sable under wraps," Murphy said from her closet. "Aside from the fact she'll be mortified because of all she's revealed already, what if I risk it and tell her and she turns out to be some…some…I don't know—"

"Exactly. A one-night stand doesn't necessarily tell you much—"

"I don't do one-night stands."

"You mean you *haven't* in ages."

"The point is, what if I—"

"Oh, I get your point. If she turns out to be some giggling ditz—"

"I seriously doubt it."

"Well, she could be the stud who can't wait to tell her posse she fucked the famous Sable."

Murphy threw a hairbrush from the bathroom.

Razor picked up the brush and leaned against the bathroom door, watching Murphy apply mascara.

"Look, Murph. At least she said she likes Sable. This doesn't have to turn into an international crisis. Just keep your cool."

"Sable makes her swoon, makes her melt."

"Hm. I see some good potential here. Nice."

"It's not nice. It's a problem."

"For fuck's sake, Murph. No, it's not. Should you happen to whisper sweet nothings, just don't use your 'Sable the Seductress' voice."

"Thanks, you're a huge help. And we won't be whispering sweet nothings."

"Hey, your voice is your voice. Over the air, everyone's is a little different, and I always modify yours, remember, drop it a smidgeon. You said she didn't recognize Sable when you met before, now did she?"

"No, I'm sure she didn't." Murphy tried to edge past her in the doorway, but Razor pinned her shoulders to the wall.

"Stop for a Jesus Christ minute and listen to me."

"She'll be here in a few, Razor. Let me go. What time is it?"

"Time for the engineer to talk and the DJ to shut up."

Murphy sagged against the wall and closed her eyes. It was hard to breathe. Inviting Riley home seemed like the easiest, most genuine thing to do at the moment. She never thought it would make her crazy. And she didn't want Sable interfering. She wanted that little knickknack tucked far out of sight.

"First of all, you wouldn't have invited her here if you didn't like her. Second of all, she wouldn't have accepted if she didn't like you. That's all that matters. It's just drinks and a light dinner. *Plus*, she's fucking hot." She tapped both Murphy's shoulders with finality. "See? Simple."

"You have to get out of here." Murphy led her by the arm through the house, and Razor grabbed her backpack off the couch before they reached the door. "Oh, wait," Murphy said, stepping back. "Shoes. What should—"

"Barefoot. It's sexy."

"Swell." She put her hands over her face. "Shit. I feel like a sixteen-year-old."

Razor laughed and squeezed her arm. "You're just out of practice. Quit worrying. And no sixteen-year-old could ever look as good as you do."

"Really? I look okay?"

"Stop, already! If Tina finds out what I seriously think, I'll be sleeping in my car for life." She kissed Murphy's forehead. "The blouse is just the right fit and it's your color. Peach always gives you this natural blush. And the shorts show off those screaming hot legs and your sinful ass. Ten bucks says she won't be able to keep her hands off them."

"I don't want to get mauled, Raz, I just want to look…you know…"

"Uh-huh. You're a class act, Murph. That's obvious no matter what you wear. Now relax, will you? And have fun." She winked as she left.

❖

The lancing pain in her leg just reminded Riley of how irresponsible she'd been. *Big shot Ms. Fix-it, slacking off. Can't afford to be so careless.* Maybe I *should* take a damn Percocet, she thought, and cover up my idiocy, too. But she'd taken two last night, and they'd exposed more idiocy than she remembered having, turned her into a blubbering fool, so she'd vowed not to risk tonight being a smashing success by popping any more of that demon stuff. Tonight just had a special feel about it she couldn't explain. *Too many times, she's been the face in the crowd, driving the Beetle in traffic, even the visitor in dreams. No way I'm screwing this up.* She groaned as she sat on the edge of the bed and straightened her leg into her best jeans. *Suck it up.*

Tucking in her last clean undershirt, she hobbled around the loft and collected the cash and change off her little table, her wallet from atop the television, and then the seldom-worn Tevas from the bottom of her closet. She groaned again when she wiggled the sandal onto her left foot. She leaned against the closet doorframe, wishing it wasn't too late to take a second shower and flush the sludge of those damn drugs from her brain. It was a chore to choose the right shirt from the limited selection hanging before her. *Wonder if she likes yellow. The green or red Polo? White, blue, or black Oxford? T-shirts in the drawer…uh-uh.* She grabbed the cobalt Oxford.

She found her watch on the toilet tank and strapped it on. Listing onto her right hip and wincing into the mirror, she brushed her teeth and double-checked her shirt. *Hope this blue doesn't blind her like it's blinding me.* She straightened her collar and rolled back her cuffs. *Not bad, but shit, I need a haircut.* She ran both hands through her wet hair and spotted the time in her reflection.

"As if you'll look halfway decent by the time you get down three flights of stairs." She swallowed four ibuprofen, took a breath against the twinge in her leg, and headed down to the Jeep.

Occasional jabs of pain accompanied her as she drove, each gear change causing her to grit her teeth. Stops at the liquor store and florist were a challenge, but she took them as practice for the night ahead. Besides, she had no choice. The wine was a must, the flowers…well… *Okay, so, yes, I think this* is *a date, and maybe you don't, but who needs a reason?*

Riley stopped the Jeep before driving down Murphy's street. She set the brake, lifted her foot off the clutch, and gasped at the pain. She straightened her shirt, tucked it in better in the back, smoothed the denim over her thighs, and tried in vain to tame the mess her hair had become during the ride without a roof.

"Useless," she growled into the rearview mirror. Settling back behind the wheel, she grimaced again when she put the Jeep in gear. She found Murphy's quaint little oceanfront house within a minute, seeing the name on the mailbox ratchetted up her nerves. *What's to be nervous about? She's only the finest woman you've ever met, spectacularly beautiful, and thinks you're special enough to invite you to her home. That's all.*

She climbed out gingerly, cradling two bottles of very expensive burgundy in her left arm, and had second thoughts—a second time—about the colorful bouquet on the passenger seat. *Shows appreciation, right?* She limped toward the door, flowers in hand, too.

The inner door opened as Riley assessed the first of three steps, and when the storm door swung out wide, she looked up. All the way up, from the pink toenails to the sleek legs, the trim white shorts, the form-fitting sleeveless blouse with its hint of cleavage, and the big brown eyes, and absolutely dazzling smile. Riley's breath caught.

"Wow." *Not a bad intro, considering the jackhammer in my chest.*

"Riley, hi. It's so good to see you. I don't know which to remark about first, what you're carrying or your injury." She reached down and steadied Riley with a hand at her elbow.

Riley swallowed a hiss of pain as she climbed the steps. Close now, she stopped within the arc of Murphy's arm holding the door open, and cringed inwardly when she heard herself fumble.

"I…um…you…" Murphy grinned expectantly. *Busted.* "Honestly, I don't mean to embarrass you, but…you're just gorgeous." She laid the flowers in Murphy's hands. "I'd like you to have these." Murphy's expression softened as she looked down. Those sweeping, graceful lashes weren't tipped with droplets of melting snow now. They fluttered slightly, and Riley couldn't look away.

"Oh, Riley. Come in, please." She backed up into the house, and Riley forced herself to concentrate on not tripping over the threshold. "Boy, a breathtaking compliment and spectacular flowers with you on my doorstep? A girl can't dream of a lovelier greeting. Thank you. Please make yourself at home."

"Thanks for tonight, Murphy." She cleared her throat and prayed her nervousness didn't show. "I know it's pretty impromptu, so I hope you didn't go to any trouble."

"Not at all, and it's my pleasure. It's better this way anyway. We don't have people bumping into us and loudspeaker distractions, and all that, and we can relax and actually listen to each other. *You* can get off that bad leg and be comfortable. Let me just put these in water. Have a seat."

Riley watched her leave the room but couldn't part with the view. She hobbled after her and hitched a hip onto a kitchen stool while Murphy filled a vase.

"Look at all these," Murphy said, arranging the long stems. "They're amazing—and so very sweet of you." Her reverent touch and avid concentration revealed her appreciation of Riley's gesture, said she shared the sincerity with which it had been made, and Riley couldn't have been more pleased. *Once in a while, I do something right.*

She found herself captivated by this alluring woman she felt she knew better than she actually did. *A far cry from wide-eyed desperation in a parka and floppy-eared hat.* The oranges, yellows, and reds of the flowers warmed Murphy's creamy complexion. *Jesus, if just her face does this to me...*

"I...I suppose this isn't really a *date* date, but I don't believe you need a reason to give flowers to a lady. Definitely not to someone special."

Murphy stopped arranging to look at her evenly. Riley noted the hike in her pulse and wondered if her "someone special" comment had been too presumptuous.

Murphy set the vase on the counter nearby and fluffed the blossoms one last time.

"Before you have me so flustered I can't think," she said with a sideways look, "I'd like to get us drinks so we can sit. You need to rest your leg and I *really* need to sit."

CHAPTER FIFTEEN

Murphy read the label on Riley's wine, a much-needed act to hide the tremor in her motion. She added Riley's "someone special" to her collection of most-private memories, flattered to be seen as such. It wasn't an especially unique compliment, but Riley's sensitivity and the shy tip of her head was endearing.

"This wine is wonderful, Riley. You shouldn't have done this."

"I wanted to. I sampled some of it at a Memorial Day party." She deliberately coughed and spoke against her fist. "I was lucky to remember the name."

"Then I'm excited to get to it." Murphy put a corkscrew on the counter and went for glasses. When she turned back, she was pleased to find Riley's capable, weathered hands at work on the cork, her smooth, bronzed face determined and totally engaged. She looked up before pouring, and Murphy's heart skipped a beat.

"This is a beautiful home, Murphy. The location is to die for."

"Thank you. It's pretty special to me. A little small, but I dream of adding a second floor someday." Murphy steadied her excited nerves with an exhale into the refrigerator as she reached for the fruit and cheese tray, and then waved for Riley to follow her onto the deck. "Come sit. Let me show off my view."

Riley steadied herself off the stool, then hurried to open the sliding screen door. *And they say chivalry—*

"God. Look at this view." Riley practically fell into the Adirondack chair. The ocean met the beach several hundred yards away, the sun now just several inches from setting over the Atlantic. "How lucky are you?"

"No kidding." Murphy set the tray on a little table between their chairs. "Trust me. I thank my lucky stars every day, every morning when I come out to this, and every evening when I say good night to it."

"Aw, Murphy. I'd live out here. I'd camp on this deck," she said with an easy chuckle. "The outdoors makes you feel so alive, makes everything *real*."

"Hard to stay inside, that's for sure." She held up her glass. "This is very, very good. Thank you again. It's a treat." She shifted in her seat to face Riley more directly. "So…" she frowned as she jutted her chin toward Riley's extended leg. "What's up with the injury? Spill."

Riley grinned sheepishly, and Murphy loved the look of it, how it softened that rugged face.

"Chainsaw."

"Oh, Riley! Ewww!" Murphy scrunched herself into a ball for a moment. "Ouch!"

"Well, yeah, there were a lot of big ouches. There still are, in fact, but it was my own damn fault. I should have been harnessed, working on that tree, but I was in a hurry and just went with a belt. When it slipped, I went down." She motioned with the blade of her hand exactly how and where the saw struck her leg. "I'd let the saw go, so at least the chain wasn't running when it landed on me."

"Lucky you. Is the pain still really bad?"

Riley laughed and Murphy liked the sound, hearty and rather suggestive, like the woman. She bit her lower lip. "It's okay to laugh," Riley said and shrugged as she reached for a piece of cheese. "I'm coping. The Percocets they prescribed sent me into outer space last night, and I'm trying like hell to avoid another trip."

"Last night?"

"Yeah." She grinned at Murphy over the rim of her glass. "All because I was in a hurry to meet this hell-on-wheels hot babe."

"Uh-huh." Murphy felt color rise in her cheeks and took a drink.

"No complaints, though, except for following the doctor's orders. Lying around the house kills me, and one spacey night was enough."

Riley dazed and silly didn't compute easily for Murphy. Her only image of Riley off her game was from the hoedown, when alcohol was a factor, and she gazed off toward the colorful horizon, trying to envision a homebound, drugged-out Riley last night. *Last night I dealt with my own buzzed friend.*

"I don't blame you," she managed.

Teased by an image of Arby, Murphy vacantly popped a hunk of cheese into her mouth. "Oh," and she stood quickly, "you should have that leg up on something." She dragged a footstool closer, lifted Riley's leg by the ankle, and placed it on the stool. "Does that help?"

Riley stared up at her with uncharacteristic wonder, a vulnerability that nestled into Murphy's chest and embraced her. If there was a moment for a camera, this was one, to capture this magnetic image. The setting sun heightened Riley's deep tan, drew a white-gold sheen to her hair, and intensified the blue of her eyes. A contrast of seagrass and ocean, she mused, appreciating the brilliant color of Riley's shirt. *And the tailored fit says she's comfortable in that body.*

"Um…yes. Much. Thank you."

Murphy pointed to the grill in the sand nearby. "I'm going to put on the steak tips, so you stay right there." She stole a chunk of cantaloupe and disappeared into the kitchen, eager to regain control of her wandering thoughts.

"Let me help. I'm pretty good with a grill."

"No, gimpy. You sit. Talk to me."

"Damn, you're tough."

Returning with a tray of meat and utensils, en route to the steps, Murphy bent down to Riley's ear. "Butches don't have a monopoly on grilling." *Where the hell did that come from?* She noted Riley's grin as she walked on, knew she was being checked out. She looked back over her shoulder. "Stereotypes be dammed." *Okay. I'm officially flirting. I can't believe this.*

Riley bolted upright in the chair and stared down at herself. "Is it the shirt? What gave it away?"

Murphy laughed roundly. "Gee. Lucky guess. And I'll have you know I've been cooking outside since I was a little girl."

"Over a barbecue rig like that? Or a real fire?"

"Grilling. On a grill. Yes."

"Ahhhh. I see."

Murphy laid the meat on the grate and turned to face her. "You see what, exactly?"

"That's not a *real* fire. Do you like to camp?"

"This is so a *real* fire." Murphy trotted up to the deck for her wine. "What do you think cooks the food?"

Riley chuckled under her breath, and the soft, muted laugh struck a chord. Murphy stopped short, glass in hand. *Do that again.*

A whisper in her head insisted she press. "So, you're a camper?"

Riley immediately averted her eyes from Murphy's legs.

Caught you.

"Ah...um. Sorry." Riley's cheeks colored adorably and she shook her head at herself. "My mind was elsewhere for a second."

Murphy grinned. "So I saw." The headiness of Riley's obvious review overtook Murphy's focus on that familiar chuckle, and kept her standing right where Riley wanted her to stand. This just felt too good. She had no desire to change Riley's view, made no modest retreat to a chair or down the steps to the grill. She knew she had a toned, trim figure, and even at forty, still turned a head or two, but turning Riley's meant something. *What, exactly?*

"I'm sorry," Riley said. "What did you ask?"

"You're a camper?" Murphy repeated. She sipped her wine and her original thought returned, though minimized by her own flirtation.

Riley nodded. "Since I was a little girl, too."

"And where were you a little girl?" The breeze carried the aroma of grilling steak, and Murphy quickly went back down to tend to it. *Why didn't I do this in advance? Oh, yeah. Too busy freaking out.*

"Worcester," Riley answered from the deck.

"Central Mass, huh?"

"If I'd grown up around here with this," she said with a wistful lilt, and nodded toward the ocean, "I'd have become a lazy beach bum."

"I doubt you've ever been lazy in your life."

"My dad was a self-employed landscaper, and my brother and I were his employees as soon as we could be trusted to carry potted plants."

Murphy returned to the deck, tongs in hand, and leaned against the railing. "Hard work's in your genes then." She crossed her ankles and abruptly wondered if she was posing. *So what?*

"I suppose. I enjoy working with my hands, creating or fixing things."

"But how did you end up as the go-to girl for Provincetown property owners?"

Riley shifted in the chair. She picked up a piece of cheese and stared at it, as if searching for something written there.

"My girlfriend's father hired me onto his construction crew on the Cape, building houses, docks, sheds, everything. I learned hands-on from some terrific craftsmen, great old guys, and I made a ton of connections, including the one that ultimately put me in P-town many years later."

"And the girlfriend?"

"Ah, well…" She sighed hard. "I think Cape Cod was a bit too confining for her. I couldn't blame her, I suppose. We were young." Her voice dropped to a humbled drone and Murphy leaned closer. "I wanted a future here, but she wanted more elbow room. It hurt, but you move on, you know?" The tone of her voice rang a bell. Loudly, this time.

Murphy leveled a long, keen look at her as she replayed the sound in her head. It rolled through her mind as crisply as if from her headset. Pitch, diction, and resonance of voices played an integral part in her profession, the tools she had worked with for years, and her skill with them homed in on the familiarity of Riley's. *This cannot be what it sounds like. Pay attention. This flirting business is messing with my head.* She set her glass aside and returned to the grill to turn the steak tips. She glanced up, almost expecting to see someone else sitting in Riley's place. *I owe you an equally honest response.*

"I guess I may have broken a few hearts—including my own—during my twenties, too." Riley straightened attentively. "God, they were wild years, especially coming from a suburban, white-picket-fence upbringing, your typical Girl Scouts, soccer, music lessons…" She offered Riley a feeble grin. "But then came college…and the classic sex, drugs, and rock 'n' roll."

"Where was the scene of your crimes?"

"Manhattan. Talk about temptations. I fell into the 'scene' pretty deeply, managed some bands, promoted some, even sang in one for almost a year, but the drugs turned things dirty. And scary." She piled the meat on a platter and returned to the deck. "That wild, kinky scene just wasn't for me. I found I just loved playing music and settled into the disc jockey world for the last ten years or so."

"No kidding?" Riley's tone lifted. "Is that what you do now? I saw all the boxes off the living room. You can't possibly cart all that around to various gigs." With effort, she stood and followed Murphy into the kitchen.

"No. That's merchandise for my eBay store. I work from home."

"People can do that? Have an online store?" She chuckled, and Murphy mentally recorded the sound. "Being out so much has left me pretty ignorant of the Internet world, but…I suppose so, huh? Why not?"

"Of course." Murphy handed her a knife. "Slice up the meat for me?" She produced a massive bowl of salad from the refrigerator. "I'll admit, inheriting this place from my aunt has meant the world, but my store keeps me afloat. Plus, you can't beat being your own boss."

"No argument there. I went on my own about two years ago now. Wouldn't have it any other way." Sliced steak tips piled up on the platter, Riley's work efficient and precise. "Going solo's never bothered me. Like going for a ride or to the beach or camping." She shrugged. "It's an independent streak, I guess. Your line of work says you've got one. Does it extend into your personal life?"

Murphy's attention drifted, along with her focus, as she struggled to *hear* Riley. She tried to take in everything about her, ran her gaze along Riley's corded forearm and across her chest before pausing on her lips and then looking up. She saw Riley swallow hard. *Jesus, will you get a grip? Any more suggestive and I'll be in her lap.* The back of her neck grew damp, and she thought the temperature in the breezy kitchen had risen ten degrees.

"So what's a 'good time' for you? What do you do for fun?" Murphy piled salad on both plates and Riley topped it with meat. "You work nights mostly, don't you? That must put a damper on dating."

"I work days, officially, but take after-hours and emergency calls. Most P-town shops are just too tiny, too cramped to have repairs going on around customers, so a lot of work happens after closing. And I haven't done much dating in quite a while. I'm hoping to start building a house next spring, so I'm taking every job I can get."

"Really? How exciting." Impressive, Murphy thought as she put everything on a tray to take outside. "Daunting—and exhausting." When Riley uttered that low, gentle half-laugh again, Murphy couldn't help but notice.

"Yeah, exhausting at least, and I already crash at weird times of the day." She grabbed the wine bottle and slid the door open. "I can't get into TV, but I read a lot. The radio is good, too."

"Oh, that's right," Murphy said, stepping out and moving to the patio table. "You're a *Nightlight* listener, aren't you?" Murphy mentally booted herself in the ass. *Real smart, broaching this subject.*

Riley laughed brightly. "Yeah, I confess. That show's not as bad as the *Enquirer*, but it can get pretty dicey some times. Hey, hold on. You listen, too, if I remember correctly."

Murphy offered a Cheshire grin. "You never know what Sable will bring up, do you?"

Riley laughed again as they sat and dug into the food. "No, you certainly don't. Her voice is just so seductive, half the time I think she lulls callers into saying some of the things they come out with."

Murphy poked at her salad and took a leap of faith.

"Have you ever called in?"

"I'll tell if you tell."

Murphy's heart pounded and she had to force food into her mouth. Her appetite had abandoned her.

"I asked first."

"Okay, yes. I've thrown in my two cents a few times. She's hard to resist." She leaned closer. "And I'd be lying if I said I'd ever turn her away." She brought a forkful of salad to her lips. "Your turn."

"Well, I…"

"Yeah…Fess up, girl."

Murphy's fixation with identifying Riley's voice again took a backseat. Now she was forced to focus on preserving Sable's identity. "It's hard to keep the personal and business lives separate, but I do my best. I can't afford to mix the two."

Riley nodded as she chewed, then reached for her wine. "I can appreciate that, the need to keep them separate. Working at home must make that a constant challenge."

"I work at all hours, including nights, but my days are flexible. That's a big bonus."

"Wow. Your eBay business has you working the overnight?"

"I…ah, well…it can." Her heart raced. *Damn you, Sable.* "I'm often out late. I-I do volunteer work."

"Really?" Riley glanced up as she sliced into a piece of steak. "What kind?" The look of innocence on her face nearly forced Murphy from the table. *Go ahead. Make things worse.* "For a home care agency…for the elderly."

"Wow. That's great. It takes a special kind of woman do to that, Murphy." *Special. Yeah, right.* "I actually prefer working the odd hours, without the hustle and bustle around me. Except in the winter."

Murphy felt her heart rate level off. "The snow." It was good to be back on comfortable *honest* ground.

"Right." Riley refilled their glasses. "The blizzards are my least favorite. I'll take a hurricane over a blizzard any day."

"You know, if I had to choose, I'd do the same. The cold is merciless."

Riley dipped her head. "Even when you're dancing on snowbanks in the dark with a beautiful woman."

The words and their sound dropped Murphy's stomach like a roller coaster plunge. She raised her glass for the compliment, but her wine shimmered with the quake in her hand. *There's no way, is there? She easily could have heard Arby on the show. It's just a dancing analogy, after all. But isn't it really too coincidental?*

She met Riley's eyes and felt their playful affection take hold. She wished they would take her away from this predicament, back to the snow on that winter night so they could start from scratch. But that wasn't happening. Not as long as Sable and Arby stood between them.

Riley set her empty plate aside. "Have you ever looked back on that night? Ever wondered, if our rescue hadn't gone off without a hitch...? I have."

"I have, too."

"Once in a while, maybe when I'm just worn out and fuzzy, I see us arguing in the blowing snow. You really were kinda cute in that damn hat."

Murphy had to laugh. "As were you with your runny nose."

"And you with no phone."

"You with no coffee."

"Your hands blocking the heater."

"Your huffing and puffing steaming up the windshield."

"It's like a dance ended too soon," Riley said softly.

Murphy's breathing shortened. *Oh God. Why did I doubt it?* Her glass trembled against her lips as she sipped her wine, and she prayed her voice wouldn't shake.

"Riley, you were my hero, you know. I should have tracked you down right after that and thanked you."

"You did thank me."

"Well, nevertheless, I should have—"

"Hey." Riley held her glass to Murphy's. "Here's to no longer being strangers in the night."

CHAPTER SIXTEEN

Murphy stared into her reflection in the bathroom mirror, searching for direction and the composure to see her through the rest of the evening. Splashing cold water on her face would only ruin her makeup, so that wasn't an option. Riley—*and Arby*—sat on the deck, awaiting her return, and here she stood, short of breath, heart doing flips in her chest, and her conscience spinning so fast, she was dizzy.

"Dear God. Some strength here, please." Her hands were cold and they shook. "How do I handle this? Would you like to dance, *Arby*? And why *Arby*? Where did that name—*your initials*."

She tightened her grip on the edge of the sink.

"Now, Sable *shouldn't* confess. There's no way." *How could she? Embarrassing you as Riley was a horrible enough proposition, but now Arby? Totally humiliating. Shit. And then I panic and invent that elderly care thing. How fucking stupid was that?* She rubbed her temples with her fingertips.

"Breathe." *One person, one great voice, one dynamic, enthralling woman.* "Stop making it harder than it is." She straightened her necklace, the tiny sapphire solitaire Bryce had given her on their six-month anniversary. "She's charming, engaging, isn't she? She would have been a good friend of ours back in the day. I like her a lot." Suddenly, she stared hard into her reflection. "You don't mind, do you? That I feel...well, I guess, at ease with her? Maybe even a bit *enchanted?*"

Don't complicate things any further, for God's sake. It's just an evening of good conversation, a nice connection. Simple. Enjoy.

She inhaled and exhaled with purpose, collected herself, and returned to the deck, the sunset, and Riley. Arby. RB.

At the screen door, she took a moment to study the woman in repose, stretched out in the chair, face turned to the first stars of the night. *I know so much more about you than I can say. And I like it all. Why does life always have to be such a challenge?*

She slid the door open and Riley sat up, a broad welcome on her face that melted Murphy where she stood.

"Twilight is magnificent here, Murphy."

"It is, isn't it?" She strolled to the railing. "It never ceases to amaze me. I'm sure the artists who have flocked to the Cape for generations worship this as much as the dawn. The light is ethereal."

Murphy set her left hand over her right on the rail and found herself fidgeting. Uncertain if memories or this mind-blowing scenario were at play, she forced herself to stop.

"I love this time of night. Well, it's not completely night yet, but… The pastels in the sky, the change in the air off the sea…"

She heard Riley rise from the chair and tried not to grow tense. Having her close—bodily—created waves in her stomach and a serious sexual craving that she hadn't felt in far, far too long. *Since Bryce.* She suspected those heavy conversations with Arby, packed with innuendo, had gradually revived her these past months, and now, with Arby's fantasy persona and Riley's desirable reality morphing into the same person, Murphy knew she was in some serious trouble.

Riley moved to her side. "I've spent a lot of time at beach houses, watching sunsets, watching the night roll in like the tide." She leaned on her palms, studying the darkening horizon. "It's true that there's something magical about it."

Murphy crossed her arms. The breeze had turned cool. The slight, hesitant movement of Riley's arm said Riley had considered encircling her shoulders. *No, intimate conversation doesn't necessarily entitle you to physical intimacy, but it sure would have been nice.*

The tactile memory of Bryce's arms around her, the warmth and security, drew a shiver. She didn't want to relive those days, not even in fantasy, because they were best left perfectly preserved where they were. Those memories were a part of her that she wouldn't trade for the world, but moments here, like this, always threatened to break her.

"When my partner Bryce became too ill to handle the beach, we'd sit here for hours, looking at the sky, the changes." Riley watched her closely and Murphy dared an appreciative glance. "I bought her a color swatch wheel to use outside. She didn't want computer-generated colors. We enjoyed her last few weeks right here with some pretty heavy debates and lots of laughter…lots of laughter, over which specific tints matched the streaks across the sky."

Riley turned a hip against the rail and faced her. "How long ago?"

"Three years. We'd been together for nine. Pancreatic cancer took her."

"Jesus. I'm sorry, Murphy. But she'll always be with you, you know."

"No matter how well I think I'm coping, it still…" She sighed at herself. "There are times when I see these colors, I have to look away."

"Oh, but no. Don't," Riley said gently, that familiar easy alto now so close to Murphy's ear. She lightly moved a wisp of Murphy's hair back from her cheek, and Murphy's eyes drifted shut. The tingle of the fleeting touch lingered. "Don't look away, Murphy. Don't close your eyes." Riley turned to the last throes of sunset. "All these colors are for you."

Murphy cleared her throat and fought to keep her emotions in check. Memories of Bryce always befell her here, and they rode head-and-shoulders above everything. But she'd never had to place them into perspective with the likes of Riley.

"Thank you," she said. "That's heavy stuff."

"It's okay that it still gets to you. Hearts don't have rules." She chuckled. "Well, if they do, they don't always play by them. We're just along for the ride."

Murphy looked down at their feet, her own bare and Riley's strapped in leather, and thought of life's twists and turns, the mixes and matches. *What are the odds that the fantasy woman who's flirted and courted, aroused you for months, turns out to be real woman, someone you shouldn't have to resist at all? What are those odds?*

"Unbelievable," she answered out loud. She realized it wasn't an altogether appropriate response to Riley's insightful comment and wished she'd kept her mouth shut. Or that someone had stopped her. *Bryce, why didn't you?* "Thank you," she said again, and lifted her head. "I never expected a conversation like this tonight. I apologize, really. Thanks for indulging me."

"Do not apologize." Riley cupped Murphy's elbow and turned her toward the house. "Time to go in."

Without thinking, Murphy unfolded her arms and slipped her palm into Riley's hand, and when Riley laced their fingers together, Murphy wanted to walk just like that for hours.

Riley pulled open the sliding door with her free hand, led them inside, and closed the door. She gave Murphy's hand a little squeeze.

"I wasn't indulging you," she said quietly. "It's called sharing and it's good. It means a lot."

Murphy squeezed her hand in return, and Riley grazed her fingertips along Murphy's cheek. Murphy tipped her head into Riley's touch, could hear her own heart pound, the blood rush in her ears. She couldn't dismiss the tenderness of Riley's touch or the growing desire to feel it on her lips, to deliver some of her own.

"You make it easy to share," she said. "You give of yourself so naturally and that means a lot to *me*." She didn't want to consider how much sharing she *hadn't* done, not with Riley this close and holding her hand.

"I'm glad we did this tonight, Murphy." Riley clutched their joined hands to her chest. "I don't want it to be the only time, either. Say you'll let me take you out sometime soon."

Murphy nodded, responded from the heart. "I'd like that very much." She didn't want this night to end but doubted she had much stamina left. Emotionally drained was a very loud condition screaming from inside. One of them. The other, surprisingly the most vocal and definitely the most impatient, pleaded for satisfaction while Murphy craved time to regroup. "I'm glad we did this tonight, too. I'm very happy we've finally met."

"Me, too. Finally." Riley walked them to the door, fingers still entwined between them.

"I like you, Murphy Callahan, even if your taste in hats boggles my mind." She flashed her a sly grin as she opened the door.

"Oh yeah?" Murphy thrust out her chin. "Well, since when do Rough Riders look like boys from the 'hood, huh?" Riley blushed and Murphy smiled. "You know, I had no idea you were a blonde that night, it was so dark and you had this double-covered." She combed her fingers back through Riley's hair. She'd fought the temptation for propriety's sake all evening but didn't even hesitate now. *A cool, light crown of spun gold...Bryce's was so thick and black.* "I like it."

"So the lady likes blondes."

"Hair color doesn't make the woman," she answered, "but this suits you perfectly."

"That so?" Riley's voice dropped an octave and rolled over Murphy's skin like a deep massage. "What makes the woman for Murphy Callahan?"

"Oh, let's see…She has to be smart and considerate, sensitive…"

Never losing eye contact, Riley toyed with a button on Murphy's shirt. "Is that right?"

"It is." Murphy struggled against the quiver in her voice. "She should have a sense of humor, too."

"Uh-huh." Riley edged closer. "You don't say."

Murphy took a step back and her shoulders met the door. Riley inched closer and leaned both palms on the door, sandwiching Murphy's shoulders, and lowered her head to whisper in her ear.

"Is that all, Ms. Callahan?"

Murphy exhaled carefully in anticipation, her insides roiling with need.

"She should be decisive and…and strong." Riley's forehead met hers. "And she should be honest…kind…"

Riley trailed her nose along the side of Murphy's.

"And…?"

The feel of hard, unwavering thighs, of small breasts against her own sent Murphy into a tailspin of excitement and want. She could barely think, move, or breathe, and didn't give a damn about any of them.

"And…um…" She knew a transfer of power was under way inside, her brain stepping down, her body rising to the call. She swallowed, trying to think. "And…devoted…"

Riley touched her mouth to Murphy's and kept it there, without pressure, a feather's intangible kiss, brimming with anticipation. Murphy ached for the real thing. Soft and enthralling, Riley's lips parted against Murphy's as she spoke. "And…?"

"And tender," Murphy said on a breath, thinking it just might be her last.

Riley's lips skimmed across hers, almost tentatively, as if searching for the perfect spot to land. With a barely perceptible tilt of her head, Riley kissed her fully, seriously.

Broad, warm palms on her shoulders kept Murphy from dissolving into the floor, but nothing could stop her from dissolving into Riley's chest. Her arms traveled around Riley's solid torso, and she hung on as Riley stole the ground from beneath her feet.

Hardly cognizant of her body's response, she opened to Riley's kiss, kneaded her back, squeezed her closer. Want surged and awakened nerve endings and emotions she hadn't acknowledged in years. Riley captured each one of her lips, tugging gently and smoothing her tongue lightly, reverently, across their surface, and Murphy reveled in their connection. Her own eagerness to give and receive surprised her.

She welcomed a renewed kiss that pressed her head into the cup of Riley's hand. Riley leaned in and they bumped the door to the wall. She might take me right here, Murphy thought fleetingly, and the realization that she'd welcome it startled her. *God, I'd give myself to you right now.* Riley's tongue beckoned, flicked against hers, and Murphy encouraged it with her own.

In awe of what she knew and didn't know about Riley, Murphy thoroughly enjoyed exploring the muscled shoulders and sides, flexing her fingers into Riley's waist, all through a very steamy shirt that hinted of a balsam forest. And for the first time since…in a long time, she wanted to let go, to take and be taken…*by this woman.* The feel of her, deliciously solid yet pliant in her hands, had Murphy lost in sensation until a thigh slipped between her legs and made her groan, exquisitely aroused, into Riley's mouth.

The sound must have roused Riley in a very different way, however, because she gripped Murphy's shoulders in her fingers and stepped back, her face a mixture of emotions.

Riley fumbled for words. "I…You…Wow, Murphy. I…"

"If…if you say you're sorry about that…spectacular moment, I swear I'll hurt you."

Riley grinned toward the floor and ran a hand through her hair. She chuckled as only Arby could.

"I had to stop. I-I was losing my mind."

"Probably wise. You'd already blown mine."

"Amazing, having you in my arms. Kissing you is heaven."

"Kissing you is…*very* dangerous, Riley."

"So, you might still be that damsel in distress?"

Murphy seized a pinch of Riley's shirt. "For such a romantic Rough Rider? I think yes."

"So…it's a date?"

"Absolutely."

Riley twirled a wave of Murphy's hair behind her ear. "Your hair's so incredibly soft. I love the feel of it on my face."

They were seconds away from starting all over again. Murphy felt it, and once she laid both palms on Riley's chest, she knew Riley felt it, too. She put two fingers to Riley's lips.

"Shh." She stood on her toes and kissed Riley lightly. "We have a date."

"We have a date," Riley repeated, and hobbled out to the top step. "Thank you for a great night, Murphy."

"Thank *you*. You made it very special. Please drive safely."

"I will." Riley maneuvered down the steps and limped backwards all the way to the Jeep. "I'll call you."

"I should hope so." She hung in the open doorway, watching Riley back out to the street, wanting to call her back and ask that she stay.

CHAPTER SEVENTEEN

Murphy knew that a cumulative total of four hours' sleep wasn't enough to survive the upcoming day, but through her jumbled, wine-induced fog, she managed to recognize two important facts: it was Sunday, she didn't have to be coherent or even vertical; and Riley Burke rocked her world. She *could* haul herself into the early summer sunshine on her deck and try to return to that dream of tender hands and consuming lips, or even guzzle a gallon of espresso and lose herself in that erotic novel, but either way, she figured she'd end up frustrated. *Besides, nothing beats just lying here, remembering.*

"After all this time, how ready and willing was I?" She flopped onto her side and wrapped her arms around the pillow. *And she knew it. She was, too. Jesus, thank God one of us stopped.* She groaned. *Too bad.*

She rolled onto her back and stared at the ceiling, saw them pressed together against the door, tasted the wine on Riley's tongue. The breadth of Riley's chest seeped into her bones and was still there. Riley's reverent squeeze of her hips rushed into her core like a rogue wave—*again.* Murphy squirmed between the sheets.

"Shit. Talk about being swept away." She exhaled with gusto and her attention fell upon the photo on the bureau. *It was an emotional night, a lot to handle. I never expected her to…Never thought I'd—*

Her ringing cell phone pulled her from Bryce's picture. The compulsion to rationalize her actions, however, insisted she linger over the embrace she'd offered, the ardent kisses she'd returned, the moan that had broadcast her pleasure. *God.*

"Razor. Really?"

"Morning to you, too. Are you alone?"

"Oh, you're imp—"

"Listen, we're on our way to breakfast and the flea market, but I need to hear about last night, so we're paying you a quickie visit."

Murphy pulled the pillow over her head. "It's still early. Have a heart."

"It's after eight. Get up and make us lattes."

The pillow only brought Razor closer. She flung it off and sighed. "Am I allowed time to shower?"

Tina yelled from somewhere in the car. "Sorry, Murph. I tried."

"Tell Tina I love her. You, I hate."

"I know. See you in a few."

Murphy dropped her cell on the bed. Damn it, she hated waking up and finding herself already behind. It made her cranky. *Especially this morning.* She had to sort out last night's events in a hurry, tear herself from images and sensations that awakened rejuvenated and insistent. She grumbled as hot water sharpened her senses and restored a semblance of order. *So much for a lazy morning between the sheets with thoughts of your mouth, your hands on me.*

"Probably for my own good." Murphy slapped the wall. "Damn it!" She grabbed the shampoo and lathered her hair. "Yes, Razor, I know for a fact that she's tender and sweet, that she's built like a freakin' rock, that she's gorgeous and soft-spoken…" Her hands fell to her sides as suds flowed off her head. "And she's Arby."

Murphy set her forehead against the tiles. How to cope with Arby's future calls to *Nightlight* was the newest dilemma. Without a doubt, she knew Razor—with all good intentions—would cut Arby off like some ninja assassin before she'd allow any "carrying on" over the airwaves. And, being totally honest with herself, the last thing Murphy wanted was to turn Riley away. *This is bad.* It was hard enough, fulfilling her obligation of Sable's secrecy and keeping Riley in the dark about her, but now, Murphy felt compelled to keep Razor in the dark about Arby. *What happened to my nice, steady, routine life? I'm going to lose my freakin' mind.*

Her cell beckoned from the bedroom and she dragged herself from the shower. "Coming, Razor." *Coffee's cheaper than a therapist, so I suppose getting me up is a good thing.* She yelled at the phone. "I don't need this DRAMA!" She calmed herself with a sigh before answering. "You can never just call once, can you?"

"We were thinking you should join us for breakfast. We'll wait."

"I'd suggest you do breakfast and the flea market and let me be, period, but you got me up now, so do you want lattes or not?"

"Thought you'd be a stick-in-the-mud, so we got cinnamon buns from Trish at Patty Cakes. A-ha! That made you pause. Your mouth's filling with saliva right now, isn't it? A little drool on your lip?" Murphy pulled clothes out of her drawers. The last things she needed to think about were mouths and saliva and lips. And on top of it all, Razor was in her merciless mode. "Do I hear the grumpy DJ's stomach rumbling? A yearning for sweet decadence in her loins?"

"Hunger has nothing to do with loins."

"Do we have lonely loins this morning?"

"Leave my loins alone." *One of these days, Razor...*

"Okay. We're here."

Murphy jerked upright, a pair of mint green bikini briefs in her hand. "What?"

"Open the door, lover girl. We need to feed."

Murphy disconnected and purposely took her time dressing and getting to the door. Crossing the living room, though, she was waylaid by a vivid flashback: Riley holding her hand, Riley's face, a warm satin against her cheek, Riley's lips...*so soft*. How the thrill had skyrocketed. The door itself bore witness, and Murphy caught herself placing a palm on it, reconnecting with the moment.

The doorbell startled her. It rang three more times in rapid succession before she could yank the door open.

"Only because Tina's here as a witness do I *not* kick your scrawny pain-in-my-ass butt down these steps."

Tina preceded Razor inside. "Hiya, sweetie."

"How do you put up with her?" she asked her, and scowled when Razor waltzed past, grinning.

"Mornin', Ms. Grumpypuss." She passed the pastry box beneath Murphy's nose. "Yum-yums. Come on."

Murphy followed them into her kitchen.

Tina uttered a little gasp and went directly to the flowers on the counter. "Oh, Murphy! Are these from her? They're fantastic."

"Yes, they certainly are." When her cheeks warmed, Murphy hurried to the espresso machine in the corner. "Lattes, coming up."

Razor was at her shoulder immediately.

"I saw that...that 'ohhhhh yeah' glazed look on your face. You had fun, didn't you?"

Murphy nodded. She bit back a smile and refused to show Razor.

"By the looks of these," Tina said, "I'd guess it went well. Happy for you, Murph. I'm glad she turned out to be as nice as you expected."

Expected? Oh, dear Lord.

"Riley's terrific and great company. It was good to get to know her. Kind of strange, in a way, because we'd met last winter, so this was like…like finishing a conversation. We shared a lot and it was fun."

Razor hovered. "And…?"

Murphy turned abruptly, the leading question throwing her right back to last night, right into Riley's kiss. "You do *not* have to know everything."

"Don't be ridiculous. Of course I do. How'd the steak tips come out? Or did you zoom off to La-La Land and turn them into shoe leather?"

"My steak tip salad was outstanding as usual, thank you very much."

Razor snatched up one of the empty wine bottles by the sink and eyed Murphy as she prepared their drinks. "This is primo stuff, y'know. The woman is hot for you." She leaned against Murphy's shoulder. "You both got a nice buzz on and she stayed the night, didn't she?"

Murphy shoved her away. "No, now shut up."

"I bet she blew you into orbit. It's just like riding a bike, right? Tell me you at least went for a ride."

"Razor," Tina said from the counter, "come and sit down and leave her alone. You're badgering, for God's sake. Ask the basic questions, and if Murph wants to answer, she will, and then you're done. No more."

"Okay." Razor seemed satisfied with that. "So, is she a good kisser? Did you see her at least partially naked? And did you fuck?" She grinned at Tina and turned back, expectantly.

Murphy placed their drinks on the counter and sat. She frowned at Razor.

"How are you still my friend?"

"Because we've been friends for too long to remember why."

"You know? You're right." She raised her cup and shook her head at Tina. "How you do it is beyond my comprehension."

"Well?" Razor still stood beside her stool. "Are you going to answer my questions or not?"

"Not."

"Aw, shit." Razor sank onto a stool. "Tease."

"I am *not* a tease! Stop being such a nosey teenager."

Razor sulked. "I was rooting for someone to ring your bell,

Murphy, someone who'd put pizzazz into your life, give you a whole new outlook."

Pizzazz is an understatement.

Murphy slung an arm over Razor's shoulder. "Slow down, tiger. Riley and I basically just met." She tried not to grin at Razor's empathetic disappointment. "The world-changing epiphany might take a second meeting." *Who are you kidding, you who were so wet and legless against the front door?*

"I'm just psyched for you, Murph. I want you to live again—and not settle for some fantasy radio woman with a sappy night voice."

That "night voice" ran through Murphy's mind like a favorite song. She felt it gloss her lips on the whispered stroke of Riley's tongue. But appreciation of such undying friendship was what she needed to convey right now, not the headiness of an arousing evening—or the anxiety of someone withholding a shocking truth. She gave Razor a reassuring squeeze and flicked a finger at the pewter labrys dangling from Razor's ear.

"Okay, Razor. I'll tell you that Riley is an absolutely amazing kisser and we could've kissed all night, but didn't. And that's all I'm saying. Happy now?"

A slow, conniving grin spread across Razor's energetic face.

"You slept with her, didn't you?"

"Dear God." Murphy dropped her head onto her arms.

❖

"What do you mean, she has to be home by nine?" Didi tossed her bar rag onto a shelf and guffawed. "Is she still in high school, for Christ's sake? You that desperate, RB?"

"She works nights a lot. *She* suggested Saturday, but I can't. This is the weekend a bunch of us are building that ramp for a friend in Quincy. And then, he gets out of Mass General on Monday morning, so we're all staying over to see he gets into his place all right."

"So, you're a damn Girl Scout. I hope this gal appreciates you. God knows, the last one didn't."

"This one's not just some *gal*, Didi. I told you that."

"Oh, right. Excuse me. *Lady.*"

"That's better."

"First date?"

"Friday, yeah. Officially. Even if it has to be quick, she's worth it."

"But you were at her place last weekend." Didi snorted. "She nurse your leg all night?"

"No nursing. And it wasn't all night. We just hung out, sort of caught up, filled in the blanks. We met last February, actually, and our paths have crossed since, but we never got together at all."

"So, she's local? What happened in February?"

Riley nodded and drank. "She lives in Wellfleet. I hauled her car out of a snowbank on Bradford, four o'clock in the morning during one of those lovely storms we had."

"Whoa. Four o'clock? Shit, I'd remember her, too. Is she hot?" Didi stopped washing glasses when she didn't get an answer. "Well, what's her name?" She waved a hand through Riley's distant stare. "Hey, Romeo. Wherefore art thou?"

"Ah...yeah, she's...she's sensational. In every way."

"You're scaring me, buddy."

Riley rotated her glass in her hands absently. "Murphy Callahan is her name."

"Hm. Don't know a Murphy. You really like this one, don't you?"

"Ever meet someone and things just click? Like the teasing is fun and just pops out? You find yourself opening up, saying things you'd probably never say in a million years?" She paused, expecting a response but not really wanting one. "Y'know, like you're on the edge of your seat, waiting to learn everything about her, and you're taken by the way she wears her clothes, puts her lips to a glass...The way she says your name."

Didi put her hands on her hips and frowned. "You got another job tonight or are you done?"

"Done."

"Good."

"Why?"

"Your first *official* date is three nights away?" Riley nodded and Didi shook her head. "Go home and start taking cold showers."

CHAPTER EIGHTEEN

Murphy cleared boxes of her eBay inventory into a corner, thinking Bryce would have never tolerated such disorganization. In earlier times, Bryce had helped Murphy keep their household neat and spotless, running smoothly, ever efficient. *This much has changed without her.* She sat and watched Razor routinely "set up" paperwork over every available surface of the living room. How Razor functioned in disarray more drastic than her own always amazed her, but, at the moment, Murphy's train of thought advanced beyond Bryce and clutter.

"Is she naked?" Razor's voice fell upon her like a wet blanket.

"Huh?" Murphy looked up. Razor stood with hands on her hips, waiting.

"Riley. Is she—"

"Oh. No, you ass. She's just…"

Razor nodded knowingly. "*Just*. You've got her bare-chested in boxers, stretched out on your bed."

Murphy sat forward, shook off the image. "I do not."

"I'm happy she's got you dreaming, but whatever it is you're busy doing, you've gotta stop and come back here for the next few hours. We've got to work up these show ideas before management starts harping. You know *that's* just too ugly."

"I told them I won't do this gig unless I can do it my way, and I'm standing my ground. They'll cave. I know they will."

"Seems they're set on the dominatrix thing, Murph." Razor shook a catalogue at her as proof. "I had these in my in-box this morning. Pictures of outfits that Toys of Eros is offering to lend you."

"No. No. No. What's so bad about my vampire idea?"

"Look, all I know is that they've worked out something already with the Pied. I'm sure the bar doesn't care what costume you choose, as long as it gets *you*, live and in person. Personally, I think the dominatrix bit is a great play on *Nightlight*'s mystique, but your vampire idea works, too." She spun to a different pile of papers. "The theme for Carnival Week is 'Give It All You've Got,' so we can make it fly." She finally found the brochure she was looking for. "Costume options are right here. Let's go for it, then."

Murphy sat back into the couch, relieved Razor was on her side. No way in hell would she portray a sex queen for this masquerade bash—hosting *Nightlight*'s first-ever live broadcast—even if it was a fundraiser for a worthy organization.

Razor gazed sadly at the pictures sent from Toys of Eros. "Kinda looked forward to showing you all this great, hot stuff, but now I don't dare."

"No. I don't need to see sex toys. Not right now, at least."

"No shit. We don't have time for you to run and change your pretty pink panties."

Murphy stuck out her tongue and flipped her off.

Razor's wicked laugh bounced around the living room. "Hey, you know, if Ms. Hunky is the real deal, you'll probably *have* to come clean soon. You could turn her on as 'Sable the Dominatrix.' Y'know…a little role play."

"Yeah, right. Like *that* would be the perfect way to tell her." She reached for her water bottle. *No way to any of it.* Thoughts of Riley wouldn't go in that direction. Instead, she remembered how soft that shaggy blond hair had felt in her fingers, how rousing it looked against that blue fitted shirt. "She's got a shy side that's just…She'd probably be embarrassed by a dominatrix. She's very soft-spoken, you know, sensit—"

"Uh-huh. Embarrassed my ass. Hello, earth to Sable."

"Well, she's just easy to be with, to talk to. Cripes, I almost made a fool of myself. I told you how I got all maudlin on her, but she—"

Razor sighed, pen poised above a clipboard. "Murphy. Bringing up an ex on a date isn't—"

"Bryce isn't my ex. She's my late partner. There's a difference. And I wasn't flaunting her or anything, and I don't think I sounded pathetic. It just came out. Riley was a sweetheart about it. Actually, very compassionate and I was touched."

"Hm. I wouldn't have thought she… Well, that's good, Murph."

"Yes, it is. And *she* is."

"For now, would you please try to spare some thought for this?"

She handed her another costume brochure. "Now. In case you haven't read your email lately, we need the promo spots ASAP, so let's run through the script again."

"Yeah, yeah. I got the memo." Murphy scanned the pictures of available costumes. "I think you're pushing it with the script, by the way."

"It's been approved." Razor tapped the brochure. "Check out the fourth page. It's you."

Murphy turned to said page and sat up straight. "No fucking way."

"Yes, fucking way. I was thinking maybe…pull your hair back severely, or maybe you'd rather wear a wig. See that half-mask? We'll go overboard with makeup for your eyes and the lower part of your face."

Murphy stared at the costume, or what little there was of it, and its revealing black lace. She turned to her, wide-eyed. "I can't do this."

"Of course you can. It'll be a blast."

"You said…Jesus. Thank God we've got over a month for me to wrap my head around this. And what if she…?" The prospect of Riley identifying her made her stomach turn. "You said no one will recognize me. You're sure?"

"Murph. We'll do a total makeover on you. Don't worry."

"And you said I'll be up in their DJ booth, overlooking the crowd, unapproachable, right?"

"Right. There's an outside staircase in the back, so you could swoop in and out like a true vampire, if you want." She laughed at herself. "We'll meet with the Pied manager and work it out."

Murphy played the scene in her head, remaining shadowed throughout, scurrying around in the dark, especially dressed in the outfit displayed in the brochure. How Bryce would have fussed. *You wouldn't want me leaving the house, wearing so little, would you?* "Razor. I…I've never worn anything like this." She held up a hand. "Look, I'm already shaking."

"Don't be such a pussy. Embrace it. Pretend it's your alter ego or something. You *have* to get into it."

"Wow. For four hours? No wonder you want me panting over the damn radio."

"The script is fun and you know it. I'll add more bottom to your sound when you get to the hot part, that's all. Come on, let's try it again." She handed her the script.

"I can't sound like someone I'm not for hours, Raz."

"For these commercial spots only. Please. You just need to emphasize certain things…like the foxy, hungry vampire queen that you are."

Murphy threw the script at her. "Screw this!"

Razor whirled. "That's it! Vehemence, girlfriend. Vehemence." She tossed the script back. "Read it now."

Murphy cursed, but stood up from the couch to project. "'You *know* you want it, so satisfy that ache. *Don't* be left out. Let go and give it all you've got. *Nightlight* will be burning hot for you. *Come.*'"

Razor's eyebrows rose. "Well, at least that's better than the last time."

"Better? What more do you want?"

"Depth, Murph. You lose that sultry tone when you project. Your voice rises an oct—"

"Oh, fuck me!"

"Save that for Riley."

"Do *not* make me think of her while I'm doing this."

"Listen: Lower your volume but keep the emphasis."

"Did you actually write this shit or steal it from some phone sex TV commercial?"

"Just try it again. Will you, please? And this time, include the intro."

"This is the meanest thing anyone's ever done to me."

"Stop bitching and speak."

"Help me, Lord." Murphy took a long swig of water, closed her eyes, and settled herself. She summoned her low-key *Nightlight* tone and pace, and focused on putting the heaviest seductive hint she could muster into her voice. *Don't listen, Bryce…Riley…*

"Hello, everyone. This is Sable, host of WCCD's *Nightlight*, reminding you all to mark your calendars for a very special fundraising event to kick off Carnival Week this year. We'll be on the air that Saturday night—and, yes, I said *Saturday night*—from nine to one, with *Nightlight*'s first-ever remote broadcast from the Pied Bar's gigantic masquerade bash. Proceeds will benefit P-town's Help Our Women organization, so be sure to don your most creative persona and stop by. Join me for what promises to be a *very a*-rousing night." She inserted a suggestive pause and spoke through a slower, deeper breath. "Consider this a personal invitation from me. You *know* you want it, so satisfy that ache. *Don't* be left out. Let go and give it all you've got. *Nightlight* will be burning hot for you. *Come.*"

Murphy slammed the script onto the coffee table and flopped onto the couch. "I'm done. Toast. Finished."

Razor glowed. "Absolutely fucking perfect!"

"If you make me read it again, I'll rip those studs off your face."

Razor jogged around the room, waving the script. "Perfect! Perfect!"

"You are insane."

"That's why you love me."

Murphy dropped her head back and blew out a breath. "True."

CHAPTER NINETEEN

When their wine glasses clinked together, even the subtle, intimate atmosphere of Ciro & Sal's Restaurant faded away. The promise in Riley's eyes spoke of a newness and surety Murphy hadn't anticipated. She returned the salute, genuinely pleased to hold her glass to Riley's for an extra beat and connect with her. But something told her the gesture meant more than the usual "Glad to be here with you."

Why? I'm attracted to your attraction? Only Bryce's attention and sincerity ever felt this real, so am I substituting here? Damn. Maybe I am, it's been that long...so long, since my company was sought by someone who mattered this much.

She wondered when Riley had begun to matter. *When you saved me in the snow? When Arby's soft side told me who you really were? When we shared our thoughts...such deep kisses?* She didn't know when, but Riley had slipped beneath her covers and into her life where another hadn't been for a very long time, where there hadn't been room. And Murphy knew she'd made room, unconsciously, granted, but she'd let it happen. *And the world didn't shatter.* She didn't know if she could keep it up, if splitting her heart in two risked her sanity. *Not like I have a choice, really.* The security, the devotion she and Bryce had built stood strong in her mind, while Riley's invigorating, liberating stature grew right before her eyes. *Liberating is just how it feels, but what does that say?*

She searched Riley's face in the candlelight, and stopped thinking about hidden meanings and subconscious signs. There was nothing hidden or subconscious about what she saw, and she raised her glass again.

"To a fabulous dinner with a fabulous woman."

"The pleasure's been all mine, Murphy. Why didn't we meet long ago?"

"Oh, it's a good thing that we didn't. We were very different people, long ago."

"Yeah, on second thought, I prefer who we are today." Frown lines formed beneath the wisps of hair taunting her forehead, and Murphy wanted to smooth them away. Riley raised an eyebrow and drew her attention. "I confess, though, Ms. Callahan, I wish I could've seen you as a rocker. Wow." She shook her head at the missed opportunity.

"It's best letting the past stay where it is." *Some things are best left undisturbed.* "God, the things we did back then...Some were pretty outrageous."

Riley sat back, her head cocked slightly, apparently considering the possibilities. Murphy thought she could look at her for hours. Riley's appreciation and respect for Murphy's company on this early evening came through in her attire as much as her gaze or her bearing. Wearing a steel gray V-neck tee and matching black linen blazer and trousers, she easily was the most arresting woman in the room. She absently ran a hand down the front of her open blazer, and when she caught Murphy's gaze, she didn't look away.

Her heart beat a little harder. *She is* so *dangerous. I hope you like what you see as much as I do.* "I'm often amazed by life's hidden agendas. How we didn't meet until we both were single..."

Riley sighed into her wine. "You're right. It's a good thing. The temptation would have been criminal."

"Don't make me blush, Riley Burke."

"Sometimes the good *and* the bad need to take a back seat." Riley lifted Murphy's fingers into her hand on the table. Her thumb trailed across each one. "I just want us to enjoy this time. And look forward to more."

"So do I. You make me smile more than I have in ages, Riley. It feels good. Yes, I'd like to see more of you, too."

Riley leaned forward and squeezed Murphy's fingers. "I enjoy spending time with you, too. Very much. Hearing you laugh, learning how and what you think, hearing your voice—"

"Oh my God!" Murphy jerked back. Frantic, she dove into her purse.

Riley straightened, looking ready to engage whatever enemy had thrown Murphy into a frenzy. "What? What's wrong?"

Murphy pulled out her cell and searched for messages. Against her better judgment, she'd turned the ringer off during dinner, and now she saw five voice mail messages and twelve missed calls. And she had nine minutes before *Nightlight* went on the air.

"Murphy, what is it?"

She turned to Riley, panic emptying her brain of any semblance of explanation. But she had to say something and fast.

"I-I completely lost track of time. I'm sorry, Riley. I need…"

Riley looked at the phone in Murphy's hand.

Murphy looked at it, too. She had to get to the studio, but Riley had picked her up at home and driven to the downtown restaurant. She couldn't let Riley drive her home to her car; there wasn't time. But she couldn't let Riley drop her off at the studio a half mile away, either.

"What, Murphy? What do you need? How can I help?"

Jesus, I have fucked this up royally. Poor Riley, enchanting, drop-dead handsome Riley is now almost as much of a wreck as I am. Son of a bitch!

"I can't believe I lost track of the time. I…I have to be—I need to…I have a-an appointment. Shit!"

Riley stood up and waved for the waiter to bring the check. "I forgot you said you couldn't stay. I'll get you right home. Let's go. I'm sor—"

Murphy shook her head and tried to stop kicking herself long enough to think straight.

"Thank you, Riley, but no. Please don't worry. It's not far. My appointment…My client. She's…frail, and I, ah…I'm on call, whenever her daughter needs coverage. I can just run over to her house." She stuffed her cell back into her purse as she got to her feet.

"I'll get the Jeep," Riley said, backing away. "Tell Thomas, the waiter, I'll be back to pay him."

Murphy grabbed her sleeve and shook her head again. "No, Riley, really. I'm sorry to upset you—Christ, upset *everything* after such a wonderful evening. It'll actually take less time if I hustle over to her house."

"But how will you get home? If you want, call me later and I'll—"

"God, you're the sweetest thing. Thank you, but when her daughter gets back, she can run me home." She urged Riley back toward her chair. "Please sit and finish your wine. Everything's okay."

"Well, I…I feel awful, Murphy. I should've paid more attention to the time. I remember telling Cinderella not to worry about the pumpkin thing."

"Oh, Riley. Please do not apologize. It's my bad." She drew Riley to her by the chin. "Thank you so much for a truly special evening. You're definitely Prince Charming." She kissed Riley on the lips. "I'm *so* sorry," she whispered, and hurried out.

At the sidewalk, she flipped off her heels, scooped them up, and ran. She'd just make it to the studio in time, she knew, and once her head stopped spinning, she'd figure out how to fix the mess she made.

❖

Riley sat as if shoved. Thomas arrived with the check, and she handed him a credit card while staring at the empty place setting. Murphy's elegance lingered in the seat opposite her, ravishing in the turquoise dress and delicate feathered earrings, the matching necklace nestled into plush, beckoning cleavage. Her presence still warmed Riley, hell, still held her to the chair. Tender fingers and magical lips had stolen her very breath and waltzed away on gorgeous legs.

Murphy's soothing voice came to mind as Riley walked to the Jeep. Riley sighed, feeling soulfully incomplete as she started the Jeep, as if a hand had suddenly clamped over her mouth and stifled her laughter.

Prince Charming. I'd be honored. There'll be more dates. She wants them too. These things happen. We all live crazy lives.

She shook her head at just *how* crazy and hoped optimism would overtake the numbness that had set in during the insanity of the past ten minutes. "Didi, I could use a shot of something good right now." She turned on the radio and drove to the Den.

"...This is Sable, looking forward to hearing what's on your mind tonight. Give us a call, why don't you? 555-201-1112 is the number, or drop us a note at nightlight-dot-com. Let's settle in together for the next four hours. We'll be right back after a few words from our local sponsors, so stay close."

"I'll tell you what's on my mind, Sexy Sable. A very fine lady— the most scorching hot date I've ever had—just left me high and...well, not so dry, if you know what I mean. What do you have to say about that? No date has ever run out on you, I bet. And I doubt you'd ever run out on her."

She turned down the narrow side street, thankful, as always, for the absence of sidewalks, and parked as close to the building as retracted side mirrors would allow. "Didi, don't fail me now." She ran a hand back through her unruly hair and trotted down the few steps to the cellar bar.

"Hey!" Didi's shout turned the half-dozen heads in the room. "Look what the cat dragged in tonight." She slapped down a shot glass as Riley settled onto a stool. "The usual?"

"Dewer's."

"Whoa. Rough night for Romeo? Pretty early to be seeing you." Didi reached up for the bottle and switched on the radio nearby. Sable's whiskey voice flowed out into the room and Didi chuckled. "That woman's a piece of work, y'know? I just love that voice." She set the scotch in front of Riley. "So what's your story, or would you rather call Sable and pour your heart out to her?"

"Thanks. The big date was cut short, that's all."

"Hm. Looks like your puppy died. Shame, too, with you all spiffed up." She leaned over the bar and sniffed. "You smell good, too."

"Yeah, well, we lost track of time and she had to rush off."

"Eh, things happen, hon. She'll be back."

Didi cocked her ear toward the radio.

"Thanks for the call, Digger. Now, who else has a wild night to share, since Digger's got us reminiscing. Hello, you're on Nightlight. *This is Sable."*

Didi laughed roundly. "Oh, I could give that girl a few memories."

"Didi, you're a wild one, you are." Riley sent her a smirk and thought of her own wild escapades many years prior. The libations were quite different back then, along with the dance scene, the attire. She chuckled, remembering how her leather pants and vest made her sweat yet attracted women like a magnet. Suddenly seeing Murphy as a rocker covered in leather and the sheen of exertion, she downed her scotch in a flash.

"Hi, Sable. It's Belle. My birthday party at Herring Cove, back in 2012, comes to mind. Quite a few of us reminisce about it all the time. We went from Friday night right through to Monday morning. The cops finally kicked us off the beach, those of us still conscious, that is."

Riley enjoyed Sable's laugh.

"You all survived the weekend without getting arrested?"

"Well, two women were. They refused to get dressed. They don't appreciate it when we bring that up these days."

"Woo-hoo!" Didi stopped drawing a draft beer to punch the air. "Those are my kinda gals!"

"Can't say as I blame them for not wanting it mentioned," Sable said. *"Some things are better left to memory. Let the past stay where it is."*

Riley looked up at the radio. *Odd, hearing that line twice in an hour.* She recalled Murphy's compassionate expression when uttering the same words.

"Got that right, Sable. Hey, I think it's your turn. Got a hot night you want to share?"

Didi refilled Riley's glass. "Oh, I bet she does. Plenty of 'em."

Riley nodded and sipped her scotch. "I'm sure you're right."

"Ah, well, let's see what I can dredge up that's acceptable for the air. This is FCC-licensed radio, remember. Um...Well, there was the time—in a previous life, mind you—I spent the night on stage, topless, with a heavy metal band."

Didi and two other women in the bar applauded. Riley laughed and shook her head before drinking.

"Hope it was a women's band, Sable."

"Oh, absolutely. And I confess, it was shamelessly outrageous," Sable and Belle shared a laugh, *"especially because I was the lead singer at the time."*

Riley stared at the radio dial, wishing she could see what had to be a mile-wide grin on Sable's face. But she easily conjured Murphy's face instead. Murphy, the rocker. *One hot image.* She grinned at that thought and downed the rest of her scotch.

Chapter Twenty

Razor threw her clipboard on the desk and rolled up to the soundboard in her chair.

"Take six."

"I still don't see what was wrong with the last one," Murphy said, hands on her hips, glaring at Razor through the glass.

"It wasn't good enough. Take six."

"You know it was, Raz."

"Let's get on with it. We only have twenty minutes of studio time left. Now, ready?"

Murphy read the script again, and even though she thought it sounded exactly like the previous run-through, Razor seemed satisfied this time.

"Got it. You're done. I'll polish this up and we'll start airing it tomorrow night."

Murphy went into the booth and leaned against Razor's desk.

"On what schedule?"

She had to ask because Razor still steamed about the other night and wasn't offering much of anything. She didn't call yesterday, either. Murphy literally had run into the studio Friday night, flung herself into her seat, and had just taken a breath when Razor began the countdown to air. She knew Razor well enough to keep her distance, and she had. But enough was enough.

Razor grabbed the clipboard and flipped some pages while Murphy watched and waited.

"On *Nightlight*, at first, it runs once a week. At two weeks before the event, it runs once a night. The week *of* the event, *Nightlight* runs it every hour. Day shows get the shorter, G-rated version, to run once each, morning, afternoon, evening, every day." She tossed the clipboard back down and returned to the soundboard.

Murphy sighed. "How long are you going to hold Friday against me?"

"I'm over it."

"The hell you are. Look at me." Razor didn't. "I apologized till I turned blue."

"Should've been till you passed out."

"Oh, come on. I just lost track of time."

"I was a nutcase, getting ready to go on myself, you know."

"And when has that ever been necessary, hmm?"

"Twice."

"I was hospitalized with frigging pneumonia, for God's sake!"

"You weren't Friday night."

"Razor."

"Don't 'Razor' me. Aside from sending me into fucking cardiac arrest, we almost blew this prime studio time. I needed to confirm right before air time, and my brain was frying. I had to commit without you. I doubt I was even coherent. I believe I told you this cost me an arm and a leg and an ounce of great weed."

"And I told you I'll reimburse you."

Razor blew a breath up to her forehead. "Okay, fine."

"It won't happen again. I promise."

"It can't, Murph."

"It won't."

"Even if you two are tied in knots on the brink of ecstasy."

Murphy grinned. "Cut it out."

"You really like her, huh?"

She nodded. "It's killing me that I can't reach her. Leaving messages sucks. I've left four. I just hope she hasn't decided to ignore my calls."

"Ouch. You owe her big time. Do you know where she lives?" Murphy shook her head. "Well, find out. Go pop in."

"Yeah, right. *Really* show her how considerate I am."

Razor shook her head at her. "Wish I could've seen you running up Commercial in that dress."

"How to turn heads." She slumped into Razor's chair. "I still can't believe how I lied to her, blew her off like that. How horrible."

Razor crossed her arms. "Y'want me to say it?"

"No. I don't. I feel like such a shit. I know it's only fair that I tell her."

"It might be time you did."

"I'm going to, really."

❖

Riley sat on her cooler and wiped the sweat off her face with the hem of her tank top. *Too damn hot, too early.* She took a long drink of water, poured some onto her head, and rubbed it into her hair.

"How much longer, Burke?"

The shop manager was impatient, and Riley had reached her last nerve. Friday, her dream date went south, Saturday her cell phone fell out the Jeep window on Route 6 and was immediately run over, Sunday she spent in Cape traffic visiting her re-hospitalized Boston friend, and now this: a "reno" job that was claiming her whole life instead of four hours.

"You'll be decorating in the morning," she said. He paused, seemed to think about it, and spun back inside. "Should've done this a month ago," she mumbled after him.

She couldn't wait to shower and spend the rest of the night playing with her new phone. It was a far cry from her Android, and she worried about the differences for the next few hours as she cut and stained trim board, primed and painted the walls, and tacked on the trim.

It was almost dark by the time she packed her tools and lugged everything down the alley and around the corner to the Jeep—and saw her flat rear tire.

"Son of a bitch." She set all her gear inside and stepped back and stared. "Why now?"

"Well, that sucks. Need a hand?"

Riley turned to the tall, sharp-eyed woman and tried not to be distracted by her multi-colored hair.

"Eh…well. Thank you. I'm not exactly sure yet."

The woman gave a hefty shoulder bump to the spare tire attached to Riley's tailgate. "Tire still good, y'think?"

Riley grinned at her effort. "Yeah. Should be. I think I'm good. This was just the last thing I needed."

"Long day, huh?"

Riley nodded. "Long *few* days."

The woman surprised Riley by offering a handshake. "You're

Riley, right?" Riley shook her hand. "I'm Razor Delaney. You know my grandfather. You worked his West End place."

"Nice to meet you. Yeah, Ray Delaney. A sweet guy. He made it through the winter all right? I never got a call."

"He did. He lucked out." She turned and pointed at the flat. "Luckier than you."

"No shit, huh?" Riley retrieved the jack, and again was surprised when Razor dropped her backpack on the curb and got to work on the spare. "Aw, hey. You don't have to do that. Gets pretty filthy back there and you'll—"

"No problem. Listen, you've been there for Granddad enough times." She balled up the tire cover and put it in the back of the Jeep. "And I bet we've both been through worse shit than this."

Riley snickered. *Ain't that the truth.*

Together, they changed the tire in only a few minutes, but Riley was more than ready to call it a day.

"You're good at this," she said, rummaging through her large toolbox. "Thanks a lot, really." She passed her a container of pre-moistened towels to clean her hands. "Let me buy you a drink? You have time?"

Razor checked her phone. "As a matter of fact...sure. I'm not due home for another hour. Got a nine o'clock date with my better half. Sunday is our *Orange* night." Riley was baffled. "*Orange Is The New Black.* The TV show."

"Oh. Sorry, I don't watch much. My schedule is too weird."

"Well, do *you* have time for this drink? You don't need to call anyone?"

"Plenty of time, and there's no one." Riley pointed to the Pied Bar down the street and they started walking. "Besides, at the moment, I'm phone-less. My Droid took a skiing trip out on Route 6, and I haven't set up my new one yet. I just got it this morning."

"I hate losing a phone. Either you lose all your stuff or it takes forever to find it."

"I was pissed beyond words. And I'm lost, because this new one's an iPhone. I'm praying the guy at the store loaded all my stuff."

"You can transfer contacts from your home computer."

Riley shook her head at herself. "I'm not too savvy when it comes to phones or computers."

"Y'know...if you want, I could try taking a look. I'm a geek for a living."

"That so?" Riley grinned. "Do you have a shop?"

"No. I work at WCCD." They turned into the bar's boardwalk alley. "Give the station a call some evening when I'm there and come by."

"Wow. I appreciate that." She enjoyed Razor's company, her lively demeanor, and saw their exchange as the highpoint of her entire lousy weekend. "That's very generous. Thanks so much. I'm kind of desperate."

Razor laughed and pulled out her cell again as they ordered drinks.

"See?" She held up the phone and indicated the attached chain clipped to her belt. "Loser Line. That's what I call it."

"I need one of those. Obviously." Beers finally in hand, they leaned back against the bar. "So, WCCD, huh? What do you do?"

Razor grinned toward the rear deck and the ocean beyond. She seemed ready to burst about something.

"I'm a producer, but really just a glorified sound engineer."

"Really? Cool job. How'd you end up here? Sorry, but you don't seem like a native."

"No?" and she chuckled as she raised her bottle.

"No. I'd peg you for New York."

"Well, you'd be right. I, ah…I had a friend who migrated here, and I landed the job on her recommendation."

"Nice. I always have the station on in the Jeep. I practically live in the damn thing anyway. Is your friend a DJ? Someone I'd recognize?"

"Oh, I think you would. It's Sable." She took a long drink.

"No! You two have…history?"

"Not *that* kind of history. We've been buddies for years."

"So, are you *her* producer?" Razor nodded. "Damn, this is cool. She's…well, please let her know that everyone loves the show."

"Thanks. It's worked out great. We've been doing *Nightlight* for two years now. I think it's CCD's top-rated show."

"I bet it is. A lot of places in town have it on when they don't have a live DJ in house. The calls that come in can be priceless."

"There never really is a dull moment. They keep me on my toes." She eyed Riley curiously. "Have you ever called in?"

"Sure. She's fun to talk to. And a voice to die for."

Razor leaned her shoulder against Riley's. "A little inside scoop for you: we have an on-location broadcast coming up in August to kick off Carnival. A masquerade dance. We don't air on weekends usually, but part of the cover charge is going to HOW, so our management agreed."

"No kidding? *Nightlight* on location?"

"Right here, in fact." Razor pointed up to the DJ booth.

"Sable will be here?"

Razor grinned playfully. "Absolutely. So get yourself a good costume."

CHAPTER TWENTY-ONE

Murphy lowered her headphones to her shoulders when Razor switched to commercial.

"So you two went to the Pied yesterday? Please tell me you didn't—"

"No, Miss I-Promise-I'll-Tell-Her, I didn't give away your secret."

"Thank God. I'm going to tell all tomorrow when I take her to lunch." Razor nodded absently, preoccupied with her controls in the booth, but Murphy wondered if Razor believed her. *Hell. Do I?* She turned back to her mike and lowered it into position. "You helped her change a flat?" She chuckled. "Like she needed help."

"I didn't mind. Gave me a chance to check her out. Pretty nice in tank, shorts, and work boots. She's got the best arms and shoulders. She's built like a brick—"

"Will you cut it out?"

"She trashed her phone, you know. That's why she never returned your 'forgive me' calls. I bet she's got every skill a woman could want, but she's not the tech type. So I offered to help her with her new cell. She might come by."

Murphy spun around. "To the studio?"

"Chill. She'll call first. Probably tomorrow night. You'll have confessed about Sable by then, won't you?"

Lost in thought, Murphy again turned back to her mike. "Right."

"Fifteen seconds. Oh, hey, don't forget the photo shoot we've gotta do with the *Banner*. Have you put your costume together yet, Ms. Vampira?"

"Christ, not now, Raz."

"And three, two, one…"

"Welcome back," Murphy breathed into the mike. "Looks like you're in a talkative mood tonight. We've barely started and the board is lit up. Let's see what's on your mind." She clicked a call button. "Good evening. This is Sable and you're on *Nightlight*."

"Hi, Sable. Thanks for taking my call. Just wanted to say I heard your commercial for the live show during Carnival and think it's great."

"Thank you. We're very excited to join the Pied for this fundraiser. It should be a really fun night."

"We're looking forward to meeting you. We'll be able to, won't we?"

"Oh, I'll be there." She glared at Razor. "We're hoping listeners will come by and say hello—and make the evening a financial success for HOW."

"You bet. See you there."

Murphy shuddered. Visions of herself dressed as she'd never dressed before, cowering in the shadows of the DJ booth, threatened to close her throat. She hit the next button.

"Welcome to *Nightlight*. This is Sable. What's on your mind tonight?"

"Hi, Sable. A bunch of us here at Recovering Hearts heard the commercial, too, the racy version on your show. We're dying to know if you'll be wielding any special toys."

Murphy laughed. "I've been told that details are still being worked out about special raffle items, so…who knows?"

"Aw, come on. Give us the dirt. What's up your sleeve for that night?" Several women laughed in the background. "Or will you even be wearing sleeves?"

"You'll just have to swing by and find out, won't you?"

"Oh, we will. Thanks, Sable. Be seeing you."

"Looking forward to it. Thanks for the call." She shook her head at her plight and pressed the next line. "Good evening. This is Sable and you're on *Nightlight*."

"Hey, Sable! Finally, you're coming out!"

She grinned at the delight in the gruff voice. "Hi, Digger. Yes, they're dragging me out of my cave. Hope you're planning to stop by."

"Sure am. Wouldn't miss it."

"Well, thank you, but first and foremost, we want a great turnout for charity. Dress up in your finest, Digger."

"Don't you worry. I like all things leather."

"Why am I not surprised?"

"Bet you do, too."

"I prefer it over vinyl, actually." *God, where did that come from?*

"Yeah! I agree with the callers from Recovering Hearts. Hope you'll be demonstrating some of the *finer* arts."

"Now, Digger. This will be a public event, remember."

"Yeah, yeah. You just put me at the top of your list for *assistants,* when the time comes."

"My 'list,' huh? You're right up there, Dig. Not to worry."

"Excellent. Thanks, Sable."

Murphy stole a sip of coffee before clicking the next button. Another look at Razor caught her beaming like a fiend.

"Good evening and welcome to *Nightlight*. This is Sable and you're on the air."

"Good evening, Sable." That very special alto warmed her ear, and Murphy sat up straighter. *Funny how it only takes a few words now. I've missed your voice.*

"Well, hello, Arby. Thanks for calling."

"This event sounds pretty wild. Do you have a bodyguard lined up?"

Murphy laughed. *Volunteer, please.* "I seriously doubt there'll be a need for security. I think *Nightlighters* will display the proper decorum, don't you?"

"With the sultry Sable sharing the room? I'm not so sure. The temptation will be…well, just short of criminal, having you there in person, finally."

"Criminal. Wow." Murphy smiled at the memory of Riley using the word. "Well, I'm flattered, but hardly think we'll have any issues. Besides, my engineer once taught self-defense, so we'll be just fine. Thank you for your concern, though. I hope you'll stop by and say hello." *Right. That's just what I'll need.*

"I work an odd schedule, but I'm going to try. I'd love to put a face to your voice."

"That's sweet of you, Arby. I'm glad you called."

"Pleasure's mine, Sable. You have a good night."

Murphy watched the button on her call board go dark and sighed. *Are you home now? You don't rely on memories for company, do you? No. You call me. Jesus, if you only knew.*

"Phew. All this flattery has me in need of a breather," she managed.

"Let's take a quick one and give our sponsors some airtime. We'll be right back. Stay close."

Razor spoke from the ceiling speaker. "You're determined to meet her, aren't you?"

Murphy flexed her shoulders against the back of her chair. *I need the most complete costume money can buy.* "Eh...well, I'm curious. After all this time, aren't you?"

"Not if it means you'll fall back under her spell. You need to focus on reeling Riley in, Murph, not on Radio Romeo."

"Stop worrying. She probably won't even show up."

"I just lost it. I mean, I actually burst out laughing as I drove. Jesus, Murphy. I've never heard anything so suggestive on the radio." Riley leaned back as a waiter delivered their elaborate sandwiches on Pepe's second-story beachfront deck. "You must have heard it. The night-time version, that is."

Murphy nodded obligingly, still unable to broach the combustible subject of Sable. Her palms were damp and she clung to her poise. She'd much rather ponder the telling fit of Riley's yellow Polo shirt.

"Actually, I have."

"She's such a tease, Sable is. Fantasy material, if you know what I mean. Makes you wonder. I wouldn't be surprised, if...well, you know."

"What wouldn't surprise you?"

"If she's really into it, sex play."

Murphy nearly choked on her ice tea. "You think?"

Riley shrugged and her face began to color. "Well, she's just so provocative. She's so good, it can't be an act entirely. The commercial is pure foreplay, I swear." Riley took a bite of her sandwich and looked to Murphy for comment.

"It certainly is stirring up interest, which must please them, considering the event is still more than a month away. I've heard it's already the talk of the town."

"More than talk, too, in some cases."

"Oh?"

"This bar owner I know says, one of these nights, she's going to take the radio into the bathroom with her."

"Oh, God."

Riley laughed. "She even dared me to do it." Riley blushed fully and Murphy grinned. Shy looked so deliciously sweet on her. "I told her to get a grip, but..." She leaned forward slightly and whispered, "I have to admit, for Sable? Well...when I'm exhausted in bed..."

Murphy forced a grin as she swallowed the lump in her throat. The last thing she needed was the image of Riley naked, vulnerable, willing, and horny.

For her.

"It's quite the entertaining show, isn't it?" Murphy said.

The fear of humiliating Riley rose to a new high, and Murphy practically shook with anxiety. Leveling with her now, with Riley's shared intimacies still ringing in the air, would embarrass them both. Riley, most of all, and no doubt piss her off. As it was, Murphy had spent the first ten minutes of this lunch apologizing for Friday.

The longer you wait...

"I met Sable's engineer Sunday night."

"I—you did?" Her temples throbbed as a headache rose. *Now, there's no way out. Coward. Such an ass.*

"Really nice woman, Razor Delaney. Quite a character, but genuine, really friendly. And right out of the blue, too." Murphy could practically see Razor's ulterior motive. "She helped me change the Jeep's flat tire and even said I could stop by the station and she'd try to help with my new phone."

"Are you going to?" The pounding in her head increased.

Riley nodded. "Tomorrow. I really need the help. I'm..." She shrugged. "Well, I'm not too swift with tech gadgets." She winked and Murphy almost sighed. "Maybe I'll even get an introduction to Sable out of it."

"Ah," Murphy said, wine glass poised at her lips, "and here I was, thinking you were going to stalk her at that live broadcast."

Riley raised her own glass. "Originally, I'd hoped you and I might go to that together, but I might not be able to make it. I'll be out of town most of that weekend, but if I get back early enough, I'm going to try. How about you? Will you go check her out?"

"I...I already have plans for that Saturday night, too, so I'm afraid not." She wiped her hands and rummaged through her purse for Tylenol. Her mind snarled. Riley might not make the party after all, and Murphy noted the twinge of disappointment, not relief, that nudged her.

Did she *really* want Riley to meet Sable, the vampire? *Right. On top of everything, I have a death wish.*

"Damn," Riley said. "I'll have to find somebody to tell me what she looks like."

Murphy showed her the pills in her hand. "Please excuse this. A rising headache. No reflection on you, trust me, just work stress."

Riley's gaze was sympathetic, her lips moist, her hair disheveled in the breeze off the ocean, and Murphy yearned to be facing her in a lounge chair with the sound of waves breaking on shore providing familiar comfort. Just as quickly, however, the image turned, and she saw herself as the busty, hungry vampire, mouth poised at that hardened neck.

She swallowed the Tylenol with a sip of water. "She'll be…well, I'd suspect Sable would be in costume, too. Don't you think?"

"Oh." Riley looked crestfallen. "That's right. Damn it."

"I bet people will be talking the next day," she added. The thought made her stomach clench. Early next week, she would be dressed for the event, having photographs taken for the cable TV commercial and the newspaper ad due to appear at the end of the month. *Oh, Sable will be the talk of the town, all right.*

"So," Riley began, sitting back, "you already have big plans for that night? Hot date?"

"Hm? Oh, no. Well…yes." *Jesus.* "I mean, not hot, just…just old friends. Something scheduled a while ago."

"Ah. You must look forward to getting out, seeing as how you mostly work from home."

"I do. I enjoy going off-Cape. You must, too. What's taking you out of town that night?" She sipped her wine again. Her subconscious didn't want to hear Riley had a hot date of her own. But she tried to concentrate on the issue at hand: diverting the conversation from Sable and avoiding more lies.

"I'm seeing friends, too, in Fall River. They're having a get-together like we used to have—back when we were all wild and crazy."

"Good luck with that." Murphy laughed. "Sounds like fun, though."

"God help us. We're too old for that today, so we'll probably all be asleep by midnight. It's supposed to start Friday and wind up Monday morning."

"Ah, yes. The three-day weekend that turns into a mini-vacation."

"I'm back Saturday night, though, giving myself a Friday-Saturday escape from work."

"How do you ever manage to really get away?"

"I have a couple of people I call to fill in when there's an emergency, but I really love my job, the flexibility, the people in town, and try never to let them down."

"I don't imagine you ever do."

Riley gathered herself closer to the table and reached for Murphy's hand, her touch light and warm as she entwined their fingers. The urge to tug Riley to her across the table rose automatically, and Murphy tightened their grip. *I truly don't want to hurt you.*

"Murphy. Our evening at your place was wonderful. I think about it a lot."

"I do, too. And I apologize again for bringing up my past. Something just...I don't know what came over me, but it wasn't appropriate."

"Do you really think it bothered me? Actually, I was flattered you shared something so personal. Thank you." She squeezed Murphy's hand. "That's only a small part of a great evening—and not the part that lingers in my mind."

Murphy looked down at their inter-locked fingers and recalled Riley's broad hand at the back of her head, the strong fingers so gentle in her hair. Her face heated, but she looked up anyway, wanting Riley to know their night had moved her as well. "It's not the most memorable part, I agree."

"I was wondering...if you're free on the night of the Fourth, would you want to do the fireworks in town? I know a great spot on the beach and..." Her voice faded as she studied Murphy's expression. "No?"

"I can't, Riley. I'm sorry. Thank you, though. That's Friday and...I have to work." Murphy took an internal breath. *This hole of mine just keeps getting deeper.*

"On the holiday?"

"Well...I...It's my client's daughter. *She* has to work, so I've been called in."

"Where does she live? Could you use a little company?"

Murphy's nerves twitched. "Oh. Well, that would be nice, but... I'm sorry. Can't. Privacy rules and all that." *I fucking hate this.*

"Damn. Well, I'm booked solid on Saturday, but...Sunday? If you don't have plans, would you like to get away for the day?"

As much as Murphy doubted she could escape her nagging

conscience, getting away with Riley sounded refreshing and fun. If she couldn't be honest with Riley, she could at least be fair, and Sable's guilt-filled interruptions weren't fair at all. *Neither are comparisons to Bryce.* She had no idea if she'd be able to avoid either, but Riley deserved her best effort.

"Sunday would be perfect. What did you have in mind?"

"I have absolutely no idea. Something totally spontaneous."

Murphy loved the playful message in Riley's smile, and the luscious memory of kissing it. Riley's adventurous spirit and suggestive intent were contagious. "I'm game. Let's do it."

CHAPTER TWENTY-TWO

Running that spot kills me." Murphy tossed down her headphones. "She's all I can think of whenever we play it."

"No comment."

Murphy flung her head back and swore at the ceiling. "How can I tell her the truth when she's said so much about how Sable affects her?"

"You mean how Riley gets off in bed listening to her?"

"Aghhh!" Murphy put her hands over her ears. "She didn't say that, exactly."

"Oh, then you mean how she thinks Sable's an erotic goddess?"

"Please stop."

"You asked for it, keeping this damn secret."

"It's become a nightmare."

Razor appeared at her side. "Well, at least she said she'll probably miss the event and won't be drooling in front of you."

"Yeah. Highly unlikely. I don't know what I'd do. God. I really like her, Razor."

"I'm happy for you, Murph. You know that, but shit. You're overdue in tell—"

"I know. I know." Murphy looked up at her, horror-stricken. "If she *does* show up and recognizes me…"

Razor shook her head. "Look, I'm sure she won't recognize you, not in the outfit you'll be wearing. You *did* decide on black leather, didn't you?"

"Sort of. I'm still looking." She sighed hard. "The white vinyl made me feel like a reject from the sixties."

"Good. No cold-blooded vampire would survive in the sunshine of white vinyl anyway." She chuckled at herself as she returned to her booth. "Oh, and don't screw around leaving here tonight. She called and said she'll be coming by."

"What?"

"Ten seconds."

"She did?"

"Six seconds."

"Razor!" She snapped the headset onto her head and spun around to face the mike.

"She's working some big job, so it'll be late. And—you're on."

Murphy infused a heavy dose of seductive charm into her voice and spoke words out of habit. Her mind was nowhere near the subject of "dream vacations," the *Nightlight* topic of the evening. By the time she put the caller on the air, she'd decided to fade out tonight's show with music, just to speed up her exit. Of course, Riley could ring the outside buzzer at any time and suddenly appear in Razor's booth, and then…game over.

Murphy glanced at the clock. One hour to go. She decided to fade out the show with *two* songs. *Long ones.* And she turned her attention to the ongoing conversation and the music library at her disposal.

❖

Riley rang the front door buzzer of WCCD's studio at precisely eight minutes to two. She ran a hand through her hair and laughed lightly at herself, a bit unnerved by the prospect of meeting Sable. She checked her watch and pressed the buzzer again. A few lights were on upstairs, and she knew Sable was still on the air. That come-hither voice was still speaking when she'd jumped out of the Jeep just now.

Riley stepped back to look up at the building, an historic old schoolhouse. She wondered if she should call Razor, if they hadn't heard the buzzer. She rang it once more. A full minute later, she checked her watch, then decided to make the call.

Someone pounded down the stairs inside and pulled the door open.

"Hey, Riley." Razor looked rather exasperated, maybe even flustered, and Riley wondered if anyone could ever really tell when she was. "Sorry. Were you waiting long? I didn't hear the buzzer until just now."

As she stepped inside, Riley thought she heard another door shut somewhere in the building just when Razor shut hers. The thought of Sable upstairs had her feeling like a silly, idol-worshipping teenager.

"No problem. I appreciate you taking the time. It's late and I'm sure you'd rather be headed home."

Razor led them upstairs. "I don't know the meaning of the word 'late.' My Tina does, though, but not to worry. To us it means after three, so you're good."

"Jesus, your hours are as crazy as mine." She sat beside Razor at her computer and handed her the new cell phone. "I hope you can figure this damn thing out."

"We're going to try." She started in on the phone, but reached to an adjacent computer, which carried the current WCCD broadcast, and lowered the volume. "Old-time radio shows are priceless, but most people can't take more than a couple hours. Teddy in there," she tilted her head toward the doorway, "he likes to run them all night so they let him. Fills the air till the wake-up DJ comes on at six."

Riley looked across the hall to the studio and wondered if Sable would appear soon. *She wouldn't take off without a good night to her friend.* She wandered around the room, reading posters and various awards while Razor worked magic on her phone.

"Good show tonight," she offered, "not that I could listen to all of it, but you had a few hot calls."

Razor chortled but didn't look up. "Input your password for me so I can start transferring your stuff." Riley typed in the information under Razor's watchful eye. "Did you hear the woman give us a hard time about the Carnival commercial?"

"No. An irate caller?"

"Yep. Really chewed us a new one for putting 'trash' on the air. Said she was going to report us to the FCC."

"Wish I could've heard Sable handle that one."

Razor laughed. "She invited the caller to the event. The woman hung up."

"Love it. Good for Sable."

"Hell, with our luck, the woman will show up and picket the damn place. You think you'll make it? Got a costume?" She glanced up, and her crooked grin struck Riley as particularly cunning. It suited her and Riley chuckled.

"No. I expect I won't be back in town until, well, late."

"After three." Razor grinned.

"Right. If the old gang lets me go at all."

Razor lowered her head and returned to work. "Too bad because it's shaping up to be a fun time."

"I'm disappointed that I'll miss meeting Sable. Actually, I was holding out hope of meeting her tonight."

Razor shook her head. "Man, you just missed her. She...she wasn't feeling so hot, so she took off a little early."

Riley chuckled. "Even when she's off her game she sounds hot. Does she ever find fans waiting outside at night?"

"Not any more. A year ago, we started having the cops come by when we signed off and left the building. Women used to gather on the sidewalk out front once in a while, but then this goon started showing up. No one loiters now, thank God."

"Good. Small town, but still that stuff can get nasty."

Razor sat back as she swiped a finger across the phone's screen, apparently testing her work. "Deep down, Sable's always been a pretty private person. She's got a heart of gold, too, and this job suits her perfectly."

"The anonymity, you mean?"

"Yeah. And nowadays, with *Nightlight* such a success, she works hard to maintain that. It's a requirement, actually, although that's not public knowledge. And she's only doing this fundraiser thing because she can be in costume."

"Ah. I get it. I can appreciate that." Riley picked up a small, framed photo on Razor's desk. "Oh, hey! You know Murphy Callahan?"

Razor looked up sharply.

"Eh...Ah, yeah. You—you know her, huh?" Riley only nodded, captivated by the image. "Well...that's...um. Her partner Bryce and my Tina were friends years ago. That's a pretty old picture."

Riley set it back in place. "Small world." The two laughing, well dressed couples in the night time photograph looked relaxed and very happy, posing beside a limo in some city. Riley couldn't take her eyes off Murphy's, the sparkle of contentment evident as she stood with an arm linked through her late partner's. Bryce was slim, dark, and tall, and seemed quite proud to have such a beautiful lady on her arm. *The expressions say so much. Is she your type, Murphy? Well, at least you like this blonde.*

"She's still gorgeous."

Razor looked up at her for an extra beat before speaking.

"Murphy?" She chortled. "You can say that again. And she'd be the last one to admit it."

Riley agreed and remembered the bashful reaction to her compliment on Murphy's doorstep. *Drifting. Snap out of it.* "Man, your Tina sure is a cutie."

"She is, isn't she?" Razor beamed. "Hasn't changed a bit. That shot's maybe…oh, six years old."

"What did Bryce do for a living?" *Make it obvious you're fixated on her best friend, stupid.*

"When we all met, she was a public defender in Manhattan, but she'd gone into practice for non-profits when that picture was taken."

Riley dared to wonder how she measured up to Bryce. Riley had needed six years for a four-year business degree while building houses on Cape Cod and never sought more education or work expansion because she loved what she did and was exceptional at it. She tamped down a wave of inadequacy and chided herself for even entertaining such thoughts.

"They look so perfect together."

Razor nodded. "It took Murphy quite a while to recover after Bryce died."

"I don't know Murphy that well, but I'm not surprised. She's a very sensitive woman, very sincere."

"That she is."

"We met accidentally during the winter but have started seeing more of each other lately."

"Is that right? So…you two are…dating?"

"We are. It's all still new, but I think she's as eager for us to get to know each other as I am." She grinned. "She seems pretty reserved, but I just know there's so much more to her than she lets on, and that makes it exciting. I do think she's very special."

"She is," Razor said, rising from her chair. "I'm sure you'll see." She handed the phone to Riley with a triumphant grin.

CHAPTER TWENTY-THREE

Murphy turned in the seat of the open-top Jeep and faced Riley as she drove. She'd greeted Riley at the door with a hug and a lingering kiss just moments earlier, a kiss like the one after their luncheon, when she'd hummed some random tune all the way home. Now, the sensation of them pressed together, albeit fleeting, lingered just as pleasantly. The very sight of Riley, smiling that devilish way behind black sunglasses, looking rough-and-ready as always in a white button-down and jeans, seemed to perform miracles. It successfully pushed her pervasive conscience aside and allowed her desires to brew freely.

Riley sent her a glance. "So did you have to work late on Friday night? I bet it killed you to hear the fireworks in the bay." The sincere inquiry repositioned Murphy's anxiety back into her chest like a lead weight. She absolutely hated this deception.

"Ah...yes, it did."

Riley glanced at her again, as if expecting more, but Murphy just didn't have the heart to expand the lie.

"How about you?" she countered. "Did you end up working, too?"

"Eh, no. I hit the beach for the fireworks then went home. I tried to read a while, but I guess I was more worn out than I realized and fell asleep."

Murphy wondered if Riley had tuned in to *Nightlight* and listened to the many Fourth of July stories callers offered. Arby hadn't called in, and Murphy remembered daydreaming about what Riley was doing and with whom. She wished they'd spent the holiday on her deck.

"Sometimes we have no choice but to recharge. I'm sure you needed it."

"Probably true, but, God, some of the women I know can still party till all hours. And things can get a little wild for my taste, if you know what I mean."

"A bit on the hot 'n heavy side?"

"Yeah, a lot. I'm not into that much public display."

"Neither am I. A little is nice, exciting. Maybe I'm just old-fashioned, but I think the heavy action should be kept private where it belongs."

Riley nodded as she drove. Knowing Riley respected intimacy between partners had Murphy willing to put her trust—herself—in Riley's hands anywhere. *And* still *I draw the line at a full confession.*

"I like old-fashioned." Riley sent her a grin. "Some of these women, though…they can go overboard. The last time my old friends got together, they started joking around with vibrators, and then the clothes started coming off in the pool. I…" She shrugged. "I had to call it a night."

Murphy's mind spun. *If we had a pool to ourselves, could I be swayed into outrageous acts with Riley?* "Not your fantasy date, I take it."

"Quit it, Callahan. I think I'm blushing."

"I see that and it's adorable. I take it you like the private, seductive type of woman." *How often has that vixen Sable satisfied you?*

"Well…"

"Uh-huh. And the sex play?"

"Um, maybe—"

"Hm. Now Riley Burke gets real."

"Oh. No. Now, that's not really…Look, I mean, I-I don't—"

"Oh, you're even stuttering now. You're busted." She laughed at Riley's fluster and poked her arm. "Some Rough Rider you turned out to be."

Riley stopped at a red light and looked at her. Murphy silently cursed their sunglasses.

"This Rough Rider doesn't do rough."

Murphy lowered her glasses slightly and reached for Riley's. She slid them down the bridge of her nose just enough to meet her eyes. "Good. I don't either." She pushed Riley's glasses back up.

An impatient driver behind the Jeep beeped, and Riley quickly returned her attention to the road.

"Boy, I like the seductive Murphy Callahan."

"Do you? Well, since we're being so candid, I like the blushing Rough Rider."

Riley turned into the gates behind Dennis-Yarmouth High School and joined the line of traffic waiting to enter and park. Murphy looked around curiously.

"What's going on here today?"

"The last day of their July Fourth Fair," Riley said, paying the girl at the booth and driving on to a parking space. "Live bands all day today, and I thought, since we're both music fans, we'd check it out, see what else we have in common—since we're being so candid and all."

"Spontaneity is a wonderful thing." She leaned across the console, kissed Riley's cheek, and sat back. She didn't have a chance to contemplate what she'd done before Riley followed her back across the console and lightly kissed her lips.

"Jesus, Murphy. Is it ever. Candor is a wonderful thing, too."

Murphy's heart lifted with their impulsive behavior. The spontaneity was invigorating and promising. And candor counted for a lot. Murphy believed it always had, that it was her nature to be frank, honest, and Riley made being herself so easy. *So, when did that all change?*

❖

Murphy patiently held the lamp by its jade bowl base, but Riley finally had to ask for help. As much as her ego insisted she heft the Craftsman coffee table into the Jeep by herself, the task simply was too awkward for one person. Riley paused, took a breath, and sent her a sheepish look.

"Oh, sure," Murphy said, and rolled her eyes. "*Now* you realize you need a hand." She set the lamp on the ground and lifted the other end of the table. "Just when I was beginning to think you weren't the stubborn butch I met last winter." Riley grinned as they finagled the table into the Jeep. She'd happily take any teasing Murphy dished out. "You *do* realize that the butch is a given," Murphy continued, hand on her hip, "and you *are* stubborn."

Riley felt her pulse rate kick up a notch. She couldn't change the stubborn or the butch, and she dared to hope Murphy really didn't want her to. In fact, Murphy stood there in her sassy stance, a playful smirk across that delectable mouth, and practically challenged Riley to throw all restraint aside.

Behave. Don't screw this up. She's like no one else.

"Stubborn runs in the family."

"And the butch is all you."

Somehow, Murphy always managed to press those arousal buttons without even trying. Riley fought the urge to take Murphy into her arms. *God, this is hard.*

"And the lady is all you."

Just being herself—even more than the baby blue tank top and white shorts, Murphy reached in deep and tripped all Riley's senses. Murphy's voice had a touch of its own and never failed to lull Riley into a warm, hazy world where their emotions and inner thoughts surfaced and merged, pulsed on a single current. She wanted to go there, stay there. That realization nearly took her breath away, the draw was undeniable. And growing. She wanted to hear Murphy's voice more often, softly at her ear, whispered against her lips…

Murphy shook her head slightly. "You're too sweet for my own good, Riley Burke. I almost forgot this." She picked up the lamp and tucked it into a snug space between the table's legs.

Riley struggled to stay efficient and sharp. Murphy's attention made her heart pound, her breathing erratic, and that dammed arousal in her depths intensify by the second. She pulled a beach towel from the emergency duffel bag in the back and packed it around the lamp for cushioning.

"Are you ever *un*prepared in this vehicle?"

"Rarely. I did take out all my work gear though." They settled into the front seats, and Riley drove away from the antique store before they went back inside and continued their spontaneous spending. "You noticed I tidied up, I hope."

"Yes, Ms. Burke. I noticed."

"Wanted to make a decent impression."

"You did and I'm flattered."

"Good. Are you hungry, too? Shall we find someplace for dinner?"

"Hm." Murphy relaxed in her seat and slapped a palm over her stomach. Riley was tempted to feel it, too. "Since my evil date tortured me with that hot fudge sundae an hour ago, I'm not really."

"Maybe later, then," Riley said, slowing to take in the quaint shops and placid harbor in the heart of Wellfleet. "When's the last time you went for a boat ride?" She parked at the end of the dock, facing the sloping late afternoon sun.

"Oh, that's a hard one." They admired the array of boats in nearby slips and followed the progress of an incoming catamaran. "I was… probably…well, in my early thirties, I think."

"Last year?"

"Right." Murphy laughed. "I think I was thirty-one. Nine years ago."

"A couple of years ago for me." Riley turned to face her. "I'm thirty-nine."

"I confess, I *was* curious."

"What else are you curious about?"

"Hm. Let's see." Murphy took Riley's hand from the steering wheel and clasped it on her own thigh. Pleasantly surprised, Riley treated herself to the look of her, head back against the headrest, staring out at the harbor, utterly relaxed and comfortable. Riley's heart thrummed as the impulse rose to stroke her cheek, to make a physical connection of her own. "Well," Murphy began, "I'm curious about all these lucky people who own these beautiful boats, where they go…"

"How they can afford them."

"Yes," Murphy said with a chuckle. "I'm curious about whether they're really happy, if they're satisfied to have this in their lives. I don't really know if I would be. It's dreamy fun, for sure, but…"

The hint of uncertainty, of longing bothered Riley almost to the point of taking remedial action. She yearned to "fix" whatever it was that stole the confidence from Murphy's voice, that infectious smile from her face, and she abruptly wondered if sitting here in the oncoming sunset was a bad idea. *Those pastel skies.*

She entwined their fingers and squeezed. "You have a beautiful home on the ocean, the kind most people dream of."

"I am lucky, I know. Satisfied, I suppose." She looked over at Riley. "What about you and your place? It's a loft, you said. Are you happy?"

Riley shrugged. "I have a coffee table now."

Murphy blurted a laugh that warmed Riley to her toes. *Damn, I love that sound.*

Murphy broke their handhold to lightly slap Riley's arm. "And I have a new lamp I don't need. Be serious."

Riley reclaimed her hand but drew it to her own leg this time.

"Well, I love my job, I'm obviously independently wealthy, and I live in a hideously expensive loft. So, am I satisfied with that? I guess there's not much reason to be otherwise. Happy is…It's all relative, isn't it?" She knew her poor job of avoiding the topic revealed a lot more than she'd intended, but once again, the solitary parallel in their lives seemed to merge fluidly and she was tempted to empty her soul. *How does she do this to me?*

Murphy nodded. "There hasn't been anyone special in my life for a long time, and it's taken a while, but I've become okay with that."

Riley wondered about the truth of that statement.

Murphy rubbed her thumb over the back of Riley's hand and turned her gaze toward the lowering sun. "Happy is a different concept, isn't it?"

Determined not to let this spectacular, lighthearted day end with a thud, Riley pushed her thoughts passed the heavy subject.

"I've got an idea." She squeezed Murphy's hand and let go, sending her a grin as she started the Jeep. "I'll give you a happy concept. You with me?"

That optimistic look returned to Murphy's face, expectant and appreciative, and exactly what Riley hoped to see. She tried not to squirm like an excited kid as she drove.

Murphy tugged on her shirtsleeve. "What have you got up here, Burke? Where are we going now?"

"You'll see."

CHAPTER TWENTY-FOUR

Murphy bounced forward in her seat and grabbed Riley's arm with such excitement, she nearly misdirected the Jeep. "I don't believe you! The drive-in?"

Riley grinned all the way through the entrance and up to the ticket booth. "Just cute animated movies this weekend, but who cares? It's the experience, right? Bet it's been ages for you, just like me."

"I can't believe it. I pass this so often for work and haven't seen a movie here in…Oh, uh, not since…I was a kid visiting my aunt." Again, she leaned across the console and pecked Riley's cheek. "You are a true joy, Riley Burke."

Riley paid and drove on, still grinning. Delight consumed Murphy. Sharing this nostalgic adventure with someone who obviously appreciated it as much as she did just overwhelmed her. In truth, she'd been to the Wellfleet Drive-in only three years ago, with Bryce, and they'd come several times that final summer. But she wasn't about to cast a pall over Riley's pleasure, the joy she was taking from this treat. Riley's eagerness to please was written all over her, as much a part of her as that little swagger in her walk, the clench of that strong jaw when she pondered a thought, and the brilliant light in her eyes. Murphy couldn't get enough. *This definitely will feel different.*

Riley sighed and shook her head at the scene, acres of moderately maintained asphalt rolling in graceful waves toward the mammoth white screen in the distance. Cresting each paved wave, cement posts offered two speakers each to moviegoers who stationed their vehicles alongside. In the middle of the site, the legendary "snack bar," projection house, and playground composed an island that already was attracting early arrivals.

"I only come by here once in a while. I wouldn't be able to pass this too often without making it a habit," Riley said, and Murphy's heart skipped. A bolt of guilt crackled down her spine.

Riley turned the Jeep around, looked over her shoulder at the movie screen, and backed up to the top of the rise. "You work in your house, then hit the road at night for work, and I bet you don't do enough fun things." She tossed her sunglasses onto the dash, set the brake, and shut off the vehicle. "I know *I'd* rather you not turn into some mystery lady no one ever sees." She lifted Murphy's chin with a finger, sending a tingle down Murphy's throat to her shoulders. Her ears heated. Close now, Riley's smile beckoned. "I can't let that happen, Ms. Callahan."

She winked before jumping out and walking around the Jeep. Murphy took another breath. *God, what the truth says about me.* She scrolled through her memory of their conversations, tallying the amount of crow she'd have to eat. *Lies. That's what they are. Who am I kidding? And I'll be left with the integrity of a dirt bag, not to mention the hurt and embarrassment I'll deliver.*

"Check this out." Riley stood at her door with a speaker in hand. She turned the volume knob and old-time rock 'n' roll from the fifties blasted into the warm evening air. "Isn't this just the coolest?" She hung the blaring speaker back on the post and hustled to others still unclaimed nearby. She turned them all on full. "Rock Around the Clock" by Bill Haley and the Comets flooded the vicinity.

Murphy couldn't help but grin at her, and she realized how long she'd gone without this happiness in her life, how much she missed it—and how easily Riley created it for her.

Dig to China yet? Lie or hurt her. Choose.

"Hey, good lookin'!" Riley trotted back to her door and Murphy eyed her warily as she was tugged from the Jeep. That mischievous grin definitely said she was up to no good. "Dance with me, baby!" Riley swung their joined hands over Murphy's head, spinning her.

"Riley!"

Riley's strong hand slid across her back, and the sensation weakened Murphy's knees. Swept up in the crook of Riley's arm, Murphy squealed with surprise but held on as Riley danced them around the post, and then the Jeep, till the song ended. They separated and fell against the door, laughing.

"Dance a lady right off her feet, why don't you?"

"I couldn't resist."

"Well, it was fun. You're fun." She moved a strand of hair back off Riley's forehead. "I've got to ask. Why are we parked facing away from the screen?"

"Ah!" Riley held up a finger. "We'll be more comfortable watching this way," she said, darting away to open the tailgate. She put the lamp on the driver's seat, then hauled the coffee table out with a huff and what looked to Murphy to be pure adrenaline, and set it on the ground behind the Jeep.

Murphy grinned at Riley's energy. Watching her was a pleasure. Hell, just looking at her was an exercise in sexual restraint. These weren't cargoes Riley had on. These rugged whitewashed jeans fit her like a glove, and it took no effort whatsoever for Murphy to imagine her hands on those muscular thighs, on that tight ass. Or kneading into that lean torso…or both hands on those shoulders, taking off that classy white shirt… She shook her head at herself. *Earth to Murphy?*

Riley produced two long thin drawstring bags from her duffel and handed one to Murphy. "Chair for the lady?" She pulled a collapsible chair from the bag and helped Murphy with hers. She set them at the table and shut the tailgate. "Our patio lounge."

Murphy laughed. "You are something."

"And for the second movie, when it gets chilly, we can lounge in the back of the Jeep. Not having a rear seat comes in handy."

Murphy just crossed her arms and shook her head, unable to stop smiling.

"Come on." Riley took her hand again. "Let's get some God-awful munchies and settle in."

❖

"How much junk have we eaten today?" Murphy dipped a French fry into a pool of processed cheese and dragged it across Riley's lower lip. "So bad. You love this stuff, don't you?"

"I love junk food." Riley accepted the French fry and wanted to take Murphy's delicate fingertips with it. Sitting shoulder-to-shoulder inside in the dark was much better than having a coffee table between them out in the open. And if this playing with food didn't stop soon, she was bound to bring them a lot closer.

She raised the cheeseburger in her hand. "Another luscious taste of heat lamp burger?"

Murphy leaned toward it and took a bite. She found her napkin when she sat back and wiped her mouth. "You know? That's not so bad. And why am I so hungry?"

"Maybe because all we had today was a sausage and beer at the fair."

"And doughy crab cakes. And don't forget the cotton candy you insisted on."

"And then later, ice cream."

"And popcorn when we got here."

Riley glanced thoughtfully at the roof she'd drawn up over them. "Quite reasonable that we'd be hungry." She nodded as they stared out at the movie on the big screen.

"Makes perfect sense."

"It does. Plus, being outside always makes me hungry." Riley looked her over. "Where does it go on this perfect body?"

"Perfect?" Murphy laughed. "Oh, if you only knew." She edged closer and settled against Riley's shoulder. "There's no sign of it on you."

Riley turned her face into Murphy's hair. The moment was perfect, Murphy was perfect, the scent of lavender in her hair intoxicating, their connection at once calming and exciting. Even the salty evening air, wafting into the window-less Jeep couldn't chill the shared warmth where their bodies met, shoulder to hip to thigh to calf. She couldn't predict how this glorious day, this perfect evening would end, but it didn't matter, really. So far, their time together had been the most exhilarating she could remember.

She searched hard for words that wouldn't sound as wanton as her libido was acting. "So you've checked me out?" Aiming for a casual air to disguise her excitement, Riley picked a fry out of the box in Murphy's hand, stuck one end in her own mouth, and turned to her, leaning very close.

Murphy set the box of fries aside and touched her forehead to Riley's. "I have." She bit off the opposite end of the fry, their noses bumping. When their lips met, everything in Riley's world but Murphy disappeared.

"I'd confess to doing the same, but it might get me in trouble."

"Since when does the Rough Rider shy away from trouble?"

Since you mentioned it...

Riley extricated her arm from between them, encircled Murphy's shoulders, and drew her in tightly to her side. She tipped her head onto the silky waves and wondered if Murphy could feel her pulse racing. So surreal was this moment, she heard her heart whisper aloud.

"You're very special, Murphy Callahan, gorgeous, smart, thoughtful, fun. You have me acting like a kid again, happy just making you happy."

Murphy shifted her hips and turned to her, and Riley's hold slipped lower, settling securely around Murphy's waist. She squeezed and Murphy acknowledged it with a growing smile. Riley drifted beneath Murphy's gaze, as it roamed her cheekbones, eyebrows, nose, and each lip. Murphy trailed a fingertip along her jaw, then down her throat, and rested her palm on the opening of her shirt. The intimate tenderness consumed Riley so fully, it blanked her mind of every word, every chivalrous gesture she'd considered, and left her knowing, without doubt, what was about to happen.

"You're right," Murphy whispered. "That stuff could get a Rough Rider into trouble."

"And what about Murphy Callahan?" Riley brushed her nose across the tip of Murphy's. "Does she shy away from trouble?"

"Is that what this is, Riley? Trouble?"

"No, Murphy." She enclosed her within both arms and spoke against her lips. "This is amazing. Just like you."

Riley kissed the delicate surface of her upper lip, lightly enough to request permission. Murphy met her kiss without hesitation, just as softly, and Riley thanked God for the welcome. She prayed her lips wouldn't tremble as she delivered a kiss that said more. She tilted her head and carefully pressed her mouth to the moist silkiness, and she reeled when those sweet lips parted and claimed hers in return.

Murphy's palm grazed upward, along Riley's neck to the back of her head, and when those elegant fingers searched into her hair, Riley almost fell away from their kiss. The sensation across her scalp shimmered down her spine, and the desire in Murphy's kiss stirred equally vital nerves elsewhere, combining to heighten Riley's arousal almost beyond control.

And she didn't want to control it. She didn't want Murphy controlling her own desire, either. She wanted, needed them each to let go. Now.

Riley drew her onto her lap as they kissed and Murphy's supple form shifted to settle weightless and relaxed upon her, snug in her arms.

Leaning into Riley's chest, Murphy laced her arms around her neck, her pleasure revealed on a tiny, hushed moan into Riley's mouth.

Craving full contact, Riley ran splayed hands across her back, along her sides to the slight curve of her hips, and back again, pressing her closer still, absorbing the feel of Murphy's gently muscled frame, enjoying the softness, the movement brought by each breath, each lift of her arm, and stroke of her hand. She let her fingertips gauge the delicate skin at the back of Murphy's neck, touching reverently behind and along her ear, and slipped her fingers into the rich waves of her hair. *Every part of you is a thrill, Murphy Callahan.*

She captured Murphy's lower lip between hers, slid the tip of her tongue along the inside. Murphy licked it and covered Riley's mouth with her own. She cupped Riley's cheek as they kissed, as her tongue swept across Riley's, tentatively at first, and then with intent. Lost in the palm of Murphy's warm hand, Riley tasted each lip before kissing her deeply.

Murphy groaned, an aroused rumble Riley felt on her tongue, and she drew back and placed a long, smiling kiss on Murphy's jaw.

"What planet am I on?" she whispered, and kissed Murphy's mouth lightly.

Murphy ran a fingertip along Riley's lower lip. "I couldn't care less."

"Wherever it is, there's only this," Riley said against her lips.

"Yes, only this," Murphy answered, and sealed their kiss.

Murphy's acquiescence flooded Riley's senses, sent such a rush of heat through her body, she nearly rolled her onto the floor. Yearning became fire between her legs, in her lungs, on her lips. She felt control slipping away.

"Murphy." She kissed her hungrily. Her only reality became *this woman*, the warm, inviting reality of her everywhere. Riley stroked her sides, reached upward, traveled the plush curve of her breasts, and the resultant encouraging sigh sent Riley's heart rate soaring. Murphy's deep, excited breath inadvertently lifted her breasts into Riley's hands, and Riley reveled in the feel of them through the cotton tank and bra.

Slowly, Murphy lifted her head. "Riley." She kissed her lightly, pressed her mouth to Riley's cheek. "Please...wait."

Riley wasn't sure she could. Blood rushed so hard through her system, she felt like a downhill train trying to brake and she feared loss of control. She steadied herself and lowered her hands. "If I've overstep—"

"No," Murphy whispered. "Take me home." Riley's lungs began to constrict as disappointment set in. She leaned back to see if Murphy really meant it, and Murphy grazed a fingertip over Riley's lower lip. "Stay with me tonight?"

Chapter Twenty-five

Excitement and arousal gave a little ground to common sense and inner thought when Murphy led Riley into her bedroom, and she wasn't thrilled about the intrusion. She worried about whether she was doing the right thing, if it was too early to be doing *this*, if she *really* could trust her motives, if she was actually trying to prove to herself—and Bryce—that she could. And the worry irritated the hell out of her. *Don't you dare have second thoughts now.* She consciously dismissed her hesitation about where they were, the memory of the last time she'd made love in this bed and with whom, and focused on the hand she held and why.

She purposely avoided glancing at Bryce's picture but a plea for understanding ran through her mind nonetheless. *We'll always have something special, you and I, and nothing could ever change that. She's special in her own right, not your substitute, and I want this with her. The invitation just came out.*

Murphy clicked on the nightstand lamp, and Riley's arms slipped around her waist, captured her when she turned, and she enjoyed the feel of it, being enveloped by a strength that rendered her compliant, willing. Unencumbered.

Murphy combed back Riley's windblown hair with her fingers, pleased to see her touch soften Riley's ardent expression.

"I like it when the Rough Rider melts in my hands."

Riley drew Murphy's hips against hers. "I want to melt all over you, Murphy Callahan." She kissed her deeply, and her hands drifted across Murphy's back until they found their way beneath her tank, and explored her skin. Riley paused at the bra clasp, and Murphy's heart hammered. Her mind flitted in several directions, from Riley's hands, to the fresh air scent of her skin, to the last time she'd surrendered so easily.

Slow, warm kisses lingered on her neck. *Dear God, yes.* Murphy tightened her arms around Riley's shoulders and found herself stepping into her fully, sending permission.

Riley released the hooks and Murphy shivered with anticipation when fingertips slipped beneath the garment and touched her breasts. *How long has it been?* She sought sanctuary in Riley's mouth, anchored herself to Riley's solid presence, and heard herself moan when Riley's fingers found her nipples. Murphy wanted their clothes gone. Immediately. She wanted those long fingers, those broad, powerful hands to possess her breasts, bring them to Riley's amazing mouth, and set them free.

Riley slid her palms over Murphy's breasts, scissored the nipples between her fingers, and squeezed gently. Murphy gasped as arousal shot through her.

Riley dropped her hands and lifted tank top and bra off in one motion. She edged away slightly, brushed the backs of her hands upward over Murphy's stomach, and cupped her breasts.

"I want you melting all over me, too," Riley whispered before kissing her. "Jesus, Murphy. You're so beautiful." She bent slightly and set a long kiss within her cleavage.

Murphy ran her fingers through that mussed hair, and her knees almost gave out when Riley placed a reverent kiss on each nipple. Tremors loosened her hips, had her so wet she could hardly stand. Dire need swept up from her sex and demanded attention. *Anything and everything you want.* When Riley straightened, her chiseled features were taut with restraint, and Murphy acted instinctively to answer both their needs.

She ran her palms across Riley's chest, across her shirt, her breasts, and met her eyes as she began unbuttoning the Oxford. "Clothes need to be off." Riley hooked a finger around the button on Murphy's shorts and Murphy struggled to remain on point. "Do not distract me. This shirt, first."

Riley gripped the front of Murphy's waistband with her whole hand. "This distracts you?"

Murphy cocked an eyebrow at her and worked her way down Riley's buttons. "You might say." No woman had ever reached for her so possessively. *Not even Bryce.*

Riley unbuttoned, then unzipped Murphy's shorts. "How about now?"

Murphy exhaled hard. "*So* wicked." She slipped Riley's shirt off her shoulders and let it fall to the floor. A white athletic undershirt hugged Riley's body, and Murphy couldn't resist running her hands up Riley's arms to her shoulders. Slowly, she trailed a fingertip down the center of Riley's chest to her belt buckle.

Riley pressed her mouth to Murphy's forehead. "Who's wicked now?"

And I'm loving every damn second of it. Maybe even a bit beside myself, loving it.

Heat blazed off Riley's skin as Murphy opened her belt and unbuttoned her jeans. She tugged the undershirt free and peeled it off. Gazing at Riley's toned chest, the modest breasts with their dark tips, the defined abs, Murphy just dropped the undershirt where she stood. *Sweet Jesus.*

Riley reached out with both hands and gave Murphy's shorts a little yank. They went to the floor, too, and so did Riley, to a knee. She palmed the cheeks of Murphy's rear and drew her in. Still dazed by Riley's perfection, Murphy practically staggered a half-step forward and felt Riley's lips caress her stomach, her bikini briefs being dragged downward. Absently, Murphy stepped out of them and hoped with everything she had that Riley was taken by what she saw.

More than anything, Murphy wanted to please her. Hell, she thought, I want to put any "babe" she's had to shame, turn her inside out like she's never enjoyed before, give her all of me.

Sable, too? Reality slammed her so hard, she couldn't tell if her insurgent conscience or Riley's sublime attention was making her tremble. *What does that say about me? What will she think of me some day, if...What would Bryce think of all this?*

Riley kissed her stomach, licked her hip, nuzzled into the moist curls between her legs. Fighting back her anxiety, Murphy wanted to take and be taken. Baring her body, that willingness to share came so effortlessly with Riley. Murphy had virtually stopped expecting to have such a deeply fulfilling connection in her life again. And now here it was, kneeling before her, innocently believing Murphy offered all of herself, when, in fact, a key part remained withheld.

She scolded herself; going *this* far without full disclosure said something about her that neither she nor Riley would want to learn. *I know better. Could I have done this to you, Bryce?*

Those heated eyes roamed up her legs, and Murphy looked on helplessly as they smoldered their way into her sex and sizzled across her stomach and breasts. Riley's gaze engulfed her and there was no escape. None that would come to mind, no considerate route to take, and certainly no place to off-load the burden of deceit she bore.

Riley pulled off Murphy's sandals before standing and shedding the rest of her clothes. Her conscience now smothered by escalating desire, Murphy could only watch, hungrily. Riley steered her backward to the bed, and Murphy lay down, riveted to the movement of each defined muscle in Riley's body. Her words barely came out above a whisper.

"You're carved like a work of art."

Riley knelt astride her hips and leaned over her on outstretched arms. Murphy couldn't resist, and reached out and smoothed Riley's thighs with her hands. She slid them up to Riley's hips, her sides, then onto her back, and uttered a hushed, awestruck sigh.

Riley grinned down at her, hair threatening her forehead.

"Make you a deal, Ms. Callahan."

"Oh, this had better be good."

"I'll give you this body, if you give me yours."

Immediately, Murphy pulled Riley down on top of her, didn't allow her conscience a second to intervene, and connected with a deep, searching kiss that roused both of them. She lost herself in it, let it provide the reality she desperately needed. Weighty, hot, and dominant. Murphy's hands wandered over Riley's shoulders, along her torso, kneading, wanting this remarkable body closer still, to have absolutely nothing between them.

"Jesus, Riley. You feel…"

"Shh." Riley lowered a soft smile to her lips, and rocked into her, slid against her in their combined damp heat and ground their sexes together. She withdrew from a kiss, and groaned as she buried her face in Murphy's neck. "Words can't express," she whispered between delicate kisses to her ear and neck.

Murphy lifted her chin when Riley arrived at her throat, and spiraling arousal made it hard to keep still. *No, even if I could find the right words, they wouldn't do this justice.* Riley took her hands in one of hers and pinned them to the mattress beyond her head. The devilish grin was back and Murphy loved the look of it.

Riley slipped off to her side, straddled Murphy's thigh, leaving it wet when she rocked her leg into Murphy's sex. *She's as wet as I am. Thank God, because there's more where that came from.*

Riley kissed her way to Murphy's breast and licked her nipple, tugged it with her teeth until Murphy squirmed. Riley muttered a soft chuckle, and Murphy caught the familiarity in that brief, muted sound. *Arby. I know you now. And you know...*

Riley moved to her other breast, brushed her cheek against the nipple, and claimed it, along with Murphy's full attention. Riley's free hand grazed downward, rubbed several light circles on Murphy's stomach, and Murphy's hips opened with invitation. *Please.*

Riley traced the curve of her hip bone, slid her hand along Murphy's thigh and fanned her fingers around it. Her mouth at Murphy's breast, Riley gently squeezed her thigh, first near her knee, and then higher. Murphy's head dropped back, her eyes closed, and feeling Riley playfully tug her hair, she knew she'd surrendered.

Riley's fingers dipped between Murphy's legs, slid expertly to either side of her clit, and tightened. Murphy hissed at the sensation. Her hips jerked against Riley's hand, and Riley rose over her. Murphy pulled her arms free to draw Riley to her with both hands.

"God, yes. Kiss me."

She ventured into Riley's mouth, licked her tongue, captured it, relished every second she owned it, and nearly lost her mind when Riley began stroking her sex. Locking her arms around Riley's neck, unable to get close enough, Murphy met Riley's firm kiss eagerly and parted her legs farther. She drifted, delirious with sensation, when Riley traced two fingers through her wetness and slid deep inside her.

Riley lowered her head, taunted Murphy's nipple with her teeth, and Murphy drove her hands into Riley's hair and pressed Riley's mouth to her. Riley complied and sucked the puckered flesh as she reached deeper and explored. Murphy's mind spun at the dual stimulation, deciding neither one should ever end. But then Riley shifted to lie between Murphy's legs, and dragged her opened mouth along Murphy's ribs to her hip, sliding down on the bed as Murphy writhed beneath her. Propped up on her elbows, Murphy watched Riley settle between her thighs, watched Riley's wet fingers emerge.

Riley spread Murphy's lips and glazed the engorged tissues with her essence, circling over the head of Murphy's clit with a little extra emphasis. Murphy's head fell back at the stimulation.

"R-Riley...God."

"You're incredible, Murphy," Riley whispered, breath hot on sensitive flesh. "We're good for each other." She plucked at her clit with two fingers. Murphy gasped and Riley repeated the tease.

"God, Riley! You're seriously going to make me scream."

"Serious...is good, too." Her thumb pressed to Murphy's clit,

Riley leaned toward her. Murphy lurched up and they came within inches of a kiss. Riley spoke softly. "I'm very serious about you," she said, her subdued tone so much like Arby's in Murphy's whirling mind. "I'm serious about pleasing you." She released the pressure on Murphy's clit.

Murphy gulped a breath as she reached for Riley's face.

"I'm serious about you, too. Everything about you."

Truly.

Riley inched closer and Murphy met her with a kiss full of honest intention. She loved the way Riley kissed, her lips so sure and unwavering, yet so supple and indulgent. *How strong and confident in her sensitivity she is to reveal so much.* She realized how much she, herself, put into every kiss, that holding back wasn't possible, that she wanted to please without reservation, and dared to wonder how Riley interpreted *her* kisses. *Is it wrong to care more about what they say today than…ever before?*

Her insides tingled as Riley withdrew her fingers again, and kissed her way down to Murphy's pelvis. Riley dipped her head and Murphy's nerves spiked. A lingering kiss on the tip of her clit made her quiver. Riley's tongue lolled through her sex, flitted into her opening, and darted around her clit, and Murphy found herself rocking into Riley's mouth for more.

Riley responded promptly, her fingers gliding inside as she slid her lips the length of Murphy's distended shaft. She sucked so hungrily, Murphy arched hard off the bed, trembling with excitement when Riley persisted and rose with her. Riley pressed into her again, began a deep, thrusting rhythm that heightened her onrushing orgasm.

From all points in her body, current scorched into Murphy's sex. Only seconds remained, she knew, before her senses exploded. Her muscles contracted and Riley stiffened her thrusts, her long, hardened fingers penetrating so deeply. Murphy's breathing shortened as contractions lengthened, until both peaked and held.

"Riley!" Her voice cracked.

She fisted the comforter, her muscles strained against Riley's steel-like arm around her hips. She groaned as Riley sucked hard, unrelenting. Each heavy stroke of Riley's tongue across her clit made her twitch, her nerves spark in rapid succession. She shuddered against Riley's mouth, against the fingers plunging inside her, and a brilliant display of lightning she hadn't seen in years lit up the night sky in her mind.

Riley nestled a long, deliberate kiss into her sex, and Murphy felt the last of her tremors dissolve into the wetness of Riley's face. *Jesus, you're incredible.*

Now studying her expression closely, Riley licked the inside of her thighs, and gently eased her fingers out, a tender motion Murphy appreciated immensely.

Life returned slowly to Murphy's limbs, and she flexed her legs. *God, has an orgasm ever been so good?* She blinked and the room came back into focus. Riley still lay between her legs, slowly massaging her sex.

A finger slipped inside her, and Murphy gripped Riley's hand and kept it there.

"You are magnificent, Riley Burke. I think you could make me come all night, but there are a couple rules you should know."

"Rules?" Riley's rugged face softened irresistibly.

"Yes, rules." She bit back a grin.

"Fuck the rules." Riley wiggled her finger and Murphy moaned. Riley looked down at Murphy's sex and kissed it. "I want more of you, Ms. Callahan. Now."

Murphy drew Riley's hand from between her legs and urged her to lie beside her.

"Rule number one: Murphy gets a minute of recovery time."

Riley laughed as she leaned against Murphy's side. "Understood." She reached across to Murphy's opposite hip, rolled Murphy to face her, and drew Murphy's thigh up over her own. "But I bet you could come right now. Your minute's almost up." She slid her hand between Murphy's thighs and gripped her sex.

"Oh, that feels awfully good, so it may be true, wise guy." She captured one of Riley's nipples between forefinger and thumb. "But rule number two says Murphy gets Riley—now."

CHAPTER TWENTY-SIX

Half her face buried in the pillow, Riley felt the heat of July sunshine on her back—and the luscious presence of an amazing woman. She smiled, eyes still closed, arms beneath the pillow, and absorbed the plush feel of Murphy's cheek on her shoulder, the arm and leg that draped across her, the body that breathed slowly, fully relaxed against her side. *Wow.*

She wanted to let her sleep but ached to hold her, to have Murphy in her arms, playfully affectionate and seriously hungry just like they'd been last night. She grinned at how they'd nearly rolled off the bed, arms and legs tangled in the sheet, and hurriedly reorganized the bedding, eager to reconnect. They'd collapsed soon after that incredible mutual orgasm and Riley remembered falling asleep, thrilled just to watch Murphy drift off.

She sighed at the memory, at how perfectly they fit and felt together. *It's never been like this.* There was no desire to slip away from a "typical, hot night," as in her younger days. Quite the opposite, and Riley wasn't sure if she should be exultant or worried. She did know their evening had been spectacular, and she wanted more. A lot more. With *this lady* and only her, and the idea of Murphy giving herself to some other woman just sank like a rock in Riley's stomach. *Does the word exclusive ring a bell?*

What it all meant created a fog in her mind and threatened to spoil this brilliant morning after. She replayed last night in her head, and her insides stirred. Sensations returned full force, of Murphy's soft, yearning kisses on her chest, of those refined fingers exploring her, stroking her to shattering heights, and easing her clenched muscles into mush. Dark, enticing eyes claimed her very soul. How right it had felt,

Riley thought, nursing Murphy's sweet essence from her sex, being submersed in her slick arousal. There can be nothing more humbling, more profound, she pondered, than when a woman offers you her most delicate flesh, chooses *you* to take her, hot and pulsing in your mouth.

Fingers splayed, Murphy's palm slid down Riley's back so slowly Riley wondered if she was dreaming. It grazed softly over the curve of her ass, left cheek to right, and back again before resting. Then Murphy squeezed.

Riley grinned, still half-buried in the pillow. "Mmmmagic hands."

Murphy turned her face onto Riley's shoulder and kissed it. "Good morning."

"Ah. The angel speaks."

Murphy extended her leg farther over Riley's hip and settled into a seated position on her ass. She kneaded Riley's back, sides, and shoulders.

"How can you be this hard and this soft?" She lay forward on top of her, and Riley thought she'd died and gone to heaven. "Riley, I'm *so glad* last night wasn't a dream." She stretched her arms along Riley's, beneath the pillow, and Riley clasped her hands.

"No dream's ever felt this good." She squeezed Murphy's fingers. "You're doing okay this morning?"

She felt Murphy's lips curl against her neck. "I feel amazing, thanks to you." She withdrew her hands and dragged them down Riley's back as she sat up. "Turn over, Ms. Rough Rider."

Murphy hoisted herself up just enough for Riley to flip onto her back, and reseated herself on Riley's hips. Her phone vibrated on the dresser and Riley was very glad she ignored it.

"I'm not ready to share you," Riley murmured. *Did I just say that?* She flexed her fingers into Murphy's thighs as high as she could reach and brushed the underside of her breasts with her fingertips. Thankfully, the phone stopped vibrating. "Every inch of you is as delicious as it looks," she lifted both nipples, "and I want to savor every taste."

Her arms braced against Riley's shoulders, Murphy leaned forward again, her center hot and wet on Riley's abdomen. Riley lifted her hips to grind against it, and Murphy lowered her breasts into Riley's palms. Riley curled her fingers around them possessively and watched Murphy's elegant face react. *Such a high, pleasing you. An addiction I'm willing to nurture.*

Murphy's lips hovered above hers, auburn waves tickled Riley's cheeks. "I don't think I can call you Rough Rider anymore."

"But I like it. Gets my butch all riled up."

Murphy laughed. "You're butch is absolutely perfect, just the way it is. Trust me." She shifted her hips suggestively, and Riley's clit hardened. "You're not rough at all, Riley, not your kiss, your touch, definitely not this body." She kissed her lightly. "You're a certified member of the Softie Club, and you're simply irresistible."

Riley warmed from the inside out. Being irresistible to Murphy meant everything. And it was okay to be in the Softie Club if it pleased Murphy. Her membership really wasn't a secret anyway, she figured, because Sable had initiated her not long ago. *Am I just a pushover for a seductive voice? Well,* this *seductive voice, for sure.*

"Still rough around the edges, though." She gripped Murphy's ribs firmly and pulled her down into a searing kiss.

She struggled to concentrate with Murphy's fingers in her hair. They dizzied her and her mind was already spinning with Murphy's tongue in her mouth, her baby-soft ass in her hands. Murphy raised her head and slid her cheek along Riley's jaw.

"All right. You can still be a Rough Rider."

"*Your* Rough Rider."

Murphy sat up slightly and palmed Riley's cheeks. "Seems I'm destined to be the damsel in distress in need of your rescue."

The phone vibrated again, and Riley growled and tightened her arms around Murphy's waist.

Murphy grinned and flicked her tongue against Riley's lips.

"Was that grumble for the interruption or is your hungry belly complaining?"

Riley chuckled softly. "Both, I suppose." She lifted her head and kissed her. "Mm-mm."

"We should eat before we run out of gas, don't you think?" Murphy sat back and rubbed Riley's stomach.

Jesus, I love it when you do that.

"Eating sounds great." Riley reached between Murphy's legs and cupped her.

Murphy lurched slightly. "Down, woman! Food first," she said, grinning as she slipped away and twirled into her robe. "Do you put bacon in that body?" She used both hands to flip her disarrayed hair out from beneath the collar.

The robe swung open and Riley enjoyed the view immensely. *Do. Not. Wake. Up.*

"Eh...bacon. Yes."

"Such delicious thoughts." Murphy winked, flashed open her robe, and closed it quickly.

"Dear God!" Riley threw herself onto her back.

Murphy laughed and tied her robe. "I'll put coffee on," she said as she left the room. "Feel free to jump in the shower if you want."

Maybe I don't need to if we're going to spend the rest of the day on the kitchen floor.

❖

Murphy opted for no clothes, just her robe, when she finished her shower. *My, my, how we've loosened up.* Monday mornings don't get any better than this, she thought, not when all you have to face is one hot woman who's hot for you.

Cripes, what she does... Her sex clenched and she had to stop brushing her teeth to take a breath. *God damn.* She ran a finger over her puffy lower lip and grinned. *Probably not the only part of me that looks like this.* She ran a hand over her breasts, found her nipples rather tender to the touch, and shook her head at her reflection. *How long has it been? Has it ever been this fine?*

The shower provided much-needed rejuvenation and soothed some of the ache from muscles that had forgotten what it was like to give and take. However, the shower also liberated some of the common sense Murphy had locked away yesterday. And now that common sense broached subjects like honesty and secrets.

Murphy countered that train of thought as she brushed her hair at the mirror. Although she hardly had a basis for it, her intuition said Riley was not the long-term-lover type. *Why can't I see you unloading a U-Haul behind a white picket fence? It can't be wise to risk taking this beyond what it is. You're just so unlike what I'm used to, so unlike Bryce.*

She straightened against a twinge of that heartache. And, just as powerfully, disappointment replaced it, thanks to that nagging doubt about Riley. She squinted at herself in the mirror.

"Why are you always making mountains out of molehills?" she whispered. *So she's not Bryce, but a fling with Riley Burke wouldn't be the end of the world. Razor's probably right. And if I'm just another woman in her life, there's no need to unveil every aspect of mine.*

That heavy matter of conscience answered, Murphy reverted to the here and now and the woman with whom she experienced profound bliss in bed, whose spirit and companionship created a contentment she hadn't experienced in a very long time.

She found Riley at the deck railing, surveying the ocean through binoculars. Two mugs of coffee and plates of bagels and bacon waited on the table nearby. *Are you always this thoughtful?*

Murphy hated to disturb the picture before her by sliding open the screen. Riley stood barefoot in boxers and her form-fitting undershirt, wet hair slicked back, and oozing so much sexual energy, Murphy felt herself grow wet. *Muscle memory.* With arms raised to her eyes, the toned definition of her biceps, shoulders, and back stood out in relief. A swimmer's shape, Murphy mused, assessing the slim hips and the chiseled legs. *All of that so incredibly tender and gentle, just as sweet to taste as to touch.*

Riley reached for her coffee and spotted Murphy in the doorway. She picked up Murphy's cup instead.

"Hi, gorgeous." She handed her the coffee. "It's okay to be out here dressed like this, I hope."

"Thank you. Sure it is. My only neighbors are back up on the corner and on the other side of the street. And you dressed like this is very, *very* okay with me."

Riley took her hand and led her to the railing. "Believe it or not, I don't have clothes in the Jeep, no shorts anyway, and it's hot as hell out here." She tugged on the knot that secured Murphy's robe. "Aren't you roasting in this?"

"If you expect me to toast all my lily-white you-know-whats out here, you've got another think coming."

"Show me."

"Sorry. The wild child retired many years ago."

Riley pulled one strand of the knot loose. "I don't buy that for a second."

Murphy quickly set her cup down to grab the tie, but her hands landed on Riley's instead and couldn't stop her from untying the knot.

"Now," Riley began, and opened the robe and looked down at Murphy's naked form. "Jesus." She slid her arms inside, around Murphy's waist, and drew her close. "Now, Ms. Callahan, exquisite lady who called my name in the throes of orgasm, may I kiss you?"

Murphy stepped into Riley fully, aroused by the contact of warm cotton on her bare skin, and laced her arms around her neck. *Asking like that could get you anything.* She brushed her lips across Riley's mouth. "Four times, I think," she whispered, and kissed her.

Her enthusiasm made Riley moan, and Murphy hummed in agreement. Riley's hands drifted up and she gripped a portion of the robe at Murphy's neck and peeled it down and off her shoulders.

"Riley," Murphy said, a tight exhale into Riley's mouth.

"More." Riley kissed her lower lip, her chin, and dipped her head to kiss her throat. She withdrew her arms and gently took Murphy's from around her neck. The robe fell to Murphy's waist and Murphy let it. Riley grazed her palms over Murphy's breasts. "Four times, yes."

The sun bore down on Murphy's skin, heating her throughout, but the breeze off the ocean came as a refreshing, invigorating change. Murphy didn't think, she simply acted. She lowered her arms, caught the robe when it dropped, and tossed it onto the deck with a flourish.

She knelt on the robe, pulling Riley down to her, and pushed Riley's undershirt up and off. "Three for you, as I recall." She urged Riley to sit and then knelt astride her. "Don't misunderstand, Ms. Burke. By no means is it a matter of keeping score. Honestly."

Riley grinned up at her and fondled her ass. "Oh, no. Of course not."

"*Someone* with an amazing mouth knocked me out last night, ran me right into the ground—"

"Wore you out, did she?"

Murphy nodded severely as she slid her palms across Riley's shoulders. "And I hadn't finished."

Riley's sandy eyebrows rose adorably. "Is that so? The nerve of her. You should always let a lady *finish*."

"Glad you agree." Murphy pressed Riley's shoulders to the deck and rocked back on her heels. She gripped the edge of Riley's boxers and pulled them off. "I always finish what I start and when I can't…" She spread Riley's legs and knelt between them, rubbed her hands up her thighs.

"Wh-when you can't?" Riley asked, head raised off the deck to watch.

"Well, then I make a point to get right back to it. And give extra effort."

Murphy's heart pounded with an eagerness to thrill this woman who had reached inside her, literally and figuratively, and delivered such unexpected, consuming joy. She was just as captivated as she'd been last night, as intoxicated by the surrender and perfection before her as the awakening of her own hunger.

You get to me, Riley. If this is just a simple fling, why do I feel so lucky?

She slid her fingers through Riley's sex and Riley groaned. Murphy leaned forward and kissed along the ridges of her abs, felt them seize tightly against her mouth, and worked her way down. Riley's thighs, so firm against her palms, softened in surrender when Murphy's mouth settled over her, and trembled with each flick of Murphy's tongue.

"God, Murphy."

Murphy only hummed into her, sucked Riley's clit deeper. She threaded her arms under and over Riley's hips, and hugged them closer to nuzzle into Riley's wetness as deeply as she could. A guttural moan and tremors in the tender flesh said Riley was close. Her pelvis rocked against Murphy's mouth.

Riley slapped her palms to the deck as her torso bowed.

"Murphy! Y-yes, I'm—" Riley's words stopped, replaced by a grinding of teeth and a long, tortuous groan as her body stiffened to stone.

Murphy raised her head, a breath away from Riley's clit. "Come to me, Riley."

CHAPTER TWENTY-SEVEN

Razor threw her backpack in the corner, flipped the audio switch for the studio, and cursed.

"So much for getting here early, God damn it. No time for us to catch up. I need *all* the details."

Murphy laughed as she jotted song selections on her clipboard. "Tina's folks get off okay?"

"Yeah, yeah. Think they cared what I said about Monday traffic leaving the Cape? Nooooo. 'We just *have* to go out to breakfast first,' her mom says. Tina reminded them that *we're* driving, that *we're* the ones looking at a whole damn day on the road." She shook her head and swore colorfully.

Murphy bit back a grin as she pulled a log book off the shelf. Poor Razor, tired, irritated, and in need of entertaining distraction. Recounting sixteen hours of five-star sex would do the trick, Murphy thought. She knew Razor supported everything about that, but there was only so much Murphy was willing to share. They didn't have much time before going on-air, anyway, so she decided a few generalizations might restore Razor's usual mood.

She jumped when Razor barked through the speaker.

"Hold it! Is the DJ humming? As in…as in are you humming?"

Murphy ignored her and opened the book as she returned to her seat.

"I repeat, 'as in humming'?" Getting no reaction, Razor hurried to her side just as expected. "Humming, as in…I slept with Riley Burke and we fucked like rabbits?"

Murphy dropped her chin to her chest briefly. "God. You need to take it down a notch before you have a stroke."

"You fucked like rabbits?"

"Razor!"

"Why the humming? You're not Mrs. Cleaver. You don't hum."

"When we went out yesterday morning, I actually considered inviting her back to the house, but—"

"But? Aw, Murph."

"Well," Murphy shrugged as she stepped around her and slid the book back into place, "I didn't think we were...I wasn't sure if I was ready."

Razor scrutinized her movements.

"'Ready'? What the fuck's 'ready' mean? No clean sheets? You're hot for each other. You didn't forget what that means, did you? You at least got *somewhere* together, you're humming, you know."

"Jesus, who are you? My coach?" She sat down and picked up her pen. *Sometimes teasing you is such fun.* "We went to the drive-in."

"Huh. Well..." Razor shook her head and went back to her booth. "Tell me it was more than two fifteen-year-olds on a first date. Please say you at least got your hands on that body." Murphy could feel the stare coming at her through the glass. Predictably, Razor sighed. "Did you guys even get to second base? Did you even let her know you wanted it?"

"I didn't shove my boobs in her face, if that's what you're getting at."

"Well, why not? Did she at least try to cop—"

"She's very considerate and polite."

"Right. You went to the damn drive-in with a nun."

"She's not some horny frat boy." She started to write but paused and her gaze fell away. "We learned a lot about each other."

The silence in the studio struck her. She found Razor frowning.

"Hm" was all Razor offered.

"What? Are *you* humming now?"

"That was a 'hm,' not a hum."

"What for?"

"It's serious, isn't it?"

Murphy caught the word "yes" that nearly popped out. "We're going to date, is that okay?"

"Yeah, right. And you're going to see other women?"

"We didn't get engaged, for God's sake, Razor," and suddenly, Murphy flashed back to the commitment ceremony she and Bryce had held in Key West. Her heart thudded as her mood threatened to crash. "She's not…I'm…"

"She, you, what?" Razor asked, hanging on her every word.

"Never mind."

"Oh, don't do that. She, you, what?"

"She's not Bryce, okay?"

Razor's face went blank. Then she frowned. "Shit. Don't go backwards on me, here, Murph. Tell me you didn't spend the evening comparing them. That'd just be so wrong."

"No. I didn't." She recalled glancing away from the photo on her dresser that night, and images of making love with Riley surfaced pointedly. "We had a terrific evening, actually," and the statement almost made her laugh. "We…we spent…"

"Good. Thank God. Two minutes to air, by the way. So…? You spent what?"

The reaction she knew she'd get from Razor made Murphy grin. "Riley left my place about four o'clock this afternoon."

Razor tossed her headset down. "Holy—" She bolted out of the booth, yelling, "For fuck's sake!" Murphy was laughing by the time Razor skidded to a stop at her chair. "You *did* fuck like rabbits, didn't you?"

"Sweetie, rabbits can't come close to what we did."

Razor threw her arms around Murphy and lifted her from the chair. "No fucking way!" She squeezed her hard, then jerked her out to arm's length. "I knew you could do it! I am so proud of you, I could scream!"

"You *are* screaming. Calm down." Murphy patted her cheek and sat. *With all this recall, sitting is wise.*

"Oh, man, you need to spill, girlfriend." Razor paced to the door and back. "This is big, Murph. I mean, this is…this is so great!"

"Great…well, great falls a bit short."

"Really?" The mischievous light was back in Razor's eyes. "How about incredible? Is that a better word?"

Murphy nodded. "Absolutely."

"I love this! How about—" Razor spared a glance at the clock when Murphy tapped her watch. "Was it earth-shattering?"

Murphy held up her headset and pointed at the door. "We're under thirty seconds. Get going."

"The muscle groups got a workout, didn't they? You're walking rather well, considering. Wow, Murph. How many hours?"

"You need to shut up now."

"I have to call Tina." Razor scurried out.

"No, you don't," Murphy said to her back. *And, frankly, yes, earth-, moon-, and star-shattering.* She pulled the mike toward her, knowing the upbeat lilt in her voice would be heard in her words. *And if Arby calls?* She cleared her throat and tried to concentrate.

"So…you're seeing her again when? Tomorrow?"

Murphy prepared a sarcastic comeback but cringed at the memory of putting Riley off until the weekend. Weeknight dates were risky. God knows she'd already screwed one up badly. If she lost track of time and was late getting to the studio again, Razor would flip out and probably reveal the Big Secret to Riley just to teach Murphy a lesson.

"Saturday night. I'm making lasagna."

"Saturday? Not till then?"

"*Mom* says I shouldn't go out on weeknights. Remember?"

"Oh, yeah. Jesus, Murph. You still haven't told her, have you? You guys went through the pearly gates and you *still* didn't tell her?"

"Stop, Razor. It's complicated." *So much more than you know.*

"Hm."

"Don't 'hm' me."

Razor mumbled "God" as she shook her head. "Well, dinner at home is good. Don't blow it."

"You love my lasagna."

Razor threw her pen at the glass between them. "I don't mean the God damn lasagna." She picked her pen off the floor. "The night. Don't blow the *night*. Jesus."

"It's not *all* about sex, Razor."

"The hell it isn't. Do Tina and I have to come over Saturday night and direct?"

"You stay away."

"You deserve a wild time. I hope it's so good, you're struggling to walk in here Monday."

That was more of a probability than she dared consider right now.

"You're impossible." She pulled the mike into position. "Have you even prepped yet? You've been so damn busy organizing my sex life, you probably—"

"Fifteen seconds, smartass. So, she's a great kisser, huh?"

"Knock it off."

"Hard body and nice strong, *long* fingers?"

"Shit, Razor! Will you please shut the fuck up?"

Razor snickered, obviously enjoying her role. "Lasagna is good butch food."

Murphy flicked a fingernail on the head of the mike and sent a sharp crackle into Razor's ears.

Razor yanked her headset off. "Ow!"

"I'm discussing 'date meals' tonight. We'll see."

"It's good energy food, all those carbs, so you bulk up. I'll bet five rounds, at least."

Murphy whirled out of her chair.

"Okay!" Razor said, laughing. "Sit down. Five seconds."

Murphy returned to her seat. *Five rounds. Jesus, four was...* She blew out a steadying breath.

"And three, two, one..."

"Good evening and welcome to *Nightlight*. This is Sable coming to you for the next four hours from WCCD's Provincetown studio, ready and willing to share conversation and music as we put another Fourth of July behind us and charge into summer." A button lit up on her call board and she arched a brow in surprise. "So let us know what's on your mind tonight. Summer plans? How you spent the Fourth? A song dedication for someone special? Give us a call at 555-201-1112 or drop a note at nightlight-dot-com. I've got a topic for your consideration tonight, too, and we'll get to that right after we indulge in some of k.d. lang's 'Constant Craving.' Stay close."

"Digger on the board already," Razor said, once the song had begun.

"Please just keep my voice out of the basement tonight, okay? I think you were a little heavy-handed for that last show. I sounded like I was talking from my shoes."

"Very sexy, though, Sable, and deeper is safer, seeing as how you've given Ms. Hunky everything but the truth. And remember: you're Murphy when you whisper, so don't."

Murphy cleared her throat and stamped "don't whisper" in her mind's eye. With a flash of panic, she wondered if Riley was listening and what would happen if she picked up on a familiar whispered voice.

❖

"We're back and already we have company." She clicked the lighted button. "Hello, you're on *Nightlight*. Welcome."

"Sable. It's Digger. Couldn't wait to say hi."

"Good to hear you, Digger. What's got you so eager to jump in tonight?"

"Your secret's out, girl. Saw you Saturday night with a hot number from town."

Murphy's heart skipped. "Oh, is that right?"

"That's right. I thought listeners should know you *are* the knockout you sound like on the radio." Murphy sent Razor a worried look. "You two were going strong, too. Way to go, Sable."

"And where was I supposedly going strong?"

Digger chuckled. "Like you weren't finding sand in your...you know...the next day."

Murphy exhaled beneath the mike. "Sorry to spoil your fun, Digger, but I wasn't at the beach over the weekend."

"Huh? No way. We were sure it was you. I mean, the woman was *hot* and had your bedroom voice, even when her date...um...hit the magic button."

"Okay, careful, now." She shook her head at the mike as if Digger could see. "Not this girl, Digger."

"Bummer. Well...your mystique remains intact, I guess. That's good, too."

"Thanks, Dig. Hey, while you're here, let me toss out my topic of the night. You game?"

"For you?" Digger's chuckle rumbled in her ear. "Shoot."

"What do you think is a special date night meal?"

Now Digger laughed roundly. "Y'want me to say it on the radio?"

"Be serious. I have a friend who's looking for advice."

"Hm. Seriously, huh? Well...a lady I was seeing a while back served me pork chops on our first date. That's one of my favorites, y'know? But they're messy. You sort of lose your cool status when you're gnawing on a bone. Same goes for ribs. So not them."

Murphy bit back a laugh. "Good point to remember."

"I'd say fish."

"Fish?"

"Yeah. Easy to cook, to eat, and you're not all bogged down when it's time to hit the sheets. Y'know what I'm sayin'?"

"Got it. Thanks, Dig. I'm writing it down."

"You bet."

"And thanks for checking in. Have a good night."

Razor clicked into her ear. "Lasagna's heavy."

"Shut up, you." She hit the next illuminated button. "Hi. You're on *Nightlight*. This is Sable. Thanks for joining us."

"Hi. Sable. This is Bangles. I called last winter—but we listen to you all the time. My girlfriend said pasta primavera is a good choice, especially if it's a first date. And easy to show off."

"Thanks. Adding it to my list right now."

"Cool. I made it for her the first time I showed off my cooking. It's hard to screw up," she added with a whisper.

"Gotcha. Thanks." She clicked the next line. "Good evening and you're on *Nightlight* with Sable. Thanks for joining us. What's on your mind?"

The white whooshing noise of moving air preceded the voice on the line. "Hello, Sable."

Murphy sent a curious look at Razor but received only a head shake. She leaned forward and pressed one of the earpieces to her head, hoping to hear more clearly.

"Hi there. Hard to hear you, but thanks for the call."

"Just thought I'd add my two cents as a regular listener. I'm a sucker for Italian food. Steak's always my first choice, but can be tricky on a date."

"I see." She wondered if the steak tips she served Riley that first night were overcooked. "Do you have an Italian dish you'd recommend?"

"Chicken parm gets my vote." The white noise stopped and the caller's voice came across unimpeded, smooth and low enough to curl Murphy's toes. "Unless she can pull off a great steak while being distracted."

Murphy sat upright with a start. The rich alto warmed her ear. *Riley. It's been seven hours. I can still feel you.* "Arby?"

"Yeah. Hi. Are you a steak fan? My guess is you're a filet mignon woman."

Murphy laughed. "It's a favorite, yes."

"Thought so. And I bet you prepare it perfectly."

"As a matter of fact, I *do* know my way around steak. Thank you."

"Tips are another favorite, and I was impressed to have them on a first date. I mean…please don't think I'm some kind of chauvinist, because, I'm really not," *you have nothing to worry about, Riley*, "but we talked through her entire cooking process and the meal was terrific. She," Murphy heard her sigh, "well, the lady's terrific, too."

Murphy caught herself staring at the far wall, seeing Riley on her deck, injured leg on the footstool, wine in hand, and sunset warming her face while they chatted and she worked the grill. The night they really met. The night she discovered Arby. The night kisses said so much. Suddenly, she heard her own silence and blurted out a response.

"So you think she was rather brave to tackle that for a first date meal?" The white noise returned and clouded the transmission, and Murphy inwardly cursed the interference. *She's in the Jeep, damn it.*

"I was more caught up in her than the food, but, yes, definitely. You have to be good at it and she's…she's exceptional. But chicken parm is all advance work, so you can spend your time concentrating on each other."

"Excellent point." *My exact thought about lasagna.* "Well, I hope your steak tip salad led to a successful evening." She grinned toward her lap. *Am I blushing?*

"It certainly did, but her cooking skills aren't what matter. A first date meal can help you through those occasional awkward moments, I guess, as long as it turns out all right, but beyond that, it's all up to each of you. And she aced every part of that evening. I'm hoping we'll see a lot more of each other."

For how long, Riley? You left just as deep an impression on me. Are you talking to yourself now, like I am?

"Well, I…" Murphy's mind raced for a comeback. She only heard the blood thrumming in her ears. "I'm putting chicken parmesan at the top of my list. No sense risking a good evening with overcooked steak."

"Wouldn't be a risk for you, Sable. I get the feeling you'd handle cooking during a date like a pro."

"And I get the feeling *you* aced every part of that evening as well." *Understatement.* "I'm betting your lucky lady didn't miss a trick. My vote says you two are off to a great start, Arby. Good luck."

"Thanks for the support, Sable. As always, it's been a pleasure."

"And it's all mine. Thanks for the call, Arby." Murphy held up a palm to Razor. She needed to take a breath. "And we'll be right back after we pay a couple of bills, so please stay close."

"We're clear. Three minutes." Razor entered the studio and leaned against the door. "I was praying you two wouldn't veer off from eating food to eating something else. Sounds like she's got a woman in her life, so maybe she'll stop seducing you on the radio."

Murphy set her elbows on the counter and dropped her head into her hands. Didn't she want that voice to seduce her away from her reservations, from comparisons, from thoughts of long-term improbabilities? All night. She wanted to feel that voice on her lips, her breasts, her thighs. Now. Tonight. As soon as she fumbled through her front door, and when she dragged herself back to that bed…with all its memories, new as well as old. She wanted to feel it far beyond that, too, and the thought made her pulse race. *How much of an investment is a fling?*

"Murph? You okay?"

"Hm? Oh. Just beat, I think."

Razor grinned. "I'm not surprised. How much sleep did you actually get?"

Murphy shook her head. "I have no idea."

"Nice! Did you at least eat—food?"

"A bagel, I think…and bacon."

"Uh-huh. You should've thrown filet mignon on the grill. Or some tips." She chuckled. "Hey, you served Riley a tips salad that night she came over for drinks, huh?"

Murphy sat back. She didn't look at Razor, didn't want her reading her face.

"I did. They were good, too."

"Well, that's no surprise. You're a magician with a grill."

"Right."

"So, tell me you're not feeling even a tad dumped, now that Arby's got somebody."

"Please. It's just that voice."

"Well, that butch voice might still be around, anyway." Murphy considered herself fortunate. "But I'm glad to see you're not taking her seriously." Razor handed Murphy the headset. "Get back to funny special meal stories." She paused before leaving for her booth. "Don't be giving that one another thought. You've got a real live heartthrob to think about now."

CHAPTER TWENTY-EIGHT

Riley held a large, unwieldy bundle of scrap lumber wrapped in a blue tarp on her shoulder and found her way out of the East End alley by flashlight. She crossed Commercial Street to her Jeep at the curb and dumped the load inside like a dead body in a rug. "Take that," she mumbled, shutting the tailgate. She tossed in her work gloves as an afterthought. Oncoming headlights illuminated the narrow, empty street, as well as Riley, as she wiped the sweat off her face with a paper towel.

The street quickly darkened, and Riley looked up to see the yellow Beetle leaving Commercial by way of a side street. *Not many cars like yours, Ms. Callahan. What brings you out at two thirty in the morning?* She stared at the empty intersection and wondered how Murphy missed seeing her and the Jeep, not that far ahead. *Preoccupied, evidently.* Finally, her parched throat reminded her there was water in the Jeep and she jumped in, pulling out her cell phone. *Just a quick hello.* She downed half a bottle as her mind wandered. *No work keeping you in tonight? Visiting a client...friends...a lover? Now that thought sucks.* She tucked her cell phone back into her pocket, started the engine, and headed home.

Riley sank onto her futon with a cold Coors, hardly aware she'd parked the Jeep and climbed the three flights. "Who is she, Murphy?" She drank heavily and told herself she didn't want to know, didn't need to know, and had no right even to a twinge of jealousy. "Damn it." A night of breathtaking passion did not turn a fledgling connection into a steady relationship, and she felt like a fool for thinking otherwise. *Talk about premature...jumping the gun.* "But will you be 'the one' who got away?"

She stared out at the sea of black rooftops, knowing the harbor rolled just beyond them, and that, across the bay, beachfront homes in Wellfleet looked back. She thought about Murphy's cozy house with its deck and picturesque view, a home to call her own with pride and accomplishment. Roots. She took a deep breath. "Next year." She sipped her beer slowly. "Will I still be your occasional date?" *I want to be your only date, Murphy Callahan.*

"What the hell am I doing?" she shouted at the coffee table, the Craftsman she bought *with Murphy*, their "patio table" at the drive-in. "Going overboard, stupid, that's what. You can't always get what you want." *But you'll never get it if you won't even admit what it is. Slow down and take a good long look around. Face it.* "I really am done bouncing around."

Damn, Riley Burke sticks her neck out one more time.

She looked back at the coffee table and the closed laptop.

You, beautiful lady, have so much in common with Sable. Have friends told you that? Much the same confidence, same playful manner. You're a great listener and have such an easy delivery, such a subtle sensuality. Riley grinned as she recalled Sable's reference to them. "She seems to think you and I are on the right road. Just on the success of your steak tips salad."

Riley turned to the window again, as if searching for something in particular, but only heard Sable's words—and her own. *I never told her anything about salad. Damn if she didn't just come out with an assumption like that and nail it correctly.* She snickered into her beer. "Either you've gone totally soft, Burke, or the woman's an expert at reading people too well."

❖

Forearms on the railing, Murphy let her wine glass dangle from her fingers and tried not to fantasize about which distant building had a loft with Riley in it—if Riley was even home by now. She very well could be working the next maintenance crisis. Or not. She wished controlling her mind was a little easier. She'd much rather see Riley in bed, naked, that body relaxed in sleep, than see Riley in bed, somewhere, that body wrapped around a faceless lover. If she'd just driven another hundred yards, she wouldn't be standing here counting on wine to soothe her nerves and ease her into sleep.

And just why she was on the deck was no mystery. *Not at sunset but at full dark.* Murphy sent a sardonic smile toward the familiar sound of waves on the beach. She wondered if she'd ever get past the lonely pull of pastel memories and, in a way, hoped she wouldn't. *"Don't look away...These colors are for you."* She sipped her wine, grateful and impressed that Riley somehow had understood.

"I think you're amazing, too." *Only Bryce ever had me in such a state, mooning like this. You occupy so much of my mind, already. You're here in my house, and, God knows, at work, and I love that you're around me, but...only if you're the real deal. What if you're out there right now with someone else?*

"See? A fling? Me?" *Not sure I can handle it, giving myself to a woman and simply moving on. Moving on is never simple.*

"Jesus. Overreact much?" She hated how often she pictured Riley in unknown places with unknown women. *Based on...what, exactly? Regardless, that's what a fling is all about in the first place, dummy, so wrap your head around it.*

"Guess I should try." She stared out at Long Point and Bryce's favorite lighthouse. "Oh, Riley. For nine years, I knew what was real, and now, look at me. I'm afraid to find out if you are." She swirled the burgundy in her glass and watched the stars' reflection sparkle up at her. "*Really* would be nice to find out without losing my mind, having to be someone I'm not."

She sighed and downed a final mouthful of wine, deciding to go to bed before she ended up drunk and crying herself to sleep on the deck.

But turning on the bedside lamp brought such an onslaught of memories, she had to pause and gather herself. Riley's beautifully muscled form, her sweet flirtation, so invigorating and full of life, flashed at Murphy from the bed. Just as quickly, she saw Bryce's long, shallow body punished by sickness, her fathomless brown eyes clinging to happier times.

Perspective. The fun and frolic have their place. No matter what, I can't afford to lose perspective. That's one price I can't pay again.

She took a pillow from the bed, shut off the lamp, and headed for the couch.

CHAPTER TWENTY-NINE

She'd never left flowers on a woman's doorstep before, but Riley wasn't going to let that stop her. She wanted the old-school affectionate gesture to say she cared, that she wasn't just hooked on the languorous kissing and exquisite orgasms. She was serious for the first time in…maybe ever, she thought with a little start. And as crazy as it was to think long-term about a woman she barely knew, she *had* to make a sincere statement.

Actually, she'd hoped to lay the flowers in Murphy's arms, kiss her, and leave, because just appearing unexpectedly on her doorstep would probably intrude upon that baffling work schedule Murphy kept and defeat Riley's purpose in a big way. But Murphy didn't answer her doorbell. Riley obviously saw that the Beetle wasn't in the driveway, but she'd had to try.

Disappointed, she set the small bouquet on the top step and headed back to the Jeep. This was the second time she'd found no one home. Earlier in the week, on a trip back to town, Riley had stopped by to surprise Murphy with a quick hello, but turned around in Murphy's driveway and continued on when she didn't see her car. This time, returning from an evening mid-Cape supply run, Riley had felt lucky, and arrived bearing flowers at nine fifteen.

Weeknights can't be date nights, you said, so where might you be on this Thursday night, Ms. Callahan? Another elderly call-out? A trip to the store? You're so hard to catch, but damn, if it doesn't feel like someone else succeeded. Does she bring you flowers? Well, corny as it may be, this woman does and she's hoping you will give her a shot.

She returned to the front steps and took her flowers to the backyard. A watering can, an old flower pot, even a forgotten coffee cup would do, she thought, but the empty wine bottle near the railing boosted her spirits—and nearly dashed them in the same moment. *Did you enjoy this with someone, Murphy? Maybe you were out here alone, drifting with the colors of the sky. Maybe you left this here for me.*

She found the hose in the dark and rinsed and filled the bottle, then squeezed her flowers into it. She positioned it on the little table between the Adirondack chairs on the deck, directly opposite the sliding screen door where Murphy couldn't miss it.

She stepped back and looked around the deck, remembering every step they took, every intimate thought and gaze they shared, and the masterful way Murphy had blown her mind that morning, gloriously naked, right here where she stood.

Jesus. Riley rubbed her eyes, as if the physical stimulation would help her see exactly where she was and what she was doing and why. She'd never been so taken by a woman so quickly, never been this swept away, not to the point where bewitching sighs, delicate touches visited her every waking moment, had her doing things like this, standing in the dark in Murphy's backyard and seeing things so clearly.

She turned toward the bay, peered into the black void that hung from sky to sea grass, and listened.

Somewhere between the two, waves stroked the shoreline in a steady rhythm, reached through the dark to ground her. That relentless breeze kept her drive from sinking. Land and sky merge with ocean out there, she pondered, as if their fusion channels that massive life force to this destination, like the heart guides the spirit. Or tries to. So alive in such an indefinable world, tireless and persistent, determined. *We don't have defined boundaries, either, Murphy. We're just as free to follow our hearts, and part of you knows that. I can feel it. I felt it with you in my arms.*

She inhaled a deep breath of salt air and exhaled with care, sharpening her thinking. She didn't want even a semblance of boundary separating them and felt the imperative to scale any that existed. That thought had her gripping the railing, and the tangible connection to Murphy's life.

Sometimes the dark sheds just the right amount of light to see where you're going.

❖

"Here. Try this one." Razor offered a floor-length halter-top sheath, slit open to the upper thigh on the left side. The black satin number shimmered in the boutique's recessed lighting as Murphy held it open at the slit.

"*Plus*, it's cut to the navel, Razor. No way."

"Sure, way." She pressed it to Murphy's shoulders. "Oh, yeah."

"No." Murphy stepped back. "I'd fall out of it, for one thing. And what would I wear under it?"

"Wear nothing under it." Murphy growled. "Okay, a thong. And I don't think you'd fall out. I mean, you've got an awesome set, Murph, but I still think you can keep those girls under control."

"What if Riley ever recognized me?"

"You said she probably won't show. But even if she does, you'll be in full costume. Oh, I get it." She cupped her own right breast. "She'd recognize your girls."

"Stop." Murphy turned away to search through more evening dresses.

"She might, huh? Since you spent so many hours getting them acquainted and all."

"Be serious, please."

"Has she called you back yet?"

"No, and I've left two messages. I *so* wish I'd been there. The flowers were…just perfect." A hand on the next dress in line, she stopped and stared at the floor. "I can't stop thinking about her."

"Obviously, she can't stop thinking about you, either. Hell, you met for lunch Tuesday, right?"

Murphy nodded. "And I called her Wednesday morning."

"And then the flowers last night? Lord help us. Dinner's still on for tomorrow night?"

"Definitely." *Keeping things in perspective is so hard.* "We just have a great time together. That's all it is, really."

"Sure. That's all. Well, before you two 'have a great time together' house hunting on Sunday, you'd better come clean. She deserves to know now, no matter what's at stake, and if you keep this up, it will have a painful end."

Perspective is supposed to prevent pain.

Murphy tried to envision the look on Riley's face when she learned Sable's identity. *And if she confesses to being Arby, I have to remember to act surprised. God.* Murphy massaged her temples.

"Razor, please."

"Just saying, Murph. It's a bestie's job to nag for your own good."

Razor held up the sheath again. "Now. I think this black satin is a keeper."

Murphy eyed it warily. "And I still worry she'd recognize me."

"Not unless she has X-ray vision."

"Look at it. You don't *need* X-ray vision."

"Nobody's going to know it's you, Murph. Not behind the mask. Plus, you'll have that trampy blond wig and enough makeup to make a clown jealous."

Murphy dropped her hands to her sides and sighed at the lineup of clothes, frustrated. "This is our fourth stop and we've still got nothing." She turned in a circle, scanning the shop for more options. "We have to be at the damn ad agency in an hour. Why did you ever agree to the photo shoot?"

"Because they're up my ass. As your *producer*, it's my job to haul Sable out from under her rock, convince her to expose herself, so to speak."

"Yeah, right. I got that memo. The freaking vampire queen." She held the sheath out from the bottom. "Expose herself for sure."

"Come on." Razor practically dragged her to the shoe department. "Can't check the dress without something decent on your feet." She snatched the first sexy pair of stilettoes she saw, and marched Murphy back to the changing room. "Now, go for it. I'm telling you, the dress is going to fit like a glove."

Murphy mumbled an obscenity as she disappeared to try on the sheath and four-inch spiked heels. Within five minutes, she swore a bit louder, and when she appeared in the doorway, Razor's jaw dropped.

"Oh, fuck."

"Razor!" Murphy hissed, and slammed her hands onto her hips.

"No, Murph. Really. Let's. Right now."

"That's it! Forget this." Murphy spun back into the changing room.

"Wait! Murph!" Razor ran after her. "Jesus H. Christ." She stood in the narrow doorway, staring at Murphy's reflection in the tall mirror. Murphy stared, too. "Have to tell you, Ms. Callahan. Sable is the sexiest female I have ever seen. We're buying the dress."

"Razor, it's skin tight. I can't wear *anything* beneath this."

Razor's grin widened. "Nope. Not a single thing. Strike a pose."

"What?"

"You heard me. Let's see Sultry Sable hungry and horny."

"Absolu—"

"I bet you've done it to tease Riley."

Murphy felt her face heat. "Well…that's different."

"Oh, Callahan. I knew there was a naughty girl in you."

"What I show Riley and what Sable will show a crowd are *vastly* different things."

"Yeah, but Sable's show will be easy. She's got a costume. What's Murphy got?"

Chapter Thirty

My plan is simple. I'd put a second floor on my little house for a guest bedroom and a new master overlooking my beach. Oh, and a second bath, a luxurious one." Murphy smiled at the sketch she had pinned to the wall nearby. *Someday.* "Then, I think I'd bank the rest of the money until my head stopped spinning."

The caller laughed. "If I won the lottery, I'd buy a yacht, the kind that my helicopter can land on and my jet skis can float up inside."

"Basic necessities."

"Yup. And I'd dock it in Coral Gables and cruise away from the hurricanes, if I had to."

Murphy chuckled. "I'll loan you my boat slip in Newport."

"Thanks, Sable. It's great that we're so independently wealthy, isn't it?"

"I tell my driver the very same thing, every time we're out for a joyride in my Bentley. Thanks, caller." She opened the next line, still grinning. "Welcome to *Nightlight*. This is Sable. What indulgence would you make with your lottery millions? How would you splurge?"

"Hi, Sable." The lilting voice almost giggled. "I've always dreamed of buying all the latest fashions in Paris."

"Oh, now *that's* different. Paris and shopping, an exciting combination."

"God, yes. I went on spring break two years ago and swore I'd go back one day when I was rich. Have you ever been?"

"Never been to Europe, unfortunately. My money, when I had some to spare, was always required elsewhere. But it's on the bucket list—after my home addition—when I win my millions."

Now, the caller did giggle. "Hey, when I win, I'll buy you the plane ticket."

"I'll be waiting. Thanks, caller." She clicked the blinking button and the next line opened. "Good evening and welcome to *Nightlight*. Feel like a big spender tonight?"

"As a matter of fact, I do. Good to talk to you, Sable. How are you?"

Murphy cleared her throat off-mike. "Arby. I'm well, thank you. And thanks for calling." She reached for her coffee. *Do not envision a thing.* "You're in the mood to spend your lottery cash, I gather."

"Definitely. I'm going to build the home of my dreams. It might take a year just to find the right acreage, but the search will be one hell of an adventure."

"Narrow down the region you'd search."

"Oh. Hm. Cape Cod would be my first choice, but only if I can find an oceanfront-woods combination, and that's rare around here, unfortunately. I prefer the ocean, but a lake will do, so that expands my options."

"New England? Not, say…the Blue Ridge Mountains or…I hear Michigan has some beautiful parts." *Would you like to travel, Riley, see the country, at least? And would you go alone? So many topics we haven't hit yet.*

"Eh, love to visit, but I'm a local at heart. If I did venture off to live, I'd go as far as the Northwest Kingdom in Vermont or Maine's Alagash."

"How about upstate New York?" It was a favorite of Murphy's, and she wanted to know if Riley shared that opinion. *This keeping-my-wits-about-me stuff is rough,* she thought, chin in her hand, fighting a losing battle against the imagery in her mind. *Riley shin-deep in a stream, hair mussed by the wind… Get a grip.* She sat up straighter.

"Yeah, upstate. That would be in the running, too, I guess. Actually, I've spent a lot of time there and once planned to retire up that way."

"Retire, huh? Well, since we're all big lottery winners tonight, you can retire right now. What's this dream home you're going to build?"

"A log cabin."

"Really?" *How did I not guess this?*

"Not too big, though. Just going big with the kitchen and bathroom."

"I see."

"And I don't want Carnegie Hall for a great room. I like a cozy feel, with a good-sized wood-burning fireplace, couches close by." *I can see you there so clearly. You do "cozy" very comfortably.* "There'll be a couple other rooms, too, regular size, for bedrooms or whatever."

Murphy grinned at the mike. "No game room? Home theater?"

"No. The basement can be used for that, if I want them someday, but who needs that when you have the outdoors? There'll be fields and woods around for cross-country skiing and all that, and I'll probably buy a canoe or a cat-boat, because there will be water right there, remember."

"I got it."

Riley's passion for the outdoors drew Murphy back to her childhood years, to times filled with excursions and curiosity, before college lured her to an exotic, urban life. With surprise, she realized how long she'd been away and that she actually missed those adventures. She respected Riley a great deal for not dismissing what really mattered in her life, for dreaming big and taking aim.

"Do you have a design already?" Murphy again glanced at her own sketch.

"I do, as a matter of fact. I'm going to do as much of the work as I can myself."

Murphy sat back and drew the mike with her. "Build the cabin, too?" *Is there anything you won't tackle?*

"I've thought about tracking down an expert and learning how, so I might, but I can do all the other stuff already. This way, my costs won't be outrageous—won't eat up all my millions."

"But if you put your log cabin on Cape Cod, the land alone might." *You don't need millions to build your dream, Riley. It'll happen.*

The muted chuckle threatened to bring *very* intimate moments to mind.

"So, Sable, you're content to just add on to your house?"

"Just for a bit more room inside. I doubt I could ever part with my beach or the gorgeous sunrises and sunsets. They hold very special memories." She heard her last words and held her breath. *No more descriptions of the house.*

"On the Cape, they're like no other. I think we all see special things in them. And no lottery windfall could ever provide what they offer."

Murphy stopped doodling on her clipboard. Sea gulls and setting suns filled the margins, and now a log cabin sat in the upper right corner.

"Oh, Arby. Gently poetic as always."

"Thanks for letting us dream tonight, Sable."

"There's no giving up on dreams, you know," she added, and pictured Razor pacing, impatient for her to wrap this up. "Buy those lottery tickets." She laughed lightly. "Hey, dreams *do* come true, now and then."

"I believe that, too."

"As you should. Why don't you send along a copy of your plan? I'll keep it here next to mine. We'll rely on *Nightlight* pressure to shame us into seeing them through."

"I like that." The laugh warmed Murphy to her core. "Consider it done. Again, thanks, Sable."

"You're welcome. Good night, Arby."

Razor punched in a commercial, and Murphy sat staring at the metallic mesh that covered the tip of her microphone. Not that she actually *saw* it, but rather looked toward it. It was simply just there, like her attraction to Riley, as up-front and centered as Riley's unassuming, unpretentious manner. *The woman has a way of taking me someplace else. It's something different about her every time we connect, no matter how we connect.*

Over the running jingle, Razor's voice pulled Murphy back to reality.

"Well, that ran long, but it was okay."

Murphy looked up. "Sure, it was." She saw the initials "R.B." on the top of her clipboard and quickly scribbled them out.

"The bit about sending her plan, though, Murph…You had me worried there for a second. I'm glad you shut her down when you did." Murphy hoped Riley didn't feel "shut down." Her pulse rate increased a bit as she acknowledged that was the last thing she wanted to do.

❖

Didi poured a draft beer for Riley and delivered it with a smirk that said something smartass was about to come out her mouth.

"What?" Riley asked, thinking she'd beat Didi to the punch.

"So, call up your radio lover and offer to build her addition."

Riley didn't dare admit that working with Sable would be a rush. Such a job had actually crossed her mind. Of course, she had no idea if Sable owned a sprawling ranch or a three-story Colonial, but knew she could put a second floor on your average little beach house single-handedly. Done it before. Twice, in fact. And had all the trade connections to do everything else necessary, as well. *I will send her my cabin plan, though, just for kicks.*

"You've been sampling your merchandise, Didi."

"Uh-uh. When you're on the line, she's sexier than ever. Everybody hears it."

"Not true. She's got a sexy voice, period." *But not as sexy as someone else I know.*

"Noel at the A House says his pool is up to two hundred and seventy bucks on you two."

"Oh, for Christ's sake."

Didi leaned closer. "Look, just promise your best pal Didi that before you and Sable do the deed, you'll let me know so I can get in on that pool. I deserve the inside scoop, I think."

"Sorry. Nice voice, nice woman, but not interested."

"Still hot for your new lady friend, huh?"

"I told you. She's special."

"You've got that glazed look in your eye, RB. Don't tell me you're hooked already?"

Riley looked up to speak, but only managed to smile before returning to her beer.

"Whoa!" Didi reared back. "You bring this woman in here, Burke, or I will bust your butt. That's as serious an I've-got-it-bad look as I've ever seen, and I ain't *never* seen it on *you!*"

Still smiling, Riley stood and opened her wallet. "I gotta go." She flipped cash onto the bar.

"Yeah. Sure you do. She's waiting, isn't she?"

"Jesus. No, she's not waiting. I'm seeing her tomorrow night."

"Uh-huh."

"It's been a long day and a longer night, Didi. I'm crashing, since you need to know all my business."

Didi laughed as she snatched the bills off the bar and put them in the register. "Yup. You go home and get lots of rest."

"I intend to." Riley headed for the door, shaking her head.

"Hey, RB? You could call your *other lover* and practice by yourself."

"Good night, Didi."

CHAPTER THIRTY-ONE

See this connection? Here's your leak." Riley shone her penlight onto the drip under the kitchen sink. Murphy left her crouch, turned onto her hip, and squeezed into the cabinet beside Riley to look. "Here," Riley said, and Murphy leaned against her shoulder to see the water glistening in the light. She enjoyed every second of this close-quarters connection, to hell with the problem at hand. Riley had removed her dress shirt and was down to a black athletic undershirt that hugged her the way Murphy wanted to. Body heat and the invigorating scent of a woodsy cologne had Murphy struggling to pay attention.

"I…I see. I need a plumber, don't I?"

Riley moved her head just enough to make eye contact. Murphy felt the full body rush instantly and wondered if Riley picked up on it. They lay stretched out, hips and upper bodies pressed together, legs extended onto the kitchen floor amidst all the wet spray cans, cleanser bottles, and other miscellaneous items Murphy had removed from the cabinet. Not the ideal finish to a romantic meal, but a sure way to fire up one's engines. Murphy made a point not to let their legs entwine.

"If I had my gear with me, I'd take care of this now," Riley said, just inches from Murphy's cheek, "although, I know I don't have a replacement elbow for this. Not even in my inventory."

"No, you're not here to work. I appreciate you diagnosing the damn leak, though." She couldn't look away from Riley's face, the smooth glide of her jaw, the set of her lips. "You have no idea how embarrassing this is. I'm so sorry, you're—"

"Please don't be. I'm not." Murphy fought back a sigh. "I get to show off for a beautiful woman, lay against her, breathe in the sweetness of her skin, have her *this* close…" She kissed her lightly and hummed against her lips. "Trust me. I love it."

Murphy swallowed hard. *No. Swooning under the sink is not how I saw this night.*

Riley turned away when water dripped on her arm. "I don't have plumber's tape in the Jeep, but I do have duct tape. It'll have to do for now."

"I'll get it." Murphy pushed herself backward, out of the cabinet, and knelt beside Riley's legs. "Where do I look?" She grinned at the shaggy head watching her every move. "Besides at you."

Riley grinned back. "In the console."

Murphy steadied herself with a hand on Riley's knee as she stood and then hurried off, taking a breath to calm her rising pulse. She was halfway across the living room, tempted to change her iPod music from romantic jazz to something more upbeat, when she remembered a roll of tape Razor had used months ago. She returned to the kitchen and riffled through a utility drawer until she found it.

"How's this?" she said, back on her knees and offering the roll.

"Gee, you're fast." Riley inspected it. "Glad you had some. Thank you." She stuck the penlight in her mouth, pointed it at the leak, and rubbed the spot dry with a rag.

Murphy edged in beside her again, took a breath against the sensation of fitting her hips to Riley's, and delicately lifted the light from between her teeth. "Give me this. It's *my* job," she said, and kissed her.

"Wow. If this isn't the best job I've ever had." Riley brushed her nose across Murphy's. "Let's get this done and get out of here."

Propped up on her elbow and limited to the use of one hand, she pulled out a length of tape, bit it off from the roll, and let it hang from her mouth as she dried the pipe again under Murphy's light. She wrapped the leak repeatedly, melding the material to the pipe by clenching her fist around it each time, and Murphy looked on, completely enthralled. She almost shook her head at herself, so taken by the motion of Riley's hardened fingers, the rise of muscle along her arm, the flex of her shoulder. All so near. She could practically taste the power emanating from Riley's upper body.

"Done," Riley said on a breath, staring at her work as if daring the leak to reappear. "But this is only a temp fix, remember. This needs to be replaced." She rapped the pipe with her knuckles.

"Will do. Thank you, Riley." She shut off the light and they backed out. "I should have checked more thoroughly and tackled it myself, instead of letting you get into all this."

"Stop. It didn't amount to anything, really, and it was a pleasure."

Murphy looked at the products cluttering the floor and knew she could have done the job, avoided the whole mess, if she'd tried—and missed this extremely arousing interaction. She shook out a trash bag. "I'll just put everything in this for now."

Riley helped her put items in the bag. "I can swing by Monday and fix things the right way, if you want. I'd like to do that for you."

"Thank you, but you have your own work to deal with. I'm fine with calling a plumber." She stuffed the bag into the cabinet, feeling very spoiled by this royal treatment.

"Why spend that much money for just a simple thing? In fact, if you need anything done around here, please don't hesitate to ask."

Murphy cupped Riley's cheek. "You're too good to be true, you know." She kissed her lightly, taken by the physical need for such contact.

Riley grinned and shook her head as she washed her hands. "Just know that I don't mind."

"There's really nothing but this damn leak, although I have big dreams about a second story someday." Riley looked up at the ceiling and exposed the smooth, tanned expanse of her throat. Murphy trailed a finger down it, remembering the salty-sweet taste on her tongue. "You've already come to my rescue—again. Thank you."

Riley wrapped her arms around Murphy's waist. "For you, I work for kisses." She lowered her head and Murphy threaded her arms around her neck, drew her in as their lips met. *God, you never have to work for this.*

"I thought you were going to say food," she said, and sighed as Riley's lips tugged at her throat.

"Your chicken parmesan tonight was inspiring, a favorite of mine, just like this." Riley kissed her jaw and lingered, her hands melting into Murphy's back, and Murphy felt arousal swirl up from her depths and blot out her conscious thought.

"I know."

Riley kissed her lower lip. "How did you know?"

Murphy's focus returned so sharply she stiffened in Riley's arms.

"Really, just a lucky guess." She teased Riley's lips with the tip of her tongue. Her nerves simmered with multiple stimulation, not the least of which was the unsettling awareness of having said too much. She nipped at Riley's upper lip, licked it slowly, and won a lengthy kiss and a tight squeeze from Riley in return.

❖

"I'm the lucky one, Murphy." Riley buried her face in the crook of Murphy's neck and hugged her.

Murphy moaned at the feel of them fitted together. *Your tenderness literally takes my breath away, Riley Burke. I could get used to this and that's just so dangerous.* She slipped her hand up into Riley's hair and held her head in place. "You make me feel so much without even saying a word."

"Sometimes you don't need words." Riley swayed them to the music from the living room and lifted her head when the song ended and pressed her cheek to Murphy's. "Sometimes the song just ends too soon."

"The good ones are never long enough," she whispered.

Riley drew back slightly. Her studious look said the words had struck a chord.

They struck a chord with Murphy, too. They blasted from memory. Her suggestive exchange with Arby about dancing returned verbatim. Panicked, Murphy scrambled to say something that sounded like herself and not Sable.

"So, Rough Rider." She took both Riley's hands in hers. "Do you like to dance?" She prayed the subject of a certain radio personality had left Riley's mind.

"I'd do anything with you." Riley moved them to the music with slight, fluid steps, and set her mouth to Murphy's. "I don't want our song to end, Murphy. Not tonight, not for a long, long time."

The softness of her lips, the depth of their kiss silenced Murphy's conscience completely. The words lost their connection to the radio conversation and delivered an entirely different message to Murphy's dazed mind. *You really expect this—us—to go somewhere, don't you? Do I dare?*

She kissed Riley's cheek and jaw, wishing she had answers to questions she couldn't formulate. She brushed Riley's hair from her forehead, drawn nearer when Riley's eyes closed as they always did when Murphy stroked her hair. This woman at her fingertips, virtually at her command, brought emotion to life, awakened desire so long asleep, it felt new and empowering. Foreign. Murphy hardly knew how to cope.

She heard herself whisper against Riley's lips. "God, Riley. You steal my mind, make me *feel* so much." She kissed her, locking her arms around Riley's neck.

Riley groaned, her hips shifted restlessly, and Murphy's heart pounded with pleasure. Riley responded with a deeper kiss, urged her back against the refrigerator, and Murphy returned the groan when Riley fitted her thigh between her legs and curled her fingers around her breast.

"Murphy." Quickened breathing flared against Murphy's mouth. Riley's fingertips touched her cheek reverently, traced the rim of her ear, slipped into her hair, and the contact in so many places overwhelmed Murphy's self-control. *So easy to surrender to you.* Riley kissed each lip carefully, kissed her chin, her neck, and opened Murphy's top buttons to kiss downward from her collarbone.

Yes. Murphy tugged Riley's thin shirt over her head and ran her palms heavily down the front of her chest, back up to her shoulders. Riley finished unbuttoning Murphy's blouse and trailed her fingers to the front clasp of her bra. *Yes, I was hoping.* She set a kiss just above the clasp, opened the bra, and moved each cup aside.

"So beautiful, you are." She lifted a breast in her palm. "Let me cherish you, Murphy. Only you." She claimed the nipple with her lips as Murphy reeled from both the touch and the sentiment. She held Riley's head to her breast with both hands, her thighs tight.

She moaned as Riley kneaded her stomach, and when her shorts were unzipped, her hips arched against Riley's thigh in anticipation. Riley's broad hand, that sturdy forearm reached deeply between her legs, slid through her wetness, and Riley hummed against her breast when she finally slipped fingers inside. Murphy's head dropped back against the refrigerator, hands lost in Riley's hair, and through a sensuous haze, she glimpsed the pastel sunset beyond the sliding screen door.

She closed her eyes. She didn't need the reminder of a past love. Not now. Not as Riley kissed her stomach and knelt before her, nuzzled into her hair and stroked her sex. *Never in the kitchen, Bryce, I know.* She felt Riley's tongue dip between her folds, circle her clit, and Murphy twitched.

"Oh, God," Murphy said, her voice strained, "you're so...so good."

Riley leaned against her, pressed Murphy's hips to the refrigerator door, and licked her steadily, her tongue firm, eager. She drove her fingers inside her with a determined rhythm, and Murphy's knees shook. Muscles coiled tightly and her pelvis rocked against Riley's motion as her body clenched.

So quickly. Jesus. Never this fast. It doesn't mean it's never been good...Bryce...

Riley's hungry focus on her clit had Murphy's legs trembling. She knew it was noticeable because Riley withdrew her fingers and wrapped an arm around Murphy's thigh.

"Please...don't stop," Murphy said on an exhale.

Riley tipped forward, drew Murphy's thighs over her shoulders, and knelt upright. Her feet leaving the floor, Murphy grasped fistfuls of Riley's hair and leaned back against the refrigerator. Tremors rippled through her beneath Riley's tireless attention. Sun warmed her eyelids, forced another glimpse of the sunset, and she squeezed her eyes shut against the vision imprinted on her mind. *Bryce's sky...* But dazzling colors erupted in her backlit darkness, accompanied by the strain of every muscle. Riley growled into her and Murphy's breath caught. Her heart raced as she arched hard and crashed into a thunderous orgasm, and heard her own wrenching cry.

"Y-yes, God, Bryce! Yes!"

Riley stopped. She gently withdrew and lowered Murphy's feet to the floor. Her hands drifted down to rest on her thighs as she sat back.

Her chest still heaving, Murphy fought back tears. The kitchen smoldered in the abrupt silence.

"Oh, Riley!" Tears escaping, she dropped to her knees but Riley stood and urged Murphy up. "I'm so, so sorry," Murphy cried. She cupped Riley's cheek, ran her other hand through Riley's hair. The lost expression didn't change. Murphy swiped at her own tears. "Riley, I have no explanation for that. I'm just so incredibly sorry."

Riley cast a half-smile toward the floor and shook her head. "Not exactly what one hopes to hear, you know?" She edged away, picked her shirt off the floor, and put it on.

"Please, Riley, don't go." Murphy's hand shook as she pressed it to Riley's arm. "Won't you please stay? I need to explain, somehow."

"I...ah." Riley ran a hand back through her hair. "I guess, maybe, we both have some thinking to do, Murphy. It's best if we do it separately." She found her dress shirt on the stool and returned to where Murphy still stood, frozen to the floor.

Wiping away tears with her fingertips, Murphy could only feel, not think. *I'd never want to hurt you. God, what's wrong with me?* She'd extinguished that consuming heat in Riley's eyes. Fear and despair pressed into her and made her shake. She gathered her bra and blouse across her chest.

Riley lightly rubbed away another of Murphy's tears. "You're very special to me, Murphy, like no other woman I've ever had in my life. The thing is…I'm pretty sure I don't want to share you. With anyone. Just…just so you know. And I probably should deal with that, but… Let's give us some time, okay?"

She went to the front door and Murphy managed to follow, never feeling more helpless. She watched Riley step out. Her heart leapt in her chest when Riley turned at the bottom of the stairs and spoke.

"Take care of yourself, please?"

"Riley. I can't stand this. I'm so sorry. You deserv—"

Riley held up a finger. "Shh. I understand, but we each need to do this, Murphy. I'll call you."

Chapter Thirty-two

L ori something." Didi snapped her fingers. "Yeah, Lori Hathaway. Now strut on over and say hi."

Riley just sipped her beer and continued to count the glasses behind the bar, knowing Didi was far from satisfied.

"Listen, RB. She's got a great sense of humor for a cop. Hell, this is her third or fourth time here, and if the guys brought her in, she's got to be cool. Go on and introduce yourself."

"Didi, give it a rest."

Didi leaned so close Riley could smell the rum on her breath. "You listen to me, God damn it. It's been…two weeks? Call your girl, for cripes' sake. I'm sick of lookin' at your mopey ass hanging off the end of my bar. What are you trying to prove? That you're some pious prima donna? You punishing the poor girl?"

Riley pushed off her elbows and stretched her back. "Are you done?"

"No. What exactly happened, anyway? You owe me an explanation."

Riley snickered. "Explanation is the key word. And I don't owe you anything except for these three beers."

"You ain't even called your radio girlfriend, have you?"

"Nothing to say. I'm calling Murphy tomorrow, satisfied? I know it's cliché, nowadays, but we needed some space to think things through."

"Oh please." Didi slapped the bar rag over her shoulder. "Well, you'll come down off your high horse once you meet Officer Hathaway. Go broaden your horizons." She laughed at her choice of words.

"Thanks for the effort, Didi, but there's only one woman on my horizon, and I have no interest in looking elsewhere. Unless I hear otherwise."

"Well," Didi turned her back to the handful of other patrons, "your horizons are about to be broadened whether you like it or not." She hurried to the far end of the bar.

Riley downed the rest of her beer and stood up. "I don't think so."

"Oh, how to give a lady a complex."

Riley turned at the lilting voice and into the playful look of a petite blue-eyed blonde.

"Hi. I'm Lori. You're Riley Burke, they tell me."

"That's me." She offered a handshake and found Lori's grip surprisingly firm. "Pleased to meet you. I don't mean to be rude, but I'm—"

"Oh, no." Lori sat and patted Riley's stool. "If you don't give me ten minutes of your time, I'll never hear the end of it from the guys." Riley sent a surreptitious scan around the room, noting the two patrolmen in the corner. "Yeah, those guys," Lori said. "They bet me ten dollars I wouldn't come over here and chat with you."

"So, I'm what? And what does that make you?"

"One lesbian to another, Riley. I'm new to the department, and apparently, they think you should be a 'person of my interest.' All I know about you is that you like girls."

Riley snorted. "This *is* Provincetown."

"Well, do you play the field?"

"Are you offering?"

"Are you available if I am?"

"No."

Lori laughed. "And I'm not offering. But I wasn't about to pass up a quick ten dollars just because I refused to say hello to a very handsome woman."

Riley shook her head. "I know those guys. They're all right. They joke around a lot, but they can take it, too." She pushed several bills across the bar for Didi. "Hey, I really am sorry, but it's past my bedtime. You tell those clowns they owe you twenty."

"Twenty?" Lori chuckled. "I'd love to, but they won't part with that much."

"Sure they will." Riley cupped the back of Lori's head, and drew her into a prolonged kiss. Lori steadied herself with a palm on Riley's chest. The patrolmen hooted from the corner.

"Wow. Ah…well." Lori straightened on the stool. "*That* was worth a lot more than twenty."

Riley offered a congenial smile. "A pleasure meeting you, Lori. Good night."

❖

"Our fourth email of the night is from Venus in Truro," Murphy said, scrolling down the text on her monitor. "She writes, 'I wired four milk crates together, and that's been my coffee table for the past two years. When company comes, they leave their shoes at the door, and we all sit on the floor around the table. I think that says a lot about who I am, because I'm neat, practical, and I recycle.' I'd have to agree with that, Venus. My guess is you have at least one metal sculpture in your home and you're vegan. Drop us a note and tell us if we've got you pegged."

Murphy took a breath before opening the next line. Friday nights were always popular, the lines always busy, and she hoped this would be the night Riley finally decided to call. Razor had grown increasingly edgy these past two weeks, knowing Murphy and Riley had yet to decide where their relationship was headed, and Razor feared any renewed interest in Arby that might arise in Riley's absence. Murphy wrestled with how to assuage Razor's concern, but reminded herself, that Razor's worries took a backseat to her own. The anxiety that preceded each call was making her crazy.

"Welcome to *Nightlight*. You're on with Sable. Joining in tonight? Or making a request?"

"Hi, Sable. This is…um…Gabby, first time caller."

"Hey, Gabby." She relaxed back in her chair. "Welcome. What's on your mind tonight?"

"I'm joining in. I have a Tina Turner poster—a big one—right over my kitchen table. Everybody sees it right away when they come in. I think that says a lot about me." She laughed.

"Great taste in women, first of all. Up-front, direct, and honest."

"Yup. To a fault, sometimes, but, hey. It's who I am."

"I like that. Tell us about the poster. I had one back in the day."

"From an old movie. She's in the desert, sitting on this beast of a motorcycle."

"I know the poster. It's a collector's item, Gabby. You hang on to that one."

"Sure will. Thanks, Sable. Nice talking to you."

"Same here."

Razor's voice rattled privately into her ear. "Hey there." Murphy looked up and Razor frowned. "Took her a while, but she's back."

Murphy felt her pulse jump. She took a quick sip of coffee and inched closer to the mike as she opened the line, fervently hoping she'd get through the call.

"Good evening. Thanks for joining us on *Nightlight*. This is Sable and you're live."

"Sable. How are you?"

Murphy tightened her grip on the armrest of her chair. *I'm missing you terribly, that's how I am.* She took a breath and released it slowly.

"Arby? It's been a while. I'm well, thank you, and you?"

"I'm getting by. I think just living in a loft says something about me. I haven't really had a need for much furniture these past few years, so…"

Murphy thought the casual, personable tone was lacking in her voice, and she tried to keep her own strong. "You have a log cabin in your future, I thought. Which reminds me that I haven't received that plan you said you'd send. It says a lot about a person when she's determined to build the home of her dreams." *Tell me your dreams haven't changed.*

"Oh. I forgot to send you a copy. I've been…a little preoccupied lately, but I will."

"Good. Don't forget. Now, you want to tell us about this loft of yours?" She'd been curious since first meeting Riley and often wondered why the subject never came up. *This could be the only way we ever talk about it.*

"It's not much, really. A futon, flat-screen, an old wingback chair. Oh, and my Craftsman coffee table. That's my prize possession."

"Sounds special." Murphy bit her lower lip.

"It is, actually. I had help getting it into my Jeep, but she wasn't around later when I lugged the thing up three flights of stairs."

"See? More determination on your part, although it sounds like she…she should have stuck around." Murphy purposely rotated in her chair, slightly farther from Razor's eyes. *I'm doomed. Razor knows everything we did that day in the Jeep. If she hasn't picked up on who this really is by now, she's asleep.*

"I didn't mind. She made the day and the night fantastic. I wouldn't trade it for anything. So, the coffee table makes me smile a lot."

Murphy lowered her head. *I want to do that, Riley.*

Razor's instant message on the monitor drew Murphy upright.

Commercial next

Murphy focused on the mike. "Well, you were right, Arby, about the loft saying a lot. And treasuring a Cape Cod antique, does, too. You keep smiling." She moved away slightly to clear her throat. "That's what a woman with your kind of determination does."

"I'm working on it, Sable." *I hope so. I'm trying, too.* "Thanks for taking my call."

"My pleasure, Arby." Murphy blinked as moisture blurred her vision. *Do not fall apart.* "Please don't be a stranger." She took a breath and disconnected the line. "Time for us to pay a few bills, everybody, so we'll be back after a few. Stay close."

CHAPTER THIRTY-THREE

Deep in thought, Murphy jerked with surprise and spilled wine over the deck railing when Razor appeared in her backyard. It had been a quiet, contemplative Saturday. No work or shopping or housecleaning, just thinking and brooding and sulking, with sobbing thrown in for good measure, and now she added exhaustion. She sank into an Adirondack chair, not ready to hear what she knew was bouncing around in Razor's head.

"Hey. Figured I'd find you out here." Razor climbed the stairs, watching her. "Another spectacular sunset." She went into the kitchen, returned with a glass, and poured herself a little wine from Murphy's bottle. She sat beside her and sighed. "So."

Murphy sipped her wine and nodded. "So."

Razor looked toward the ocean, took a sip, and set the glass on the table. She pulled a cigarette lighter from her jeans pocket, then a battered pack of Marlboros and a joint, which she proceeded to puff to life under Murphy's apprehensive eye.

She inhaled, held the lungful of smoke, and passed the joint. "Here. I know you'll fall asleep after four hits, but just do a little. Tonight, it's a necessity."

Murphy obliged and handed it back. She hadn't spoken with Razor since their reserved, awkward parting last night in the parking lot, so Razor's appearance really wasn't a surprise.

"Okay." Razor sipped more wine. "We're going to talk and I'm going to start." She took another hit, paused in thought, and passed the joint. "Why didn't you tell me about Arby? Or should I say Riley?"

Murphy exhaled a stream of smoke toward her feet. "Because I was afraid you'd shut her off."

"You wouldn't think I'd be amused, want to let you play it out?"

Murphy simply passed the joint. "Yeah, right."

"Of course, I'd have to keep things 'acceptable' on the air, but I wouldn't—"

"I don't want to lose the connection."

Razor nodded. "Well, that's obvious." She squinted through the smoke that curled around her head. "At least you admit that much." She handed Murphy the joint. "It's a start."

Murphy peered at Razor in the half-light and took a hit. "Don't start, Razor. Please."

"Hell, I probably *should* stop putting her calls through—for her sake as well as yours. You can't get your head on straight and she's out there spinning her wheels." Razor shook her head as she took back the joint. "Shit, Murphy. Riley wouldn't call if she knew she was talking to you. How fair is this?"

"You don't think I realize that?"

"She'll feel like a fool—a duped fool. How's she going to react when she learns *both you and Sable* have been taking her for a ride?" She gulped half her wine. "Jesus, Murph."

Murphy rested her head back in the chair and stared up at the early stars.

"I never wanted to hurt her, Razor. God, never."

"You're not even sure what you want."

"You know I'm not the kind of person who'd use—"

Razor snickered. "Too late, honey. When she finds out the score, she won't know *who* you are." She inhaled and passed the joint again. Murphy waved it away and Razor stabbed it into a flower pot. "She's already trying to figure out your first disaster."

"Thanks a lot."

"Well, you've got to admit, calling someone else's name when you come...Hell, that'll leave a mark, mess with your head."

"Stop already. Please don't remind me. Such a nightmare." She folded her arms across her chest. "Razor, I can't string her along. She's so...God, she's wonderful and doesn't deserve this." She sat up and wiped tears away with her T-shirt sleeve. "I know I'm being so unfair all the way around. What I've done to her with Bryce is the real killer. I just can't seem to get beyond the past. Bryce comes to mind when I'm with her and that's...so not right. There's too much history."

"Hm. History, sure. That's okay, you know. You're supposed to cherish that, and I know you do, but there's pain there, too, and no one should keep dwelling on the pain. You're too smart a woman, Murph, too sharp to take the easy way out."

"Easy? You think painful memories are easy?" Now the tears rolled down her cheeks and Murphy didn't care.

"Of course not. But are you going to pass up a really fine woman—who thinks the world of you, I'd say—just because fighting back memories is hard?"

Murphy lifted her head and assessed the varying shades of pink and orange that streaked the sky. "It's *very* hard."

"You're scared, Murph, afraid to let go, even of the pain. Think about it. You've come to associate a relationship with pain and that's not what it's all about. You've got to get past it."

"Well, I can't use Riley to do it, Razor. I *do* know that's not right."

"No, you can't. This is a one-woman war." Razor sipped her wine and went quiet.

"My only recourse is to end this between us now, before…before my pathetic truth hurts her even more. My struggle is bad enough. Inflicting it on Riley—more than I already have—is out of the question."

"I'm not sure that sending Riley on her way is the right answer, Murph. Hey, if you want the easy way out, just tell her how you and Sable have been stringing her along. That way, she'll walk, resentful, pissed off, thinking you're a piece of shit, and you can keep right on dwelling in the past."

"There is no easy way out." She rubbed her eyes. "Maybe I *should* tell her about Sable. I'd rather she be mad than hurt."

"The Sable deception isn't one of your brightest moves, that's for sure."

"Tell me something I don't know."

"Either way, she's going to hurt."

"Unbelievable." Murphy shook her head. "I know my real problem is handling the past. I see that. And ending things with Riley will save her from the nutcase I apparently am. The Sable issue won't have to come up, then."

"Look, Murph. I have to disagree. You have some hurdles to clear, not avoid, and I don't believe saying good-bye to Riley is the clever, end-all solution you think it is." Murphy just sighed. "But if you're hell-bent to do it, make sure you do it for the right reason—not as a handy excuse to make everything 'go away.' Do it to get your head on straight, so you can level with Riley, so you can offer her or whoever comes along, *all* of you, not just whatever part's available."

Murphy turned to her, saw the concern and the loving enthusiasm Razor had for seemingly everything in her life. "Who are you and what have you done with my whacky best friend?"

"Hey, I'm here to give you that boot in the ass you need." She set her hand on Murphy's arm and winked. "Life *does* go on, girl. See? You've acknowledged the issue. You've made it to this point," she gestured across the bay, "and, in case you haven't noticed, Riley's right over there."

Riley took a measure of comfort in dropping off her log cabin drawing at the WCCD office. She'd prefer to share the plan for her dream home with a certain someone, but knew Sable had a similar goal and would be amused by the signature, "Making dreams come true." Sable had told everyone that night about her wish for a new master bedroom that overlooked the ocean, a second story on her beach house. *Just what Murphy wants.*

Blueprints came to mind as she returned to the renovation job on the opposite end of town. Creating two back rooms in the tiny restaurant had her daydreaming about options for Murphy's addition, and, once again, she caught herself overstepping. *Calling in a favor and having a plumber fix her sink for free is one thing. Designing her second floor is another, especially when she's obviously having second thoughts about us.*

She called Murphy earlier in the week but had to leave a message. Five days without a call back told her Murphy still wrestled with issues and wasn't ready to meet, maybe wasn't interested period. But Riley wanted to be told in person, wanted to see Murphy's eyes when she admitted her heart still belonged to Bryce. Riley frowned as she worked. She found it impossible to believe Murphy could cast them aside after they had connected so well and said such heartfelt things. *She's not the kind of woman to say or do things she doesn't mean.*

Riley checked out the two women nearby, sharply dressed in business attire, conferring over paperwork about the restaurant, and she saw Murphy in such a role, professional, focused, and self-assured. Murphy knew her own mind and it showed, except when it came to their budding relationship, and Riley felt driven to help her resolve that problem. No one had ever drawn her in this way, compelled her to invest her heart and take such a risk. *Part of you does want to move on, Murphy. You've shown me that much. Give us a chance.*

Determined, Riley refused to go into a fourth week with things still unresolved between them.

She hammered studs into place and remembered Sable calling her determined, how she thought Riley's appreciation of that damn coffee table said something about her character. "Cape Cod antique." She chuckled. "Damn. I could build a replica in a heartbeat." She stopped and stared at the nail she'd just pounded flush. *Did I say it was an antique? I don't think I said I found it on the Cape, either.* She reached for another nail in her pouch and banged it into the two-by-four. *Another lucky assumption. Sable knows me better than I do. Maybe I should ask her* out.

She snickered at herself and pulled her ringing cell phone from her thigh pocket. The name on the screen brought her up short. She stepped out back to take the call.

"Murphy. Hi."

"Hi. I'm sorry to call now. I'm sure you're working, but I—"

"It's okay. I'm glad you called. You got my message?"

"I did and would dinner tonight be all right? I really want to talk, too."

Riley tried to remain levelheaded, but having that familiar voice in her ear made her smile. "Tonight?" Murphy normally shied away from weeknight dates, and Riley dared to hope their situation meant enough to Murphy to break her own rule. "Sure. I should be done here sometime around five."

"I...I was thinking of Devon's, someplace...quiet."

The drop in Murphy's tone was unsettling. *She's serious, not excited. There's too much depth in her voice.*

"Fine with me." *Suggest a time—and don't sound so eager.* "Six o'clock? Seven?"

"Um...well, seven...Devon's starts to pick up by seven." The warm, hushed timber of Murphy's voice had Riley clinging to every syllable. "So, would six be okay?"

If it weren't for this damn foreboding feeling, I could get lost in this sexy voice. We should talk on the phone more often.

"I'll be there at six. I'm looking forward to it."

The pause in Murphy's response didn't sit well. Riley ran a hand back through her hair. *Was that too much to admit?*

"Riley, I…I'll see you at six. Thank you. I know—"

"Let's talk later, Murphy, not like this."

CHAPTER THIRTY-FOUR

Murphy sipped her water and checked her watch. Exactly six, and she wiped her moist palms on her shorts. All the talking she'd done around the house today failed to coach her courage high enough for what she was about to do. She glanced out to the sidewalk, and reached for water again. Her hand trembled. *Oh, sure, this looks like a woman set in her convictions.*

She dreaded this. Hated it. Her heart pleaded, but she'd put her head in charge, and now it throbbed and her stomach rolled with dissention. *Remember: it's this way or worse.* She took a deep steadying breath and tried to steel herself against succumbing to her first sighting of Riley in three weeks.

She watched two men with a Rottweiler stop on the sidewalk and offer handshakes to Riley as she approached the building. Murphy exhaled slowly, thankful to have this private moment to enjoy the look of her.

As Riley walked to the table, Murphy stood, wondering if she was simply being courteous or expecting to be taken in those arms. Riley stepped close and took her hands, didn't move to hold her or even kiss her cheek.

"Hi. It's really good to see you, Murphy."

She sat opposite her and Murphy sensed the gap between them widen.

"You look well. I'm happy to see you, too."

A waiter appeared, and Riley ordered a margarita, and Murphy, a Manhattan.

"Serious drink, Ms. Callahan." Riley sat back and eyed her curiously. "I don't know who's more nervous about this, you or me."

Murphy managed to smile past the ache in her chest. She shook her head, mostly at the entire mess this had become. "I need to thank you for sending the plumber. I didn't forget."

"She's great, isn't she? We lucked out that she had a free spot that morning and your job was a quickie. Bet she talked your ear off, though."

"As a matter of fact." Murphy laughed lightly. "She was pretty funny." The waiter delivered their drinks and left promptly. "Ah…did you want to order dinner now?"

"So we won't be interrupted later?" Riley moved the place setting aside and leaned on folded arms. "Food is the farthest thing from my mind." She lifted Murphy's hand, held her fingers on the table. "I've done a lot of thinking since the last time we were together. Have you?"

She stroked Murphy's knuckles with her thumb, waiting patiently for an answer, and Murphy fought to concentrate. Riley's gentle touch always distracted her. *Sensitivity is why you're here, remember.*

"Yes, a lot." She cleared her throat and withdrew her fingers, knowing that in itself spoke volumes. "I've hurt you, Riley, and you have no idea how sorry I am. God knows, I never meant to be so inconsiderate."

Riley didn't dispute the claim. She sipped her drink and folded her fingers around the stem of the glass, and Murphy pushed out more lines she'd spoken into her bathroom mirror earlier.

"I guess it's pretty obvious to you now, that I have, well, unfinished business. It's become pretty painfully clear to me, too, and I can't put you in the middle of my mess. I…" She took a breath. "I need 'us' to stop until I learn to handle things better."

Riley sat back. "You're putting an end to this?"

"I believe it's for the best, Riley. I've already hurt you. As much as I truly want to, I can't tell you it won't happen again, or…or get worse, if I don't finally deal with how I've been coping these past few years."

"I don't want 'us' to end, Murphy. I want to be in your life, not shut out of it. You don't have to be alone to deal with your 'unfinished business.' There are two different issues here."

"No, Riley. One's affecting my response to the other, and I need to separate them to put them in proper perspective. It's already driven a wedge between us, and I'm scared that it will again, unless I come to terms with it."

Riley looked at her so steadily, Murphy turned to her drink. A substantial sip burned its way into her stomach and smoldered.

"I don't want to take Bryce's place, Murphy." The tenderness in her voice brought Arby to mind, and Murphy almost shuddered. "No one ever will or should. She deserves that piece of your heart. But there are plenty of other pieces—ones you are free to give."

"That may be so, but…but not now, not yet. I have some work to do first."

Consternation looked out of place on Riley's usually sunny face. She looked pained and confused and Murphy's heart clambered for her to do something about it.

"Murphy…" Riley blew out a breath. "Okay, um…Look, I'll confess something, too." She set her hand on Murphy's, lightly, cautiously. "I'd love to be the *only one* in your life, but if I've crowded you…I mean, I know we haven't been seeing each other very long but if I've pressured you into this…this withdrawal, Jesus, I never meant to. I'll back away. If I've come on too—"

"I'm not ready for this…for us to become something more, Riley." Hoping that hadn't come out of her mouth as harshly as it sounded, she mumbled toward her drink. "That became very obvious in my kitchen."

Riley's hand receded off the table to her lap. "So, this is the 'we can be friends' talk."

"I…I'm not even sure I can risk that, Riley. At least not right now." She offered a weak smile. "You mean a lot to me already and…I'm not handling my feelings very well."

The waiter appeared and offered to take their dinner order.

Riley looked up at him, her expression blank. "Ah…no, thank you." He nodded and moved on. She sipped her drink and trailed a fingertip around the salted rim. "Well…what does 'not right now' mean? A month from now? I'll call you next summer?"

"I don't know, Riley. I've never had to face it like this before."

"Does it feel like I'm forcing you? Because I—"

"No, no. I need—I *want* to get a grip on this because…" Murphy clasped her hands over her plate. "I don't go into relationships easily. I don't take them lightly, Riley, and I don't believe anyone should invest less than one hundred percent."

"I know this seems awfully fast, but we've been honest with each other, and we're old enough to know what we feel."

Murphy folded her fingers together tighter to stop them from shaking. Honesty was much more a part of this than Riley knew, and Murphy fought the shocking, desperate urge to run.

"I'm being as honest with you as I can, Riley. You mean so much to me, I…I can't hurt you. I think you're—"

"Stop." Riley raised a hand briefly. "Please." Stress wrinkled her forehead.

Murphy thought the bewilderment she saw, the angst, appeared out of character. She blinked away tears as she watched Riley drink and push her glass away.

"Murphy, I'd hoped tonight we'd talk about moving forward, not stopping." She looked up, defeat evident in her strong features. "If we can't even be friends right now, I...Well, there's not much left to say."

She slid her chair back and stood. She reached to the tabletop and lifted Murphy's hand, kissed her fingers, and placed her hand back down.

"Making you happy has made me happy from the moment we met, Murphy. If this is what you need, what you really want, I won't interfere. Just know how much I care for you and that it just doesn't... *stop*. Maybe, down the road, our paths will cross again and...we'll see what happens."

CHAPTER THIRTY-FIVE

I bumped into CCD's sales rep at the Wired Puppy yesterday morning. She said the A House is all bent out of shape over *Nightlight*'s soap opera."

Murphy poured more paint into Razor's bucket and went back to work on her bedroom wall, part of her "new outlook" project she hoped would help steer her onto the right emotional track—and keep her too busy to think. "The closet needs some touch-up. What soap opera?"

"She went there on Tuesday about their ad for Carnival and found out that customers have been betting on when Sable and Arby will get together. Guess they're pissed things have gone quiet."

Murphy stopped her roller halfway up the wall and looked at her. "You're not serious."

"That's what *she* said to *them*. But evidently it's true."

Murphy resumed painting. She didn't know what to say to that. *Soap opera.* Their conversations hadn't gone *that* far. The idea that they'd been good for business turned her stomach.

"Serves them right, getting all caught up in some stupid betting thing."

"She said she was going to email you about it." Razor climbed the stepladder to paint across the top of the closet.

"She hasn't yet, and I caught up with all the mail last night."

"Oh, I forgot. Every single lesbian spends her Saturday nights going over email from work."

"Don't."

"Apparently, now there's some serious cash in the pool they started, so they're hot for you two to get back at it."

Murphy kept painting, but could tell Razor eyed her warily, hoping for a reaction. Drawing none, Razor continued with a sigh.

"So...do you think she'll still call?"

Murphy didn't want to get into it. The shows after the episode at Devon's had been utter torture, hanging on every incoming call, praying she could hold it together if it was Riley. But with the passing of Thursday and, then, Friday, Murphy felt her emotions swing from resigned to empty.

"I suppose she will. Why wouldn't she?" she said, trying for as cavalier an attitude as possible. She dipped her roller in the tray and started the last wall. "I mean, Sable is always a great listener, the good friend. I don't see why she wouldn't call."

Razor glanced at her. "Unless Riley can't or doesn't want to verbalize what she's going through."

"She always shares personal things with Sable."

"She does, doesn't she? And Sable shares with her." Razor waited for her to react.

"Yes, she does. Sable's always been there for her."

Razor stepped off the ladder and gripped Murphy's roller. "You're scaring the crap out of me. Stop this third-person shit."

Murphy turned to her sharply. "It's just as well she doesn't call, isn't it? How am I supposed to react if she does?" Her voice grew louder by the second. "I can't very well sob into the mike, now, can I? Shit. I don't even have a frigging *right* to sob, Razor. I brought this on. All of it." She tossed a hand toward the room, and her voice cracked. "I've made one colossal mistake after another and it's cost me dearly. And it's cost Riley, too, God damn it! I-I could fall in love with that woman!"

Razor dropped her brush into the bucket, set the roller in the tray, and pulled Murphy into a hug.

❖

Murphy clicked the next lighted button on her monitor and sat back. "And you're live on *Nightlight*. Hi, Digger. What do you have for us tonight?"

"Ironing."

"Ironing? Okay, how did ironing contribute to making you such an independent woman?"

"I did it for a living when I was young, earned enough money for my first truck."

"Have to say, Dig, I'm surprised. Ironing just doesn't sound like something you'd do. How did you get into it?"

"Hell, I was about twenty. I was playing with my four-year-old niece, and we had the real iron on the bed, moving it all around. Problem was, we walked away and left it and I didn't know she went back and plugged it in. Nobody knew—until we smelled the bedspread burning."

"No!"

"Oh, yeah." Murphy laughed with her and realized it felt good for a change. "I had to go to their house and do the whole family's ironing for a month. My sister and brother-in-law, their two kids, and my other sister who lived with them. It sure sucked. All the adults had white-collar jobs, you know? Dress-up clothes. It was awful, but boy, I became an expert."

"I'm impressed. I know who to call in a pinch, because I hate it. Everyone I know hates it."

"Sorry to disappoint you, Sable, but I wouldn't touch an iron today, even if you *did* pay me."

"Well, it's safe to say there is a whole town's worth of people who are happy you do what you do today, Dig. It's a lot more important to the public welfare than ironing."

"Thanks, Sable. Good talking to you, as usual."

"Thank you for sharing a fun story."

Razor's instant message appeared on Murphy's monitor just as she was about to connect the next caller.

Take a breath. It's her.

A shiver trickled down the back of Murphy's neck and she flexed her shoulders. She rubbed her eyes against the onslaught of images that came to mind and dragged her cursor over the lighted button. *Do this right. I broke us up to spare you this, however wrong that might have been...* She clicked the line open.

"Good evening and welcome to *Nightlight*. This is Sable. What's on your mind tonight?"

"Hi, Sable. Good to hear your voice."

Murphy swallowed. "Arby. It's good to hear yours, as well. It's been a while."

"Yeah, well. We all have stuff to get through. Your topic tonight had me thinking, and I guess I was in the mood to talk." *If it wasn't for this job, Riley, I wouldn't be talking much either.* "I can't contribute something as special as some of your other callers, or as funny as burning a bedspread, but building a tree house went a long way for me."

"A tree house, you say." Murphy rested her forehead in her hand. The trembling in her palm vibrated in her head, so she sat up again. Nothing felt comfortable, just Riley's voice. "Did you build it yourself? How old were you?" *Focus.*

"I was eleven." Murphy leaned her head back. She could see the eager, vibrant little girl. "I had some help from my dad and brother, but yes, by myself. I drew up the plans, saved my allowance for supplies, and just needed some guidance with a few power tools."

"I bet you climbed that tree a little recklessly, too, and probably with tools in hand."

The soft, brief chuckle made Murphy grin. Her eyes filled. *I miss you.*

"I suppose I'm still a little reckless, now and then."

"I hope not with power tools, like those nail guns…or chainsaws—or drills," she added quickly, and slapped both hands over her face. *What was I thinking?* The silence on the line lasted just long enough to replay the words in her head and she squeezed her eyes shut, trying not to hear them, longing to retract them.

"Eh, well, I've learned a lesson or two with them."

Murphy couldn't tell from the brief response just how Riley had received her reference to chainsaws. She thought it best to move on quickly.

"And today, you're building, fixing things for a living—and intend to build your dream home yourself." She spared a quick look at the cabin sketch that now hung beside her beach house plan. *"Making dreams come true."*

"Did you get my drawing?"

"I did. It's here on my wall." *Next to mine.*

"Someday, right?"

"Definitely, someday, Arby."

"I think our past helps us with our independence every day, more than we realize. I mean, yeah, there are some things we don't want to refer back to, but even they offer lessons."

Murphy stared at the mike. *Riley, if you only knew.* She could feel Razor watching, no doubt wondering where Murphy was going to take this. *Hell, are they both that deep in my head?*

Turning away briefly, Murphy tried to clear the logjam in her throat. "I couldn't agree with you more…Arby. As usual, that was well said." She wished her own difficulties hadn't exacted such a toll. "I do think, however, that extracting a life lesson from a painful experience can revive that pain, and that's probably why so many people fail to 'see where they've been,' so to speak, and miss those important messages."

"No one wants to relive the pain, you're right, Sable, and it's a shame when it has to come to that, but sometimes life demands it of us. Those messages can be very important."

"But that demand…" she heard the wobble in her voice and took a breath, "that demand often comes with a heavy price, unfortunately." Murphy muted her mike. The unspent tears at the back of her throat made her cough. She yanked a tissue from the box on her counter.

Another instant message popped up on her monitor.

End this before you lose it.

Murphy strained to hear the lengthy sigh in her headset. Riley struggles, too, she thought, and wished this whole nightmare—*that I caused*—was behind them.

"But, Sable, there's no denying we gain from our past, we lean on it, sometimes, and in the end, that's usually a good thing. Don't you think?"

I'm working hard on it, Riley. How I love your spirit. It's as strong as you are.

"I do." A tear slipped down her cheek and she swiped it away. "We all have things in our past we lean on, some we lean on more than we know and that can make it awfully hard to see our way clear. And seeing our way clear is what life is all about."

"And having dreams."

"Yes, Arby, dreams."

"Don't forget, Sable. Some dreams we actually *can* make come true. Even a kid's tree house."

Nodding at the mike, Murphy smiled through her tears. "Yes, exactly like your tree house."

Riley exhaled hard. "Well, let's raise a glass to tree houses, Sable. Thanks for listening, for being here tonight."

"Raising my glass, Arby. As always, it's been my pleasure."

CHAPTER THIRTY-SIX

Still mostly asleep, Riley fumbled for her ringing cell phone and knocked it off the nightstand.

"Shit."

She leaned too far to reach it and fell out of bed. Her hurried "hello" came out as a deep "ohhh" when her head hit the floor. "God damn it. Sorry. Hello?"

"Riley? It's Jack from Pawz. Are you all right?"

Now on her knees, Riley scrubbed at her face and threw herself back across the mattress. *Thank God he's a good guy.* "Hi, Jack. Sorry. Not too coordinated yet." She cleared her throat and fought to wake up.

"Late night, huh?"

"Geez, yeah. I got sidetracked on some plans here and…Cripes, the sun was coming up."

"Oh. Not good."

"Mmm. I know I have your job today." She looked at the clock and winced. "Was going to be there at nine."

"It's ten thirty."

"Thanks a lot." *Wake the hell up.* She pushed herself into a sitting position, then headed for her dresser. "I'll be there in fifteen. I'm so sorry, Jack. Really."

"I was getting worried. Thought you might have forgotten us."

"No, no. I'm sorry. Just let me jump in the shower. I'll be right over."

Jack's bright laugh was a relief to hear. "Get a decent cup of coffee."

"I'll bring you one, too. See you soon." She shoved a hand through her hair and swore at the bruise on her forehead.

She threw clean underwear and socks on the bed, and found a not-too-wrinkled T-shirt in the next drawer. Turning to the bathroom, she took in the disaster she'd made of her loft after that heavy conversation with Sable.

Wads of paper were everywhere, snowballs of wrinkled ideas and reworked concepts dotted the carpet, chair, her kitchenette's counter, and clustered around an overflowing trash bin. The coffee table and her laptop cowered somewhere beneath a blanket of sketches, interrupted only by the remnants of a Coors twelve-pack. She congratulated herself for drinking only four last night, credit for the other empties going to several previous nights.

"That's gotta stop," she mumbled, turning on the shower. But ideas for her cabin would not stop, and she was eager to plow through the mess and find the best ones and fine-tune her dream home.

"It's all your fault, Sable." She lathered her hair and listened to that conversation again, the one about past life events getting in the way of dreams. It had inspired her to draw, but the hot shower delivered a serious splash of reality, forced her to see she'd just been avoiding what had kept her awake for too many recent nights.

"You're entitled to new dreams, too, Ms. Callahan. You lean on your past so much you can't see what's ahead." She sighed hard as she toweled off. "You haven't come close to letting anyone in since Bryce died, have you?"

She pulled on shorts and shirt, while that concept swirled in her head. *I know you felt it, Murphy. Jesus, we're good together. I don't want to give up and I don't think you do, either. I hope you won't be upset if I remind you.*

She pounded down the stairs and squeezed the Jeep through Commercial Street's summertime bustle. *Were you listening last night, Murphy? Did you hear what Sable said? Did you hear me?*

"You probably wouldn't even know it was me." She shook her head. "Cripes, Sable seems to know me like a damn book, even though last night she seemed...different."

Chainsaws.

Riley pulled over across from the Wired Puppy and bolted in for coffee. *I guess the tree talk made her think of them, but, Jesus, she hits so close to home.* She hurried back to the Jeep, deep in thought, and suddenly remembered the picture on Razor's desk. She shut the door, started the engine, but didn't move.

"Holy shit. They're friends." *Took long enough to see it! Stands to reason they would be, with Razor being both Sable's engineer and*

Murphy's friend. Friends talk. Damn. Murphy's probably told Sable what a turn-on I think she is.

"Isn't that just great." *They share stuff, that's how Sable's known things I never said, the damn chainsaw, the salad Murphy made.* "The 'Cape Cod antique' coffee table." *Bet they have things in common, too.*

"How do you do, Sable?" Riley said, mocking. "It's me, RB, your radio stalker. Could you put in a good word for me with your pal, Murphy?" She laughed at herself. "Uh-huh."

She drove toward the center of town, advanced carefully through the congestion of tourists, locals, dogs, and a sea of vehicles, and when she parked in the alley beside Pawz, had no recollection of the trip.

❖

Tina held up her bottle of Sam Adams to interrupt the conversation. "Excuse me, radio people, but *my vote* is no. You'll depress all your listeners, Murphy, and the ones who *do* call, will depress *you*."

Razor chewed a mouthful of hamburger quickly and swallowed. "I agree. It'll be one hell of a long night, if we're dwelling on breakups."

"I don't think so," Murphy said. She propped her feet up on the lone vacant chair at her patio table. "People want to commiserate, and Sable's their girl." Razor and Tina exchanged a look. "What? She is. She's been the local Dr. Phil here for—"

She stopped when Razor went to the little table between the Adirondack chairs, snatched the vase of new flowers, and thumped it down beside Murphy's beer.

"Face it. You just want to lure her to call. Obviously, she still cares."

Tina hid a grin behind her fingertips. Murphy noticed and Tina shrugged. "She's not giving up, Murphy, but she's not hassling you, either. Very romantic."

"Knowing she was on this deck again yesterday just makes me…" She blew out a breath.

"Makes you what?" Razor said. "Horny? Sad? Mad?"

"Does it feel like harassment?" Tina asked.

"I don't know. I like that she was here. I think. But she shouldn't have been." Murphy waved her beer bottle at the sky. "How am I ever going to get my head on straight if she's around?"

"Really. How 'around' has she been?" Tina sighed. "Look, hon. When's the last time she called Sable?"

"It's been almost two weeks ago now."

"And you've only seen her once—just that horrid evening at Devon's—in what, over a month?" She sipped her beer, but her steady gaze made her point.

"If you ask me," Razor said, "and I know no one did, but…If you ask me, I'd say snap out of this and go get her. You *know* you want her, Murph. So what, you've got an issue. You've finally redecorated the damn bedroom, you've rearranged every stick of furniture in the house. It looks like the new start you were after. Now, let Riley—hell, let love do its magic."

Murphy picked at the label on her bottle. She knew there wouldn't be much room left for anything like love once she leveled with Riley about all of it. But she did wonder if she'd used her memories of Bryce to avoid coming clean. *Would it be so impossible to move on if I really tried?*

"I may have made too big of a mess to overcome."

Razor and Tina leaned forward simultaneously.

"You don't know that," Razor said.

Tina knocked the tip of her bottle against the vase. "She's determined, Murphy."

Murphy looked from one to the other. "It wouldn't dishonor what Bryce and I had, would it?"

Razor squeezed Murphy's arm. "No. You've got to work on that line of thinking."

Tina had rounded the table and now hugged Murphy from behind. "You know Bryce would absolutely freak to see you this lost and confused. She'd hate to see you so alone and unhappy—especially when there's someone as sweet and sincere as Riley Burke out there waiting for you."

Murphy eyed each of them and nodded. "Riley makes me happy, makes me feel again. She's…I don't want to let her go, but, Jesus, just because I can't—"

"Hey. Work through it together. Sure looks like she's willing." Razor finished her beer and leaned close. "Most of all, remember her name is Riley, next time she blows your mind." She grinned. "And I recommend lots and lots of practice."

CHAPTER THIRTY-SEVEN

Riley's workday felt twice as long with the headache that had arrived by late afternoon. Repairing the steps at Patty Cakes in the dark—and the rain—capped off a grueling string of small jobs that stole too much of her concentration from a subject that meant far more to her than money. Tylenol she'd found in her console hadn't touched the throbbing at her temples, and she conceded that the pizza on the passenger seat wasn't about to help, either. It simply reminded her of the late hour and to never be a pizza shop's last customer of the night. Soaked through to her work boots, she grumbled as she headed home in the unrelenting downpour.

"Damn mess is still there," she said, anticipating the disarray that awaited her in the loft. "And I think I can handle a whole house?"

Sure would be nice to come home to you, Murphy Callahan. Did the flowers upset you? Did I overstep again and piss you off?

"Hey, Sable. What should I do?" She reconsidered the idea of aligning Sable to her cause. "She understands." She turned on the radio, and *Nightlight* came through clearly. *Can't ask for a much stronger signal, with the studio just around the corner.* "Nice meeting you, Sable. I'm RB."

Without a second thought, she curled the Jeep off of Bradford Street and down the tiny cross street beside the WCCD building. Razor would let her in, she was sure. Even if there wasn't time to meet Sable and chat about their mutual friend, Razor might offer some insight about how best to approach Murphy.

But the Jeep's headlights sent enough indirect light through the chain link fence ahead for Riley to see the two vehicles parked behind the studio. She stopped abruptly. She hadn't expected to spot the yellow Beetle.

Her windshield wipers cleared her vision, but the image didn't change. It was *very* clear. She set the brake and stepped mindlessly out into the rain. From the fence, she could make out the "Engineers are not of sound mind" bumper sticker on the Subaru. She knew who owned the car beside it. Riley gripped the cold, wet steel links as if to prove the setting was real.

"Well, I'll be dammed."

Stunned, she backed away and returned to the Jeep. Sable's voice reached her even before she opened the door, and when Riley settled behind the wheel, that soothing seductive sound enveloped her completely. She stared at the radio and then at the building.

"I've been so blind." She crept past in first gear, dazed, her headache overwhelmed by an unrelenting assault of recollections and equations that battled to make sense.

On autopilot, she rounded the block and drove home. The chaos of her loft didn't exist as she shoved papers off the coffee table and made room for the pizza, and then peeled off her wet clothes. Her mind had gone blank, like the emergency shutdown of a nuke plant, a self-preservation tactic, threatened by an overload of too much to process.

She leaned on both palms beneath a steaming shower, desperately in need of clarity. *It helped this morning.* But back in boxers and undershirt, seated on her futon, she found herself still hopelessly adrift. The pizza box challenged her self-control. The aroma teased her senses, and her empty stomach rolled loudly, pleading its case.

She saw only Murphy's welcoming face, heard only Sable's voice.

She flopped back onto the mattress and stared at the ceiling.

"Shit."

The recollections and incomplete equations returned full strength and raced through her mind, whipping her headache into a blinding migraine. She folded her arms across her face.

Friends with Sable. Right. Friends, my ass. All this time, and you couldn't tell me? Me?

"How could I *not* have seen it, Murphy?" She dropped her arms to her sides and spoke toward the ceiling. "It all makes sense and I was too...too stupid to put two and two together."

Too busy falling in love.

She saw the pieces—and there were many—fall into place like dominoes, toppling forward and leaving...what in their wake? The beach house addition, the overnight work schedule, the abrupt end to their dinner date...steak tip salad, the Cape Cod antique table, chainsaws...the "I know" about chicken parmesan, the dance that ends too soon...

"No!" She lunged off the futon to pace. "You had to be anonymous even to me? And let me make a fool of myself with all I said about Sable?" Stricken by another thought, she squared off with her own frustrated, confused expression in the black, rain-spattered window. "When did you know? I gave you my initials, Jesus, when was that?"

She rifled a hand through her hair. "God damn it. Have you been playing with me all this time? Those special conversations we had. Were they just part of Sable's act?"

She stalked around the room. "Did you and Razor get a kick out it? Stringing me along?" She stopped at the trash bin. "And at your house? Was *that* all entertainment, too?" She kicked the bin across the room and rubbish flew everywhere. "Fuck!"

She eyed her keys on the coffee table and considered getting dressed and just driving anywhere all night. The disastrous loft crowded her, stuffed her with anxiety and anger she needed to vent.

But it was just as miserable outside as in, and she dropped onto the futon, defeated.

"Jesus Christ." She buried her face in her hands. "Were you going to tell me?" *Easier to kick me to the curb, wasn't it?*

Their last tender moment sprang to mind, and she heard Bryce's name ring through Murphy's kitchen. Riley still reveled in the feel of her, the taste of her as she climaxed, as euphoria overtook her physically and mentally—and *that* name emerged. Riley firmly believed Murphy's attachment to Bryce was genuine. *She couldn't have just played it that way to break us up. She wouldn't have.*

"It saved you from having to confess about this...this charade, though. Didn't it?"

Was it all just too much for you to handle, Murphy? I certainly can see where it would be, but I'm not some dupe who falls for superficial women, and I just know the real you is in there. And I want her. Give us a chance, damn it. No more hiding behind masks, not Sable's, not Bryce's. I don't know how to go about it, and maybe flowers weren't the smartest idea, but I'm not giving up.

"God, Murphy. We've been talking for months. It didn't have to go like this."

❖

The prospect of being talkative for one more hour practically sent Murphy to the ladies' room to throw up. Even Razor was losing patience with her. Riley hadn't returned Murphy's calls or called in to chat with Sable, and this show had become a tedious chore.

Razor rapped a backhand on the memo on the wall as she returned to her booth.

"Yes. The fundraiser is Saturday," Murphy said. "I saw it." A numbness crept over her and she decided it was for the best.

"The betting game at the A House folded, you know."

"Good."

"One call in three weeks, Murph."

"I'm aware." She put the log book away and returned to her seat.

"When did you leave the second message?"

"Saturday."

"Did you say something other than 'I'd like to talk'?"

"This time, yes." Draping the headset around her neck, Murphy glanced at the dark call buttons on her monitor.

"Well?"

"Well, what?"

"Jesus. You better get the lead out of your head in the next thirty seconds, girlie. What the hell did you say?"

"I asked for forgiveness, okay?"

"Hm. Did you say you have stuff to tell her?"

Murphy sighed. "I implied that, yes."

"Implied?"

"Not now, please."

Razor grumbled as she settled her headset in place. "Fine. We're back in ten."

Murphy stole a sip of coffee. Riley now had taken up residence in her head, as well as her heart, but she couldn't afford to attend to her right now. She was exhausted from nights of interrupted sleep and throwing herself into projects at home, not to mention the preparation involved for Saturday night's live broadcast at the Pied. She urgently needed elbow room to maintain the personality listeners expected, to get through yet one more show with a semblance of concentration.

"I'll get you another cup," Razor said in Murphy's ear. "Pep it up, okay? And you're live in three, two, one…"

"Welcome back to our final hour. We've had some rousing contributions tonight. 'How did you know?' has turned out to be quite the popular topic." A call button lit up on her monitor and momentarily distracted her. "We, ah..." *Cripes. It won't be her.* "Let's see. So far, I'd say Chef-tell's was the hottest, wouldn't you agree? Kind of hard to ignore the signals when your best friend puts a ring on your finger in the shower." She nodded a thank-you to Razor for delivering a fresh cup of coffee. "And we're far from done. So let's keep it rolling." She clicked on the first button. "Hi there. This is Sable and you're on *Nightlight.*" She sat back and cradled the cup in both hands.

"Hi, Sable. This is...um...I've never called before, so I'm kind of nervous."

"Not a thing to be nervous about. Relax. You don't have to give a name, if you'd rather not. *Nightlight*'s happy you called. What's on your mind?"

"Well, my wife and I had been friends for years, helping each other through dyke drama, you know?"

"Oh, believe me. I know."

"So, one day, she started telling me how much she loved this new book she'd found, and that I *had* to read it. Of course I was intrigued, especially when she said I reminded her of one of the main characters. She blushed to high heaven."

"I gather she was referring to a love interest in the book."

"Ohhhhhh, yeah. A hot one. Neither of the main characters had been in a serious relationship before, and neither had we. Needless to say, I got the message."

Murphy grinned. "You said your *wife* gave you this book?" She tensed when Razor's instant message appeared on the monitor.
Holding on line two.

Murphy watched the button blink. She sipped her coffee and the cup vibrated against her mouth. She set it down quickly.

The caller chuckled. "Uh-huh. I got the message *and* the girl. Twenty-seven years now."

"Gotta love a happy ending. Smart women, you two." She exhaled away from the mike, relieved her mind hadn't disengaged.

"Always make time for a good book," the caller said with a laugh. "That's my motto."

"Great advice. Thank you for calling and don't be a stranger."

"Thanks, Sable."

Now, Murphy prayed for strength and composure. She opened the second line and tried, unsuccessfully, to will herself to relax. "Welcome to *Nightlight*. This is Sable and you're on the air."

"Hello, Sable."

"Arby?" She swallowed hard. "We've missed your contributions lately. Good to hear your voice." *Dear God, yes.*

"Well, thank you. I enjoy yours, too, Sable, even more so on the phone than over the radio."

Same here.

"Careful, Arby. You'll have me blushing. Do you have a 'How did I know' story?" Her lips brushed the tip of the mike. *Can't get any closer.* She forced herself to back off, lean into her chair.

"I do, although I haven't been seeing this lady for long. We met last winter and finally connected several months later." *You're telling our story, Riley?* She took a long, quiet breath and glanced at Razor. She received a thumbs-up but it didn't instill much strength. "Sounds premature, I suppose," Riley went on, "but...when it's right, you know it."

This is where I'm expected to speak, to agree.

"So they say."

How lame.

"I guess I knew right from the start, I mean, when we finally spent some time together. She told me about the passing of her partner and it embarrassed her to do that, I think. She apologized, but what struck me was how she reacted to everything. She felt she could speak about very personal memories in that beautiful sunset, shared them with me, and even appreciated *my* feelings as she reminisced. I was taken by that. Through all that difficult emotion, she thought of me. I realized just how big a heart she has. I did a lot of soul searching that night. That's how I knew."

Murphy gripped the arms of her chair and fought the constricting of her throat. She couldn't hold back a sob and speak at the same time. When Riley continued, Murphy muffled a whimper with a tissue at her mouth.

"I guess I could have chosen the first time I felt those incredible eyes take hold of me. Or her kiss, when it first took my breath away. The touch of her mouth was...magical. But, really, it was that sunset on her deck. Not that her look, her kiss don't absolutely melt me into my shoes. Holy crap." She chuckled. Murphy pressed the tissue to her eyelids. "But that night, I think she shared a piece of her soul with me. And that meant so much. It always will."

"She—she's very lucky to have someone like you in her life... Arby."

"Well, she's having some trouble finding room in that heart of hers—I understand, though. No one comes away from a deep loss unscathed, but you can't hide from it, either. I'm just hoping that, with time, she'll see what I see in her and let me in."

Hide from it? She looked at Razor and Razor pointed directly at her. Murphy turned back to the mike.

"Y-you're a good person, Arby."

"I hope she's listening."

"I'm sure she is." She bit her lip and toyed with the tissue.

"Thank you for hearing me out."

"Any time, Arby. I'm very glad you called."

"Good-bye, Sable."

The light went out on Murphy's monitor and Razor started the promotional piece for the Pied fundraiser. Murphy dropped her head onto her arms and cried.

Razor arrived at her side and put an arm around her shoulders.

"One step at a time," she whispered. "You'll come out of this. You both will. Together. That woman's in love with you."

"Nothing ever sounded so final, Razor." She sniffed against her arm and lifted her head.

"Murph, you heard her. She's giving you time. However you sounded in those messages must've told her you need more."

"But...I want to try."

"Did you say that?"

Murphy held the tissue to her nose and shook her head. "Not exactly."

"Why? Because you're still not sure?"

"I-I don't know."

Razor squeezed her shoulders. "Then she's right. You *do* need more time."

"Do you think I'm hiding?"

Razor shrugged. "Subconsciously, maybe, yeah, but I can't say if you're hiding Sable behind Bryce or the other way around. Only you can figure that out."

CHAPTER THIRTY-EIGHT

Winded, Razor returned to the DJ booth high above the Pied Bar dance floor. She swirled her cape around her body and threw herself into Murphy's chair, then removed her Darth Vader helmet and fluffed up her red and gold hair.

"How many more raffles? I'm exhausted."

"Two more, I think." Murphy scanned the items on the table nearby. "The Lobster Pot gift certificate and the nipple clamps." She shivered and tugged the sides of her dress closer across her chest, but nothing was going to minimize the chill or the view she provided the crowd below. "I have to open this door for a while," she said, and propped open the back door to the exterior staircase. "If we can't cut the AC, I'll end up poking right through this dress."

Razor laughed. "The mask is very Elizabethan, Murph, and the blond wig is definitely slutty, but that dress..." She shook her head. "Mother of God, you're hot." She ran an appraisal down the deep V-opening that presented most of Murphy's breasts, and then down her hip and the long stroke of bare leg to her stilettos. "Wow."

"Stop. I'm already shivering. That ice-cold breeze through the vent—"

"Colder than a—"

"Yeah." Murphy laughed, grateful for the humor. "Now I know the meaning of the phrase." She lifted her black cape off a chair and debated covering up. The tall collar would keep the draft off the back of her neck, but the red satin lining wouldn't help the rest of her much.

"Don't even think about it. You'll start a flipping riot. From down there, they can only see you from the knees up, but it's a scrumptious view. Just one cue from you, Ms. Vampira, and they'll volunteer to be sucked dry."

"God, Razor. You're bad." She absently pinched the slit at her thigh closed. "They got their look when we waltzed in. That's enough."

The bar had only been half-full when they arrived hours earlier—and she'd never been more thankful for a full costume in her life. She'd followed Darth Vader across the dance floor, gliding regally, silently, and offered suggestive grins and eye contact over her high collar. Tina had outdone herself, having drawn Murphy's eyes into heavily shadowed, ebony pools. She'd accented Murphy's mouth until the scarlet lips simply beckoned—until Murphy smiled and her blood-sucking incisors stole center stage.

The rock star treatment had been a rush, and she had to admit she enjoyed the role play. Being able to focus on nothing but that moment had been a welcome relief, and knowing that her identity had been thoroughly concealed, she'd allowed herself some raucous teasing. When she reached the interior stairway to the booth, she took two delicate steps up, turned to the crowd, and whisked off her cape to roaring applause.

Long white-blond hair, severely pulled back and gathered behind her head, flowed over her left shoulder and created a stunning, bright slash against her dress, and black satin evening gloves matched the eerie mask that hid all but her mouth and chin. The rest of her, she displayed shamelessly, especially when she turned her back to the room and climbed the stairs in the tight sheath with its revealing slit.

Murphy surveyed the crowd through the glass and waved to the many women who shouted her name over the driving music. "It's like a feeding frenzy down there."

"Yeah, no kidding." Razor pushed herself up. "The only reason I'm doing the stairs again right now is alcohol."

"Bring me back something. We've got"—she checked the LED numbers on the play-back deck—"four minutes after this segue. And then there are two calls in queue."

Razor read the numbers over her shoulder. "We should take that first one. She's been holding the longest. The second one just popped in before I ran downstairs with that last prize."

"Got it. Go. Hurry. Something cold and big!" she yelled, as the world's skinniest Darth Vader swept down the stairs.

As required, Murphy stood at the glass, posing with arms crossed, looking foreboding and hungry as any good vampire should. She pointed at specific women, sent provocative waves, and grinned with satisfaction when they turned to each other, excited to have caught the bewitching Sable's eye. *Talk about leaving reality behind.*

She snickered at herself and continued perusing the crowd through the flashing, multi-colored lights. Every costume imaginable had turned out, it seemed. She rolled her fingers in greeting to Trish from Patty Cakes, when she realized she was the firefighter in full turn-out gear, and then to Maria from the Portuguese Bakery, a risqué angel in nothing but white lace. A well-equipped dominatrix prowled the packed room, blatantly assessing a cowgirl, a leather-clad biker, and a trio of zombies.

A tall, slim woman in US Marine Corps dress blues waved up at her and Murphy cocked her head suggestively, before recognizing developer Chris Ross. *Jesus, thank God for costumes.* Her leisurely look through the crowd grew more intent, and she found herself searching for the one handsome face that mattered most.

Even if you didn't have that party with your old friends tonight, I doubt you'd be here. Not with all the thinking you've been doing. She dared herself to believe Riley wasn't interested in mingling with women, that *she* was the only one on her mind. *How she loves to dance...*

"No." She sighed and turned to the array of equipment, cords, and lights on the table beside her.

"No what?" Razor handed her a flute of something blood-red.

"Nothing." She looked at the drink. "I needed big, Razor."

"Oh, it's bigger than it looks. Trust me. It's pure vodka—and I had them color it appropriately." She grinned. "Ms. Vampira gets her fix in style tonight."

"God help me." She sipped the drink and battled a grimace to raise the glass to the crowd, which cheered at the sight of Sable joining the effort. "Let's take this call now."

Razor was speaking to the caller already, as music came to a close simultaneously on the dance floor and over the air. Murphy settled the wireless headset on her head and returned to the window and the crowd.

"You're live in three, two, one..."

"Hello." Murphy's deep croon oozed through the room. "Welcome to *Nightlight*. This is Sable." As it did every time she introduced herself, the dance floor erupted with cheers and whistles. "We're partying for a good cause at the Pied Bar tonight, raising money for P-town's own

Help Our Women. In keeping with this year's Carnival theme, 'Give it all you've got,' we're taking donations as well as stories of perseverance and triumph. Care to share?"

"We're celebrating a victory in my discrimination case against my ex-boss," the caller said, and the crowd applauded.

"Well, congratulations. A long time coming, I gather?"

"Yeah, eight months."

"Sounds like you gave it all you had."

"No way was I letting him off the hook. I'm mailing HOW a contribution of two hundred dollars tomorrow morning because we settled out of court for big money, all my back pay, and legal expenses, too." Women cheered.

"Thank you, caller! You're a saint. And we'll be right over to party at your house!" The crowd yelled its agreement.

The caller laughed. "You bet, Sable. Party on!"

"Thanks so much for the call and the very generous donation. And congratulations again." She nodded to Razor and the next line opened. "Good evening and welcome to the party. This is Sable and you're on *Nightlight*." The throng below cheered again.

"Hi, Sable. It's Digger."

"Digger, hi."

The crowd yelled "Dig-ger, Dig-ger," and Murphy and Razor grinned at the audience recognition.

"Can't make it to the party and I am *so* bummed, I can't stand it."

"Aw, so am I, Dig."

"But listen, I just had to call and say you're sounding extra seductive tonight."

"Ooo. I appreciate that, especially from you. Thank you. Being surrounded by a swarm of hot lesbians must bring out the vamp in me." The crowd hooted and whistled. Murphy winked at a particularly attractive ballerina, and the woman's date slid a possessive arm around her.

God, I'm getting too into this.

"Sure wish I was there, Sable. Sounds like a wild time."

"That it is, Dig, but you're here in spirit and I'm glad. Wouldn't have been the same without your voice." *Seriously, whose voice?*

"Thanks, Sable. Have a great night, everybody!"

The crowd yelled Digger's name again as Murphy disconnected.

She raised her glass to the window and spoke through her headset mike to the dance floor. "It's raffle time, so fish around in somebody's favorite pocket and find that ticket." Razor joined her at the window and they watched the women laugh and squirm, reaching into the pockets of others. "The Lobster Pot's legendary food, people! You *know* you want it!" She held the gift certificate against the glass.

A Xena warrior yelled up from the crowd. "Bend over more so we can see it!" Women began chanting Sable's name.

"My pleasure." Murphy offered a teasing smile. She bent as far forward as she could, pressing the envelope to her breasts for safe keeping, and the crowd roared its appreciation. Murphy straightened and fanned her chest with the envelope.

Razor whispered from behind her Darth mask. "Maybe we should take this act on the road. You're surprisingly comfortable in front of a live audience."

Murphy put fingertips over her mouthpiece. "Remember the old days, Razor? There wasn't anything we wouldn't do on stage. It's a little different today."

"A little, yeah." She turned away and lifted her mask to take a long swig of Heineken. "Hey, the bartender said they collected a ton of money tonight. They're really happy with the turnout."

"Did we push the fire law limit?"

"Probably, but it doesn't look like that out there now. A lot have left already. We've only got another thirty minutes left."

Murphy scanned the crowd again. Seventy, maybe eighty women, she guessed. *Easier to see that she's not here.* She took a steadying breath.

"Okay! Everybody out there ready?" The crowd shouted back. Razor held up the glass fish bowl and Murphy plucked out a ticket. "The winning number is—zero, six, two, six, five, three!"

Somewhere a woman shrieked and everyone laughed.

"There," Murphy said with a tip of her head toward the rear of the room. "The cowgirl next to Trish, the firefighter." Razor grabbed the gift certificate and raced down the stairs. "Coming at you, hon!" Murphy said. The women made way for Darth and clapped as the prize was awarded. Razor looked up at Murphy and signaled her with a nod.

"Enough of this standing around, now. Let's dance!" Murphy sidestepped to the table and hit Razor's pre-set button. Music boomed into the room and the crowd came alive.

CHAPTER THIRTY-NINE

Digger nailed it, Riley thought. *Sable's more seductive than ever tonight.* But then, maybe the voice only seemed different because they'd spoken so seldom lately. She hadn't called regularly in a long time, and Tuesday night's call had been an impulse she couldn't resist... when she told Murphy—through Sable—how she felt about her.

"I don't regret that, Murphy, and I meant every freakin' word, but damn, it's still so easy to be mad at you." Riley ran a hand through her blowing hair as she drove along the empty road to Provincetown. "But I can't be mad. I don't want to be. Frustrated, yes." She pounded the steering wheel. "What I wouldn't give for you to make a stand."

She'd listened to Murphy's voice mail messages until she knew every pause, every breath recorded, and then listened some more, every chance she had, believing there was more to be heard that wasn't spoken. *I know you wrestle with the past. And I also know you wrestle with this stupid deception. You want out from under the pressure. I can hear it in your voice. Is that all you want?*

"It's not in your radio voice, Murphy. You're managing to cover it up so well, especially tonight." She envisioned the wild crowd she could hear rumbling in the background whenever Sable opened the line. "Jesus, you can't show Sable to *me*. You must be wearing one hell of a costume to come out in public." She tossed her head back and growled at the night sky. "You've put on quite a show for me, though, hiding with *no* costume."

She crossed the town line on Route 6 and vacantly focused on the asphalt that led through the dunes. She knew the solitary road like the back of her hand, knew that it soon would end, with no optional destination. *The end of the line...or the beginning, depending on how you look at it.*

The dance music on the radio ended and *that* voice seized her.

"Raffle time, people! Our last one of the night! We thank Toys of Eros for these beauties. They're a hot little number, stainless steel nipple clamps. Let's find the wild woman winner. Search those pockets and get your tickets ready!" As Riley downshifted and turned off the highway, a voice in the Pied crowd yelled something unintelligible. *"No,"* Sable said. *"Sable's not demonstrating. And neither are any of you! Not here, at least. Of course, I strongly endorse their private use."*

Riley heard the crowd cheer as she drove along the shore. "If I ever showed up with those, you'd turn every shade of red, Ms. Callahan. You're not fooling me. Not about nipple clamps, anyway." She turned the volume up to hear the crowd comments, but had little luck. "Maybe I *should* surprise you with them. Catching you off guard might just shake things up."

Riley arrived at the fork in the road and faced going home on Bradford Street, or into town on Commercial. Without thought, she found herself cruising slowly down Commercial, hardly conscious of driving. More like the damn Jeep is taking *me*, she thought.

Stop kidding yourself. You know exactly where you're going.

She rolled beyond the center of town and into an alley she often used when working at night. Music from the Pied pulsed down its boardwalk alley and out to the street, accompanied by a rousing cheer. Riley figured the nipple clamps had found a new home.

Two couples approached on the boardwalk as she started down, and one woman hailed her.

"Burke, you lazy dog! No costume?"

"Hey, Trish." Riley stopped and they shared a hug. "I just got back to town."

"Well, here." She plunked her firefighter's helmet onto Riley's head, and shook off the matching coat. "Put this on. It'll look better on you than me, for sure."

"Thanks, but, I don't—"

"Sure you want to. You can drop them at the bakery during the week. Now you're prepared for something hot in there to catch fire, huh?" Riley just shook her head. "You called it close, you know. You couldn't be much later."

"No kidding. But I had to catch a look at Sable."

All four women spoke at once.

"Jesus, she's a goddess," Trish said with a laugh. "Any time, any place, you know what I'm saying?" Her date punched her shoulder playfully. "Go! Get in there. You'll see." She slapped her arm. "Enjoy!"

Riley stopped to pay the cover charge but the young woman she knew at the door made a face.

"It's late, Riley. Forget it."

"No," she said, and pulled money from her wallet. "Take this as my donation. It's a fundraiser, after all."

"Gee, thanks. Here, take your ticket 'cause there's still time for a free beer."

Riley stepped into a wall of sound, refrigerated air, and some fifty women, all dancing. *Everyone came to see you, Sable, and now it's my turn.* She edged around them to the bar and redeemed her ticket.

The cold brew was a refreshing relief, and she admired the gyrations and innovative dance moves in the crowd. But she couldn't see the DJ booth from her vantage point, so she made her way to the opposite side of the room.

Settled against the wall, she looked up.

A striking blond vampire laughed freely with Darth Vader behind the glass. Her fangs gleamed between fiery red lips, and the mask shielding most of her face only enhanced the mystery of her black eyes. They were almost as hypnotic as her mouth-watering cleavage, as tantalizing as those full, luscious breasts—all of which Riley knew so very well. Memory conjured urgent need and desire, and Riley's fingers moved restlessly.

She took a deep, slow breath, and remembered she held a beer. She straightened off the wall and downed a serious mouthful. The vampire moved gracefully, confidently, as she busied herself with paperwork and her mouthpiece, all while bobbing to the music. Her body shimmered in a skintight dress that offered her toned, creamy thigh for everyone's viewing pleasure.

Riley removed her helmet and finger-combed her hair. "Jesus, Murphy." She wiggled the helmet back onto her head and slumped against the wall. *Give me strength.*

CHAPTER FORTY

"Last call for alcohol!" Murphy clicked off her mouthpiece and downed half a bottle of water. "If I don't get out of this costume soon, I'm going to jump through the glass, I swear."

"No shit." Razor knocked on her helmet. "This thing is like an oven." She reviewed their status on the monitor. "We'll take this last call up here, keep the music out on the floor, and then close with two tunes. Hang in there." Razor leaned away to speak to the caller on hold. Murphy collected their papers, glasses, and cups, and dragged their equipment cases to the center of the room while she awaited Razor's signal.

What a night. I can't blame her for not showing. Not sure I would have shown, either. Something else to keep me awake all night. Maybe one more message tomorrow.

"Ready?"

"Yeah." Murphy positioned her headset and mouthpiece and pulled up a chair. She sighed as Razor counted down, glad to be off her aching feet.

"Hello and welcome to *Nightlight*. This is Sable and you're on the air."

"Hey, Sable. My name's Sasha and I'm just calling to give a shout-out to my wife. Since you and the Pied are doing this fundraiser for HOW, I figured it was appropriate. See, my wife's a survivor and she made it through a horrible past with the help of HOW's fine, fine people."

"Glad you called, Sasha. Yes, HOW's a great organization and never gets enough credit. We and all of WCCD are proud to help such a worthy cause."

"My wife had two little girls when we met and, well, if it wasn't for HOW, we probably wouldn't all be happy and healthy today. Those people, they give it everything they've got, you know what I mean? I know my sweetheart's grateful, but I am, too. And, well, that's all I wanted to say."

"No doubt you and your sweetheart have given everything you've got, too, and I'm so happy you called and shared that. Your story was perfect for tonight, Sasha. You're part of the *Nightlight* family now, so please do call again, any time."

Murphy saw the light go out and wished she had the guts those women displayed, the drive to give it all she's got. *My past can't compare to theirs, but moving forward with life certainly does. How many callers tonight spoke of having what it takes and giving it all? What's the matter with me?*

She stared blankly at the monitor, searching her mind for an answer, and another call lit up.

Razor blew out a breath. "All right. *One* more?" Murphy nodded and cleared her throat.

Razor greeted the caller, but looked back as she spoke to her. "Okay, but please turn the background down, all right?"

Just the expression on Razor's face told Murphy who was on the line. Her blood pressure soared and her hands trembled. *Here it is. Time to give it my best shot.*

"Put her through, Razor."

"Murphy. You sure you can do this?"

"I'm going to do my best."

"If you fall apart, she'll realize you know her. Everything will come tumbling out, Murph."

Murphy nodded and fussed with her mouthpiece. "I can do this." *I better.*

Razor mumbled a skeptical "okay" and counted down.

"Welcome to *Nightlight*. This is Sable. Thanks for joining us tonight."

"Hi, Sable. I appreciate you taking my call. I know…I know I'm probably your last one."

"Hello. Arby? It's hard to hear you. You're correct, but…I-I was hoping you'd join us tonight." *Sounds like you're at a bar. That's where you've been all night?*

"Somehow, you manage to come up with subjects for your shows that I can't resist."

"We love hearing that, but credit for tonight's topic goes to the

Carnival committee. What's on your mind?" She lowered her face into her hand. *Cripes, what a question.*

"The Carnival theme is great this year and...I was thinking about it tonight while I was driving, coming home from the city. Coming here, where I've worked hard to build my business and hopefully, a home." Murphy frowned as she struggled to hear. "I've given everything I've got to have the life I've always wanted, and I suppose, I'm satisfied, but then I wonder if I've given enough."

Murphy started pacing. The background noise was so loud, it made deciphering Riley's words extremely difficult, but what she could gather had her near tears. She wasn't sure she'd make it through this conversation, after all. The angst in her system threatened to suffocate her. She inhaled and exhaled deeply, silently.

"Not given enough?" She wandered to the glass. Several dozen women danced joyfully to the night's final song. She labored to keep her voice from quaking. "What makes you say that, Arby?"

Razor produced a tissue box and Murphy hurriedly pulled one out. Dabbing her tears through the holes in her mask maddened her. *Concentrate. Don't miss a single word.*

"Because I haven't given it all I've got."

"I'm sorry, Arby. I didn't catch what you said. Could you repeat that please?"

"I said it feels like I haven't tried hard enough."

Oh, Riley, you have tried.

"I d-doubt that, Arby. You're a sincere, generous person. You deserve the best for all you do."

A squeal of radio interference pierced Murphy and Razor's ears, and Murphy squinted. *Wherever she is, that damn bar has us on the radio!*

"Tonight, I decided happiness has been missing and I'm going after it, no matter what."

Murphy fought for composure and a tear slid down behind her mask. "You've what?" She pressed an earpiece tighter to her head. "What does that mean?"

"It means there's a difference between being satisfied and being happy, Sable." Murphy's heart sprang into her throat as their weighty, metaphoric conversation about boats came to mind. *I want to make you happy.* "So," Riley added, "I'm going after it because...because happiness is having the lady I love in my life."

Oh, my God, Riley. She gulped a breath and more tears escaped.

"Does sh-she—" The last song of the night ended and the broadcast automatically went out to the dance floor. "Does she know this?"

Women shouted their thanks up to her, filled the room with boisterous applause for the evening's entertainment, and compounded the noise Murphy fought hard to ignore. And signal interference again squealed in her ear.

"Arby? We've got a feedback issue over the air. It's hard to hear you." *I can't lose you now.*

She flashed a pleading a glance at Razor, and returned to struggling with her focus. As desperate as she was to hear Riley more clearly, she *had* to respond to the grateful audience now clustered below. Xena thrust her sword upward; the ballerina curtseyed. Women jockeyed closer for a better view as they cheered for Sable.

"Happiness is having the lady I love in my life."

Numb, Murphy went through the motions, waved, forced a smile, and made fleeting eye contact, but hardly *saw* anyone as she struggled to multi-task.

She grew frantic as her heart slammed against her chest. Riley's declaration echoed in her head, shortened her breath. *"...the lady I love..."* Still live on the air, Murphy had a show to close, and needed to acknowledge the appreciative women remaining on the dance floor.

She looked down, registered the faithful followers who remained, the firefighter in her helmet and coat—Trish, she remembered, and the bedraggled zombie trio. Xena bowed graciously to her.

The damn transmission interference again whined in her headset, threatened to crush her.

Determined to hear through it, Murphy refused to let her question go unanswered. Several women hooted up at her and flashed their breasts. Murphy tried to sharpen her concentration with a slow blink.

"Arby, does...does your lady know how you feel?" The firefighter squeezed between two women directly below her. "Arby, *please* turn that ra—"

The *blond* firefighter. Now, with helmet in hand. And a phone to her ear. She smiled up at Murphy.

"Yes, *Sable*. She knows now."

CHAPTER FORTY-ONE

Murphy couldn't speak. Nothing worked. Mouth, throat, lungs, brain, all failed her at once. She knew her heart hadn't, though, because it was trying to reach Riley through every pore in her body. She placed her palm on the glass, yearning for contact. *I need to be with you.*

Razor looked up from the soundboard, waiting for Sable to fill the silent airwaves with *something*. Anything. She strode to her side and took her arm, then followed Murphy's line of vision to the dance floor.

Peripherally, Murphy saw her inhale, and some innate charge in Murphy's head switched reality back on.

"Yes, Arby," she said into her mouthpiece. "She knows now." She couldn't—wouldn't pull her eyes from Riley's.

"Thank you, Sable."

"*I* should be thanking *you*."

A crowd of women now hovered around Riley. They looked from her to Sable and back, jibing each other as they followed the scratchy exchange over the dance floor's sound system.

Razor handed her a scribbled note, reminding her she was still on the air.

Riley watched, unmoving. "You're someone very special, you know."

Murphy blinked back tears. "Careful. You'll get me all f-flustered on the air." She covered her face with both hands, but not before she saw Riley smile.

"I know the feeling, Sable, so, I'm going to go now."

Murphy quickly put both hands on the glass. "Thank you for calling, Arby. You've capped off this terrific night in the m-most beautiful way."

"Good night, Sable."

"Good night and...stay close."

Riley lowered the phone. Around her, women rooted her on, and Murphy shook her head lightly at the idea of Riley needing anyone's encouragement. She heard the line disconnect.

Razor poked her arm, made a slicing motion across her throat, and Murphy knew she had to return to the present.

"Well. This—This has been one hell of night, here at the Pied with *Nightlight*'s first-ever live broadcast." Quietly, she forced an inhale and exhaled with restraint. "It's been a blast and a huge success for P-town's Help Our Women. Keep an ear open for the final donations tally. *Nightlight* will get that info to you as soon as we know it. Thank you all for coming, for listening, for calling to participate, and for donating to one of the most vital organizations in town. This is Sable signing off until we turn our *Nightlight* on again, Monday night. Remember: stay close."

The crowd around Riley dissipated, and somewhere, in the back of her mind, Murphy was cognizant of the airwaves closing, but she couldn't look away.

"Razor, a pen, please. Hurry."

She scratched "back stairs" in large letters on the other side of Razor's note and slapped it against the window.

Riley grinned, put the firefighter's helmet on, and left the dance floor.

❖

Murphy stared down at the empty room and half-heard Razor moving around her, unplugging cords and packing their gear. She should be helping but couldn't move her feet.

"I-I can't believe this."

Razor stopped and chuckled.

"Well, it's one way to settle everything. She figured it out, Murph."

"She loves me." She touched the glass timidly.

Razor appeared at her side and tapped Murphy's temple.

"Ding! Did the light come on?"

"Yeah," she said, her voice distant. "I think it's getting brighter by the minute."

"Good. Then you'll be a matching set."

"Oh, but after all I've done, Razor? She *loves* me?"

Razor whispered at her shoulder. "Makeup sex is going to cripple you."

Murphy spun and slapped her arm.

"I'm going to be apologizing till Christmas."

"Ah-huh." Razor lifted the headset off Murphy's head. "As you should. Just think of all the time you'll spend looking into that face, submitting—"

"Shush!" She gave her a shove. "I need to get outside." She hurried toward the back door. "Forgive me for not helping you?"

"I got this. Go."

Murphy swung the door all the way open and stepped out onto the second floor landing. Night air washed over her, far warmer than the booth's air conditioning, and salty, right off the ocean from some one hundred feet away. She gripped the railing and inhaled as deeply as she could.

This is what I dreamt of, hoped for, had practically given up on. Where do I start?

She yanked the mask off and wondered what her face looked like, if crying through pounds of eyeliner and mascara had given her a zebra face. She ran inside and ran back out with the box of tissues, already scrubbing her cheeks.

"Murphy." Riley stood at the bottom of the stairs, hand on the rail, looking up from beneath the broad brim of the helmet. "Blonde looks *very* good on you."

"Riley." Tears started again and she blotted them away. "You… you make an awfully sexy firefighter."

"And you're the fire I never want to put out." She started up the stairs, and Murphy's breathing grew shorter with each step. "God, you're stunning, Murphy, even with all the makeup."

"I'm so sorry, Riley. You have no idea how sorry." *So hard to face you.*

Riley draped her coat over the railing and set the helmet on it. She took the tissue box from Murphy and balanced that on the railing, too, then lifted Murphy's chin with a finger.

"Look at me, Ms. Callahan."

Murphy clenched her stomach, trembled, holding back an emotional outburst. She knew Riley could feel it in just her simple touch.

"Everything snowballed, Riley. I never meant to—"

Riley shook her head. She picked the tissue out of Murphy's hand and wiped away the remnants of tears.

"Later," she said, her voice hushed. "Tell me later. Right now, I just need to look at you."

Murphy snickered at herself. "Please. I'm a total mess."

"Shh. You're spectacular, Murphy. This outfit…You take my breath away."

Murphy shivered as Riley's fingertips grazed down into her cleavage and traced the swell of her breasts. She wanted that touch, to feel Riley's hands fan beneath the vee of her dress, curl around her breasts, and possess them. Possess *her*.

She combed Riley's mussed hair back into place with her fingers.

"I don't ever want to take anything away from you. Well, maybe a breath, now and then, but I want to *give* you everything. *Honestly*."

With an easy, perfect glide against the satin dress, Riley's arms slid around her waist. Her hold was purposeful, strong, and sure, and Murphy nearly swooned when Riley drew their hips together.

"No more masks. I want the real you. I love you, Murphy. Say we can move forward—together."

Murphy nodded and kneaded her fingers into Riley's shoulders. "Yes, Riley. I want that, too." She linked her arms around Riley's neck. "I'm so sorry it took me this long to realize just how much. I love you, too."

Riley squeezed her closer and brought her lips to Murphy's. "I *do* have one favor to ask, though."

"Oh, Riley. Name it."

"Take out your fangs."

Murphy blurted a quick, embarrassed laugh. "Oh! I can't believe I forgot." She popped each one off her teeth. "I got so used to them tonight, I—"

"Put them in my pocket," Riley whispered. "I'm going to kiss you and nothing's getting in my way."

About the Author

A recent telecommunications retiree, CF Frizzell ("friz") is the recipient of the Golden Crown Literary Society's 2015 Debut Author Award for her novel *Stick McLaughlin: The Prohibition Years*. Friz discovered her passion for writing in high school and went on to establish an award-winning twenty-two-year career in community newspapers that culminated in the role of founder/publisher. Her second novel, *Exchange*, was released in July 2016. Friz is into history, New England pro sports, and singing and acoustic guitar, and lives just an hour from Provincetown with her wife, Kathy.

Books Available From Bold Strokes Books

A Quiet Death by Cari Hunter. When the body of a young Pakistani girl is found out on the moors, the investigation leaves Detective Sanne Jensen facing an ordeal she may not survive. (978-1-62639-815-3)

Buried Heart by Laydin Michaels. When Drew Chambliss meets Cicely Jones, her buried past finds its way to the surface. Will they survive its discovery or will their chance at love turn to dust? (978-1-62639-801-6)

Escape: Exodus Book Three by Gun Brooke. Aboard the Exodus ship *Pathfinder*, President Thea Tylio still holds Caya Lindemay, a clairvoyant changer, in protective custody, which has devastating consequences endangering their relationship and the entire Exodus mission. (978-1-62639-635-7)

Genuine Gold by Ann Aptaker. New York, 1952. Outlaw Cantor Gold is thrown back into her honky-tonk Coney Island past, where crime and passion simmer in a neon glare. (978-1-62639-730-9)

Into Thin Air by Jeannie Levig. When her girlfriend disappears, Hannah Lewis discovers her world isn't as orderly as she thought it was. (978-1-62639-722-4)

Night Voice by CF Frizzell. When talk show host Sable finally acknowledges her risqué radio relationship with a mysterious caller, she welcomes a *real* relationship with local tradeswoman Riley Burke. (978-1-62639-813-9)

Raging at the Stars by Lesley Davis. When the unbelievable theories start revealing themselves as truths, can you trust in the ones who have conspired against you from the start? (978-1-62639-720-0)

She Wolf by Sheri Lewis Wohl. When the hunter becomes the hunted, more than love might be lost. (978-1-62639-741-5)

Smothered and Covered by Missouri Vaun. The last person Nash Wiley expects to bump into over a two a.m. breakfast at Waffle House is her college crush, decked out in a curve-hugging law enforcement uniform. (978-1-62639-704-0)

The Butterfly Whisperer by Lisa Moreau. Reunited after ten years, can Jordan and Sophie heal the past and rediscover love or will differing desires keep them apart? (978-1-62639-791-0)

The Devil's Due by Ali Vali. Cain and Emma Casey are awaiting the birth of their third child, but as always in Cain's world, there are new and old enemies to face in Katrina-ravaged New Orleans. (978-1-62639-591-6)

Widows of the Sun-Moon by Barbara Ann Wright. With immortality now out of their grasp, the gods of Calamity fight amongst themselves, egged on by the mad goddess they thought they'd left behind. (978-1-62639-777-4)

Arrested Hearts by Holly Stratimore. A reckless cop who hates her life and a health nut who is afraid to die might be a perfect combination for love. (978-1-62639-809-2)

Capturing Jessica by Jane Hardee. Hyperrealist sculptor Michael tries desperately to conceal the love she holds for best friend, Jess, unaware Jess's feelings for her are changing. (978-1-62639-836-8)

Counting to Zero by AJ Quinn. NSA agent Emma Thorpe and computer hacker Paxton James must learn to trust each other as they work to stop a threat clock that's rapidly counting down to zero. (978-1-62639-783-5)

Courageous Love by KC Richardson. Two women fight a devastating disease, and their own demons, while trying to fall in love. (978-1-62639-797-2)

One More Reason to Leave Orlando by Missouri Vaun. Nash Wiley thought a threesome sounded exotic and exciting, but as it turns out the reality of sleeping with two women at the same time is just really complicated. (978-1-62639-703-3)

Pathogen by Jessica L. Webb. Can Dr. Kate Morrison navigate a deadly virus and the threat of bioterrorism, as well as her new relationship with Sergeant Andy Wyles and her own troubled past? (978-1-62639-833-7)

Rainbow Gap by Lee Lynch. Jaudon Vickers and Berry Garland, polar opposites, dream and love in this tale of lesbian lives set in Central Florida against the tapestry of societal change and the Vietnam War. (978-1-62639-799-6)

Steel and Promise by Alexa Black. Lady Nivrai's cruel desires and modified body make most of the galaxy fear her, but courtesan Cailyn Derys soon discovers the real monsters are the ones without the claws. (978-1-62639-805-4)

Swelter by D. Jackson Leigh. Teal Giovanni's mistake shines an unwanted spotlight on a small Texas ranch where August Reese is secluded until she can testify against a powerful drug kingpin. (978-1-62639-795-8)

Without Justice by Carsen Taite. Cade Kelly and Emily Sinclair must battle each other in the pursuit of justice, but can they fight their undeniable attraction outside the walls of the courtroom? (978-1-62639-560-2)

21 Questions by Mason Dixon. To find love, start by asking the right questions. (978-1-62639-724-8)

A Palette for Love by Charlotte Greene. When newly minted Ph.D. Chloé Devereaux returns to New Orleans, she doesn't expect her new job and her powerful employer—Amelia Winters—to be so appealing. (978-1-62639-758-3)

By the Dark of Her Eyes by Cameron MacElvee. When Brenna Taylor inherits a decrepit property haunted by tormented ghosts, Alejandra Santana must not only restore Brenna's house and property but also save her soul. (978-1-62639-834-4)

Death by Cocktail Straw by Missouri Vaun. She just wanted to meet girls, but an outing at the local lesbian bar goes comically off the rails, landing Nash Wiley and her best pal in the ER. (978-1-62639-702-6)

Cash Braddock by Ashley Bartlett. Cash Braddock just wants to hang with her cat, fall in love, and deal drugs. What's the problem with that? (978-1-62639-706-4)

Lone Ranger by VK Powell. Reporter Emma Ferguson stirs up a thirty-year-old mystery that threatens Park Ranger Carter West's family and jeopardizes any hope for a relationship between the two women. (978-1-62639-767-5)

Never Enough by Robyn Nyx. Can two women put aside their pasts to find love before it's too late? (978-1-62639-629-6)

Love on Call by Radclyffe. Ex-Army medic Glenn Archer and recent LA transplant Mariana Mateo fight their mutual desire in the face of past losses as they work together in the Rivers Community Hospital ER. (978-1-62639-843-6)

Two Souls by Kathleen Knowles. Can love blossom in the wake of tragedy? (978-1-62639-641-8)

Camp Rewind by Meghan O'Brien. A summer camp for grown-ups becomes the site of an unlikely romance between a shy, introverted divorcee and one of the Internet's most infamous cultural critics—who attends undercover. (978-1-62639-793-4)

Cross Purposes by Gina L. Dartt. In pursuit of a lost Acadian treasure, three women must work out not only the clues, but also the complicated tangle of emotion and attraction developing between them. (978-1-62639-713-2)

Imperfect Truth by C.A. Popovich. Can an imperfect truth stand in the way of love? (978-1-62639-787-3)

Serious Potential by Maggie Cummings. Pro golfer Tracy Allen plans to forget her ex during a visit to Bay West, a lesbian condo community in NYC, but when she meets Dr. Jennifer Betsy, she gets more than she bargained for. (978-1-62639-633-3)

Life in Death by M. Ullrich. Sometimes the devastating end is your only chance for a new beginning. (978-1-62639-773-6)

Love on Liberty by MJ Williamz. Hearts collide when politics clash. (978-1-62639-639-5)

Taste by Kris Bryant. Accomplished chef Taryn has walked away from her promising career in the city's top restaurant to devote her life to her six-year-old daughter and is content until Ki Blake comes along. (978-1-62639-718-7)

Valley of Fire by Missouri Vaun. Taken captive in a desert outpost after their small aircraft is hijacked, Ava and her captivating passenger discover things about each other and themselves that will change them both forever. (978-1-62639-496-4)

The Second Wave by Jean Copeland. Can star-crossed lovers have a second chance after decades apart, or does the love of a lifetime only happen once? (978-1-62639-830-6)

Coils by Barbara Ann Wright. A modern young woman follows her aunt into the Greek Underworld and makes a pact with Medusa to win her freedom by killing a hero of legend. (978-1-62639-598-5)

Courting the Countess by Jenny Frame. When relationship-phobic Lady Henrietta Knight starts to care about housekeeper Annie Brannigan and her daughter, can she overcome her fears and promise Annie the forever that she demands? (978-1-62639-785-9)

Dapper by Jenny Frame. Amelia Honey meets the mysterious Byron De Brek and is faced with her darkest fantasies, but will her strict moral upbringing stop her from exploring what she truly wants? (978-1-62639-898-6)

Delayed Gratification: The Honeymoon by Meghan O'Brien. A dream European honeymoon turns into a winter storm nightmare involving a delayed flight, a ditched rental car, and eventually, a surprisingly happy ending. (978-1-62639-766-8)